The Living End

Craig Schaefer

Demimonde Books
Joliet, Illinois

Craig Schaefer / Demimonde Books
2328 E. Lincoln Hwy, #238
New Lenox, IL 60451-9533
www.craigschaeferbooks.com

Publisher's Note: This is a work of fiction. Names, characters, places, and incidents are a product of the author's imagination. Locales and public names are sometimes used for atmospheric purposes. Any resemblance to actual people, living or dead, or to businesses, companies, events, institutions, or locales is completely coincidental.

Cover Design by James T. Egan of Bookfly Design LLC.
Author Photo ©2014 by Karen Forsythe Photography
Book Layout & Design ©2013 - BookDesignTemplates.com

Craig Schaefer / The Living End -- 1st ed.
ISBN 978-0-9903393-4-2

The Daniel Faust Series

Prologue

Eugene Planck wasn't a danger to himself anymore, not since the day he'd chugged down a bottle of acid to burn the snake living in his stomach. He hadn't overcome what the doctors called "delusional parasitosis"—he'd just realized that the snake couldn't be killed. Twenty years later, his throat still burned, especially on hot, dry California days like this one. He stared through the wire-mesh window, watched the wispy clouds drift by, and waited to die.

Napa State Hospital was a comfortable place for it. He had a stiff but warm single bed, a little desk with a lamp, and a view of the lawns outside. He had books, four of them, hardcovers lined up in a neat row on the desk. He'd expressed an interest in art history for a while, and the staff was happy to indulge him. Between the pills and the locked doors, it was hard to stay interested in anything for very long.

A letter from the outside would always perk him up, though. Nobody had sent him any mail for almost twenty years, not until the day his new friends came to visit, asking about Lauren Carmichael and his trip to Nepal. Since then he'd gotten three letters, preopened and screened by the hospital staff, checking up on Eugene and letting him know he wasn't forgotten. They always came with short postscripts at the end, veiled comments just bland enough to slip past a censor's marker.

"Your former student isn't doing too well, Professor. One of her real estate ventures did so badly, they had to hold a fire sale. Stay safe—Daniel."

He had to smile at that one. On the ancient Magnavox in the dayroom, Eugene had watched the press conference where Lauren blamed the destruction of the Silverlode Hotel on an unknown arsonist. He didn't know anything about Daniel Faust beyond that one time they'd met and even less about the beautiful woman at his side, the one who'd told him in a Scottish-tinged brogue that they could walk in his dreams. What he did know was that they had saved his life. For just one night, they'd given him his voice back.

A metallic rapping echoed at his door. Highcastle, one of the orderlies, peered in at him through the long glass window.

"Hey, Doc. You got a visitor."

Faust. Eugene's face brightened as he ran his fingers through his long, tangled white hair and tottered over to the door.

Highcastle strolled beside him as they walked to the visitor center. Light filled the antiseptic halls, streaming in through mesh-covered windows and security glass, putting a bounce in the older man's step.

He's coming to tell me she's dead, Eugene thought. He knew he shouldn't dare to hope, but he couldn't keep the dream from swelling in his heart, threatening to burst. *She's dead, and I can leave this place. I'm going home.*

The sturdy plastic tables and chairs of the visitor center were empty, baking in the light from slanted windows high in one wall. Empty except for one.

The visitor wore a vintage black hat with a veil of French lace, like a wealthy dowager might wear to a funeral, but Eugene only needed to see the curve of her chin to know who she was. One hand, cloaked in a black velvet glove, lifted. The crook of her finger beckoned him.

"Hello, Eugene," Lauren Carmichael said. "Come. Sit down."

The door clanged shut behind him like a falling coffin lid. Eugene looked back, startled, to find Highcastle standing in front of it. Blocking the way out. They made eye contact, and the orderly looked down at the linoleum floor, his lips pursed.

"Sorry, Doc," Highcastle murmured.

Lauren's hair had gone silver before its time, but between the veil, gloves, and voluminous mourning dress, that was almost all he could see of his former student. A sudden harsh whirring sound snatched his attention, the sound of the air-conditioning kicking on.

Hissing, he thought.

He raised his chin in defiance and hobbled toward her with as much pride as he could muster. He still had a few scraps of it left, even after all these years.

"It wasn't supposed to be like this," Lauren said. "You were supposed to be right there beside me in my hour of triumph. Sharing the glory you helped to build."

"You're mad," Eugene said.

"Could a madwoman have done the things I've done? Could a madwoman have my drive, my discipline? No, Eugene. Don't be so narrow-minded, it's beneath you."

He stood before her table, but he didn't sit down.

"I've been wondering. How did you do it?" she asked.

"Do what?"

"Talk to Daniel Faust about our trip to Nepal." She held up a velvet-sheathed finger. "My efforts to silence you—for your own protection, I might add—were exceedingly thorough. You shouldn't have been able to speak a word of it or write about it, or express it in interpretive dance for that matter. What did I miss?"

Eugene's chapped lips curled in a faint smile. "You couldn't stop me from dreaming."

"Ah. There it is. Always a loophole."

"You're too late," he said. "I told them everything. Everything I saw, everything you did, the people you and those smoke-faced things *murdered*. You won't get away with it."

"Of course I will. Eugene, beloved, the years have not been kind to you. I see wrinkles where my lips once kissed smooth skin. Your eyes still light up when you're angry, though. You were always my one weakness. You know that, don't you? My one indulgence, the one soft spot in my armor that I just couldn't bring myself to destroy."

Lauren looked over at Highcastle. The orderly stood slump-shouldered by the door, staring at his shoes.

"Leave us," she said. "And lock the door behind you, please."

Eugene turned, wide-eyed, and shook his head. "Don't go," he rasped, nearly pleading.

"Sorry, Doc." Highcastle grimaced with shame, but he still turned his back on the man. "Just the way it's gotta be."

Then he left them alone together.

"Two hundred dollars," Lauren said.

"What?"

"Two hundred dollars," she said, "is what I paid that man to betray you. Another two hundred for the part-time security guard, to ensure that camera in the corner is turned off. That's the going rate for a Judas these days, I suppose. Now, Eugene, I spend more money than that on a new pair of shoes. Are you really going to stand there and lecture me about what I can and can't get away with?"

"You can't buy your way out of facing justice," he said.

She laughed. It was an ugly sound, a mocking snicker that ended in a hissing rasp from behind her black lace veil.

"I've been doing it for years," she said. "Grow up, Eugene. I own a *senator*. I realize you haven't gotten out much lately, but this warmed-over hippie nonsense is beneath you. Hard work and dedication have provided me with the resources to shape the world to my liking. Haven't you read your Nietzsche? Or Hobbes? It's entirely natural that I exert my will."

"Daniel Faust." Eugene spat the words like a weapon. His frail hands clenched into fists at his sides.

"Hmm? What of him?"

"He's coming after you," he said. "He's coming for you, and he won't stop until you've paid for everything you've done. When he does? When your hold over me is gone and I can leave this tomb? The first place I'm going to visit is your grave. So I can stand over your dead body, breathe free air, and know that *we beat you.*"

Lauren lifted her veiled face. She glanced over to the clock on the wall, an old workhorse with a plain white dial and needle arms under a dusty bubble of plastic.

"Hmm. It's eleven o'clock."

"So?" Eugene said.

She looked back at him. He couldn't see her face, but he knew from the tone in her voice that she was smiling behind the veil.

"Daniel Faust," she said, "died fifteen minutes ago."

Eugene didn't say a word. He wanted to laugh in her face, wanted to call her bluff, but he knew her too well for that. He knew the steel backbone in her voice, that old familiar confidence.

She was telling the truth.

"That's the problem with hope." She studied her gloved hand, curling her fingers. "It lifts you up to the heavens, but one good kick and you plummet to the dirt. When I've remade the Earth to my design, the concept of hope will be the first casualty. It's kinder that way. I had such aspirations for you...once. I have learned, though, that the road to success demands absolute devotion and absolute sacrifice. I cannot allow any soft spots in my armor, not when I'm about to go to war with the entire world. No indulgences."

Eugene straightened his back and stared her down.

"Am I supposed to be scared?" he said. "I've been rotting in this hospital for twenty years. Branded as insane, abandoned, forgotten by the outside world. You have no power over me, Lauren. Nothing you could do to me is worse than what I've already endured. So go ahead. Kill me. All you're doing is setting me free."

Lauren peeled off her right glove. Her arm was mottled and green, peeling in spots, the flesh of a dying leper or a snake preparing to shed its skin. Eugene's eyes widened.

"So many sacrifices," she murmured from behind her veil. "I've been going through some changes of late, my dear. Difficult changes, but the victory is only sweeter for the pain. And no, I didn't come here to kill you."

Eugene let out a held breath. Then he tried to inhale and suddenly couldn't.

His fingers clawed at his throat as his windpipe slowly bulged. His face turned purple as he struggled for air. He crashed to the floor, kicking and thrashing, one flailing foot slamming into a chair and toppling it over.

"I came to take custody of our child," Lauren said placidly. "Killing you is just the side effect."

A rattling hiss echoed from the depths of Eugene's throat. Soon the thing in his stomach showed its diamond-shaped head, swamp green and glistening with bile, as it peeked out from the professor's soundlessly screaming mouth.

Eugene made one last desperate thrash, heaving himself across the floor toward Lauren's feet, then fell still. His dead eyes stared up at the visiting-room windows. The snake slithered out from his mouth, dropping with a wet, wriggling plop onto the floor.

Lauren reached down with her bare hand. Veins pulsed under the rotten skin, like a nest of worms infesting her arm.

"Come to Mother," Lauren whispered. "Welcome home."

1.

Out in the Arizona desert, in a ghost town called Chloride, I slouched in my chair and patted my hip through my windbreaker. Reminding myself that the gun was still there.

Chloride was an old mining town off US-93. Back in the 1800s they had over seventy mines and two thousand men to work the rock. Today the mines were long gone and only a couple hundred people remained, retired to the dusty streets and clean, cool mountain air. Abandoned tractors rusted in the sun next to the ruins of a once-booming town, nothing left but clapboard, hickory, and smoke.

I wondered if gunfighters ever met out on that rambling main street back in the day, settling their scores at high noon like in the westerns. My watch said 10:32. High noon was some time off, but we still had a gunfight on the agenda.

"Eat your sandwich," Caitlin said, sitting to my right. We'd camped out a table at Times Gone By, one of the town's few concessions to the tourist traffic. The restaurant was working the old mining town angle with the decor, from the rusted pickaxes and vintage photographs on the shingled walls to the red-and-white-checkered tablecloths. I'd ordered a sloppy joe with a dill pickle spear, and a ginger ale to settle my stomach. So far I'd just sipped at my soda, eyes riveted on the empty street on the other side of the big plate-glass windows.

"Something about a double murder just kills my appetite," I murmured.

A voice crackled in my earpiece. "Aw, you're missin' out, sugar. These joes are better than the ones I make at home."

From the far side of the almost-empty restaurant, alone at her own table, Jennifer lifted her half-eaten sandwich and gave a little wave. Like Caitlin, she wore cheap tourist sunglasses, garish and oversized. I'd gone for a pair of gold-rimmed specs with plain glass in the frames and a long scar on my cheek carefully simulated with a bit of mortician's wax. Old theater trick, but it would do the job.

When dealing with eyewitnesses to a crime—like the pretty Latina waitress in the white linen bodice who took our orders, or the elderly couple talking about bird-watching a couple of tables over—you can usually rely on the fact that people are terrible at remembering faces. Give them something for their minds to seize on, like a prominent scar, an exaggerated limp, a brightly colored hat or pair of glasses, and the finer details will fall to the wayside.

Lauren Carmichael had gone into deep hiding after the battle at her house. We'd hit her where she lived—literally—and stolen her last ace card. We'd been searching for her and her psycho-for-hire buddy Meadow Brand ever since. The trail had gone ice cold until a couple of days ago, when the email server we'd bugged pinged back to life with a flurry of messages from Brand. Apparently Lauren was hiding from her, too.

R U going to keep ducking me?! one email read. *U owe me mONEY, Lauren. I know u have it. CALL ME.*

After two days of badgering, the response finally came through. It was the golden opportunity we'd been searching for.

I'm cutting my losses and liquidating all the corporate assets I can get my hands on. New name and face waiting for me in Paris. Can't meet you in Las Vegas; too many people hunting for both of us. Drive two hours southeast, small village called Chloride. 11 a.m. tomorrow at Times Gone By. I will bring $200K USD in cash, which should satisfy my outstanding debt to you. After that, consider our business relationship amicably severed.

ROFL, Meadow responded. *Just bring the $.*

This was our last chance to take a shot at both of them. Payback for the blood on their hands. We had laid out our battle plans over a crumpled AAA road map and a round of stiff drinks.

"There's going to be witnesses, no way around that," I had said. "So that means we play it mundane. No magic. Just lead."

Caitlin wrinkled her nose. "Guns? Ugh. Detestable little trinkets. Give me a good hunting spear any day of the week."

"You're on crowd control," I said. "Lauren and Meadow aren't going to show up at the same time, so that means taking the first arrival down fast and making sure any civilians stay quiet and contained. We can herd them all into the kitchen if we have to. Margaux, Bentley, Corman, I want you three on overwatch. I want eyes on the approach into town from County Road 125, and both ends of Second Street. No surprises this time."

"I'm on the kill team," Jennifer said. It wasn't a request.

I nodded. "Yeah, you are. Just one thing: I know it's not the ideal send-off, but we've got to do this fast and clean. You know what they're both capable of, if they smell something funny. Especially Lauren. So no confrontations, no discussions, no last words. We go in, we gun them down, and we leave."

That was last night. Now my watch said 10:42, and my sandwich was leaking sauce onto my plastic plate, drizzling it out in a bloody trail. I took another sip of ginger ale.

"Something funny on 125." Margaux's Haitian accent crackled over our earbuds. Wearing lineman's overalls, she was up on a termite-gnawed telephone pole. The perfect perch to look out over miles of empty road and desert scrub.

"Whatcha got?" Jennifer said.

"Rust bucket of a panel van with Mexico plates, driving for Chloride. The spirits are fretting and tugging my ear. Bad business in that van, and it's not the flavor of bad we're lookin' for."

"Cormie's headed that way," Bentley said. His astral body was, anyway. Physically, Bentley and Corman were fifty miles away, sitting cross-legged on the worn carpet of a roadside motel room. While Corman flew and spied and spoke in a breathless whisper, Bentley played translator.

Spend enough time in the game and you develop a sixth sense for when a deal's about to go bad. Think of it as an evolutionary advantage, given that the guys who didn't develop one were all sleeping on prison cots or six feet under. I tried to tell myself that I was just nervous, that it might not mean anything, but that didn't make the muscles in my shoulders unclench.

"It's definitely headed your way," Bentley said, "but it's not Lauren or Meadow. Cormie senses four people in the van, none of them magicians, but they've got Lauren's...fingerprints on them, I suppose you could say. She's touched them with her power."

My sixth sense was screaming now. I felt like I was trying to work a jigsaw puzzle with someone blasting an air horn next to my ear. Had we missed something? The email tap had worked fine for us in the past. That was how we'd gotten a heads-up about Lauren's dinner party and even manipulated messages between her and her agents to give us the inside edge—

—which she could have figured out, when she finally emerged from the wreckage of her house.

"It's a trap," I said, realizing how we'd walked into our own killing box. "She knew we were reading her emails. She was never coming here today."

"What?" Caitlin said, but I was already standing up fast enough to knock my chair over.

"Everyone!" I shouted, turning every startled face in the almost-empty restaurant. "There's an emergency. You need to leave, right now!"

They looked at me like I was crazy, not budging from their chairs. The seconds turned into a slow, nauseous crawl as I felt the trap close over our heads. A red plastic fire-alarm box hung on the wall a few tables away. I ran over, grabbed the handle, and yanked it down. That got the civilians on their feet, as a shrill klaxon whined from the ceiling.

The van screeched to a stop on the street outside. The rusted-out side door rattled open, and I had just enough time to register the two men crouched in back, red bandannas tied over their faces and sunlight glinting off the assault rifles in their arms, before they opened fire.

The restaurant windows exploded. I threw myself to the floorboards, landing hard on my shoulder and rolling, just in time to see our waitress catch the first blast. She jolted backward on her feet, dancing a jig of death with her white blouse sprouting tiny scarlet mushroom clouds, and collapsed to the floor in a bloody ruin. Caitlin and Jennifer both flipped their tables onto their sides, crouching low and using them for makeshift shields. I trench-crawled my way to Caitlin as the storm of bullets tore the restaurant into splinters.

I pulled my piece, a Taurus Judge Magnum. It was a big black bull of a gun chambered for .454, and it barked like a Doberman as I snapped off a couple of wild shots. The van's passenger leaned out his window with a machine pistol, adding a staccato beat to the basso boom of the other two gunmen. I heard an elderly woman screaming from somewhere close to the door, but I didn't have time to think about the casualties right now. The hitters were pros. As soon as one shooter spent his magazine, his partner laid down fire and gave him a chance to reload. They had us pinned like rats.

Caitlin's pistol, a sleek little nine millimeter she'd borrowed from Jennifer, clicked on an empty chamber. She cursed under her breath and jumped up, running toward the restaurant wall. I barely had time to react before she snatched one of the antique pickaxes from the wall, spun, and hurled it faster and harder than any human being could dream of. The ax whirled through the air, spinning end over end, and buried itself with a bone-crunching spurt in one of the rifleman's chests. He fell back, spitting blood, and his partner froze.

I thought it was the opening we needed, but then I saw the surprise the driver had been getting ready on the other side of the van. He stepped into sight, another phantom in a bandanna and shades, with an olive-and-black steel tube slung over one shoulder. It rattled as he leveled it in his gloved hands. He dropped to one knee in a perfect shooter's stance, priming the weapon.

"*RPG!*" I screamed, breaking cover. "Out the back, now now *now!*"

I pulled the trigger as fast as my finger could work it, the Judge's cylinders spinning and spitting out covering fire while Caitlin and Jennifer ran ahead of me. I turned and hit the swinging door, bursting into the abandoned kitchen. We'd almost made it out the back when the grenade hit.

The world twisted sideways, and I went flat as the kitchen door blasted off its hinges on a gout of fire and roiling black smoke. The shock wave hit me like a giant's fist, and for a second the entire universe was nothing but white light and the sound of a cannon going off in my ears. A hand pulled me to my feet. Caitlin shouted something, but I couldn't hear a word of it over the ringing echoes of the aftermath. We stumbled out into the dusty back lot, eyes squinting against the sudden sunlight, the restaurant a roaring inferno at our backs.

My hearing swam back just in time to catch Bentley's panicked voice over my earpiece.

"—coming around! They're back in the van and coming around the building! Get out of there *now!*"

2.

Caitlin and I were empty, and Jennifer had two bullets to her name. We stood side by side in the empty lot, catching our breaths as the van roared around the side of the burning restaurant.

"Gloves *off*," I hissed and holstered my empty gun. My deck of cards leaped from my hip pocket in a spray of red and black, riffling into my outstretched hand.

"Fucking right," Jennifer said, trading her .357 for the gleaming razor blade that dangled from a chain around her neck. She dodged to one side, using the back wall as cover while she broke into a guttural German chant.

The van rolled into sight. The passenger leaned out his window, machine pistol reloaded and ready, but as he squeezed the trigger I scattered a handful of cards into the air. Three cards caught three bullets, each one falling to the dirt with a crumpled shell buried in its heart. The fourth card sliced through the air and slashed the shooter's shoulder to the bone. He dropped the pistol, instinctively grabbing his wounded arm, and fell back into the van.

The driver aimed straight for Caitlin and me, and gunned the engine. A rattling sound filled the air, like rain pelting a tin roof, and a whirlwind of dark, syrupy blood whipped past us. The whirlwind exploded, coating the van's windshield in sticky crimson. Suddenly blind, the driver lost his nerve and hauled the wheel around, trying to get away. Tortured metal shrieked as the van smashed head-on into the burning building. Its front end crunched like an accordion against the wall, and the driver launched through the windshield headfirst. The impact snapped his neck and left him wide-eyed and dead in a puddle of broken glass.

Jennifer held out her bleeding wrist, the torn skin already knitting itself back together as she chanted around the razor blade clenched between her teeth.

The second rifleman hauled open the side door, just in time to see Caitlin coming at him with claws bared and a mouth lined with teeth like a great white shark's. She grabbed him by the throat and dragged him behind the van. I didn't see what happened next, but I could hear his frenzied screams for about three seconds before they stopped short.

Caitlin stepped back into sight and wiped her face with the back of her hand, smearing the blood on her lips all over her cheeks, like some nightmarish war paint. I took a second to catch my breath.

That was when I saw the passenger slip out of the front seat of the van, still clutching his torn shoulder, and stagger away. Jennifer, Caitlin, and I glanced at each other. I flipped one card up in the air and caught it between my fingertips. Jack of spades.

I whipped the card toward him, and it spun like a razor-edged boomerang. The gunman screamed and fell as it sliced through his Achilles tendon and winged its way back to my hand, the card freshly edged in scarlet. He was still trying to crawl away, dragging himself across the dirt, when we walked up to him. I kicked him over onto his back.

"Where's Lauren Carmichael?" I said.

He shook his head wildly, squirming in the dust, eyes bulging.

"Don't kill me," he begged. "Please, don't kill me. I've got a family!"

I held up an open hand. "We're not going to kill you. Just tell us where Lauren is, and you can walk away."

Little white lies.

Then he screamed. Not from fear. Pain. He gripped his stomach and howled as it swelled under his clenched fingers, skin buckling and bloating, the buttons of his shirt popping one by one as his belly grew like a woman nine months pregnant. He kept swelling.

His eyes rolled back, and he shrieked like he was being fed into a meat grinder. Red lines blossomed on his stomach, the skin stretched to tearing, and then they burst. I jumped back as a flood of tiny snakes cascaded from the gunman's body, pouring out onto the stony ground and wriggling in all directions. He stopped screaming. I watched as a single garter snake squirmed out of the dead man's mouth and slithered back up his nose.

Caitlin, Jennifer, and I strode away without a word. We needed to put as much space between us and this nightmare as possible, and fast. I paused, catching a glint of light in the corner of my eye, from over by the restaurant's Dumpster.

A kid, maybe seventeen with an acne-cratered face, wore a short-order cook's apron and crouched just out of sight.

He had a phone in his hand, holding it up to record the action. He froze as we closed in on him, but he brandished the camera's eye like it was some kind of protective talisman.

I snatched the phone out of his trembling hand, tossed it to the ground, and stomped it under my heel until there was nothing left but shards of mangled plastic.

"You didn't see a goddamn thing," I told him.

"I didn't—" he said, stumbling over his tongue. "I didn't see anything."

"When the cops come," I said, "all you remember is seeing some strange Mexicans in the restaurant today. And maybe, in the shooting, somebody shouted something about cocaine. You don't remember too clearly."

"Mexicans," he said, "and cocaine. G-got it."

"Good. Because if you don't? We'll have to come back and see you again. And you wouldn't want that."

He nodded quickly, his voice caught in his throat. Some sorcerers are big on esoteric forms of thought control. I'm too lazy for that. Why go to that kind of trouble when you can get the exact same result with simple blind terror?

"Well, this was a clusterfuck," Jennifer said as we walked away.

"Still time for things to get even worse," I said.

"Yeah? How?"

I tapped my watch. "Meeting with our new lawyer. Let's go, we're gonna be late."

We blew out of town just ahead of the sirens and turned into ghosts on the highway. We blended in with the traffic, leaving the burning wreckage in our rearview mirrors. I clenched the steering wheel, counted my breaths, and waited for the crazy-fear adrenaline rush to ebb away. By the time I saw the sign saying "Las Vegas 75 miles," my knuckles weren't bone white anymore.

It's amazing, the things that start to seem normal once you get used to them.

#

The lawyer had smooth hands. Not smooth like talcum powder and baby fat, but smooth like soft plastic on a freshly molded doll. When he held out an open palm, waving it over my arrest report like a magician about to do a trick, I noticed his fingertips didn't have any whorls.

"Naughty boys," he said, flashing perfect teeth and grinning like he was about to sell me a used car. "Naughty boys and naughty girls, where would we be without them?"

Perkins's office was a shabby little walk-up over a mechanic's shop on Decatur Boulevard. Normally I wouldn't have given him a second glance—he looked like the kind of guy who chased ambulances on his morning jog—but he came with the highest of recommendations.

"Nowhere fun," said Caitlin, sitting in a cheap Ikea-knockoff chair to my left. She wore her scarlet hair in a twist at one shoulder and a black silk pantsuit made by a fashion designer whose name I couldn't even pronounce. We'd made good time on the road back from Chloride, and she'd insisted on stopping to change. Couldn't blame her for wanting an outfit that wasn't drenched in blood.

"Right you are, ma'am," Perkins said. "And may I say what a pleasure it is to be working with you again—"

"Save it," she said.

"Right, well, let's start with the good news then. The initial charges—possession of an unlicensed firearm, menacing, reckless driving and endangerment, blah blah blah—these all hinge on a single complainant. Mr. Faust and Ms....Juniper? Jennifer Juniper? Seriously?"

On my right, Jennifer stared at Perkins over the rims of her blue-tinted Lennon glasses. Her sleeves were rolled up to show off her tattooed arm, an elaborate mosaic from elbow to wrist that featured Elvis Presley as the Gautama Buddha.

"My folks were hippies," she said, her voice edged with a Kentucky twang.

Perkins shrugged and flipped through the police report. "I'd change it, but whatever floats your boat. I think we can get a lot of this tossed out or reduced out of hand. The gun's questionable, and there are some strange circumstances surrounding the civilian witness...speaking of which, this 'Meadow Brand' person? As your attorney, I recommend killing her. Make it look like a drug overdose, maybe a gang shooting, something nice and unrelated, you know?"

I'm not sure what scared me more: that I barely blinked at his suggestion or that nobody else did either. It goes with the territory when your girlfriend works as muscle for a demon prince. Caitlin had called in a favor with her boss to get Jennifer and me a meeting with Perkins, and she promised us that he'd fight harder to clear our names than any other lawyer in town.

Any *human* lawyer, anyway.

"We're kinda workin' on that," Jennifer told him.

"Good! I love proactive clients! This is a partnership, what we have here, and it means a lot that you're holding up your side of things. Now, absolute worst-case scenario, you both do a couple of months in county and I get your records expunged after the fact."

"Perkins," Caitlin said. She rested a proprietary hand on my shoulder. Her slender fingers curled, nails rasping against the cloth of my oxford shirt.

"Yes, ma'am?" he said, turning his thousand-watt smile in her direction.

"Please understand that a worst-case scenario for them will result in a worst-case scenario for *you*."

The smile vanished. He coughed politely, picked up a dented paper cup from his desk, and swallowed down a mouthful of cold coffee.

"I'm more concerned," he said, "about this federal investigation. I looked into the task force that's pursuing the Agnelli syndicate and hoo-boy, are they bringing in the heavy hitters. Now, theoretically, if Nicky Agnelli were to make a deal and turn state's evidence, how much could he actually pin on you two?"

Jennifer and I looked at each other.

"It would be good," I said thoughtfully, "if that didn't happen."

"Real good," Jennifer said.

"Well then, our best bet is to stall the investigation, or toss them some raw meat to chew on for a while. The big blank slate on the team is the FBI representative, this...Special Agent Harmony Black? Any chance you can buy your way into her good graces?"

I would have laughed, if my stomach wasn't tied in a knot.

"Zero," I said. "Black makes Joe Friday look bent. She'd cut off her own hand before she'd take a dirty nickel."

Perkins leaned back in his chair. "Huh. Bad news. Might want to kill her too and hope her replacement is more corrupt. But don't do that yet! Dead feds are bad for business. Let's just keep the option in mind for now, okay? Just back-pocket that sucker."

"The real problem is Lauren Carmichael," I said. "She pulled strings with Senator Roth to launch the investigation, as payback for Nicky screwing her over."

"Far too late to stop that ball from rolling now," Perkins said. "But you should probably think about killing her too."

"Some days I don't think about much else," I told him.

I wasn't normally a vengeful man, but two of my friends and a lot of innocent people were dead because of Lauren Carmichael and her crew. As of today, she could add five or six retirees and a waitress to her bill. Payment was overdue.

"Alton Roth, though," Perkins said, thinking. "We might have a shot there. In the metaphorical sense this time. Please do not kill Senator Roth. I voted for him twice. In the same election, in fact."

I was polite enough not to roll my eyes. Just barely.

"Look," I said, "just take care of the charges. We'll worry about the task force. Can you get us off the hook or not?"

"Yes, Perkins." Caitlin stared coolly across the desk at him. "Can you...or not?"

He looked down at the police reports and swallowed hard.

"Yes. Yes, I can. I'll get a motion to dismiss underway, start questioning the police procedures, make a few phone calls to a gentleman I know in Vegas Metro's evidence lock-up. And if you could just go ahead and kill Meadow Brand, then that'll be the frosting on the freedom cupcake. Don't worry, your Uncle Perkins has got everything under control."

"Now that's what I like to hear," Caitlin said with a feline smile.

"But seriously," Perkins said. "Friends. Listen. This task force is not going away, not easily. The hammer of the federal government rises slowly, but it falls with a mighty clamor. You either need to get some kind of guarantee of silence out of Nicky Agnelli—the kind that'll sew his lips shut for life—or start checking into countries that don't have extradition treaties."

3.

Out in the hallway, standing on cigarette-burned carpet that hadn't been cleaned since the Carter administration, Jennifer took Caitlin aside.

"I just want you to know I'm grateful," she said. "I mean, you coulda just gotten a lawyer for Dan. You didn't have to help me out any."

"You're a friend of Daniel's. That makes you a friend of mine. I like to do nice things for my friends. And assuming Perkins lives up to his usual standards and gets all of these charges dismissed..."

Caitlin stepped into Jennifer's personal space. Jennifer moved backward on instinct, thumping her shoulders against the peeling plaster on the wall. Standing a few feet away, I almost didn't hear the next part. Caitlin leaned in and put her lips close to Jennifer's ear.

"...that means, when I ask, you'll do something nice for me in return. Isn't that right?"

Jennifer nodded very quickly. Caitlin smiled and patted her shoulder, then walked over to lock my arm in hers.

"What's the rest of your day like?" she said. "More apartment hunting?"

"Have to. Bentley and Corman's couch is murder on my back, and I think I'm putting a dent in their love life. Thin walls."

I liked my old place, a rehabbed motel room in the shadow of the Vegas strip. Really felt like home—until a psycho half-demon pitched a Molotov cocktail through my window. Now I was hunting for a new home to hang my hat, and my list of requirements was hard to meet. Ideally, I needed quiet neighbors, a landlord who took rent payments in cash and wasn't picky about background checks, and hardwood floors for chalking down the occasional ritual circle.

Caitlin frowned. "Not without a proper lunch, you aren't. It's after three, and you haven't eaten all day. I'm thinking Korean."

"I'll catch up with y'all later," Jennifer said. "I've got a couple of twitchy people on my payroll, thanks to this Nicky nonsense, and they need a firm talkin'-to before they go from twitchy to jumpy."

At least my crimes—the ones I committed on Nicky's payroll, that is—were all past tense. Jennifer was still a golden stone in his greedy little pyramid. Agent Black had done a bang-up job of spreading word of the investigation all over town, hoping to scare the roaches at the bottom into giving up the big man at the top.

We parted ways in the parking lot, and I followed Caitlin to her car. She drove a white Audi Quattro with two-tone leather seats. Her business card said she was a regional manager for the Southern Tropics Import/Export Company. That was a nice way of saying she was the troubleshooter, enforcer, and all-around ass-kicker for the Court of Jade

Tears, the faction of hell that laid claim to our particular patch of sand.

When she managed something, it stayed managed.

I got in on the passenger side and closed my eyes. The city baked in its own dust under the afternoon sun. It was the kind of heat that weighed on you, drying your sweat and caking it to your skin faster than your pores could flush it out. Caitlin cranked the air-conditioning up to full blast while an Art of Noise album thumped on the sound system.

"I talked to Emma last night," she said, shooting a glance to her left before pulling the Audi out into traffic.

"Yeah? How's she holding up?"

"As well as can be expected. She's burying herself in work to get through it."

The last time I'd seen Emma was the night she snapped her husband's neck. Ben was a traitor, selling Caitlin's court out to a renegade demon with messianic dreams. The demon in question hadn't fared any better. If anyone went looking for his body, they'd find it buried under twenty tons of rock and a freshly laid parking lot.

It was a pretty rough night for everyone involved.

"How's Melanie?" I said.

Caitlin shook her head. "Coping. She's seventeen. There's no way to make this easier for her, and with Emma practically living out at the Silk Ranch...I'll make a point of checking in on her more often."

"I'll go with you," I said.

The monolith of the Enclave Resort and Casino rose up in the distance, a black tower looming over the tail of the Vegas Strip like a cat ready to pounce. Construction was moving faster by the day. Last time I'd been inside, it was just a steel skeleton. Tossing Lauren's chief architect off the top floor hadn't put a dent in her stride. We knew just enough to know the Enclave was more than it seemed. That, and it'd be a really good idea to put a bullet in Lauren's head before she cut the red ribbon on opening night.

We had thought opening night was on permanent hiatus. To finish her plan, Lauren needed the help of a dead serial killer named Gilles de Rais. Thanks to a rare tag-team play between the Vegas occult underground and the feds, de Rais's soul was rotting in a bottle at the bottom of an evidence box. It wasn't the hell he deserved, but it was the best we could do.

"She's got an angle," I said.

Caitlin arched her eyebrow at me. "Hmm?"

"Lauren. We broke her cult, we stole the Ring of Solomon, we snatched de Rais out from under her—she's got no cards left to play. She *should* be running. Instead, she muscled up with some hired thugs and came at us today like she's in her fighting prime. She's got an angle."

"Everybody does," Caitlin said.

My phone vibrated against my hip. I had treated myself to a new model after my last one ended up at the bottom of the aforementioned twenty tons of rock. I tugged it out and gave it a glance. Pixie.

I slid my thumb to take the call. "Hey, Pix, can I call you back later? About to get some lunch—"

"I need your help."

I frowned. Her voice was usually terse, but this time it had an edge that grabbed my attention and squeezed. Pixie was a mercenary hacker—sorry, *hacktivist*—and she could make anything with a circuit board jump up and dance like Fred Astaire. Usually I was the one who went to her for a helping hand, not the other way around.

"You have no idea," she said, "how hard it was to say that. But yes, I need your help."

"What's going on?"

"Not on the phone. Come to St. Jude's. Look, I have money. I can pay you, all right?"

I needed the cash. Jennifer's buddy Winslow had fronted me a car and a gun when my back was against the wall, at rates a loan shark would call steep. Given that Winslow was the top dog in an outlaw biker gang, I figured paying him back should be a priority in my life.

Even so, something told me I was going to be doing this one for free.

"Twenty minutes," I said and hung up on her.

"No rest for the wicked?" Caitlin asked, giving me a side-long glance.

"Sorry, hon. Rain check?"

"I'll settle for dinner. Eight o'clock. I'll swing by the bookstore."

"I think," I said with a smile, "that can be arranged."

#

Back when the Rat Pack was headlining at the Sands, St. Jude's was a swinging dance hall called the Diesel Room. The old marquee was long gone now, replaced by a dead neon cross, and the vintage parquet floors were scuffed and faded like a worn-out memory. I could find Pixie there most days, spooning out hot meals to the city's hungry and desti-tute, the lost souls who had fallen through the cracks in the glitter.

A smell hung in the air, something like damp dirty socks and quiet desperation. The lunchtime crowd was pretty light, and I saw Pixie working the soup line, doing what she could to make sure nobody walked away with an empty stomach.

Pixie had a knack for making me feel like a pretty horrible excuse for a human being. Which I suppose I was, to be fair, but still.

She passed her ladle to another volunteer and waved me off to the side, flashing the X marked in black Sharpie on the back of her hand. Pixie was as slight as her nickname, a wisp of a girl with chunky Buddy Holly glasses and scarlet feathered hair, the tips dyed an icy white.

"I didn't want to call you," was the first thing she said. I didn't blame her. She'd been blissfully ignorant just a couple of weeks ago, until I dragged her into my world.

I sat down at one of the picnic-style wooden tables that lined the old dance floor. She swung her leg over the bench opposite me and checked to make sure nobody was close enough to overhear.

"What's up?" I said.

"Look around. What do you see?"

I shrugged. "Lots of folks down on their luck. This city only loves you as long as you've got cash in your pockets."

"Not enough of them." She fluttered an anxious hand. "Normally we'd have twenty, thirty more regulars in here. People I know by name, or at least by their faces."

"Maybe you've got competition," I said. "Consider re-branding your product?"

Her eyes narrowed.

"It started a few days ago," she said. "Some regulars, people who have been coming around for years, just...not showing up. Then more. Every day there's fewer people coming around. Now, one or two disappearing? Maybe somebody got a job or found another way out of the system. Maybe they moved out of town, or maybe they ended up behind bars for a night or ODed. But not this many. Not all at once."

"I wasn't entirely joking about the competition," I said. "You're sure there's nowhere else they might be going for their daily bread?"

She shook her head. "I've been checking other soup kitchens, the shelters, calling hospitals about the handful I have real names for. They're not there. They're not *any-where*."

"At the risk of sounding morbid, have you called the morgue? Seen if there's an upswing in John and Jane Does?"

"Of course I did," she said. "I did that *first*. And no. They're not dying. They're disappearing. These are marginalized people, Faust. Do you know what the crime statistics are like among the homeless? Not crimes committed by them, committed *against* them. Compared to other citizens, the rates of hate crimes, beatings, rapes—"

I held up my hand. "I hear you. So lay it on the table. What's your guess as to where they're all going?"

"I don't know. My skill set is all digital, okay? But my regulars live off the grid. It's like the city streets just opened and swallowed them up, and I don't even know where to start. I was hoping you could...do your thing. Look, I can pay you. Just name a figure."

I pinched the bridge of my nose. I felt a headache coming on. Or maybe it was a bad idea disguised as a headache.

"Christ, Pix, I'm not going to charge you *money* for this. Let's just call it a favor for a favor, okay?"

She eyed me the same way I'd eyed my new lawyer.

"I'd feel safer just paying you," she said.

"Favor for a favor, and you can pick the favor. I'm trying to hold out an olive branch. Will you just fucking take it already?"

Her lips pursed as she weighed a question. Then her eyes went diamond hard.

"What happened to him, Faust?"

"Who?"

"You know who," she said. "Ben. The guy I helped you set up. A whole lot of you went out into the desert that night we stole that ring from Lauren Carmichael's house, and not everybody came back again."

I folded my hands on the table and leaned close.

"Why are you asking me a question you already know the answer to?"

4.

"Because," Pixie said, "you told me we were the good guys that night. Then I find out that while I was slipping out through the tunnel under Carmichael's house, there was a *slaughter* going on in the dining room. Then, what, you dragged Ben out into the desert and put a bullet in his head? I was part of that, damn it! You didn't tell me anyone was going to get killed. You told me we were doing the right thing."

"We *were* doing the right thing," I said flatly. "And it didn't go down like that. First of all, don't be fucking naive. Lauren and Sullivan went in planning to stab each other in the back. When I exposed their game, what did you think was going to happen? They'd have a big laugh about it and go play checkers? You knew damn well there'd be a fight. All we did was even up the odds and give the Choirboys a fighting chance against Brand's mannequins. We *saved lives*. I didn't hear you protesting at the time."

"That was before I had time to think—" she said, but I cut her off with a wave of my hand.

"Second, the plan was to let Ben go into exile with his buddies in the Redemption Choir. He pulled a gun instead. That was his choice, not mine."

Ben had been a dead man walking, and he knew it in the end. Emma took him down when he tried to run. We'd agreed, between her and me and Caitlin, that the truth needed a little creative editing for her daughter's sake. The new version involved a gun in the room and self-defense, and the killer was me instead of Emma. I had enough real blood staining my hands that I didn't mind splashing on a little more, if it made things easier between Emma and Melanie.

Pixie stared down at the table. Her jaw slowly un-clenched.

"It was easy," she said slowly, "to go with the flow when we were in the thick of it. I didn't have time to think. It was only when it was all over and done, and I tried to go back to my old life..."

I reached across the table and rested my hand over hers. She didn't pull away.

"Your old life wasn't there anymore," I said, trying to be gentle. "I know. You can do all the same things, visit all the same places, but it'll never be the same. It can't be, now that you know the world isn't the way you thought it was."

"I keep thinking about what you told me in the van. About...people like me holding back the dark. So I came back here to try and help. It's all I can do."

"And that's why I'm going to find your missing people for you," I said.

Me and my big mouth. The look of relief in her eyes told me that I needed to deliver the goods if I didn't want her heart to break. I just wished I knew where to start.

She gave me everything she had to go on, which amounted to a notebook full of scribbles and a couple of digital snapshots from St. Jude's Christmas Eve party. It wasn't much, but in a world where people can vanish off the grid without leaving a trace behind, it was the best lead I was going to get.

#

I took a cab back to Bentley and Corman's place. They ran the Scrivener's Nook, a used and rare bookstore. It looked like Charles Dickens was their interior decorator. A very drunk and disorganized Charles Dickens. Corman, built like a boxer going to seed, with hair the color of faded chestnut varnish, sat on a wooden stool behind the antique cash register and watched a video the size of a postage stamp on his phone. I heard the tinny crack of bat meeting baseball, sending it flying over the digitized roar of the crowd.

"Really?" I said, strolling over. "Surrounded by thousands of books and you're watching ESPN?"

Corman stretched his arms out, stifling a yawn. "I am as long as Bentley's out on a grocery run. Gotta rest up and recharge the ol' batteries after spending that much time outside my own skin. How'd the meeting go?"

"Well, Perkins is...he's definitely a lawyer, I'll say that."

"That good or bad?"

"He's pretty sure he can squash the lesser charges," I said. "That just leaves us with the feds to deal with."

"Don't worry, kiddo. We'll figure something out. We always do." He jerked a thumb towards a stack of envelopes at the edge of the counter. "Somebody called for you about half an hour ago. I wrote their number down and put it with the mail."

Weird. I couldn't think of anyone who would be looking for me. I wandered over and flipped through the pile. Gas bill for the building, electric bill, new copy of *Publishers Weekly*, Stash Tea catalog for Bentley—then I found Corman's scribbled note at the bottom of the stack, written on the back of a greasy pizza receipt, and I furrowed my brow.

Napa Hospital call re: Dr. Plank.

I dialed the number he'd jotted down. They picked up on the second ring.

"Napa State Hospital, how may I direct your call?"

"Hi," I said. "My name's Daniel Faust. I got a message asking me to call about a patient there. Eugene Planck?"

The line went quiet for so long I would have thought I'd been disconnected if it wasn't for the faint clatter of equipment in the background and the occasional garbled PA announcement.

"Yes," the voice on the other end finally said. "Dr. Planck listed you as his emergency contact. I have some bad news. I'm afraid...I'm afraid he's dead. It happened this morning, around eleven o'clock."

While we were walking into a trap down in Chloride, I thought. I gripped the edge of the counter, holding on tight as the world slid out from under my feet.

"How?" I said.

"It looks like a heart attack. It was very quick. He didn't suffer."

Yes, he did, I thought, because I knew what really killed him. Lauren. While we were chasing her shadow two states away, she was in California, tying up loose ends. I knew she had a soft spot for her old professor, and she'd spared his life once before. I'd thought that meant he was safe from her.

So there was one more victim I couldn't save. One more name for the list of the dead, chiseled on an granite slab and dragging me down.

"Thank you," I said. The voice started talking about burial costs and Planck's family in Virginia and did I know—and I just hung up.

Corman read the look on my face. He put down his phone.

"What's what, kiddo?"

"Eugene," I said. "The guy who helped me and Caitlin track down the Etruscan Box. He's dead."

"Natural causes?" he said, but I could tell from his tone that he knew better.

"Classic one-two punch. While we were chasing our tails and getting shot at in Arizona, Lauren was out in California dishing out some payback. I think she hoped she'd kill us all off at the same time."

"We're still here," Corman said.

I slammed my fist against the counter. A jolt of pain lanced up my arm and left my wrist throbbing.

"He spent twenty years in a mental hospital," I said, seething, "because Lauren locked a curse around his neck and *put* him there. Twenty goddamn years in purgatory. All I had to do, the *one thing* I had to do, was kill Lauren and he would have died a free man. I couldn't save Stacy Pankow or Amber Vance or any of the other people her cult murdered.

She ordered Meadow Brand to torture Spengler and kill him right in front of me. We got to Sophia's house just in time to find *her* dead body. Corman, I—"

My eyes squeezed shut. A weak and rotten dam against the tears I didn't want to let flow. I'd been pushing everything down, bottling it up so I could keep fighting, but Eugene's death was that one straw too many. I couldn't keep carrying that weight on my shoulders.

"You're afraid we're going to lose," Corman said.

I opened my eyes, took a deep breath to steady myself, and nodded.

"The only game you can lose," Corman said, "is a fair game. That's fine for baseball and poker night, but when all your chips are on the table? That's when you do what Bentley and I taught you. Cheat. Rig the game. Do whatever you gotta do to come out a winner."

"What if Lauren cheats better than us?" I said.

Corman snorted and shook his head.

"Son," he said, "*nobody* cheats better than us. Now stop worrying about could-bes and what-ifs, because could-bes and what-ifs aren't worth a damn. You're burning daylight. Get out there, do what you do best, and find a new angle. Lauren Carmichael's just one more in a long line of people who thought they were immortal until they suddenly weren't. Time we proved that to her."

5.

An hour later, I was sitting in a booth at the Five Guys on Eastern Avenue, noshing on a big, soggy bacon burger and dipping into a greasy brown paper bag stuffed with Cajun fries. I'd rather have gone for Korean with Caitlin, but the fast food quelled the gnawing in my gut. The hunger pangs, anyway. It didn't do much for the sense of dread that only got stronger when Harmony Black walked in the door.

I'd figured out an angle, all right, but I couldn't do it alone.

Harmony was a short, full-figured blonde with wire-rimmed glasses and a penchant for men's neckties. Today's was forest green. She also had a penchant for putting guys like me behind bars. She gave the clientele a quick frisking with her eyes, making sure I didn't invite her into an ambush, then slid into the seat across from me.

"Tell me something I want to hear," she said. Her words were clipped, edged with a faint New England accent.

"Such as?"

"Like you're ready to take the deal and turn state's evidence," she said. "You called me, Faust. Don't tell me I came all the way across town for the burgers."

I shoved the brown paper bag to the middle of the table.

"Try the Cajun fries," I told her.

"Look at that," she said. "Another thing you won't get to eat in prison."

"I need a favor."

She reached up, pulled her glasses down to the tip of her pert nose, and stared at me over the lenses.

"Excuse me?" she said. "I'm pretty sure I didn't hear that correctly."

"The soul bottle. I need it back. Just for a day or two."

Harmony leaned back against the hard booth. She didn't answer right away.

"You want me to give you a bottle containing the spirit of a psychopath who murdered a hundred children. In what conceivable universe, Faust, would I have any reason to do that? What—please tell me, because I really want to know—what would possibly be my motivation to do that?"

It was more like five hundred children, but correcting her history wasn't going to help my argument. I bit into my burger while I worked out how much to tell her.

"I have some indication that Lauren doesn't need de Rais's help anymore. You see the construction crews working day and night? The Enclave's still going up. She's shifting gears, finding a new approach."

"All the more reason to keep de Rais locked away forever. She *might* not need him, but that doesn't mean she doesn't want him."

"Except," I said, "he knows what she's up to. De Rais can tell us Lauren's entire scheme, because whatever the Enclave really is, we know it's based on something he started to invent centuries ago."

Harmony plucked a fry from the bag. She nibbled on it, thoughtful, then shook her head.

"So what's your plan? Let him possess someone, then interrogate him?"

"Yes," I said. "Then put him back in the bottle for good."

To give her credit, she actually thought about it while she ate another fry.

"No," she said. "Too dangerous. If anything went wrong, if he escaped, the fallout would be on my head. I can't live with that. Find another way."

"The host will be chained to a chair. There'll be armed guards—"

Harmony leaned forward a little.

"I said no. Possessions can go wrong with no warning. In case you forgot, *you* let that bastard get into my partner's skin. You can't tell me, after that, that you can guarantee *anyone's* safety."

"So, what, we just let Lauren go?"

"I'm already running my own investigation on Carmichael, off the books, with no help needed from you and your little friends. For that matter, there's no way I'm putting a monster like Gilles de Rais in the hands of a pack of gangsters. Now, if you were to reconsider my offer and come inside...maybe, *maybe* you and I could come to an agreement. You know, once I felt reassured that you were on the side of the angels."

I tried not to laugh in her face.

"That's funny," I said. "Never seen an angel that looked like a rat."

She reached for another fry. Her pink fingernails pincered it as she held it up between us like the sword in the stone.

"These," she said, "really are tasty. When you get home, you should look up what you'll be eating in Ely Prison for the next thirty years. Food for thought, if you'll pardon the pun."

She popped the fry in her mouth, smiled, and winked. Then she got up and walked out the door.

#

I drove around for a while, not aimless so much as restless, trying to come up with a new plan of attack. A heist wasn't in the cards. Harmony had stashed de Rais's bottled soul in an unmarked evidence box at the FBI's Vegas field office. A bank would be easier to crack. Besides, I already had enough heat from the feds to deal with.

The sun leaned down behind the city. Long fingers of shadow stretched from the monoliths on the strip, that dusky hour before the lights blaze and the booze flows like an oasis spring. I cruised back to the Scrivener's Nook and pushed through the glass door with just enough time to freshen up before Caitlin came by.

"These are from my trip to Denver," said the woman at the counter, showing pictures on her phone to Bentley and Corman. Bentley, the rail-thin Felix to Corman's Oscar, leaned in and squinted.

"I should really get my bifocals," he said, then saw me and waved. "Daniel! Look who's here."

The woman had her back turned to me, but in the skip of a heartbeat I recognized the way her auburn hair fell in tight ringlets, the delicate curve of her shoulder.

"Roxy?"

She still had a smile that could bring me to my knees, but I barely had time to register it before she ran over, wrapped her arms around me, and pulled me into a kiss. It lingered, burning, my heart pounding against her black sundress. She trailed the back of her hand against my cheek as she slowly pulled away, fingers glittering with the antique silver rings she'd always loved collecting.

"Hey, lover," she said. "Miss me?"

My head was reeling, and not just from the kiss. The last time I'd seen Roxy was the night she packed a bag and took a bus to Reno, out of my life forever.

"What are you—" I said, my voice catching. "What are you doing here?"

She reached down and took my hand between hers, squeezing it.

"I'm back. And I want to try again. A fresh start for us."

"Roxy, it's...it's not that simple. Things are different now."

I couldn't get my footing. I felt like I was running along a freshly waxed floor in my socks, every fumbling step a prelude to a messy fall. Something in the back of my brain was screaming at me to slow down, to stop and collect my thoughts, but I chalked it up to being hit with too many surprises at once.

"Of course it's that simple," she said. "You know how good we were together. You remember. Everyone said we were a perfect couple—"

The bells over the door jangled behind me. Roxy looked over, the smile freezing on her face. I turned around, my hand still trapped in hers, and saw Caitlin in the doorway. Her expression was carved from stone.

This looked bad.

"Cait," I said, "this is—"

"I know who she is," Caitlin said.

Then she crossed the room with three quick strides and backhanded Roxy to the floor. Roxy tumbled against a bookshelf and sent a few hardcovers thumping to the floorboards with her. She clutched her bleeding lip.

"Cait," I said quickly, taking a halting step backward. "It's not what you think."

She didn't take her eyes off Roxy.

"No," she said. "*It* is not what *you* think."

Roxy grinned. She leapt to her feet, suddenly liquid, and bent backward in a spinebreaking arc, hurling herself across the bookstore. In the air she bent and twisted and rippled like a heat mirage, sprouting a coat of tawny fur striped in midnight black. She landed on all fours. Five hundred pounds of Bengal tiger crouched in the aisle now, licking her fangs with an eager wet tongue.

Now I knew why the alarm bells were going off in my head.

"Goddamn it," I sighed.

"That would be redundant," Caitlin said dryly.

I jumped at the clattering sound of a round pumping into a shotgun. Corman had his Remington up from behind the counter with its fat black barrel leveled toward the tiger's head. Bentley was just as quick to defend their home turf. A pewter talisman dripped from his raised right hand, pregnant with thrumming power aching to burst loose.

"Went on safari once," Corman said. "Never did bag a tiger. What do you think, Bentley? Stuff it, or just mount the head on our wall?"

"We could use a new rug," Bentley said.

I held up a hand to ease them down. "Gentlemen, please allow me to introduce the Baron Naavarasi. She's not from around here."

The tiger's form melted again, her body standing erect, fur receding and turning into a flowing wave of raven hair. Now she was an Indian goddess with dusky skin, draped in a jade silk sarong that matched the color of her fingernails. Her eyes were still tiger orange.

She wasn't a demon, not in the traditional sense. She was a rakshasi, a hunger spirit and apex predator. She'd been written up here and there in the occult world, usually as the "Devourer of Innocent Flesh" or the "Lady of the Foul Banquet," after getting forcibly drafted into the Court of Night-Blooming Flowers sometime in the fifteenth century. She was still pissed about it.

"Stay your hand, hound," she said to Caitlin. "I am here as a formal and acknowledged emissary, and I have Prince Sitri's permission to walk your court's lands. You can check if you like."

"I'll be doing that," Caitlin said.

Corman didn't lower the shotgun one inch.

"We've got a policy in our store," he said. "Humans only. The young lady over there? She's got an exemption. You don't."

Naavarasi smiled at him. "But you liked me when I was Roxy."

"That was cruel," I said. "That was just...that was fucking cruel."

She strode toward us. Caitlin put a hand on my shoulder. Gently squeezing, letting me know she was in control.

"Cruel," Naavarasi said, "was spinning me a web of pretty little lies. I thought we might have something together, only to discover you still in the Wingtaker's arms."

"I didn't betray you," I said. "We bargained for a traitor's name, and that's exactly what I gave you. There was no trick there."

"Oh, I know, and my standing in the Flowers benefited handsomely for it. Even more so once I realized Prince Sitri tossed away a disposable asset and left a trail of false information for my court to fight over. I've milked that and milked it well. Don't worry. I won't tell if you won't."

"If you're here for a fight," Caitlin said, "you'll be fighting me. Just so we're clear."

The rakshasi laughed. It sounded like crystal bells.

"Why would I want a fight? I profited in the end. As one with a trickster's reputation, I appreciate the value of a good trick. Still, it did hurt my feelings, just a little bit. So, Daniel, I thought I'd come over and hurt you. Just a little bit. Now we can both get over it and move on."

Bentley blinked at her, aghast. His talisman's chain hung knotted in his fingers, like a hand grenade suspended by a cat's cradle.

"You came all the way here just for that?" he said.

"No," she said, "and not just for the kiss, though it was delicious. I am here on a diplomatic mission, with a request for aid that's covered by the treaty between our courts. I need a boon, a very small and simple one."

"Name it," Caitlin said.

"No. Not you." Naavarasi pointed her finger toward me. "I want *him* to do it."

Caitlin shook her head. "Daniel isn't a member of my court. He's not subject to our rules or our customs."

Naavarasi's eyes, still a tiger's, glittered.

"Oh. So that means he's not your consort?" she said. "Be-cause...that would mean he's *anyone's* meat, wouldn't it?"

6.

Caitlin let go of my shoulder and stepped forward, standing in Naavarasi's way.

"Whatever you're thinking, rakshasi...stop thinking it."

"What? Me?" Naavarasi pouted, all mock innocence. "The only thing I'm thinking is that I need a boon. And you are treaty-bound to deliver. You can go with him, if it makes you feel better. In fact, I request it."

"What's the job?" I said. I pretended not to notice the sudden looks of concern from Bentley and Corman.

Naavarasi favored me with a smile. "A member of our court was summoned by a foolish pair of amateur magicians, not far from here. We know that he possessed one of the summoners and likely killed the other. However, he's been bound in place somehow and hasn't left the house where he was invoked. I need you to go in, erase any binding sigils, and exorcise him from the idiot's body so he can return home. I'd do it myself, but my particular style of magic isn't conducive to such work. Yours is."

It was a simple job. I'd done plenty of exorcisms in my day. If the demon was trapped in a botched summoning circle, it'd be safe enough. If he was actually cooperating, even better. I'd be in and out in fifteen minutes.

Which was exactly why I smelled a trap.

"What choir does the target belong to?" Caitlin said.

"Right," Naavarasi said. "I forget you people have that cute little *system*. Isn't it stifling? Being locked into a tiny box, your emotions and powers restricted like that? I can embody any sin or virtue I like. Often several at once."

Caitlin's eyes melted to the color of molten copper. Her voice went lower, slower, her Scottish brogue more pronounced. That was always a bad sign.

"It's more of a guideline. Some people say I'm more wrath than lust. Push me just an inch further, baron, and you'll find out why."

Naavarasi caught the tone and waved an anxious hand.

"All right, all right," she said. "Malphas told me that he's a fledgling of the Choir of Envy. Is that a problem?"

Caitlin shook her head. "Not remotely."

"Delightful! I'll send you the address. Shall we meet again tomorrow evening and talk about your brilliant success?"

"Not here," Caitlin said. "There's a nightclub called Winter. You'll meet me there. You will never come to this address again. Under any circumstances."

"But why? I like books." Naavarasi glanced over at Bentley and Corman. "And snacks."

Corman patted Bentley's back. Then he came around the counter, toting the shotgun loosely at his side. He walked right up to Naavarasi and stood close enough to feel her breath on his weathered cheeks.

"Lady," he said calmly, "I don't know what rock you crawled out from under, but I do know this: you came in here under false pretenses, then you scared my husband, and you hurt our boy. That puts you about two notches lower than dog shit on the list of things I'm scared of. You're gonna leave now, and if you ever set foot on my property again, I'll end you."

Naavarasi's eyes widened. Her lips curled as she said, "You impudent little—"

Corman swung up the shotgun, racked the pump, and pressed the barrel under her chin.

"You should probably listen," Caitlin said.

The rakshasi slowly backed away, glaring. She swept out of the store without another word and slammed the door behind her. The bells clanged crazily, bouncing off the shuddering glass.

"Guys," I started to say. "I'm sorry—"

"No." Caitlin cut me off as she turned to Bentley and Corman. "I am sorry. That was inexcusable. Court business should never have been allowed to cross your doorstep."

I shook my head. "She came tracking me down, not you. It's my fault."

"Oh for Christ's sake," Corman said, leaning the shotgun back against his shoulder. "Both of you stop apologizing. Shit happens. She got the message."

Bentley lowered his talisman, exhaling slowly as a stream of pent-up power dissolved into the air. He leaned his palms against the counter and took a deep breath.

"So that was a rakshasi," he said. "I've never encountered one outside the pages of a book."

"I think she might be the last one on Earth," I said. "Hope so, anyway. You okay?"

Bentley nodded and gave me a shaky thumbs-up. "Fine and dandy. Cormie?"

"Yeah, hon?"

"The next time you see a Bengal tiger in our store? Do shoot it, would you? I wasn't joking. We really could use a new rug."

#

We took my car.

I'd been stuck without wheels since the Redemption Choir wrecked my old ride along with my apartment, but Jennifer's buddy Winslow had hooked me up with the little passion project he'd been rebuilding behind his garage: a 1970 Barracuda with a widemouthed grill and a hemi under the hood, blacker than my heart and built for a knife fight. The car got a little more attention than I liked, making it hard to ghost my way through the city streets, but it had muscle when I needed it.

"It's a trap," Caitlin said as she slipped into the passenger seat.

"I was thinking the same thing. Naavarasi's about to drop the boom on us, but I don't see where it's falling from. Would she risk a diplomatic incident?"

She shook her head. "No. She's well-regarded by her court—despite not being one of our kind—and her star's on the rise. She could lay some sort of an ambush for us, but there's no profit in it for her. We'll go tomorrow, when it's light out. Stay alert, and if anything seems the slightest bit amiss, we pull up stakes and leave. So...how was the kiss?"

I almost dropped my keys.

"It was Roxy's kiss," I said. "I know Naavarasi had been watching me long before we met in Denver, but...it was Roxy's kiss. Like she'd studied it, practiced it until it was absolutely perfect. Kept me from seeing through the ruse until you showed up."

"Mind games are what the baron does. They're her passion and her power. But that's not what I asked you."

I fired up the ignition and felt the Barracuda's engine growl through the metal.

"It was just a kiss. Not as good as yours."

Caitlin folded her arms and smiled. "That's all I wanted to know."

We slid through the night like a knife made of ink, only slowing down once we turned onto Las Vegas Boulevard and merged with the wall of traffic along the Strip. The casinos rose up around us in a neon bouquet of flashing lights and broken promises.

Dinner was at Saffron East, in a dining room with chintz drapes and table settings that could have served the royalty of old-world France. We had a table for two by the window, overlooking a man-made lake that glimmered with reflections from the casino lights.

"We'll have the imperial Peking duck," Caitlin told our server before I could even look at the menu.

I knew better than to complain. Caitlin's habit of ordering for people she dined with would have been annoying, except that her choices were always perfect. The first course saw the duck served up in paper-thin crepes with scallions and cucumber, touched with a brown smear of hoisin sauce. The perfect combination of savory, fresh, and a touch of sweet. The next course brought diced duck meat served in wraps of butter-lettuce leaves sprinkled with shaved jicama root. While we ate, I brought her up to speed on my talk with Pixie.

"Lots of things can devour their victims whole," Caitlin mused, "but they're rarely found in this part of the world."

I frowned while I chewed.

"I know one that's here right now," I said. "Naavarasi. Eating people is kind of what she does. You think she'd do some hunting while she was in town?"

"Without permission? Never. It would be a slap in my prince's face. You're right, though, I don't like the timing. Do we have any news on Carmichael or Brand?"

"They're phantoms, and I can't figure out how to smoke them out of hiding. There's something else. I got a call from Napa State Hospital today. Eugene Planck is dead. I can't prove it, but I know Lauren killed him. She's tying up loose ends."

Caitlin's eyes narrowed and her lips pursed.

"We're being toyed with," she said. "And I *hate* being toyed with. We have to proceed as if circumstances have changed, and assume that Lauren no longer needs de Rais's soul to finish the Enclave."

I looked at her over my wineglass. "I still think our best bet is pumping de Rais for information. That's only if we could get Agent Black to hand him over, though. Which we can't."

"If we can't negotiate with her, is there any chance intimidation might work?"

"It's Harmony Black we're talking about here," I said. "Trying to scare her would just make her dig her heels in harder. She's got a stiffer spine than one of Meadow Brand's puppets..."

My voice trailed off. I raised my eyebrows.

"Pet?" Caitlin said. "You've got that look. The one you get when you've done something clever."

"The one angle we never checked. The goddamn mannequins. Look, Brand attacked us with at least twenty of those things at the Silverlode Hotel. Another two of them went with her to kill Sophia. She had another, what, maybe twelve of them disguised as servants at Lauren's house?"

Caitlin nodded, following along. "She has no trouble producing as many as she needs, with very little time to spare. Which means—"

"Which means," I said, "she's not building them from scratch! There's no way she has time to be Carmichael-Sterling's full-time public relations director, serve as Lauren's right-hand woman and hired gun, *and* sit in a woodshop for as long as it takes to carve and assemble dozens of life-sized wooden armatures from scratch."

"She's outsourcing," Caitlin said.

"Exactly. Someone builds them; she animates them. Which means somewhere, not far away, there's a woodshop getting some very distinctive custom orders."

"A shop," Caitlin said, "that will have her current address on file. How many woodworkers can handle that kind of workload? It's not like when I was a girl, when—"

She paused.

"What?" I said.

"Never you mind what it was like when I was a girl. Let's just say it was before plastics were in vogue, and skilled artisans were more highly valued than they are today."

I made a point of never asking Caitlin her age. This seemed to make her happy.

I clinked my glass against hers and took a sip of pinot noir. "Tomorrow, after we see what Naavarasi's got planned for us, we start hunting for woodworkers. When it comes to magic, Meadow Brand is a one-trick pony. That's about to bite her in the ass."

This felt good. Caitlin and me, bouncing ideas off each other, pushing each other to think of angles we never would have come up with on our own. It wasn't something we had to work at—it just happened naturally, like we were two parts of a perfectly geared engine.

The sommelier swooped in, a tall Chinese man with a pristine white cloth draped over his forearm. He expertly refilled our glasses, twisting the bottle just right so as not to spill a drop, then glided away again.

"Speaking of the baron," Caitlin said.

"I know. She's the sommelier. And she was one of the valets outside the parking garage. I'm pretty sure she was one of the tourists on the elevator with us, too. Now that I'm not being blindsided with visions of my ex-girlfriend, I can pick up on her glow. Think we should say anything?"

"No," Caitlin said. "I think she's showing off. Don't look impressed. You'll just encourage her."

"How should I look?" I said.

"You should look at me. All night long."

"That," I said, "is a plan I can get behind."

7.

I woke up in my favorite place in the world: curled in Caitlin's arms. She was already awake—she didn't sleep so much as meditate—and her deep emerald eyes flickered open to meet mine.

"Hello, sunshine," she purred. Her body pressed against mine in the swirling expanse of gray silk sheets, warm as a kitten's fur.

"Hello yourself. Ready to live dangerously?"

"Every day," she said. "Right after a hot shower and a good breakfast. Danger goes better with mushroom and spinach omelets."

I rolled out of bed. "And bacon," I said, groaning as I stretched my arms. "Bacon cures all ills. That's a science fact."

We hit the road around nine, cruising southeast under a cloudless sky with the mountains rising up in the distance. The address Naavarasi had given us was in Henderson, near the old Water Street District. With Caitlin navigating, I narrowed down the address and pulled the Barracuda up to the curb outside a prim little suburban nest with white vinyl siding and a shaggy postage-stamp-sized lawn.

The street wasn't just sleepy, it was comatose. No birds, no lizards, not even the distant drone of airplanes. The mild breeze, staving off the worst of the morning heat, fell still as we stepped out of the car.

"That's not ominous or anything," I said, peering at the curtained windows.

I didn't expect a fight, given what we'd been told, but I'd come prepared for one anyway. My deck of cards nestled in my hip pocket. The deck vibrated eagerly and sent little pins-and-needles shivers down my leg.

Caitlin tilted up her face and sniffed the air like a wolf. "Demonflesh," she said softly. "And a corpse. Not far away."

"Let's hope it's just one," I said and led the way up the short walk to the front stoop. "Okay, cover me."

I fished my locksmith's gear out of my other pocket. It was a thin folio of olive plastic stocked with a row of stainless-steel picks and rakes. The lock on the front door was a thirty-dollar model straight from Home Depot, not the top of the line but not the worst either. I picked out a torsion wrench and a half-diamond pick, bent down on one knee, and went to work. Meanwhile Caitlin stood beside me on the stoop, looking casual as she watched the street, ready to shield me with her body if a car drove by or a neighbor poked their head out.

The tumblers clicked and rolled. I pocketed the picks and slowly turned the knob, bracing for trouble. The door swung open without a sound. Just beyond, a plush burgundy rug decorated pale birch floorboards. Dust motes hung in the air and clung to a glass credenza by the door. Caitlin followed me in.

The house stank of sweaty socks and moldy pizza, like a frat party in a sauna. As we crept inside, my wrinkling nose picked up a stronger stench, that odor of gas and decay that only comes from one thing: a corpse left out to rot.

Voices echoed the next room. We froze. Then I heard the tinny echo of a laugh track and realized it was just a television set.

I poked my head around the corner, fighting to keep my stomach under control. The stench shoved its gaseous fingers down my throat. The living room might have been nice once, with a tan leather sofa set, thick shag rugs, and a sixty-inch television. That would have been before the place turned into a garbage dump of empty food wrappers, crumbs, and dirt, sweltering under the grill of a broken air conditioner.

The kid on the couch was maybe twenty. His *Call of Duty* T-shirt stretched over his bloated belly, and his cheeks bristled with a few days of rough blond stubble. He looked over, saw us, and waved.

"Hey," he said listlessly. "I'm Pete."

Most demons can't do what Caitlin can, creating their own bodies out of raw power. They need to hijack a human or an animal's skin to stay in our world for very long. Pete was a hijacker. My second sight showed me a web of veins under the kid's skin, pulsing black and red, mapping the infestation's trail.

I rubbed my forehead. The closer I got, the more tired I felt. I couldn't concentrate, could barely remember why we'd come here.

"We're here to help," I finally managed to blurt out. "Came to get you out."

Pete shrugged. "That's cool. Whatever. You wanna watch TV?"

A king-size bag of Cheetos nestled on his lap. He grubbed around inside the bag and mashed a handful between his cheese-dust-stained lips.

"No, Pete," Caitlin said, walking around the living room and poking her head in an open doorway. "We don't want to watch television."

She waved me over. My feet felt like lead bricks. Even so, the smell coming from the doorway almost knocked me flat. A dead man lay stretched out in a bed, his rotting corpse half-buried under a wool comforter. Fat black flies clung to his eyeless face, laying their eggs.

"I keep telling him he needs to get up," Pete said. "Dude's gonna be late for work."

I stumbled back. "He's dead, Pete."

"He is?" Pete said. "Bummer. I liked that guy."

I groped for a spell, something to ward off whatever was leeching my strength away, but my mind slipped around the edges. I didn't forget my magic; it just seemed like way too much effort.

Next thing I knew, I'd dropped onto the couch next to Pete's. I needed to rest, just for a second. It was such a long walk to the front door, and I just needed to rest first.

"You're not with the Choir of Envy," I said. "Are you?"

"Huh? Me? I've got everything I want right here. Just chillin'."

Caitlin made a heroic effort, but it got her as far as I did. The couch, sitting right next to me.

"Choir of Sloth," she breathed. "Damn it. And he's no fledgling, not with this kind of power. Naavarasi lied to us."

I shook my head. It was the most I could manage.

"No, she didn't. Her exact words were, 'Prince Malphas told me that he's a fledgling of the Choir of Envy.' Know how that happened? 'Hey, prince, tell me that this guy is a fledgling of the Choir of Envy.' 'Okay, he's a fledgling of the Choir of Envy.'"

"She lies without lying," Caitlin said. "And he's not bound here. He just doesn't feel like leaving."

"Everything she told us was true. It was just enough truth to fuck us over. I'm stuck, Cait. I can't get any juice."

She closed her eyes and leaned her head back. "My kind don't mesh well with sloth. This is bad. I think the man in the other room starved to death. He starved instead of getting out of bed."

"I offered him Cheetos," Pete said. He held up the bag and shook it at us. "Want some?"

"No, Pete," I said. "We don't want Cheetos. We want you to turn your powers down so we can get off this couch."

He shrugged, not quite getting it. "So get off the couch. I'm not stopping you. Hey, Judge Judy is on! She's the coolest."

We watched fifteen minutes of "Judge Judy." It seemed like the best thing to do. Everything else was too much work.

"I don't know what she's getting out of this," Caitlin murmured. She looked paler than usual. "Even if Naavarasi could get away with murdering us by proxy, why do it at all?"

I shook my head. "She's not. Remember how she wanted to recruit me for her little army? The collar she gave me, the 'get out of death free' card?"

"You mean the utter insult to *me* she gave you? Yes. Of course."

"Naavarasi will come by in about a week, give or take a few days," I said. "When I'm dehydrated, half starved to death, and delirious. Then it'll be an offer I can't refuse. She'll claim my soul, banish Pete here, and set you free. I'll be bound to her service, and you'll be embarrassed in front of your court. It's a win-win for her."

"C'mon, guys!" Pete whined from his sofa. "Save it for the commercials, will ya? I haven't seen this one yet."

While the television droned on, I gnawed at the problem, struggling to think through the layers of gauze wrapped around my brain. We needed something to overpower the aura of sloth, something to counter it, to motivate us to move.

The show cut to commercials. I watched listlessly as a parade of women rubbed a new invigorating shampoo into their scalps, the camera lingering on as much of their wet bodies as it could get away with on daytime TV. One of the models gasped at the camera, her expression almost orgasmic as her shampoo's thirteen essential vitamin supplements gave her hair new life and shine.

I got an idea.

"Hey, Cait."

"Daniel?" she said, her voice exhausted.

"I was just thinking. About the first morning we woke up together. You remember that? When we showered together?"

Her lips curled in a faint smile. "Of course I do."

"The steam curling around us in white clouds," I said. "Our naked bodies sliding together, wet, slippery. The way your skin felt as I ran that bar of soap slowly along your hip."

A faint touch of color tinted her cheek. She got what I was doing. I knew she would.

"I was surprised you could stand up," she said, "after that night. I remember the way you gasped, the way your muscles tensed and you clawed at the sheets while I rode you, again and again and again."

"Guys," Pete whined, "c'mon, knock it off, would ya?"

I found the strength to reach out and take Caitlin's hand. Her fingers squeezed mine, meeting with a faint electric spark.

"Remember that dinner at your place last week?" I said. "Both of us drunk on red wine, watching a John Hughes movie, making out on your leather couch like a couple of teenagers. Just all over each other, hungry for each other."

Caitlin's shoulders straightened. She sat up, leaning forward, turning to me with her eyes bright and her face flushed.

"I remember when I got your clothes off. The warmth of your body, pressed between mine and the black leather. Then you sank to your knees on the carpet and kissed your way up my inner thigh..."

Pete winced and covered his ears. "Guys! Ew. Come on!"

The lethargy drained away, replaced with something new. Heat. Need. A feedback loop of hunger that coursed between us, desire riding on a groundswell of magic.

"I want you," I told her. "I want you so badly I can barely breathe. I need you."

Caitlin stood up. She tugged at my hand.

"I have so many pleasures to show you," she said, breathing fast. "So many sensations you haven't even imagined yet. Just thinking about it makes me shiver."

I looked up at her like a supplicant before a living goddess.

"Show me. Right now."

She pulled me to my feet, and I slipped my free arm around her waist, wanting to embrace her, but there was no time. We moved together, cocooned in our lust, headed straight for the front door. Pete hurled a handful of Cheetos at us, but they all landed short, scattering across the filthy rug.

"Fine!" he pouted. "You guys suck. Don't come back if you're not here to watch TV. And if you do, bring some corn chips and some Coke, okay? Make sure it's diet. Hello? Guys? Are you even listening to me?"

8.

We half ran down the walkway, barely pausing to slam the door closed behind us. The fresh desert air, arid and pure, washed away the filth and the stench and left me feeling cleaner than I'd felt in weeks. Caitlin hauled the car door open and grabbed me by the arm, shoving me into the backseat. She pressed me against the hot vinyl and straddled my lap, stealing my breath with a ferocious kiss.

"Cait," I gasped. "Someone could see—"

She clamped her hand over my mouth. Her other hand worked at my belt buckle, yanking at the clasp.

"Shut up. The only thing I want to hear out of your mouth in the next ten minutes," she hissed, "is you screaming my name. Anything else is *not interesting*."

I squirmed out of my pants, fabric pooling around my shoes, while she hiked up her skirt. Then she grabbed my lapels and tugged, sending the top two buttons of my shirt flying, pressing her sharp teeth to my bared throat and growling like a wolf as she lowered herself onto me.

I lost track of time and everything else with it, everything but the feel of her body against mine and the scent of her skin. Finally we just clung to one another, shuddering, wet and disheveled, our hearts racing together.

"I liked that," she whispered, caressing my cheek.

"Feeling's mutual," I said. "But now we've got a serious problem."

She nodded. Her dreamy smile faded. "Naavarasi."

"No," I said. "Problem is I think my legs are asleep."

Somehow we got ourselves looking more or less presentable and accomplished the long and awkward migration to the front seats of the car. I drove Caitlin back home to her penthouse at the Taipei Tower. She leaned in to kiss my cheek.

"Winter," she said, "tonight. We'll have a stern talk with our esteemed visitor."

"I'll meet you there. Right now I need to get a little work done on Pixie's problem."

That was my second stop. First stop was Bentley and Corman's cluttered apartment over the Scrivener's Nook for a new shirt and a quick shower. I was glad nobody was home.

I kept ties with a few contacts on the street. Some I met working for Nicky Agnelli, some I crossed paths with in my days of busking for change on Fremont Street. I had a reputation as a man who could be useful to know.

One of those contacts was Laika. She was six foot one, wore her blond hair in cornrows, and said she was descended from Russian aristocracy. I thought the accent was a put-on. Three in the afternoon and she was already out on the stroll, poured into a purple PVC halter dress and smoking a cigarette on the corner of a dead-end street.

Lots of tourists come to town thinking prostitution is legal in Nevada. They're half-right: it's legal in twelve counties, but not one of them is anywhere within a hundred miles of the Vegas city limits. You take a limo out to the ranches if you want a certified disease-free pro, assuming you've got the cash to afford her. In the city it's the same old street game, all risk and barely any reward. Like chutes and ladders, but the chute probably looks like a pimp's fist or a heroin needle.

The ladders don't go anywhere, either.

I rumbled the Barracuda up to the corner and shifted into park. Laika came over and leaned in the open passenger-side window, shifting her body to draw my gaze toward her cleavage and away from the tracks on her arm. I picked a third option and looked her in the eye.

"Moving up in the world," she said, laying the Russian accent on thick. She dropped her cigarette to the street and snuffed it under a stiletto heel. "Where'd you get the car?"

"Favor from a friend. Speaking of, you hear anything weird on the street lately? People dropping off the radar more than usual?"

She flicked an uneasy glance back over her shoulder. "You're asking me about weird stuff? You're the magic man, everybody knows that. But yeah. Two of Half-Cap's girls? They haven't been around. I talked to Mindy, you know, the one with the teddy bear and the pigtails. She says they both split on the same night. Left their clothes behind and even a little bankroll they'd stashed that Half-Cap didn't know about."

Which means they didn't leave town voluntarily, I thought. I tugged my phone out of my pocket and tapped my way to Pixie's photos.

"How about these guys? They might be squatting around here. Any of 'em look familiar?"

While Laika took my phone and gave the screen a close look, I caught movement in the driver's-side mirror. A sweaty slab of meat with fresh razor nicks decorating his bald scalp stormed toward the car like a bull on meth. He slapped his knuckles against my door, hard enough to make the metal jolt.

"Hey!" he snapped. "You buying, or you *leaving*?"

I fished a couple of tens out of my wallet and held them curled between my index and middle fingers, holding them up so he could see before I passed them over to Laika. She made the bills disappear.

"Buying," I said. "Now piss off."

He leaned in, squinting at me. "The fuck you just say to me?"

I slouched back. "You pay twenty percent in rent to Nicky Agnelli to let your girls work this stroll. Two years ago, you were paying twenty-five to Carl DuQueene. That's a five percent improvement in profits."

His brow furrowed.

"You remember how they found Carl DuQueene's body?" I said casually.

Now he nodded, real slow. His left eye twitched, just a little. Like he was remembering a nightmare.

"Well," I said, "I'm the reason why. So I want you to look me in the eye and say, 'Thank you, sir, for the five percent.' And don't ever touch my fucking car again."

He backed away, looking at me like he'd just met the devil. I smiled, nice and easy, until he'd scurried off back to his rathole.

Laika handed my phone back.

"Sorry," she said. "I got nothing to tell you. No familiar faces."

"Thanks for trying. Keep the twenty. Hey, how about the other way around? Any strangers hanging out, people who don't fit in?"

"We're all strangers out here," she said, then held up an acrylic fingernail painted in eggshell blue. "Wait a second. There was a guy last week, going up and down the stroll. Said he was with some mission, wanted to get us off the streets, offered us shelter if we needed it. All that save-the-world stuff. I know he was talking to Half-Cap's girls till he chased the guy off. He gave me his card, but I tossed that thing away. Sorry."

"It's something," I said. "Maybe ask around, see if any of the other girls remember anything. Give me a call if they do."

I left her on the street corner. In the rearview mirror I saw a battered old Nissan pull up to the curb in my wake, another eager customer. The wheels of commerce never stopped rolling.

\#

You wouldn't know Winter was a nightclub if it wasn't for the line snaking down the block and the faint thudding of bass echoing behind the slate black doors. There was no advertising or big marquee, just a tiny brass plate and a small sloping arrow in blue neon fixed to the bricks outside.

Freshly scrubbed and shaved, wearing a navy blazer to cut the evening chill, I skipped the line and walked right up to the bouncers out front. One waved me over, lifted the blue velvet rope, and ushered me inside.

I was on The List. Given that Winter was owned and operated by agents of hell—specifically, Prince Sitri and his Court of Jade Tears—I wasn't sure if that was an achievement to be proud of.

Fractal snowflakes whirled and exploded in showers of ivory and blue on LED wall screens, bouncing to the rhythm from the pulsing sound system. The packed dance floor writhed and shook in the shadow of a glass DJ booth dangling overhead from titanium cables. I stuck to the edge of the crowd and skirted around to a side passage lit in icy neon.

Past a few twists and turns, the music quickly fading to a muffled heartbeat, the hall ended in a solid metal door. A man in a black leather apron barred the way, his features shrouded in a gas mask with tinted lenses. A rusty machete hung from his belt. As I approached, he leaned over and tapped a code into a wall panel. The door clicked and swung open for me.

There were three levels to Winter, that I knew of. Anyone could get into the club up top—well, anyone who could pass muster with the doormen. The second floor, the honeycomb labyrinth with nested rooms done up in black leather and gold neon, was given to more intimate pursuits than wild dancing and fifteen-dollar cocktails. Pursuits largely involving things like handcuffs and the bite of a whip. Access to the "hive" was strictly by invitation only. Not everyone down here was working for Sitri's court—most of them didn't even know who really ran the place—but it was where you met the more interesting regulars.

The third level was where the Conduit lived. That was the creature who could open a pipeline straight to hell if you were unlucky enough to need one. I'd been down there twice, and twice was plenty.

Instead of getting myself lost, I stayed by the stairs and called Caitlin. She came out to greet me, and I squinted at her.

"How do I know it's really you?" I said, only half joking.

She rolled her eyes and took my hand, leading me through the honeycomb maze.

"Probably," she said, "because she knows if she ever pulls a stunt like that again, she'll be going back to Denver without her teeth. And she might anyway. The night is still young."

I shouldn't have been surprised to find a conference room down there. Mahogany walls, low lights, and a long table of smoked glass. Cylinders of Voss water and crystal glasses sat out at each place setting. It was the sort of room where I could imagine some Fortune 500 types meeting for intense business negotiations. Then I noticed the manacles dangling from stainless-steel hooks in the walls, spaced out around the room.

Caitlin followed my eye and winked. "We won't need those tonight. Try a chair instead. They're ergonomic. Haworth Zody Executive models, in fact."

She took the seat at the head of the table and gestured for me to sit at her right hand. I had to admit it was a damn comfortable chair. "Only the best of everything?"

"When Emma's buying. She's got an eye for design. She also just texted to say she won't be joining us tonight. She's been out at the ranch since Wednesday supervising construction."

I blinked. "Since Wednesday? Who the hell is watching Melanie?"

"She's almost eighteen, Daniel. She doesn't need a babysitter."

"You know what I mean," I said. "She shouldn't be alone right now."

Caitlin cracked one of the Voss cylinders open. Sparkling water burbled into her glass, splashing against its curving crystal lip.

"I know," she said. "Tell you what. Let's go out there tomorrow for lunch. We'll see if we can cheer her up a little."

"Isn't tomorrow a school day?"

She shrugged, taking a sip from her glass. "And what teenager isn't cheered up by getting out of school early? I'll forge a note from her mother."

"You're a genius," I said.

"So you say, but you're the one who got us out of trouble today."

"That," I said, "you can thank the shampoo commercial for. Crass commercialism to the rescue. So what's going to happen to Pete?"

"No human host, no possession. The house developed an unfortunate and sudden plague of roaches. Fortunately, posing as the homeowner, I was able to find an emergency exterminator. They draped the house with a tarp and started pumping in gas within the hour."

"Wait," I said. "You got that kid killed? I'm not okay with that, Caitlin."

She waved a careless hand at me. "Hardly. 'Pete' realized he was marinating in poisoned meat and fled. His mortal shell stumbled out of the house, coughing himself hoarse. He's in the hospital now, being treated for chemical exposure, but he should survive. Maybe, if he remembers any of this, it'll teach him not to play with the occult."

The door swung open. Naavarasi swept into the room with her lips pursed and eyes cold. Even from my seat, I couldn't miss the faint odor of insecticide clinging to her evening gown.

9.

"Oh," Caitlin said to Naavarasi, pretending to look surprised. "You didn't come straight here, did you? No, you must have gone to the house to see about your little friend Pete. Sorry about the fumigation. But we did send him home, as agreed. Why do you look so disappointed?"

Naavarasi took a seat at the conference table. Across from me, two chairs down from Caitlin.

"I'm not disappointed at all," she said, none of her words matching the look on her face. "I'm pleased. Wonderfully pleased."

"I'm so glad to hear that," Caitlin said. "After all, I wouldn't want to think there was any kind of subterfuge involved in your request. Some of the intelligence you gave us turned out to be faulty."

"I'm shocked," Naavarasi said.

Caitlin spread her hands, showing her open palms. "Let's get on with the meeting, shall we? Baron Naavarasi, I bid you formal greeting on behalf of the eminent and merciful

Prince Sitri and welcome you within our sacred borders, under the terms of the Cold Peace."

Naavarasi's eyes narrowed to slits. "So very formal."

"We have these formalities for a reason," Caitlin said. "And tradition is important."

"Right," Naavarasi said. "Wouldn't want to miss that. Is this what you do? Parrot pretty words someone wrote for you while you pretend you're an automaton?"

Caitlin tilted her head. "Greeting dignitaries, Baron, is part of my duty as Prince Sitri's hound. And visible emotions have no place in a diplomatic conference."

I poured myself a glass of sparkling water, and leaned back. Naavarasi fidgeted in her chair, marinating in her unhappiness, and I could see why. Caitlin was treating the hunger-spirit like she was part of hell's dominion, when that was the last thing Naavarasi wanted.

"Hey," I said, "Naavarasi."

Both women looked my way. I raised my glass.

"You got us, fair and square. It was a good trick. Respect."

She blinked, uncertain at first, like I might be mocking her, but then she started to smile.

"You were both completely safe," she said, "the entire time. I wouldn't have let anything bad happen to you."

It was another lie-without-lying. Nothing bad from *her* point of view would have happened. I let that slide without comment. The important thing was that she felt safe admitting she'd tried to con us. We weren't enemies now; we were coconspirators.

Caitlin caught my angle, like I knew she would. Her gaze flitted from me to the rakshasi as a faint smile played on her lips.

"My prince is fond of cleverness. Prince Malphas, from what I understand...not so much."

"He is fond of nothing but profit," Naavarasi said. "Paper. So much passion to be reaped in this world, so much joy and terror, and he obsesses over *paper*."

"Choir of Greed," Caitlin told me with a *what-can-you-do?* shrug. She sipped her sparkling water and looked back to Naavarasi. "I understand he annexed your old realm, is that right?"

"Annexed? He *ruined*—" Naavarasi started to say, then caught herself. She wanted to let it all out. I could feel her aching to talk, but she also knew that the enemy of her enemy wasn't necessarily her friend. She was still accountable to Prince Malphas. For now.

"...my realm is no longer what it was," she said, sullen. "But they gave me a title, and a seat on a council I've never bothered attending, and twenty acres of land in hell. I'm told it's nice."

Caitlin stood, smoothed her skirt, and said, "Could you excuse us just a moment?"

She tapped my shoulder. I followed her out of the conference room. She shut the door behind us.

"You found the key to her lock," Caitlin said.

I shrugged. "You can't treat Naavarasi like she's part of the courts. You heard her—she hates what Malphas did to her, and she doesn't *want* to assimilate. Honors and awards from your people just insult her. Imagine if somebody gave you a trophy for 'making such a great effort to be a real human being.' You'd be pissed."

"That's one way of putting it."

"Praise her on her own terms, and show she's valued for what she is: a rakshasi queen. She's starving for that. We know she's plotting against Malphas. All she wants is a little understanding. Give it to her and she'll play right into Sitri's hands."

"And is that wise?" Caitlin said. "Given her designs on you, to clasp a poisonous snake to our breast?"

"Would you rather she be out in the wild, plotting and planning who knows what? Or someplace close where we can keep an eye on her? Of course we can't trust her, that's her nature. We don't *need* to trust her if we can see her coming in advance. Besides, if she thinks there's a chance she'll get Sitri's full support when she makes her move against Malphas, she has less reason to try to snare me again."

Caitlin broke into a smile and pulled me into her arms.

"You," she murmured into my ear as her fingernails played through my hair, "are learning to think like one of us."

I wasn't sure how I felt about that.

"I need to have a private chat with Naavarasi before she heads back to Denver," Caitlin mused as she pulled away. "Feel her out. Seduce her a bit."

"Can I at least get pictures?" I said, wriggling my eyebrows like Groucho Marx.

She swatted my arm. "If it was *that* kind of seduction, I might invite you to join in. Maybe. Come over tomorrow? Swing by around ten and we'll go surprise Melanie."

"Will do," I said, then paused. I pointed down a random hallway and gave her a questioning look. Caitlin took my hand and pushed it until my finger aimed down a totally different corridor.

"That way," she said. "First left, next left, then second right."

I repeated the directions in my head, all the way to the stairs.

#

I wanted a drink, but not here. Winter wasn't my kind of place. I was about one demographic too old, one decade out of fashion, and two tax brackets too poor to hang with this crowd. The Tiger's Garden was more my scene and had the added bonus of exclusivity. If you weren't a bona fide magician, you didn't get in the door. Or find the door.

Still, I lingered on the edge of the dance floor a bit, taking in the vibe and nodding my head to the spine-throbbing beat. Then I looked over toward the bar and my teeth clenched.

She'd layered on a raccoon mask of makeup and her little black dress was shorter than my temper, but I'd recognize that mop of neon blue hair from a mile away. I cut through the crowd like a shark spotting a manatee, moved up behind her, and snatched the drink from her hand.

"Hey!" Melanie shouted, turning—then she saw my face and froze. "Oh. Oh, hey."

I sipped her drink. Some kind of fruity strawberry thing with enough rum to knock out a mule.

"Hey, Melanie. Think you're a little young for this, by about three years."

"That's not what my ID says."

From the smell of her breath, this wasn't her first round. I set her glass on the bar and slid it out of her reach.

"That's what I say," I told her. "What are you doing here?"

She shrugged one shoulder. "Came with some friends."

"Yeah? Where are they?"

She squinted into the crowd. I waited patiently, or at least as patiently as I could manage.

"They're here somewhere," she said.

"Well, now you're with me. Come on, I'm taking you home."

I had to give her a tug on the arm to get her walking. Outside on the sidewalk, I took off my blazer and draped it over her shoulders to keep off the night chill. She wore it sullenly all the way to my car.

"This is ridiculous," she said as I opened the passenger door and ushered her in. "And you're a fucking hypocrite."

I walked around the car, got in, and revved the engine.

"How do you figure?" I said.

"You mean to tell me that when you were my age, you *never* drank? You never used a fake ID or went somewhere you weren't allowed?"

I almost laughed. Those were my *minor* sins.

"There is a special kind of hypocrisy," I said, "that comes from wisdom born of age. It works like this: I did really stupid shit when I was a kid, and I paid for it. I do not want *you* to have to pay for *your* stupid shit, so I intervene, knowing where your chosen road is headed."

"So you just decided to ruin my night, because you care about me."

"That sounds about right," I said.

She didn't speak to me for rest of the drive. Can't say I blamed her.

Everything about Emma Loomis's house screamed *ordinary and respectable*. That was by design. It was a spacious tan stucco house in a sleepy little cul-de-sac, with a manicured lawn and no reason for anyone to look at it twice. I pulled into the driveway and followed Melanie to the front door.

"Seriously?" she said, looking over her shoulder at me as she jostled her keys in the lock.

"Seriously," I said. "I'm not leaving until you're in bed and asleep, to make sure you don't just leave again the second I'm gone. It's either that or I can call your mom and let her deal with you."

"Like she gives a shit."

Track lighting clicked on, casting glowing circles across polished tile and prim white carpet. The last time I'd been in the Loomises' living room, it was to assemble the best and brightest of Vegas's magical and underworld communities for a single purpose: giving Melanie's dad enough rope to hang himself.

"She really does care, you know," I said.

Melanie spun to face me, waving at the cold and empty room.

"Yeah? Then where is she, huh? Oh, right. She's four hundred miles away, renovating a *whorehouse*, because that's more important than being with her own daughter right now!"

I didn't have a good answer for that. I didn't think there was one. I still had to try.

"Different people handle their pain different ways," I said. "Your mom...she's one of those people who has to be working, all the time. She's got to keep her hands busy and her head full, because she's probably afraid she'll crash if she doesn't."

"And what about what I need? I don't even know how she can stand being at that place, after what she..." Melanie shook her head. She fell down onto the sofa and stared at the dead television.

"What?" I said.

When she looked back at me, her eyes were brimming with tears.

"I need you to tell me something. And I need the truth. Swear you'll tell me the truth."

I nodded. "Okay. You got it."

The words took a long time coming, but I already knew what she was going to ask.

"I need to know," she said, "did my mom kill my dad?"

Only three people were in that room when it all went down. One was dead and two were liars.

This conversation had been a long time coming. Didn't make me dread it any less. I shook my head.

"No," I told her. "I did."

10.

Melanie's expression didn't change. She sat there, frozen. Blue veins pulsed beneath the skin of her face, spreading out in a web that resembled a butterfly's wings, as the stress drove her demonic blood to the surface.

"We were going to let him go," I said. "But he pulled a gun. He was going to shoot your mom. If I hadn't jumped him and done...done what I did, he would have killed her. He didn't give me any choice."

Her eyes were like a dam pushing back against a raging flood. Her jaw clenched, like she couldn't force the words out. I sat down next to her.

"Is that what you thought?" I said gently. "That Emma was avoiding you because of what she did?"

"She just—" Melanie stammered, her voice breaking. "She just acted so guilty, and I thought—I thought—"

Then the tears came. She fell against me and I put my arms around her, holding her close as she finally found the grief she'd been bottling up since the night her father died.

She howled against my chest and I held her, an anchor in her storm.

"I'm *sorry*," I heard her moan again and again, and I shook my head and stroked her hair.

"Shh," I whispered. "No, it's all right. You have done *nothing* to be sorry for. Nothing at all."

Not like me, I thought. *Considering I watched Emma murder Ben in cold blood, and now I'm lying to his daughter about it.* I did my best to shove aside my self-loathing for a few minutes and focus on Melanie instead.

Her sobs turned into little choking wheezes, and then they finally faded into silence.

She slowly pulled away from me. Her makeup was caked down her cheeks like an oil slick. It stained my shirt in damp smears. She hiccuped and ran her hand under her nose.

"I bet I look like shit, huh?" she said, trying to smile.

"I've seen worse. Bet you feel a little better, though."

"Yeah," she said, sniffing. "Little bit."

"Tell you what. You go get some sleep. I'll crash here on the couch tonight. If you wake up in the night, you want to talk, you need anything, you come get me. Okay?"

She nodded quickly. "Okay."

Melanie scurried off to clean her face up and blow her nose. I waited until she was out of earshot and dialed Caitlin's number. When she answered, I heard the faint murmur of traffic under her voice.

"How'd the meeting go?"

"She's sitting right next to me," she said lightly, a veiled warning to watch what I talked about. "I'm taking our new guest out on the town for a bit, showing her the sights."

"When you're done, I could use a hand. I found Melanie up in the bar, drinking her troubles away on a bogus driver's license. I took her home."

"Wait," Caitlin said, "she was drinking in *Winter*? Out of all the places she could go, why there?"

"Probably because she wanted to get caught. It was a cry for help. I'm delivering. I'm gonna crash here tonight just to keep an eye on her, but she needs her mom. Any chance you could light a fire under Emma's ass and get her back here? Don't tell her about the bar, just...just let her know that I had the talk with Melanie, about what happened to Ben, and I think I smoothed things over a little."

Melanie had more weight on her shoulders than any seventeen-year-old should ever have to deal with. I knew what that was like. Unlike me, though, she actually had a chance to make something of her life. I wasn't sure which way she'd lean in the end, which of her parents she'd take after, and I really didn't care. What mattered to me was that she knew she had choices, and she knew she was loved.

Everybody should have that.

The doorbell rang at six in the morning. I sat up from the couch with a start, rubbed the crust from my eyes, and stumbled toward the door. I thought Emma had come home, my sleep-addled brain not realizing that Emma probably had a key to her own house.

Caitlin stood on the doorstep, draped in black Christian Dior with a floppy-brimmed hat that made me think of Audrey Hepburn in *Breakfast at Tiffany's*. She gazed at me from behind a pair of dark glasses just a little too large for her face, her body silhouetted in the morning glow.

"You are *way* early for lunch," I said, "but you look amazing."

"Emma can't get back until tonight," she said, stepping past me into the foyer. "So I took the liberty of making some plans."

An alarm clock whined from up the hall. Melanie's bedroom door opened and she trudged out like one of the walking dead, with her blue hair tangled and her body draped in an oversized nightshirt that drooped past her knees. She turned, saw us, and froze.

Caitlin was Prince Sitri's hound. To his subjects, that meant she was basically judge, jury, and executioner all rolled up in one. It was a bad sign when she showed up on your doorstep unannounced. Melanie's gaze flicked toward me, with a *what-did-you-tell-her?* look on her face.

"It occurred to me," Caitlin said, taking her glasses off and staring at Melanie, "that we haven't been spending enough time together. We're addressing that. Today."

Melanie gulped and gestured vaguely toward the bathroom. "I, uh, I have to go to school."

"Not today, you don't. You're home sick with a terrible flu. Might even last two days. Meanwhile, I have plans for you, young lady."

"I'll tear up the fake ID," Melanie squeaked. "I'll never do it again!"

Caitlin blinked, then nodded pleasantly.

"Well, yes, you will, but that's not why I'm here. We have reservations at the Canyon Ranch SpaClub. Shiatsu massage, vitamin infusion facials, sauna, mani-pedi, and of course we'll get our hair done. How does that sound?"

Melanie gaped. She fumbled for words, eventually coming up with, "That...sounds pretty okay."

"Well, then, you'd best get showered and changed. Hop to it. Go on."

Melanie vanished into the bathroom. Caitlin put her dark glasses back on and studied her fingernails.

"I *know* how to make someone relax," she told me. "She'll be a puddle of happy jelly by lunchtime."

"You're amazing, have I told you that lately?"

"I'm pretty okay," she said.

"How did things go with our, ah, guest?"

"We spent the night taking each other's measure," Caitlin said. "Seduction is a slow dance, not a sprint. She's definitely eager to be courted, but she doesn't want to seem *too* eager or give me any opportunity to upset her position with Prince Malphas. She goes back to Denver this morning. We'll see what comes of it."

While Caitlin and Melanie prepared for a day of pampering, I had a less glamorous job on my plate. Pixie's missing-persons problem had kept me tossing and turning all night while I tried to find an angle. The problem, I realized, was that I was doing all the hard work. Why hunt the predators, when I could let them hunt me instead?

Passing for homeless and hungry didn't take too much work. The people who lined up for food at St. Jude's didn't look a whole hell of a lot different from me or my friends. A little more tired. A little more scuffed up and beaten down. It was mostly in the eyes.

I headed back to Bentley and Corman's place and raided their closet. Corman was a bigger guy than me, and he hung onto clothes until even the moths lost interest. I scored an LA Dodgers T-shirt with a faded pasta sauce stain and a baggy pair of jeans that frayed at the cuffs. In the mirror, I looked like a guy wearing the only hand-me-downs he could find. I hadn't shaved yet that morning, and my stubble looked more sloppy than stylish. The bags under my eyes? Those were authentic. I really needed to stop couch-surfing.

I grabbed a fifth of Jack Daniels from the liquor cabinet and trundled back into the bathroom. Not every person on the streets has a battle with the bottle, but it's a popular stereotype. When you're crafting a disguise, playing on stereotypes goes a long way. I winced as I took a heavy swig from the bottle and gargled, swishing it over my teeth and tongue like it was mouthwash, then spit it into the sink. I gazed longingly at my unused toothbrush on my way out.

I could take my pick of gutters to crawl into, but I needed visibility. That meant the Boulevard. I parked a block off the Strip and blended in with the tourist foot traffic, noticing I was already getting more personal space than usual. Any herd can tell when they've got a sick animal in their midst.

Crystals at CityCenter was a monument to ridiculous excess. A shopping mall for the elite and elite wannabes, where Gucci and Armani boutiques rubbed shoulders with Cartier, Prada, and Kiki de Montpernasse. Normally I couldn't afford to breathe the air in there, but I'd been dragged along on a couple of shopping trips. Kiki de Montpernasse was where Caitlin bought her lingerie.

Panhandlers weren't a strange sight anywhere on the strip, but they knew to go where the money was. Outside Crystals, on a pedestrian bridge riding over the nightmare tangle of traffic below, a couple of regulars were already camped out with hand-lettered signs on corrugated cardboard and empty coffee cups for collecting change.

I'd done my own sign with a black Sharpie. "Homeless hungry need work. God Bless." I walked down to the far end of the footbridge, swallowed my pride, and sat down on the dirty concrete with my back to the steel railing and my sign propped up on my lap. In a heartbeat I went from a human being to a statistic, another faceless number in "The Homeless Problem."

It was amazing how fast I vanished. I'd braced myself for stares of disdain, insults, every bit of humiliation I could imagine, but it was the exact opposite. I just *wasn't there*. As the sun rose over Las Vegas, making the sweat bead on my scalp, I became a part of the background. The tourists didn't look at me. They stepped around my sign without seeing me at all. Trying to make eye contact turned into a game— when I managed it, their gazes jerked away so fast it was like they'd touched a hot stove.

I don't know why I was so surprised. That was exactly how I acted every time I passed the panhandlers on the bridges. I just never realized what it felt like until now.

Not everyone turned away. Every now and then someone would toss a few spare coins into my cup, even a couple of rumpled and sweaty dollar bills. I'd duck my head and mumble a "God bless ya, ma'am" as they quickly moved on, their good deed done for the day.

By noon the heat was as murderous as the growling in my stomach. I'd skipped breakfast, and now I was paying for it. I almost had to laugh. For me, this was playing a part. I could get up right then and there, walk into any restaurant on the Strip, and sit down to a decent meal. Amazing, the things you take for granted.

All right, I thought, *enough. Either these guys only prey on the homeless at night, they only work the back streets, or maybe they're just staying home today. Bottom line, the fish aren't biting. Time to pack up.*

That was when I saw the Missionary.

11.

The Missionary. That was what I dubbed the guy when I noticed him chatting up the panhandlers on the far end of the bridge. He had that look: crisp white shirt, gray slacks and polished wing tips, department store eyeglasses, and a save-the-world smile. A tan canvas satchel like a mail carrier's bag dangled over one shoulder, but I couldn't read the logo on it. I stopped watching and stared down at the concrete instead, putting all my energy into looking weak and alone.

He came over and stopped in front of me, rummaging in his satchel. I pegged him somewhere in his mid forties, with a military-neat haircut and a lantern jaw.

"You look hungry, buddy," he said. "Say, what do you like better? Turkey or roast beef?"

I gave a noncommittal shrug. "Beef, I guess."

"Well then, you, sir, are in luck, because I have just one of those left!"

He offered me a sandwich, sealed in a plastic baggie. The sight of thick, rich beef and lettuce leaves poking out from between slices of fresh bread made my stomach gurgle. I looked from him to the sandwich and back again, pretending to struggle with thinking through an alcoholic haze. It was hard to pull away from his eyes. He had these big baby blues the color of a childhood summertime.

"It's okay," he said. "Go on, it's free! We make them fresh every morning. Turkey's always harder to give away for some reason, and I always pack a few lettuce and tomato sandwiches for, you know, *vegetarians*, but I knew you were going to be a roast beef man. I can always pick 'em!"

"Nothin's free," I mumbled, but I took the sandwich.

"We're blessed to have generous donors with deep pockets," the Missionary said. He offered me a business card with his other hand, his fingers cupped to hold it by its edges. "The New Life Project. Have you heard of us?"

I shook my head and took the card. There was something funny about this guy, beyond his zeal to help his fellow man. His patter was too smooth, his moves too slick, like a stage actor playing a well-rehearsed part. I didn't feel like I needed to be on my guard, though. If anything, the more he talked, the more relaxed I felt around him.

The business card felt funny. Slick on the bottom, like it had gotten damp and left to dry out. I shoved it in my pocket.

"We're just trying to make things a little better out here," he told me. I believed him. He had wide, bright eyes younger than his body, like a kid who hadn't seen enough of the world to be beaten down by it yet. "You should come by our shelter some night. We have food, cots to sleep on—it's a safe place."

"Yeah, maybe," I said, trying to move him along. I felt bad taking his time when there were real people he could be helping.

"Just think about it? And I promise, no religious hard sell, no jive, just a roof over your head and a hot meal in your belly. We're here to help."

"Yeah, man," I mumbled. I curled my legs up against me, folding into myself, changing my body language to shut him out. "Thanks for the sandwich."

He gave me a wave and strolled away, whistling under his breath as he vanished into the crowds. I sat there a minute, perfectly still, not quite sure why I wasn't getting up.

My fingertips were numb.

I thought back to how he'd offered me the card. Holding it by the edges, not with his thumb and forefingers gripping the middle like most people would. I took it out of my pocket, carefully this time, and gave it a sniff. It was faint, in the swirl of odors from the street, but I could still catch the tang of chemicals.

He fucking dosed me, I thought, pushing myself to my feet. My legs were wobbly. I would have chalked that up to the last few hours of sitting on the brutally hot concrete, but now I could tell that my reactions were off. Just a little slower than usual, just a little less steady.

Worse, now that the Missionary and his stream of patter were gone, I could sense what he'd left in his wake: a faint trail of golden motes sparkling in the air and fading fast, invisible to the untrained eye. The aftermath of an enchantment.

No wonder I'd trusted him at first sight and it was so hard not to fall into his eyes. His slick little aura spell, blended with whatever drug he'd slipped me, formed a lethal one-two punch: each one covered the traces of the other and amplified the effect. He *made* me trust him, and it wasn't until he was long gone that I could put the pieces together. A regular joe off the street wouldn't stand a chance against this guy. I stared at the address on the card, thinking about his offer of shelter.

Why kidnap homeless people off the street when you could make them come to you?

By the time I got to my car, I felt fine again. I flexed my fingers, running my thumbnail across the pads to test for sensation as I rummaged in the trunk for a plastic bag to store the card and sandwich. Then I revved up the engine, got out while I waited for the air-conditioning to kick in, and called Pixie.

"Think I've got something on our missing-people problem," I told her. "Look up everything you can on this New Life Project operation. They're running a shelter in town. I want financials, history, anything you can get about who runs it and where they came from."

"If they're a 501(c)3, that'll all be public record," she said. "Easy sauce. You want me to check out their office too, do some Dumpster diving?"

"No. Stay away from there. At least until I figure out what the hell they're up to."

My next call was to Harmony Black.

We met in a Dunkin' Donuts parking lot. I pulled up alongside her car, a dour blue government-issue Ford, facing the other way so our windows lined up. She rolled down her window and gave me a tired look.

"What unreasonable thing do you want today?" she said.

"You have access to a chemical lab?"

"I do, yeah."

I reached out the window, offering her the plastic bag.

"I need this analyzed," I said.

"Okay, you seem fundamentally confused on the nature of our relationship, Faust. You're the criminal. You're going to prison. I'm the fed. I'm going to put you there. I don't run errands for you."

"This isn't about us," I said. "I've got a line on some homeless people going missing, and I think this is related. There's some kind of drug residue on the back of this card, and I'd bet twenty bucks you'll find the same chemicals in the sandwich. I need to know what the hell it is."

"What you *need* is to refer this to the local authorities. Drugging someone is a crime. Report it and turn over your evidence."

I leaned towards her, giving a quick glance left and right just to make sure nobody was wandering close enough to overhear.

"The guy who slipped me this stuff is one of *our* kind, agent. Some kind of magician. A good one. Slippery."

That got her attention. She took the bag from me, wary, and in my second sight the silver bangles on her wrist glittered like diamonds in the sun. Warding spells.

"If you really want me to throw some blind cops up against somebody like us," I said, "maybe more than one, then you just say the word and I'll start the meat grinder. If you ask me, though, I think this is best handled off the books."

"That's not your call," she said, setting the bag on her passenger's seat. She pursed her lips, staring at it like it might bite her, then looked back at me. "All right. I'll check into it, and that's all I'm offering. I'll be in touch."

The hum of her engine hadn't even faded away when my phone started buzzing. *Nicky*, said the caller ID. I almost let it go to voicemail, then second-guessed myself and picked up on the fourth ring.

"Dan," he said. "We need to talk."

"About?"

"Not on the phone. Come to the corner of Polaris and West Russell. Ten minutes."

"I'm not in town," I said.

"Yeah, you are. Ten minutes."

The line went dead. I cursed under my breath and shifted into first gear, rolling out into the busy street. Part of me wanted to let him stew, but I needed to figure out where his head was at—for my and Jennifer's sake, not to mention everybody else who would be wearing an orange jumpsuit if he decided to take a deal from the feds before we did.

Still, I didn't like it. Nicky wasn't terse by nature, and I'd seen what happened when he thought he was being backed into a corner. That was when bodies dropped.

He was waiting for me on the corner, dressed in a gray silk sports coat and titanium-rimmed glasses, looking like a movie producer on the hustle for a hot new deal. I pulled over to the curb, and he jumped in.

"Not here," he said. "Keep driving. Take the next left. What are you wearing? You look like a bum."

"Where are we going?"

"Just a little ride, that's all. Not far."

At the next light, I casually glanced toward his hip. His jacket was custom tailored, but I could still make out the bulge of his shoulder holster.

"This isn't the way to the Gentlemen's Bet," I said, trying to keep my tone light. I knew what happened when people went for "little rides" with Nicky Agnelli. I'd been in the backseat for more than one of them.

He knew I had to be thinking it too, and that was a lousy way of setting somebody up for a kill. Even so, he didn't have a single reassuring word for me. I decided to play it cool until I could figure out his game.

"I'm not working out of the Bet right now," he said. "You know, with all this stuff going on, these wild allegations? I'm trying to stay mobile. Agile."

His directions took us out to Eldorado, in North Vegas. Lots of sleepy little suburban houses baking in the sun, far from Nicky's usual flair for glitz and glamor. We turned on-to an access road and rolled into a half-finished housing development. It reminded me of those old pictures showing the evolution of man from ape. All along a freshly paved street the development grew from empty plots, to skeletons of plywood and drywall, to vacant and shiny houses waiting for buyers.

"This is us," Nicky said. "Number twenty, right here."

I pulled into a driveway and gave the freshly built house a hard look.

"Nice place. Thought you liked living closer to the action, though."

"Thought I'd buy myself a quiet little getaway," Nicky said. "C'mon, I wanna show you something. Let's go around the back."

I wondered, idly, if I could take Nicky in a fight. I'd never given it much thought before. I only knew one thing for sure: whatever he wanted to show me, it was nothing I wanted to see.

12.

I followed Nicky into a small yard shielded from the rest of the block by a birch picket fence. He turned to me and let out a heavy sigh, shaking his head.

"Danny, I'm gonna have to ask you something, and I know it's gonna insult you, but I hope you'll take it in the spirit of the situation and accept my honest apologies."

"Yeah?" I said. "What's that?"

"I need you to raise your arms."

"So you can see if I'm wearing a wire," I said.

"That's right."

"You son of a bitch."

Nicky's shoulders slumped.

"C'mon, buddy," he said. "With all the shit that's flying around here, you know I have to check. I *have* to. Now we can do this the friendly way, or we can do this the not-friendly way. Don't make us go there. You know me, I wouldn't ask if—"

"And you know *me*," I said. "I'm no rat, Nicky."

"I know, okay?" he said. "But given this whole situation...I gotta check. For my peace of mind. So please, pretty please, put your fucking arms up."

I stared him down as I lifted my arms in a T, not even blinking as he awkwardly patted my chest, back, and hips. His hand closed over the bulge in my hip pocket.

"What's this?" he said, squinting.

He jumped back as a stream of playing cards launched from my pocket. They flashed through the air in a stream of red and black and riffled into my outstretched hand. I caught the last card and turned my palm to show him. Bicycle Dragon Backs, my usual brand.

"Just a deck of cards," I said.

I saw his throat bulge as he swallowed. Nicky knew, better than most people, what I could do with a deck of cards.

"Yeah, all right," he said. "You're clean."

"Now tell me something I don't know."

"Do better than that," he said, turning to the back door and jiggling a key in the lock. "I'll show you."

I put the cards away and followed him in.

The kitchen had never seen a speck of dirt, outside of what we tracked in on our shoes. Nicky's new place had beech cabinets, yellow-and-white-checkered linoleum, and not a single utensil to be seen. Up the hall I could see a living room with brand new carpets the color of gold leaf, unmarred by footprints or furniture.

"This place is nice," Nicky said. "The developers went bust a few months back and they're sorting out who owes what to who, so you don't have a lot of real estate agents poking around, trying to—"

Beneath our feet, someone screamed. The muffled howl was primal, mingled fear and pain, setting my teeth on edge.

"Another nice thing," Nicky said. "It has a basement. Basements aren't cheap out here, you know? It's because of the caliche. The sedimentary rock. Digging that shit out is a ton of work. You pay out the ass for the square footage."

"What's going on here, Nicky?"

He opened a door just off the kitchen. Unfinished stone steps led the way down, under the cold glow of a dangling workman's light. He looked back at me, and I couldn't read his expression.

"Follow me. I'll show you," he said.

I stood my ground.

"C'mon," Nicky said. "This little party ain't for you. If it was, you think I ever would've let you see it coming? Jeez, Dan, gimme some fuckin' credit."

I followed him down the basement steps. Another muffled scream broke the air, over a sizzling, metallic noise. The stale, humid air down below smelled like burnt pork.

A naked man dangled by his handcuffed wrists from a ceiling beam. His toes barely brushed the concrete floor. His body was a canvas of bruises, cuts, and cigarette burns. One eye was swollen shut and the other, staring out behind a clump of matted black hair, was a thousand miles away from sane.

"Danny!" cheered Juliette, waving her arms frantically and flashing a pearly smile. She would have seemed more welcoming if her face and curly blond hair weren't spattered with fresh blood, and if she wasn't wearing a black leather apron and matching elbow-length gloves. Justine, her twin sister, stood by a rolling cart and held up a pair of jumper cables like she was about to give away the grand prize on a game show.

"What," I breathed, "the *fuck*, Nicky?"

"What, this guy right here?" Nicky said. He walked over to join the twins and patted the dangling man on the back. "Dan, meet Clay Boswell. Clay ran a little crew in Summerlin for me. Or at least he did, until he decided there was more of a future in law enforcement."

Juliette handed Nicky a white silk handkerchief. He wiped his fingers delicately. Clay tried to talk, mumbling incoherently behind the filthy gag in his mouth, his chapped and bloody lips twitching.

"Which means it's time to play our favorite game"— Justine tapped the jumper cables together and showered the cement floor in a violent explosion of sparks—"*attitude adjustment!*"

Nicky walked back over to me. Behind him, Justine lunged in and pressed the cables to Clay's chest. He shrieked and thrashed like a fish on a hook. The stench of burnt flesh twisted my stomach.

"Clay's been a bad boy," Nicky said. "Offered me up to Agent Black in exchange for immunity. Of course we caught him before he could hand over any evidence she didn't already have. Right now, Clay's making a painful and life-changing discovery. You know what that is, Dan?"

"Go ahead and tell me," I said through gritted teeth.

He moved in, standing almost toe to toe with me. "There's no such thing as immunity from *me*."

Another blast of sparks. Another muffled scream. I tried not to look.

"I don't know what he's supposed to tell you with that gag in his mouth," I said.

"Tell me?" Nicky said. "Nothing. He's already told me everything he knows. I don't want to hear another word out of him for the rest of his short and miserable life."

"Then why the fuck are you still torturing him?"

"To make a point. Dan, are you familiar with the castle doctrine?"

"Sure," I said. "Somebody invades your house, you've got the right to use lethal force."

Nicky put his arm around my shoulder. To my credit, I didn't flinch.

"I'm the king, Dan. That makes Vegas my castle. And when someone invades my castle, that means I have the right—no, the moral and ethical *duty*—to use any means necessary in its defense."

While Juliette whispered in Clay's ear, Justine put down the jumper cables and picked up a cordless drill.

"Our friend Clay, here?" Nicky said. "He's an object lesson. First, to make it clear that actions have consequences and disloyalty is something I take very, very personally. Second, to reassure everyone that I have this situation under control. The feds don't have anything. They're not going to *get* anything, and everyone just needs to chill out."

The drill whirred to life. Justine held it up to the light, so Clay's good eye could see what was coming next.

"I want you to spread the word," Nicky said. "Feds or no feds, Nicky Agnelli still owns Las Vegas. When the storm blows over, everybody who stayed cool is going to get a little something special in their Christmas stocking. Those who break ranks, on the other hand? I got more basements, Dan. There's always more basements."

"Fine," I said. "Message delivered. Now I'm leaving."

His grip tightened on my shoulder.

"Just one more minute. Stay and watch this part. This is gonna be good."

Justine looked over at me. Her eyes blazed orange in the shadows, like a candle burning inside a mad jack-o'-lantern. A forked tongue slithered from her sister's mouth, tasting the blood on Clay's ragged ear.

"Stay and watch, Danny," Justine cooed. She moved closer with the drill. "We're just getting warmed up."

#

I emerged into sunshine and heat like a long-lost cave explorer, slamming the kitchen door behind me. Then I staggered over to the picket fence, doubled over, and threw up on the freshly mowed grass. I leaned against the rough wooden fencepost with one hand until I could catch my breath.

After the basement, the quiet and peaceful suburban street was surreal. Nothing seemed real, nothing but the memory of that burning-flesh stench. I could still taste it in the back of my throat, no matter how many lungfuls of dry, hot air I gulped down.

Nicky knew. I had two encounters with Harmony Black in two days, and suddenly I got a front-row seat at his little torture show? I was a magician, and "coincidence" wasn't a word in our vocabulary. He wanted to make sure I wasn't getting too chummy with the enemy. After all, I knew more of his dirty secrets than almost anyone alive. If I wanted to burn him, I could.

And I did. I wanted to burn him to the fucking ground. Problem was, hurting him meant hurting people I cared about, too, people who would get dragged down by his sinking ship. Until I found a way around that, I was still Nicky's guardian angel.

I called Jennifer from the car and asked for a meet. She hadn't been too discreet about her unhappiness with Nicky lately, and I was pretty sure that "object lesson" in the basement wasn't just for my benefit.

I cruised back to Bentley and Corman's place to grab a shower and a change of clothes. I left the stubble on my cheeks, though. I had a feeling I'd be paying a recon visit to the good folks at the New Life Project in the very near future.

Night fell and the city woke up. I parked the car and walked half a block over to Fremont Street, drawn to the roiling of the drunken crowds and the blare of hard rock from towering speakers that were all volume, no finesse. A band on the open-air stage was ripping their way through a Van Halen tribute set and bouncing around like spandex-wrapped monkeys on crack. I waded through the cheering crowd, feeling underdressed without a plastic beer cup in my hand.

Meditation in motion was an acquired skill. I focused on my breathing and let the thoughts slip from my mind the same way I slipped through the press of bodies, letting my feet carry me along to the tempo of the drums. In the space between two heartbeats, I was nowhere at all.

Then I was in the shabby little foyer of an Indian restaurant, staring at the orange cigarette-burned carpet and inhaling the rich, spicy aroma of fresh tandoori chicken. That was how a visit to the Tiger's Garden worked: you didn't find the door, the door found you.

The gang was all there. Bentley and Corman held court over a feast of scarlet-spiced chicken and jasmine rice, and judging from the empty glasses, they'd gotten an early start on the night's drinking. Mama Margaux sat across from them, nursing a rum hurricane, with her hair done up in an ornate beehive. Her profile made me think of ancient Egyptian queens. Jennifer spotted me first and waved me over to the table, gesturing to an empty chair.

Amar intercepted me halfway there. He was the Garden's only waiter, possibly the cook and owner too, but he wouldn't talk about anything that wasn't on the menu. He held out a polished brass-rimmed tray bearing a single glass.

"Your whiskey and Coke, sir."

Time worked a little funny inside the Tiger's Garden. Your order was always placed long before you arrived, and it was always exactly what you wanted. Most of us had stopped trying to figure it out a long time ago.

"There he is," Corman called out. "Have a seat, kiddo. Soup's on."

My stomach gave an involuntary clench at the sight of the food. I couldn't help but think back to my first run-in with Naavarasi in Denver. She had her own "restaurant," and to seal a deal I'd eaten...I still didn't know what, not for sure, and she wouldn't tell me. That was her game: to keep me up at night, torturing me with the possibilities until I gave her what she wanted in exchange for the truth.

The joke was on her. The idea of learning the truth scared me more than not knowing.

13.

I did my best to push Naavarasi out of my mind as I sat down at the table and took a sip from my glass. Perfectly mixed, as always, and strong on the Jack. Just what I needed to get my feet back under me. Bentley looked over and frowned.

"Daniel? Are you feeling all right? You look pale."

I didn't sugarcoat it. These people were my family. Not by blood, but blood didn't mean a damn thing next to what we had together.

"Just came back from a little face time with Nicky Agnelli," I said. "Jen, you ever do business with a guy named Clay Boswell?"

"Little bit," she said. "He runs a B&E crew out of Summerlin. Sometimes he'd snatch my kind of merchandise and I'd take it off his hands for a cut. We're gonna do lunch next week, why?"

"Cancel your reservations. Clay went looking to make a deal with the feds. Nicky found out and gave him to the twins to play with. I was invited to watch, and by 'invited' I mean they stood me right in front of the poor bastard while the twins went to town on him and Nicky made not-so-veiled threats. He wants to make sure we know he's still the king of the castle."

"Son of a *bitch*," Jennifer said. The table thumped under her fist.

"Perhaps it's time," Bentley said, "for you both to seriously consider a visit to Agent Black. Lay your cards on the table, and take what she offers."

Corman nodded. "I know you're worried about the fallout, kiddo, but me and Bentley can take care of ourselves. Wouldn't be the first time we've pulled a vanishing act. Nicky's goons will never find us."

"Not happening," I said. "One good thing came out of this little nightmare: now we know Nicky's not shopping for a deal of his own. He's convinced he can ride this out until the task force unravels or Black just gives up and goes home."

"Can he?" Margaux said.

I shrugged. "He wouldn't be the first racket boss to get taken down in Vegas, not by a long shot, but he's got access to the kind of resources no human gangster could dream of. Bugsy Siegel didn't have a direct hotline to hell."

"Actually," Bentley started to say, then shook his head and fluttered his hand in the air. "Never mind."

I looked over at Jennifer. "I know you're pissed at Nicky, but you need to dial it down some. He's feeling cornered, and you know what that means. If he thinks you're going to be any kind of a threat, he'll shoot first and ask questions never."

"That *kochon* wouldn't dare," Margaux said. The faint crow's-feet at the corners of her eyes tightened. "What about the truce? The rules are the rules. We don't rob from him, he doesn't cross us."

The Vegas occult underground had always had an uneasy peace with Nicky, mostly because of how many of us had worked for him in one way or another. It was professional courtesy backed up by the promise of mutually assured destruction. He could take out any one of us, if he put his back into it, but he knew that would bring every magician in the city down on his head at once. That was one fight nobody would be walking away from.

"Different rules, sugar," Jennifer drawled. "I pay out to Nicky to keep my business running, not that it's done me a dog's lick of good lately. That means he has a certain proprietary interest in what I do and who I talk to. I could put a world of hurt on him if I talked to the feds. Rules or no rules, if he thinks I'm gonna pull that trigger, he's gonna pull *his* trigger."

Margaux leaned back in her chair and drank her hurricane, glowering.

"*Chak kochon gen samdi pa-l,*" she said.

"Meaning?" I said.

"Each pig gets its own Saturday," she said, contemplating her drink. "When I was a little girl, back home in Haiti, Saturday morning is when we'd slaughter the pigs."

\#

Mob mentality is like wildfire. It spreads fast and hard, and suddenly you find yourself surrounded by really smart people making really bad decisions. In the middle of a riot or a mass panic, the first thing to do is get the hell out, cool down, and collect your senses. I paid my tab and headed out to taste the night air.

Harmony Black had started a slow-motion avalanche, and I didn't know how to stop the rocks from raining down. Nicky was getting panicky, so the people under him were getting panicky, which spilled over into my crowd. It wouldn't take much of a push to get everybody tearing at everybody else's throats. Pretty soon somebody was going to do something stupid, and the entire Vegas underworld would burn for it. That probably suited Agent Black just fine, but it was my family standing in the cross fire. I needed to shut this thing down before it got completely out of control.

I had twelve calls on my phone in the last hour, all hang-ups from Pixie. She didn't leave voicemails, as a general rule, because she was afraid of the NSA listening in. There was no chance of talking over the raucous din on Fremont Street, so I waited until I was away from the crowds and in my car before I called her back. She picked up on the first ring.

"Where the hell did you find these guys?" she said, sounding breathless. I heard the clacking of a keyboard in the background, her fingers flying faster than bullets.

"Nice to talk to you too, Pix. Which guys?"

"The New Life Project! Holy crap, Faust, there is some serious craziness going on here. First of all, they're not a 501(c)3. They're not a charity at all."

I shifted in the vinyl seat.

"What are they, then?"

"Nada. They don't exist. Bogus entity, no papers. Here's the thing, though: their shelter is legally owned by McMillan Trade Group LLC. McMillan is just a holding company. It doesn't do or make...well, *anything*. They're one hundred percent owned by the Nevada Heritage Coalition. The NHC's a political action committee."

"Hold on," I said. "Why would a PAC want to start up a charity and bury it two layers deep?"

"Wait for it. The NHC is basically Senator Alton Roth's reelection machine. Not only is he their sole beneficiary, they're playing all kinds of games with the campaign financing rules. Like they fund him up to the legal cap, then they pour even more funding into his street teams and sponsoring voter registration drives in neighborhoods that lean his way. On top of that, they pay for 'independently funded' attack ads going after his opponents."

The name set off alarm bells. Roth was Lauren Carmichael's bought-and-paid-for man in the Senate. It was his influence that had pointed the feds in Nicky's direction, Lauren's little dose of payback for Nicky's betrayal.

"Is that even legal?" I said.

"Legal-ish. Ready for the good part? I got my hands on their donor list, and it's uber-shady. Tons of individual contributions, but that's a smoke screen. Half these names are just pulled off a state census. The money transfers tell the real story: the vast majority of NHC's funding comes from two sources. The first is Ausar Biomedical."

I scratched the back of my neck and glanced at my rearview mirror. This wasn't a great street to be hanging out on, especially after midnight.

"Name rings a bell," I said.

"You probably remember the media coverage. Back in the early nineties, Ausar was testing a new fertility treatment. Just small trial runs, but the result was...ugh. You remember the thalidomide babies? Like that, but even worse. A lot worse. I'm gonna have nightmares for a week just from the pictures. They got sued into oblivion after that and went into receivership. The company still exists, on paper, but it's been inactive for a little over twenty years."

Twenty years. My jaw tightened. Twenty years ago, Lauren Carmichael went to Nepal, and she damn near destroyed the world with the secrets she brought back.

Like I said, I didn't have much faith in coincidences.

"If Ausar doesn't have any money," I said, "how is it making secret donations to Roth's PAC?"

"That's the million-dollar question. Literally. It looks like they hid a metric butt-ton of cash from the government, and they've spent years slipping it into NHC's pockets through offshore intermediaries, turning it into crisp clean campaign dollars."

"Money laundering," I said.

"That's a bingo," Pixie said. "Now guess who their other big corporate donor is?"

I didn't have to guess. I already knew, down in my gut.

"The Carmichael-Sterling Group," I said.

"Then we get to the outbound cash, which is where things get even weirder. Not all of it's going to support Roth."

"How do you know that?"

She fell silent for a moment, concentrating. I listened to her fingers rattling over the keys.

"Because I'm rooting around inside one of their bank accounts right now," Pixie said. "Duh. They've been making secret payments to a guy named Angus Caine. Former British Special Air Service, now president and owner of Xerxes Security Solutions. They're a private military contractor

based out of the UK, like Blackwater but with an even nasti-
er reputation."

"Mercenaries," I said. "Senator Roth's got mercenaries on
his payroll."

I'd been assuming that Roth's hands were as clean as
your average politician's—just dirt under the nails, not
blood—and that he'd helped Lauren out in exchange for
cash under the table. A simple trade of favors. Now I wasn't
so sure.

"You thinking what I'm thinking?" Pixie said.

I turned the key. The Barracuda's engine fired to life with
a hungry growl.

"I'm thinking," I said, "that I need to get inside that
building."

Fortunately, I'd been handed an invitation.

14.

I barely slept that night. I tossed and turned on Bentley and Corman's scratchy couch, nursing a twinge in my back. When I finally drifted off, I dreamed I was standing in the middle of an earthquake on the Vegas Strip, the street ripping open beneath my feet.

The fury of a shattered world turned into the staccato buzzing of my phone, vibrating against the coffee table. I reached over, nearly tumbling off the couch, and pressed it against my ear.

"'Lo?" I mumbled, head half-buried against the cushion.

"It's Agent Black."

I opened my eyes. The sunrise rubbed up against the living room curtains, painting the white gauze in shades of gold.

"I called in a favor and fast-tracked that chemical analysis," Harmony said. "You were right. The sandwich was dosed with the same chemicals as the business card. Now you need to tell me exactly what this is about."

"What was the drug?"

"Where did you get this, Faust? Is somebody actually handing this stuff out on the street? This is serious."

"You first," I said.

I might have been half-asleep, but I could still hear her teeth grind on the other end of the line.

"It's a custom mix," she finally said. "A blend of tetrodotoxin and *datura stramonium*."

"I know those words," I muttered. I pushed against the cushions, forcing myself to sit up, and ran my fingers through my tangled hair. "Why do I know those words?"

"What do you know about zombies?"

"Shooting them in the head doesn't work," I said. "You've got to completely dismember them or they'll just keep coming."

"Not *movie* zombies, Faust. I mean real Haitian zombies."

"Right," I said. "Movies. That's totally what I was talking about."

Agent Black was a competent magician, bless her noble heart, but she was a little less worldly than I was. I tried to keep her that way.

"'Zombie powder' is a drug," she said. "Induces a temporary coma, hallucinatory trance, sometimes even long-term brain damage. It's mind control, old-school style. You dose some poor victim, bury him and dig him up again, and convince him he's an undead slave who's powerless to disobey you. Presto, you've got a zombie."

"And this is the same stuff?" I said.

"Very close, but much less concentrated. A dose this light won't be putting anyone in a coma, but it will cause a sense of passiveness and heightened suggestibility. Maybe even a waking trance state, if your victim's susceptible enough."

"So if you get the right dosage," I said, "and a friendly-looking guy says, 'Hey, you should come with me,' especially if he backs it up with a little magical nudge—"

"You'll do exactly what you're told," she said, finishing my thought for me. "Your turn. Who are these people? And what are they doing with this stuff?"

"Snatching homeless people. The 'why' part, I'm still working on."

"Not your job," Harmony said. "The drugged business card is enough probable cause to buy me a search warrant. We'll raid their offices and sort this out."

"No," I said quickly. "Don't do that. Let me check it out first, my way. New Life is connected to Senator Roth and to Lauren Carmichael."

"Can you prove that?"

"I can, but *you* can't. My source of information isn't exactly legal. Give me a chance to find something that'll stick, something that'll let you hit them both with kidnapping charges, before you go in guns blazing and scare off our only lead."

It was one of those sneaky little half-truths. If she got a chance to arrest Roth, more power to her. I'd never met the guy, but everybody likes seeing a politician in handcuffs. What I wanted was a line on where Carmichael was hiding so I could track her down before Harmony did.

Agent Black wanted to put Lauren Carmichael in a ten-by-ten prison cell. I had a better idea: a hole out in the desert, three feet wide and six feet deep.

"You've got twenty-four hours," she said and hung up on me.

I stumbled to the bathroom, splashed cold water on my face, and rubbed a hand across my bristly cheeks. Two days without shaving and my face was firmly in the "too long for roguish stubble, too short for a beard" category. I mussed my hair and changed into my panhandling outfit.

Corman was in the kitchen, wearing his ragged old gray robe and boxers, pouring himself a bowl of Frosted Flakes. He watched me come down the hall. One of his bushy eyebrows rose like a flag.

"Are those my clothes?" he said.

"Just borrowing," I told him. "I'm on a job, needed to whip up a little disguise."

"What are you disguising yourself as, a Dodgers fan?"

I just nodded. It seemed the prudent thing to do.

"Well," he said, "just bring everything back in one piece. I like that shirt."

I parked the car in a side lot about two blocks from New Life, tipped the attendant an extra twenty to keep an eye on it, and walked the rest of the way. The address led me to a run-down industrial park where half the doors had big For Lease signs. It looked like those signs had been hanging there for a while.

The New Life Project's welcome sign was shiny and new, though, standing out in front of a refurbished warehouse painted battleship gray. The place was big enough to be a homeless shelter, no doubt, but the lack of windows didn't give me a lot of optimism. A chain-link fence topped with barbed wire ran around the back of the building, cutting off the Dumpsters and the back door from casual access.

"All are welcome," the sign said. Time to put that to the test.

I'd left my wallet and phone back in the car, in case they searched me going in. My gun stayed securely in the trunk for the same reason. I still had my deck of cards, though. Being a sorcerer means you're never unarmed.

New Life had a cheap little lobby with a couple of over-stuffed chairs, a reception desk on rolling casters, and a potted fern drooping in the corner. It looked more like a doctor's office waiting room than what I imagined a homeless shelter would look like. I wished I could have brought Pixie along for some color commentary—she would have known in a heartbeat if the place was wrong.

The frizzy-haired woman behind the desk had a bright smile and glassy eyes that read like two big blue Vacancy signs. I would have pegged her for a pill popper, but Valium didn't have anything on New Life's brand of chemical bliss.

"Welcome!" she said, a little too friendly to be real. "How can we help you? Are you looking for a place to stay?"

I nodded, scrunching up my face, putting on my burnout routine.

"Yeah," I mumbled. "Guy gave me a—a card and a sammich. Said I should come around, you'd help me out."

"Absolutely! Let's just have you sign in."

She gestured to a clipboard on the edge of the desk. The sheet on top was filled with scribbled names, just two vacant spaces left at the bottom of the page. Judging from the dates, they'd had more than a few visitors in the last couple of days. I wondered where they were right now. I reached for the pen, then froze.

The plastic glistened. It was wet, a trap waiting to be sprung.

I looked up at her and gave an apologetic shrug. "I, uh...I don't know how t'write so good."

"It's okay! Just do your best, sweetie. You can even just draw a little X if you want."

Picking up that pen meant getting a dose of the Missionary's zombie juice straight through the skin of my fingers, just like when I'd taken his business card. On the other hand, the effects from my first exposure had only lasted about fifteen minutes. If I kept myself together, I could probably ride it out. The receptionist wasn't going to take no for an answer, and I was about five seconds from blowing my own cover.

I picked up the pen, scribbled an X, and dropped it as fast as I could. The familiar tingling numbness hit me in seconds, making my fingers go slack.

Remember the numbness, I told myself. *If you're numb, you're not yourself. Remember that!*

Strangely, though, it didn't seem as important as it had a minute ago. I couldn't remember why I was so worried. The receptionist leaned over and clicked a little white button on her desk intercom.

"That's perfect, sweetie! Now you just wait one second, right there, and somebody will come along to help you out."

I waited. It felt like a good idea.

The door behind her desk swung open, and the Missionary came out with a big smile and a hearty "Hey there, buddy!" He'd traded in his street ensemble for a pristine white lab coat and thick white latex gloves. I thought, on some level, that his new outfit should concern me, but I couldn't figure out why. He was such a nice guy, why worry about it? His tranquil blue eyes, so big and expressive, welcomed me in.

"I am so glad you came," he told me. "Are you hungry? It's almost lunchtime! Come on back with me. Let's get you taken care of."

He led me down a green-walled corridor lined with crisp white tiles. The air smelled like Listerine and mothballs. We paused by a rolling cart stocked with supplies from a clinic: cotton swabs, tongue depressors, bandages, and a glass jar with a shiny chrome lid.

"Just one last thing, buddy," he said. "Stand right there, real still, okay?"

He pulled back the lid on the jar. Green glittery dust sparkled inside, like ground glass from a church window.

My thoughts squeezed through my brain like molasses, my reactions confused, like a deer trapped in the headlights of an oncoming car. I had just enough time to realize what was coming, but not enough time to stop it. He dipped his gloved fingers into the jar, raised them to his lips, and blew. The dust hit my face and I impulsively jerked back, inhaling sharply, pulling it in through my mouth and nose.

The world turned into an oil painting. Colors faded and blurred and ran like melted wax. My body went numb, and under the numbness came a wriggling itching feeling all over my body, like centipedes under my skin. My ears rang with a slow dull droning like a wordless lullaby.

"That's better, friend. Let's put you with the others," I heard the Missionary say as he put his hand on my back, steering me up the corridor. Sure. Put me with the others. That sounded fine.

Steel bars rattled. A cell door slid open. Bodies moved all around me, drifting aimlessly or just standing still, wavering on their feet. I walked until I came to a cinder-block wall, and then I stopped and stared at it. The block in front of my face had so many tiny ripples, imperfections in the concrete, and I wanted to count them all. That seemed like a fine thing to do.

"His mind is not in his mind," a voice whispered off to my side. It echoed, the reverb bouncing around inside my cotton-candy skull. I looked to my left and squinted.

The smoke-faced men hovered before me, their polished black leather Oxfords dangling an inch above the floor of the cell. The rest of the room was a blur of blobs and smears, but they stood out as if drawn onto the skin of the world with a calligrapher's pen.

"Yes," the other said. "He can hear us now."

15.

I'd only seen them once before, in the tortured memories of Eugene Planck's dreams. They'd appeared to Lauren Carmichael in Nepal, taught her the arts of a sorcerer, and handed her the Ring of Solomon. They'd groomed her for twenty years, guiding her pursuit of power, but it was all a long con: she would have accidentally jump-started the apocalypse if we hadn't been there to stop her.

"Objection!" said one of the men, his words buzzing like the thrum of a thousand flies' wings flurrying in concert. His face was a blur of smoke, a break in reality. He wore a smock and mortarboard like an old-time professor, while his companion dressed in Armani black.

"Lauren and we are *un-hello!*" the other shrilled. "She couldn't fail properly! Some planetary disassembly required!"

I tried to answer, but the zombie powder had my words locked in a vice. My tongue felt fat, numb and useless in my mouth, like a dead slug.

"We had to destroy the village to save the village," the professor buzzed. "Burn out the infection. We were not in the tomb. We did not give her the ring."

"We do not believe in marriage! Only divorce! Are you on our frequency, Kenneth?"

I shook my head, mute. I could feel them scrabbling at my mind, trying to take hold—no, trying to explain. They wanted to show me something, but they didn't know how to talk and I didn't know how to listen.

"Get your mind right," the professor said, "and come see us. We will teach you gardening skills. There are strange weeds to be pulled."

"Limited-time offer!" the other buzzed. "Act now or forever hold your peace!"

"What's another word for life abundant, Faust? What's another word for life abundant?"

I rubbed at my forehead. My numb fingers slicked off beadlets of hot sweat, like oil on rubber.

"When you know the word, you will know your enemy," the professor said. "But not if you die here. Wake up! Wake up and go deaf!"

Their images faded, turning blurry and vague at the edges. I felt my thoughts slowly returning as the dose of the Missionary's powder passed its peak and ebbed away.

"Come and find us," the professor droned. "We have to show you—"

Then they were gone. I blinked, trying to focus my eyes, struggling to make sense of the world. The drugs in my system were wearing off, but they were still strong enough to keep my brain locked in a straitjacket.

"Line up!" a gruff voice shouted. "Lunchtime! You're hungry! Take a sandwich and eat it!"

I stood at the end of a ragged line. I wasn't sure how many of us there were, squeezed into the prison cell, and nobody talked. We shuffled ahead, one at a time, as a man in camouflage fatigues shoved sandwiches into our hands. My stomach grumbled, and I staggered toward the back of the cell, eager to eat. I hoped I remembered how.

"You?" a voice whispered. "Holy shit, it *is* you! Dan, hey, focus!"

I didn't want to focus. I wanted to eat. The first man had said I was hungry, and I was. I ignored the new voice and lifted the sandwich, but rough hands tore it away from me and snapped their fingers in my ear.

"Don't eat that shit! They lace the food, that's how they keep you stupid. Hey, you listening? You remember me? Eric, from the storm tunnels!"

He grabbed my chin and turned my face toward him. He looked more ragged than the last time I'd seen him, with bloodshot eyes and a week's worth of scraggly chestnut beard, but his face sparked something in the back of my mind.

The Stacy Pankow murder. The job that had put me on a head-on collision with Lauren and her cult. I'd gone down into the tunnels under Vegas to check out an alleged drowning, and found an enraged wraith instead.

"You were..." I started to say, forcing my numb tongue and lips to move. "Down there."

He nodded fast. "Yeah, yeah, and you took care of that little girl. Whatever you did, man, you laid her to rest."

I didn't lay Stacy's soul to rest. I sent her to hell. It wasn't my finest hour.

"You're magic, aren't you?" Eric whispered. He shot a look over toward the sandwich line, making sure nobody was listening. "You really are. We need you, man. We need you *now*."

"Can't...can't think right. Head's not attached to the rest of me."

Eric squeezed my shoulder hard and marched me to the back corner of the cell. He pushed me down, and I sat on the cold stone floor. He squatted beside me.

"It doesn't last long," he whispered. "That's why they keep feeding us that shit. Another hour and you'll be sharp again. I figured it out. Got a couple of other guys to stop eating, too. Leroy and Bull, they're wide-awake and ready to throw down, but we need a plan. We've just been playacting, pretending to be zombies like the rest of these guys while we try and figure out how to get out of here. We ain't eaten in three days, Dan. I don't know how much longer we can hold out."

A screech ripped through the air. It wasn't human.

It came from somewhere beyond the bars, farther than my blurred vision could see. A second screech set my teeth on edge. It sounded like a pterodactyl getting its wings sawed off.

"And that's why," Eric whispered. His face went ash gray.

"What?" was all I managed to say, but the question was obvious.

He shook his head. "They take two or three of us a day, one at a time, up that hallway. Nobody ever comes back. You just hear the screaming. I think it's like that horror movie, man. The one where those sick fucks pay a million dollars to torture somebody?"

I didn't have the heart or the words to tell him the truth. Whatever was going on here, it was probably far, far worse than that.

"Just sit here and rest a minute." Eric looked deep into my eyes. "I'm gonna go tell the others. I was scared as hell, but man, now that you're here? Now I *know* everything's gonna be all right."

He left me there, carrying that weight on my shoulders while I waited for my senses to swim back through the fog.

My vision came first. I was in a cell about twenty feet by twenty feet, with maybe a dozen prisoners. No windows, and beige-painted bars straight out of a county jail. The room stank of fear and stale piss. Outside, a corridor ran off in both directions, but I couldn't see where it led. Now and again a guard strolled past, dressed in fatigues and toting a matte-black rifle that looked like something out of a science fiction movie. He barely paid us any attention beyond the occasional glance of contempt.

Eric came back with two other guys and made quiet introductions. Leroy was a big bruiser with a pug nose while Bull was short with a shaved head and a bad attitude. The kind of guy who starts bar fights to prove himself, and usually wins.

"Guard sweeps by every five minutes," Eric whispered as we huddled in the back of the cell, "so we gotta talk fast."

Bull gave me a hard look. "Eric says you can get us out of here. That true?"

"Do my best," I said. "What are we up against? How many guards?"

"Too many," Leroy said. "I know these fuckers. One rolled up his sleeves, and I saw the triangle tat on his arm. Xerxes. I was in Desert Storm, Fifth Engineer Battalion, that's where I remember seeing that logo. These guys? They're fuckin' mercenaries. They got no right to operate on American soil."

Bull curled his lip. "They do if this is a government facility. Think about it, bro. It's a FEMA camp, just like I been warning you for years."

Xerxes. Now I knew why the Nevada Heritage Coalition was making secret payments to a private military contractor. They needed help keeping their dirty business under wraps. I wondered if the crew that had ambushed us out in Chloride had tattoos on their arms, too.

"These guys are hard as nails," Leroy said. "Their gear is no joke, either. Those rifles they're toting? Tavor TAR-21s. Chop you up like a fuckin' Ginsu on full auto."

"What about a bum-rush?" I said. "Wait for them to open the gate, then we jump the guards?"

Bull and Leroy gave Eric a look. Eric turned to me like a doctor about to tell a patient he has terminal cancer.

Eric shook his head slowly. "Look up."

I followed his gaze to the sprinkler heads set into the ceiling. There were at least four of them in the cell, more than I'd expect for a fire-control system, but innocent enough.

"The guards think we're all zombies, so they feel safe shooting their mouths off in front of us. They had a new guy who was bellyaching about, you know, what happens if the cops get wind of what's going down. The other guard said they can always get more bums, so in case of an emergency—*any* emergency—the number-one priority is getting rid of the evidence."

"Get rid of it, how?" I said.

Eric nodded upward. "That sprinkler system isn't for fires. It runs to a pair of hundred-gallon tanks on the other side of that wall. The tanks are full of concentrated sodium hydroxide."

"Lye," Bull said. "If the alarm goes off, for any reason, everyone in this cell *melts*."

I leaned my head back against the cinder-block wall and closed my eyes.

"Then we need to up our timetable," I said.

"Yeah? Why's that?" Eric said.

"Because I'm just the advance scout. The FBI knows about this place, and in less than twenty-four hours, they're going to kick in the front door. If we're still in this cell when they do, we're all dead men."

16.

A metallic *bang* echoed from up the hallway, followed by another inhuman screech. Then a scream of pain, this one all too human, ending in a ragged gurgle.

"Containment breach in two," a placid voice said over a loudspeaker as a klaxon whined. "Calling all hands for immediate termination protocol. Containment breach in two."

My stomach clenched as we looked up at the sprinkler heads, poised and ready to rain down with caustic death.

"Door's closed," Eric said, squinting at the bars. "That's not for us."

Something was coming. A slithering wet stomp sounded from the corridor, and the air filled with the stench of rotting meat.

"Not us," I whispered. "The breach was the other room. The one where they're taking people."

Whatever I'd imagined was slouching its way toward our cell, screeching and limping and hitting the walls with meaty thuds, the reality was worse. The creature rounded the corner and came into sight, turning its eyeless head to face the cage and its prisoners like a butcher eying a fresh slab of meat.

It might have been human, once. It walked on two legs, though one dragged behind it, a bloated and rubbery tube of puckered flesh that twisted and bent like a crazy straw. It had two arms, though one wept with pestilent sores and the other, flailing bonelessly, was lined with hungry little mouths whose yellowed and broken teeth chomped at the rancid air. Its head and chest were overgrown with purple and black tumors and pustules the size of golf balls. The growths blistered and swelled, as if breathing on their own.

The creature forced its arm between the bars of the cell and wrapped itself around the neck of the nearest prisoner, hauling him close. Even lost in a drugged haze, the poor bastard found the voice to scream as a dozen sets of teeth clamped onto his skin and started chewing.

A pair of double doors at the other end of the hall burst open. Four men in camo ran in, two dropping to one knee and the other two aiming high, swinging their rifles toward the cell bars. I had just enough time to wave the others back toward the wall before a hurricane of bullets jackhammered through the air and left me half-blind in the muzzle flash. The creature's pustules exploded in the fusillade, splashing yellow pus and black blood across the bars, and it slumped to the ground still clutching its bullet-riddled victim. Another prisoner's corpse sprawled on the concrete nearby, his skull blown open by a stray round.

"Zombie up!" I hissed, prompting Eric, Leroy, and Bull to wipe the looks of horror off their faces and play listless. The other prisoners stayed where they stood, wavering on drugged feet as if nothing had happened at all.

"Jesus *Christ!*" shouted a voice from up the hallway. An older man in a long white lab coat and mirrored glasses stomped into view, flailing his arms as he took in the wreckage. He had a disheveled mop of black hair and fat, puffy lips that curled in disgust. "What are you idiots *doing*? We could have contained this."

"They're doin' their bloody *job*," said the scowling man who came in behind the guards. His fatigues were crisp and his black leather boots polished to a shine, his back ramrod-straight and his eyes hard enough to cut glass. He wore his salt-and-pepper hair in a buzz cut, and his accent was pure Cockney.

"Their job? Their job is to obliterate a successful test subject and potentially contaminate half the facility? *Look* at this mess!"

The military man waved his men back, ignoring the comment. "You done good, lads. None o' you got any of that shite on you, right? Good. Back to your posts."

"We're going to need a full toxic scrub here," the man in the lab coat fretted, his eyes concealed behind his glasses. "An atmospheric workup—"

"Oh, come off it and quit your grousing. The only mess here is comin' out of your lab. If this is what you call a success, you're a long way from getting paid."

The man in the coat strode up to him, poking a slender finger against his chest as he spoke.

"Pardon me, *Major*, but I think I know a little more about the intricacies of this project than some hired gun. What we're attempting here, on a quantum-chaos scale, has literally never been—"

The major's hand shot out in a blur, locking around the other man's finger like he was snatching a fly with a pair of chopsticks. The man in the coat yelped as his finger bent backward, slowly, hovering just shy of the breaking point.

"Nedry," the major said, his voice a leathery growl, "the senator pulled me and my lads onto this job because we know what we're about. I've been to the Temple of the Black Mother in Mogili. I've drunk the cold sweat of the ten dead saints. So don't talk shite to me about black magic like I ain't never seen it. And don't *ever* touch me again unless you want to lose your finger *and* your cock, not necessarily in that order."

He let go. Nedry took a stumbling step backward, shoulders hunched, clutching his finger to his chest. I had a pretty good idea of who the major was, now. If the hired thugs were his "lads," then this had to be Angus Caine, Xerxes's president. Senator Roth and Lauren were calling out the big guns. Literally.

"Sorry," Nedry mumbled with his reddened face turned toward the carnage on the floor. "I'll just...I'll just get this cleaned up."

"You do that," Angus growled. He turned and strode away, leaving Nedry with the mess.

Whatever the hell was happening in this freak's "lab," I didn't want any part of it. Even so, it was my best and only chance to get out of this deathtrap of a cell and hopefully— if I was really good and really lucky—get the others out too.

"Eric," I whispered, crouching low behind a couple of the zombies, "how do they pick who gets taken out next?"

He huddled next to me, nodding toward the bars. "They just grab whoever's closest to the door. They ain't picky. That's how we've been staying alive. We just keep to the back of the cell. Thing is, they're taking more people out of here than they're bringing in. Sooner or later..."

"I'm going next."

"What?" he whispered, eyes wide. "Are you crazy?"

"I've got to get to a phone and call off the feds before they spook these guys. You three just hang back, keep up the zombie act, and get ready to move. When things start to happen, they're gonna happen fast."

Two men in yellow decontamination suits, their faces blurry behind visored hoods, dragged in some black nylon body bags and a cart of cleaning supplies. They had to come into the cell, pushing the prisoners back, to get at the two corpses inside the bars. That was my chance. I made my jaw slack and unfocused my eyes as I gently pushed my way through the tight crowd, slipping a little closer every time the cleaners' faces turned away. Eventually, inch by inch, I made it to the front of the pack.

"It's ridiculous, having to work under these conditions," Nedry said to the cleaners. "They toss me table scraps and expect me to cook a gourmet meal with them."

The cleaners, preoccupied with their grisly work, ignored him. I tried not to wrinkle my nose as they lifted the creature's bullet-pocked corpse and wrestled it into a double-sized body bag. The room stank like someone had put a week-old piece of meat under a broiler and turned up the heat. Nedry looked over toward the cell. I saw my doubled reflection in the lenses of his mirrored glasses.

"Time for one more, I think. Let's see. Eeny, meeny, miny...you."

His finger pointed my way. I stared straight ahead and acted like I wasn't aware of anything. The only thing I couldn't control was the pounding of my heart.

"Come on, come on," he said, reaching in and giving my sleeve a tug. I stumbled forward like a wind-up toy, letting him guide me along.

My deck of cards grew hot against my hip, but I let them sleep. I wasn't sure what this guy's background was or what he could do, but right now my life—and the lives of all the people back in that cell—depended on making myself look as harmless as possible.

An armed guard stood outside the door at the end of the hall. To the left, a second door hung open on one twisted and broken hinge with its screws ripped from the wall. Dents hammered the reinforced steel like it was made of tinfoil. I wanted to get a better look, but I didn't dare turn my head or show interest in anything beyond my own breathing.

Nedry's lab looked like a mad interior decorator with a chrome obsession got loose in a doctor's office. My reflection bounced back at me from mirrored cabinets and walls, distorted and warped in a wall of burbling beakers and flasks connected by polished brass piping to a pair of stainless-steel vats. A surgical gurney stood in the center of the room, laid out with fresh white sheets and ready for an operation, lit by a dangling light fixture on a swing arm. Difference was, most gurneys in my experience didn't come with leather restraints.

Nedry stood me in the corner of the room and shut the door, putting two inches of steel between us and the gunman outside. He didn't lock it. If the room was soundproof, I had a chance at taking him down without drawing the guard's attention. If not, I might as well hang a target around my neck and brace for the gunshot.

Nedry put his back to me. He puttered around the shelves, laying out a hypodermic needle sized for a horse and arranging a scattering of jars and vials as he hummed tunelessly under his breath.

"Take your clothes off and lie down on the gurney," he said, not looking back.

I was taking a hell of a risk going up against an unknown mage with armed backup ten feet away, not knowing how or what could trigger the alarm and the lye deathtrap, but I'd tilted the odds as far in my favor as I could. Unless I wanted a firsthand experience of what that dead monster in the hall had endured, it was time to make my move.

I hesitated, just for a heartbeat.

Nedry smelled the change in the air. His head jerked up, taking in the room's reflection in the chromed cabinets. The image bounced off his glasses and back again, redoubling into an infinite void with all of his attention on just one thing: the expression on my face as I dropped the zombie act, hardened my eyes, and called a spark of magic to my fingertips.

17.

It all happened in the space of a breath.

Nedry's face contorted in rage, his puffy lips peeling back in a grimace as he lunged for a scalpel. He twirled and whipped it through the air with perfect aim. The gleaming blade streaked toward my eye like an arrow. My cards crackled with energy, and the queen of spades flung herself into my outstretched fingertips, carrying my hand up with her momentum.

The scalpel's blade punched through the card's face, stopped dead in its flight. Then the hex Nedry had laid on the scalpel kicked in and sent a vicious shock down my arm that left me numb and reeling, like I'd just clamped my palm over a Taser and pulled the trigger.

Fight-or-flight kicked in, and the adrenaline flowed. I gave the gurney a savage kick, sending it rolling into Nedry and knocking him against the counter. He fell back, fumbling for his hypodermic needle as the lab door flung open and the guard's silhouette loomed on the threshold.

I reached up, grabbed the surgical light fixture, and heaved. The boom arm flew, and Nedry had to throw up his hand to keep the fixture from slamming into his head. The guard's rifle swung up toward me, but he paused, frozen in surprise for a second, as another card leaped out of my pocket and into my hand.

That was all the time I needed. The gun clattered to the floor and so did the guard, clutching at the card buried halfway in his throat as arterial blood guttered down the front of his camouflage fatigues.

Nedry was on his belly, reaching for the needle where it had rolled between the gurney's wheels. I stomped down on his hand hard enough to feel bones crack under my heel. Then I dropped my knee onto his back, grabbed his other hand, and wrenched it behind him.

"If you want to die today," I hissed in his ear, "go ahead and scream."

He wheezed out his pain through gritted teeth. His fractured hand flopped on the tile like a dying fish.

"We're going to play a game," I said. "It goes like this. I ask questions. You answer them. If you answer them correctly, you win valuable prizes, like the ability to continue breathing."

He grimaced and shook his head. I gave his arm a hard twist to keep him focused.

"Question one. The jets in the cell where you're keeping the prisoners. What triggers them?"

"The—the silent alarm at the reception desk," he said. "Who *are* you? Are you a cop?"

"You wish you were that lucky. Question two. How do I deactivate the system?"

"I don't know. Just go to the utility room and turn off the water main, I guess. I don't know. I'm not the damn janitor. God, you fucked up my hand—"

"Focus," I said, giving his arm a tug. "What are Lauren and Roth up to? Why are you turning these people into monsters?"

"We're not—" he started to say, then coughed. "We're not turning these people into *monsters*, you asshole. That's just a side effect. We are on the cutting edge of magical science, and you have no idea, *no idea*, what you just stepped in."

I hauled him to his feet, keeping his arm pinned behind his back. On the other side of the room, I caught his expression in the glossy chrome fixtures. Despite the pain, he had a nasty little lizard smile on his puffy lips, and I didn't like it.

"Here's what's going to happen," I said. "You're going to be a good little hostage while I free those prisoners. Then you're going to take me to Lauren Carmichael."

"Sorry, champ," he said, "but my backup just arrived."

He stared into his reflection on the far side of the room, our images redoubling and bouncing back in the mirrors over his eyes. I glanced to the doorway. Nothing there but a dead man and a pool of stale blood. The fix was in. Nedry was too confident to be bluffing, but I couldn't figure out his angle.

"What, you expecting a guard patrol?" I said. "I'm betting you're the star of the show around here. They won't shoot as long as I've got you."

"Don't look now, but there's somebody behind you," Nedry said.

There was nothing behind me but the polished chrome counter and a span of mirrored wall. I took a step back just to be safe. My hip bumped against the cold metal.

"Guess what," Nedry said. His voice dropped to a whisper. "It's *me*."

Hands burst from the mirror, six identical hands at the end of six identical white-sleeved arms, and grabbed me from behind. Nedry's face flashed on every reflective surface in sight and every mouth tittered and leered as the real man slipped free of my grip. Hands clamped down on my arms, my wrists, my throat, hauling me back against the counter and pinning me fast.

I'd never seen a trick like that before, but I didn't have time to admire the technique. Nedry didn't stick around. He broke and ran, no doubt going to fetch more of Caine's mercenaries and come back with some serious firepower.

Or trigger the alarm and kill every single hostage in that death cell.

I twisted my left arm hard, breaking loose, while the mad giggling of dozens of reflections echoed in my ears. I flailed wildly, trying to grab something I could use from the scattering of surgical tools Nedry had left behind. My fingers closed around a heavy steel shaft, and as my thumb pressed down on a toggle switch, a vicious circular blade on the end of the shaft whirred to life. Bone saw. That'd do. I wrenched my arm, leaning as far sideways as I could, and pressed the saw against the mirror.

The reflections screamed.

As the saw chewed into the glass, spitting glittering dust, the hands released me and yanked back into the mirror's depths. The spell broke on a sudden gust of heat—there, then suddenly gone, leaving nothing in the room's reflections but me as I dropped the saw and staggered away from the counter.

No time to rest. I ran for the door, pausing to crouch down and pry the sleek black rifle from the dead guard's clenched fingers. I could turn cards into deadly weapons, but they were lacking when it came to the intimidation factor. An assault rifle wouldn't have that problem. Then I patted the corpse down, dipping my fingers into his pockets, and came up with a heavy ring of keys.

I'd never beat Nedry to the front desk. I darted back toward the cell, keeping the rifle up with its butt braced against my shoulder, and tried the handle on a door marked Utility. The bare-bones and dusty room on the other side held the building's main boiler, fuse box...and two steel vats, eight feet high and half as wide, hooked to a pair of metal mesh hoses that ran up into the ceiling.

Killing the power wouldn't work. Any security setup worth its salt had the alarm system on an independent circuit, specifically so guys like me couldn't shut it down by yanking a few fuses. I wasn't dealing with amateurs here. That left the vats.

The machinery joining the vats was a nightmare jumble of pipes and flanges. Since you couldn't really hire a professional plumber to set up your deathtraps, some clever techie on Angus Caine's payroll must have done it himself with whatever parts he had on hand. The one thing that looked familiar was a valve jutting out at the bottom of the assembly, right under a pressure gauge.

It looked like a cutoff valve. Assuming I had any idea what I was looking at. Assuming it would work. Assuming the whole rig wasn't an elaborate fail-safe, a trap that would start the killing rain as soon as I turned the wheel.

That was a hell of a lot of maybes.

No time to think. Nedry would be seconds away from the front desk, probably with a platoon of thugs on his heels. I had to decide, right then and there.

A drop of icy sweat slid down the side of my face as I took hold of the valve and gave it a twist.

Nothing happened. No rattling, no gurgling sound surging through the reinforced pipes, nothing at all. I turned the wheel until it couldn't budge another inch, hoping I'd cut off the system. If not, things were about to go from bad to worse.

I got to the cell just as the alarm started to whine.

I fumbled with the guard's key ring, jamming key after key into the heavy barred door as Eric, Leroy, and Bull shouldered their way through the crowd of zombies. Leroy looked up at the sprinkler heads and grabbed the bars, rattling them as hard as he could.

"C'mon, man," Leroy cried. "Get us out of here!"

Angus Caine's voice boomed over the loudspeaker.

"All right, lads, we've got a situation gamma. Containment team to the breach point. Everyone else rally on me. Facility's compromised, full burn. Purging the cells now."

"Come *on!*" Bull shouted. I tried another key, but the lock didn't budge. My hands shook but the next key slid in and greeted me with the smooth sweet feel of the tumblers rolling over. I slid the cell door open, and the men burst out into the hall, just ahead of...

...nothing. The sprinklers dangled over the prisoners' heads, motionless and silent. The cutoff valve had worked after all.

"Don't celebrate just yet," I said. "He said a containment team was coming to the breach. I'm guessing that's Nedry's lab, which means they'll be heading this way. Leroy, you said you were military, right?"

"Long time ago, yeah, but I still got it where it counts."

I handed him the Tavor. "Here. You can use this better than I can."

Eric frowned, probably doing the same head-math I was. He looked from the closed double doors on one end of the hall up toward the bend in the corridor about a hundred feet in the other direction.

"We've gotta fall back," he said. "This is a shooting gallery. Second they come through those doors, we're screwed."

He was right, but I hadn't seen anything resembling defensive cover. We could stay here and get chewed up in the hall, or run and get bottled up in Nedry's lab. Then I snapped my fingers.

"No we're not. They don't know I killed the sprinkler feed, right? As far as they know, everyone behind those bars is dead. That means when they come through they'll be looking straight ahead, not at the cell, at least for a couple of seconds. Tunnel vision."

"So we stand just inside the bars, off to the side," Eric said. "Let 'em pass ahead of us and hit from behind."

Leroy checked the rifle's magazine and flicked off the safety. "Rock and roll, baby."

I didn't like our odds. Four men, three of them half-starved and only two with weapons, against a team of professional mercenaries?

I hoped we didn't lose the element of surprise, because that was the only thing standing between us and the grave.

18.

Crouching behind the bars of the open cell, we waited. One of the double doors swung open.

A slim metal cylinder arced over the threshold, clattering onto the stone floor and rolling to a lazy stop. I had just enough time to take a deep breath before one end burst and clouds of voluminous white smoke hissed out to fill the corridor.

I had expected trained soldiers. I didn't expect tear gas.

The Xerxes troops hustled in fast, four of them moving two by two, faces shrouded behind oval-eyed gas masks that made them look like a flock of hungry owls. By the time one glanced to the side and noticed the cell was full of living prisoners—and the door was wide open—it was too late for him. Leroy's rifle erupted in a quick three-round blast and blew the back of his skull open.

Eric barreled out of the cell and into the white fog. He threw himself onto the closest mercenary, all fists and feet and violent hunger. Bull was right behind him. Leroy squeezed off another burst as the tear gas billowed and swallowed us all.

My eyes stung like I'd stuffed slivers of fresh-cut onion under the lids. My burning lungs spasmed out the poisoned air as fast as I could breathe it in. I charged into the fight. A white-hot blast of gunfire strobed to my right and chewed into the wall. Off to the left, another rifle spat fire and sent a silhouetted body slumping to the ground. I ran up behind one of the guards and threw myself on him, yanking at his mask and ripping it off his face. He pulled his trigger, firing wild and blind, and someone else grabbed him from the front, tore the rifle away, and slammed him in the gut with it.

When the toxic smoke cleared and the fighting was done, four dead men lay sprawled and shattered across the bloodstained floor. Three of theirs. One of ours.

I slumped against the cell bars. Across from me, Eric's face was a puffy mess of tears and dried snot, and I figured I couldn't look much better. He cradled a stolen rifle in his lap, pointed lightly at the one Xerxes merc still breathing on the floor. Leroy hadn't come out so good. He sucked air between clenched teeth and cupped his free hand over a stain on his side that seeped red between his fingers.

Bull was facedown and long gone.

Behind me, the other prisoners mostly just lay where they'd fallen, gagging and spitting in the aftermath of the gas, but too far gone in their drug dreams to do anything but moan and hold their heads.

"It's a through-and-through," Leroy said, nodding down to his wound. "Hurts like a motherfucker, but I'm still breathin'. Be all right."

I wasn't sure if he was trying to be brave for his own benefit or ours, but given how much blood he was leaving on the concrete, he was anything but all right. His clock was running down.

The last living mercenary looked from me to Eric to Leroy, and to the rifles in their laps.

"You wanna stay down," I told him. "Eric, if this prick moves, shoot him in both hands and then kneecap him. I need him alive."

"Done deal," Eric said, looking like he meant it.

A walkie-talkie clipped to one of the dead men's belts squawked to life.

"Containment team report," Angus Caine's voice snapped over a bed of static. "We heard gunshots. Report in."

I pushed myself to my feet, still feeling lightheaded and sick to my stomach from the gas. I coughed wetly into my sleeve and unhooked the walkie-talkie.

"Sorry," I said. "They can't come to the phone right now. Well, three of them can't, unless you know a good necromancer. Still got a live one here, though. Want to talk about a trade?"

Angus's voice rumbled like motor oil poured over fine gravel. "Prove it."

I held out the walkie-talkie toward the merc on the floor. "Here, say hi to your boss."

"Sir!" the merc said. "I knew the risks when I went in, sir! Do not negotiate with terrorists—"

That was all I needed. I mustered what little strength I had and kicked him square in the gut. He went fetal, groaning.

"I've been called a lot of things," I said into the walkie-talkie, "but 'terrorist' is a new one. Here's the deal, Major.

I'm pretty good at reading people, and I don't think you're the kind of guy who callously throws his men's lives away. I think you *will* negotiate, especially if getting soldier-boy back doesn't cost you a thing."

The other end went silent for a minute. I hoped he wasn't getting ready to lead a full-on charge, because we wouldn't survive another fight.

"Let's talk," he said. "Come up to the lobby."

I handed the walkie-talkie to Eric and said, "You two stay here. I'll see if I can swing us safe passage."

"Hey," Eric said as I walked away. I looked back, and he gestured to one of the fallen rifles. "Aren't you gonna take a gun?"

I shook my head, showing him my empty palms.

"No guns," I said. "Trust me. I'm scarier without one."

Truth was, I was still red-eyed and throat-burned from the tear gas, and I felt like I'd been used for a punching bag. My joints ached, and it was all I could do to keep from heaving up what little was left in my stomach. I could probably pull off a cantrip or two, but right now serious sorcery was as far out of my league as a French supermodel. I'd have to fall back on the most powerful weapon I had.

Bluffing.

The doors at the end of the hall, leading into the lobby, caught my eye. I stopped just short of setting my hand against the glossy metal push plate, my palm hovering an inch away. It was wet. They'd painted the steel with a heaping helping of the Missionary's happy juice. Cute move.

I took a deep breath, pushed my shoulders back, and lifted my chin. Then I kicked the door open and strode out like a gunslinger.

Angus wasn't alone, standing in the middle of the lobby. He had a six-man squad at his back, and every one of their barrels dropped a bead on me, ready to turn me into confetti on his command. Nedry and the Missionary stood off to the side in their white lab coats. Nedry clutched his fractured hand and glared, while the Missionary looked too confident for his own good.

"Hey there, buddy!" the Missionary said with a bright smile. I could feel his aura probing at mine, trying to find a way into my mind. I scrounged up a spark of magic and gave him a wall of psychic iron in return. His eyes went wide and he flinched, drawing a curious look from Nedry.

"Now what?" Angus growled. "Did you think I was just going to let you walk out, free as a mockingbird? I don't see a hostage with you."

I shook my head. "Nope. The hostage is back in the cell, with my friends. My friends who got that zombie shit out of their systems by starving themselves for three days straight. They're really hungry now, and they're *really* pissed off. If I'm not back there in ten minutes, I can't promise your soldier's safety. Go ahead, call back there."

He nodded to the mercenary at his side, who took a walkie-talkie from his belt and held it up for Angus.

"This is Major Caine," he said. "Who's back there with my man? Report!"

Eric's chuckle crackled over the static. "Nobody here but us chickens," he said.

I nodded. "See? Not alone. Not by a long shot. And if I die, your man dies, so let's drop the posturing and talk business."

"Just shoot him," Nedry said, petulant. "Clark and I can get your man back."

I glanced over at them. "Clark? That's your name? I was calling you the Missionary all this time."

He flashed his perfect white teeth. "Gosh, thanks, buddy! That's quite the bold moniker, and don't think I don't appreciate—"

"Now shut the fuck up," I said. "Both of you. Grown-ups are talking."

"Who *are* you?" Angus said. He rested his hands on his belt.

"Daniel Faust. And if you don't know my name, there's one hell of a hole in your intel."

"Oh, yes," Angus said. "Your name came up in the briefing. Ms. Carmichael didn't think you'd be a problem, though. Not this degree of problem."

"She has a habit of downplaying trouble. I don't suppose she told you about Tony Vance or Sheldon Kaufman? They were a couple of sorcerers in her *last* crew."

Angus shook his head. "Not a word. What happened to 'em?"

"I did. Now, in this room I'm counting six guns, plus the sidearm on your hip, and your two lab-rat magicians. Tell me something, Major. Do I look worried?"

I hoped to hell I didn't, because if any single one of them decided to test me, I was as good as dead. When you're all out of options, sometimes you can get through trouble with nothing but raw confidence.

Sometimes.

"No," Angus said, "you don't. So how do you see this playing out, son?"

"Simple. You take your troops and pull out. Once you're gone, I lead everyone else out of here and drop your boy off, safe and sound, on a street corner about a mile away."

"You think we're going to let those people go?" Nedry said. "After what they've seen?"

"Yeah," I said. "I do. I'm pretty sure every computer in this building's been scrubbed with a magnet and there isn't a damn thing that can connect you or Xerxes to the property. You made a smart play with your choice of victims, too. Nobody listens to the homeless anyway, and once they start telling the cops they saw monsters here? *Nobody's* going to listen. The only thing that'll get you in trouble is if you're caught here, red-handed. Which is about to happen."

"How do you figure that?" Angus said.

"The FBI knows all about the little drugged goodies Clark's been handing out on the street, and they're about to swoop in and raid this place. I asked for a grace window so I could poke around first, but my time's almost up. If you don't want to walk out of here in cuffs, it's time to pull up stakes and go. New Life is finished."

"It's not our *only* clinic," Nedry scoffed.

Clark reached over, all smiles, and patted Nedry's back. The other man stiffened as Clark's hand slid higher, rubbing the back of his neck.

"Hey, buddy," Clark said softly, "you're all tense and angry, and I think it'd be a really good idea if you didn't talk right now, okay? Maybe just not say another word."

Nedry nodded his head, suddenly mute. His eyes glazed over.

"Thank you," Angus said to Clark. He turned back toward me and gave me a hard look. He gestured for his men to hang back as he crossed the lobby floor, standing so close I could count the bristles on his chin. He smelled like Old Spice and gunpowder.

"You killed three of my lads," he said. Crow's-feet bristled at the corners of his squinting eyes.

"Four," I said. "You forgot the one outside Nedry's lab."

"Right. Understand something, Daniel Faust. I'll do you for that. Maybe not today, maybe not tomorrow, but I'll do you for that. I'm going to cut your heart straight out of your bloody chest, and I'm going to eat it with a dollop of steak sauce. You wanted me to know your name? Well, now I know it. And I never forget."

19.

Looking into the steel flints of Angus Caine's eyes felt like staring down the business end of a double-barreled shotgun.

"Guess I'll see you on the battlefield then, Major," I said. "But if you want a piece of advice? Get out of town. Lauren Carmichael likes surrounding herself with cannon fodder. She also likes feeding her friends into the meat grinder while she skips away free. Whatever she told you, whatever she promised you, that's all you are to her."

"We aren't her *friends*," Angus growled. "We're private contractors, the best of the best, and the only thing she's promised us is cold hard cash. There's no sentiment here, boy. Don't think you can play me against her. Long as her checks keep clearing, we're not going anywhere."

I tilted my head, leaning in just a little. Showing him I wasn't intimidated, no matter how hard my heart was pounding.

"Well then. You'd better get moving, unless you want to spend those nice fat checks on cigarettes in the prison commissary."

He backed away slowly, keeping me fixed in his sight as he waved his men out of the building. He was the last to leave, and he didn't turn his back on me until he was five steps out the door.

I let out the breath I'd been holding.

Another gun barrel jabbed me in the cheek as I returned to the cell, but it was only Eric. He had the Xerxes goon kneeling on the floor with his elbows up and fingers woven behind his neck. Leroy didn't look so good. He was still sitting where I'd left him, head lolled back and eyes heavy-lidded. There was a lot more of him on the floor now, pooling out in a sticky red puddle.

"It's cool," I said, and Eric lowered his rifle. "They're gone. We need to roll. Leroy? Talk to me, buddy. Can you walk?"

"Do what I gotta do," he mumbled. He tried to stand up, and I gave him my arm.

"Your lucky day," I told the mercenary. "Your boss likes you after all. Eric, get this guy walking and cover him."

Eric pointed to the zombies sitting in the cell, watching us with listless, blank eyes.

"What about the others?" he said.

"They can wait for the FBI to show up," I said. "Until the drugs wear off, they're safer here than they would be out on the streets, wandering into traffic."

I helped Leroy all the way to the front door. That was where I left them. I ran for my car in a dead sprint. By the time I reached the lot, my shirt was soaked through with sweat and my throat burned like I'd gotten a second dose of tear gas, but I didn't have time to catch my breath. The Barracuda's chassis jolted as I swung into the office park and over a curb, tires squealing to a stop outside the New Life building. We hustled Leroy into the backseat, making him as comfortable as we could. Eric got in beside him, keeping his rifle trained on the mercenary in the passenger seat.

We went four blocks before I stomped on the brakes again. The car squealed to a stop outside a run-down gas station.

"Out," I said.

The merc stared at me blankly.

"Eric," I said, "if he doesn't get out of this car in the next five seconds, shoot him in the head, and I'll kick his body to the curb."

That got him moving. The second the door shut we took off again, leaving him in our dust.

"This isn't the way to the hospital," Eric said. "Take a left up here, it's faster."

"We're not going to the hospital," I told him.

Hospitals were messy. Hospitals meant questions. If you showed up in the ER with a bullet wound, they were legally obligated to call the cops. Leroy's story led back to a hallway filled with corpses, and that wasn't weight he needed to carry. Even if the cops called it self-defense, that'd be enough to put his and Eric's names on Angus Caine's hit list right next to mine.

I leaned over and grabbed my phone out of the glove compartment, driving with one eye on the road while I pulled up the entry labeled Doc on my contact list.

"It's Faust," I said. "You working today? Good. Got one patient, coming in hot. Gunshot, and he's lost a lot of blood.

No, I think it came out the other side. All right. Yeah, I'm vouching for him and a guest. Seven minutes."

"Who was that?" Eric asked as I hung up the phone.

"My family physician," I said.

We rumbled into the parking lot of the Rosewood Funeral Home. It sat on a lonely corner in East Vegas across the street from a boarded-up strip mall and right next door to a lonely discount furniture outlet that had been advertising the same "two days only, everything must go" sale since 1998. Doc Savoy appeared in the front door, mopping sweat from his dusky liver-spotted scalp, and waved for me to drive around back. He wore an old pair of wire-framed glasses and a faded linen butcher's smock. All ready for surgery.

I pulled the Barracuda around the building, parking behind the shelter of a vinyl fence, and the old man came jogging out to meet us. He fiddled with his glasses and squinted at Leroy as we helped him out of the backseat.

"Oh, that's not good, that's not good at all," the doc rasped. I didn't pay it any mind—he'd say the same thing if you came in with a broken fingernail. He ushered us through the service entrance and into the morgue. The steel embalming table glowed under hot lights, all hosed down and ready for the patient.

"Go and scrub up," he said, pointing Eric and me toward the big steel sink next to a row of refrigeration lockers. "Marjoline's out getting her hair done, so you two are honorary nurses today. You're all puffy looking. What'd you get into?"

"Tear gas," I said.

"*Cold* water, then. Faces and hands, cold as you can stand it. Hot water'll just bring the sting back." He looked to Leroy. "Do you know your blood type, son?"

Leroy winced as Doc Savoy helped him onto the table. "Type B? I think."

"That's just fine, then. Don't you worry about a thing. We'll fix you up right as rain."

Doc Savoy was good people, and just like Jennifer, he was one of the dozens of little reasons I hadn't thrown Nicky Agnelli under the federal bus. He wasn't one of Nicky's guys, not exactly, but every serious heister and professional villain in town had his number on their speed dial. Like most of his patients, he'd go down in Nicky's wake.

He'd been running his off-the-books fix-up service for longer than most of his clients had been alive. Rumor said that he was old-school Vegas, that he'd cut his teeth with the last of the original mobsters before the feds and the corporations ran them out of town. He had the old-school values down, anyway: he did his job, he did it well, and he'd take a twenty-year stretch before he'd ever whisper a client's name in a cop's ear.

That said, the closest he'd ever come to a medical degree was a bachelor's in veterinary science, but I figured he'd had so much practice over the years that he was basically as good as the real thing.

He pumped Leroy full of enough morphine to knock out an elephant while I used a pair of shears to cut away his shirt around the wound. The fabric was stiff with dried blood, and Leroy's skin clung to it as I gently peeled it back. Clotted black blood rimmed the bullet hole, and it quivered when he breathed, spitting out a sad scarlet trickle that rolled down his hip. Doc Savoy had Eric hold a steel water bowl and put me on instrument duty. Then he rolled up his shirtsleeves and got to work.

Eventually there was nothing left to do but wait. Eric bummed a cigarette off of the doc, and he and I went outside to wait for the final verdict. A jumbo jet cruised overhead, coming in for a landing as the late afternoon sky turned to soft violet.

"You can take off if you need to," I told Eric. I watched as he paced and stress-smoked. His worn-out sneakers crunched on the loose asphalt.

"Nah, I'm good. It's funny. Barely know the guy. I mean, we just met in that fuckin' cell. But when you go through something like that, with somebody...I'm not leaving till I know he's all right."

"Then what?" I said idly, just killing time. "Heading back down into the tunnels?"

He stared up at the airplane in the distance and thought it over. Then he looked at the stub of cigarette left between his fingers and tossed it down, snuffing it out under his heel.

"I been gone a long time," he said. "Gone from the world. Didn't think I really had anything to live for. But after what happened back there? Now I know I sure as fuck don't wanna die. I don't know, maybe I could get myself clean. Make it stick this time. Do something different."

I nodded and gestured to the service entrance. "You've got some demons to wrestle. I bet Leroy does too. Maybe you two could help each other out. Easier than going it alone."

"Yeah," he said. "Maybe so."

Doc Savoy came out a little later, rubbing a crumpled paper towel along his freshly washed fingers.

"It's all good," he said. "He's sleeping like a baby. Just make sure he keeps it clean, changes the bandages, and takes antibiotics to stave off infection. I'll send him off with a little goodie bag."

"You're the best, Doc," I said and shook his hand. He might have been pushing seventy, but he shook hands like a twenty-year-old prizefighter.

"Now," he said, "not to be vulgar, my old friend, but we've come to that time-honored part where payment is due for services rendered."

"How do you feel about barter today?" I said.

"I do prefer cash," he said. "But let's see if I feel what you're selling."

Eric's and Leroy's stolen rifles lay on the backseat of the car. I checked the fence to make sure nobody was watching before taking one out and holding it up for the doc to take a good look. He whistled as he ran his wrinkled hand along the sleek barrel.

"Hoo," he said. "Where'd you get this, robbing a space-ship? Tell me the truth now, Dan, you didn't mug ol' Buck Rogers, did you?"

"It's called a Tavor," I said. "I've got two of them here, and I can't imagine they're cheap. Take them over to Winslow at the Sunset Garage. He'll pay top dollar."

Doc Savoy grinned like a kid on Christmas morning as he cradled the rifles in his arms.

"I do believe we have a deal, old friend, yes I do. Huh. Way this neighborhood's going, I might just keep one of these for myself."

While he took his bounty inside, I offered Eric my hand.

"Good luck," I said, "wherever you end up. And listen, if you really want to get cleaned up, go over to St. Jude's and ask for Pixie. She's a good person to know."

"Thanks, man," he said, squeezing my hand. "For everything. We'd be dead if you hadn't shown up, or worse."

I got into the car, fired up the engine, and leaned out the window as I put it in reverse.

"You've got your life back," I said as I rolled on past. "Just remember that it's worth something."

20.

I had smoke on my mind, and not the kind that comes from a cigarette. The smoke-faced men had appeared to me while I was neck-deep in Clark's zombie powder, and I got the impression they'd been trying to reach out and touch someone for a while now. *He can hear us now*, they had said when the drug took hold and knocked me senseless.

I had a pretty good idea of how I could get back in touch with them. Did I want to? That was the trickier question. The faceless men had manipulated Lauren as part of a twenty-year plan to destroy the entire world, and that put them pretty firmly in the "not my friends" column. The enemy of my enemy was still my enemy. Still, if they were willing to dish the dirt on Lauren's new game, it could be worth hearing them out.

I made up my mind in the space of a slow red light. They were treacherous bastards, but they were also the only lead I had left. I'd do it tonight. The faster I worked, the faster I could throw a wrench into Lauren's gears. I dialed up Caitlin on the go, to bring her up to speed and find out how Melanie was doing.

"Happy jelly," she said, sounding smug. "Emma came back in time for dinner, and I left them to it. Emma's...not doing so well. Putting up a brave front, but Ben cut her where it hurt."

I'd been there for the final showdown. When Ben told her that he'd hated her for years, his words had hit Emma like a punch to the gut. Even when we knew he was a traitor, none of us realized how deep his loathing ran until he poured it all out in a river of bile. He'd played the loving and dutiful husband card until it was time to pull the rug out from under her in one fell swoop.

Ben had been paid in full for his betrayal, but that didn't lessen the sting.

"Daniel?" Caitlin said, sounding a little deflated. "Could you come over? I'd like to see you tonight."

She'd watched the aftermath of her best friend getting stabbed in the back by her human lover. It didn't take a genius to figure out why she wanted a little reassurance tonight. Work could wait. I hooked a U-turn at the next light, stopped at Bentley and Corman's place for a change of clothes, and headed for the Taipei Tower.

Caitlin had a penthouse on the top floor with a view of the Strip to kill for. The Southern Tropics Import/Export Company had a great incentive plan for its top employees. The ones at the bottom, not so much. She took my hand at the door and led me inside, across the expanse of black leather, ivory, and chrome. A Duran Duran album played softly on the stereo.

"Did you eat?" she said as I followed her into the kitchen. "I'm just cooking up a little something."

A little something, in this case, was a bowl of tortellini mixed with edamame and slices of smoked sausage. We sat together at her glass-topped table with a single white candle and a bottle of Argentinian Malbec. She didn't open up until her second glass of wine, but I wasn't trying to push her.

"When Emma fell in love with Ben," she said apropos of nothing, "she took a lot of snide comments for it. Relationships like—like theirs—aren't exactly favored in our society. I mean, it's generally considered, like..."

Her voice trailed off. I cracked a smile.

"You're trying to find a way of saying something like, 'It's like a human marrying their pet dog or their dinner,' without offending me," I said. "It's okay, Cait. I understand we've got some cultural issues to work through. And I know you're not like that."

Caitlin poked her food with her fork. "She didn't see him like that either. There was a lot of, 'Just wait, it'll work out. You'll see.' I backed her up, of course. Sometimes forcefully."

"How forcefully?" I said.

"You can tell someone to stop saying nasty things about your best friend a hundred times," she mused over a forkful of pasta. "But you only have to rip their tongue out once."

I poured myself another dollop of wine.

"Now she's eating crow," I guessed, "because all the people who told her the relationship was doomed turned out to be right."

"She's lost face in the court, and the shame stings almost as much as what Ben did to her. The only reason she didn't lose her position is because she helped take down Sullivan. That, and I put a word in my father's ear."

She fell silent after that. I took another bite, chewing into a spicy sliver of sausage, and contemplated my fork.

"They're saying the same things about you now, too," I said.

She nodded, eying her plate.

"Not as loudly, of course," she said, "but the grumblings are there. It's funny, you know. Emma's become your biggest fan. If we succeed where she failed, it actually vindicates her in a sense. Proves that the problem was Ben, not the entire concept of a relationship between our species."

"Does that mean she's going to stop flirting with me?"

"Of course not," she said, glancing up at me with a light smile on her lips. "We all have to be true to our nature."

"For what it's worth, I'm sorry. I don't want you to take any flack on my account."

I reached for my glass. Her hand met mine halfway, closing over it, gently pressing it down onto the table. In the shifting candlelight, her eyes glimmered with flecks of molten copper.

"My choices are mine," she said. "You helped see to that. And I choose you. Anyone who has a problem with that is welcome to challenge me on the plains of Limbo. Every notch on my hunting spear is the end of another fool's story."

After dinner we took small plates of caramel-drizzled cheesecake over to the plush leather couch, cuddling together in the television's glow. It was the only place in the world I wanted to be.

#

I woke to sunlight on my face, streaming in through the half-turned venetian blinds in Caitlin's bedroom. I was alone in the tangle of gray silk sheets, but that didn't surprise me—Caitlin didn't sleep much. I found her in the dining nook, draped in a burgundy velvet robe and pecking away on her laptop.

"I'm hunting woodworkers," she murmured, giving me a tired wave. "Rather pleased to see how many people are keeping the artisan's craft alive, even if it does make it harder to track down whoever is building Meadow Brand's puppets. Also, when this is all over, I want to go to a Renaissance fair."

"Why?"

"Nostalgia," she said, so deadpan I couldn't tell if she was kidding. "You look like you could use some coffee."

"Love some," I told her, stumbling toward the kitchen.

"Excellent. You can start a pot, then. I'll take mine with one sugar, no cream."

Once I was properly caffeinated and cleansed, after luxuriating under the pulsing twin heads in Caitlin's shower and soaking in a bath of white steam, I mussed my hair a little in the mirror and figured I could pass for a functional human being.

Ironic, considering my plans for the morning.

Jennifer texted me with directions to her new place. She'd moved out of Silverado Ranch, trading her anonymous house in the burbs for digs deeper in the city, not far from the airport. The trail led me down roads lined with strip clubs and foreclosures, dirty white concrete and barbed-wire fencing. A terraced three-story tenement squatted at the tail of a dead-end street, and I had enough street smarts to read the graffiti on the walls: this wasn't friendly territory for a man without a tribe.

I rumbled up slow in the Barracuda and got flagged down by a teenager with the eyes of a Vietnam vet. He wore yellow and brown, Cinco Calles colors. Just like the two guys loitering by the tenement door, the other one standing watch on the corner, and the three or four playing spotter from balconies and broken windows.

"What you need, man?" he asked, giving me a nod.

"Here to see Jennifer."

He squinted, sizing me up. "A'ight, you wait right here. Put it in park, okay?"

I obliged and kept my hands on the wheel so nobody felt antsy. I knew Jen used these guys as runners and occasional muscle, but that didn't mean they knew me. He walked over to the guys on the door, and one ran inside. I waited.

A couple of minutes later, he jogged back over. "Okay, you're cool. Go up to the third floor. Guy there is gonna scope you, make sure you're not packin' anything you shouldn't be. You check out, he'll tell you what room she's in today."

Today? I glanced up at the tenement and wondered how many apartments she was renting.

"Park your car right there," he said, pointing to an open spot between a pair of rusted-out junkers. "I'll keep an eye out, make sure nobody messes with it."

I slipped him a folded twenty. I didn't have to, he was on Jennifer's payroll, but it never hurts to make a good impression. Just past the front door, under the wary eyes of the thugs keeping watch, I felt like I'd stepped into a sauna. No air-conditioning in the hallways and most of the windows were broken and boarded over, leaving the tenement to marinate in sweat and decay. The air smelled like liver and onions, and a slow bass beat thumped from behind flimsy wall paneling. I took the stairs up to the top, where another guard was waiting for me with a black plastic wand in his hand.

I knew the routine and held my arms out in a T position while he ran the wand over me from neck to toe and listened to its popping and squealing. Finally, satisfied, he nodded his head down the hall.

"Three-oh-five," he grunted, then went back to sitting on a folding chair and reading a rumpled copy of *Car and Driver.*

I could have found my way there by following the music and the sound of raucous laughter. It wasn't even noon, but Jennifer had a party in full swing. A roomful of people I'd never seen before were shaking it on dirty, splintered floorboards and draped out on threadbare sofas, half of them with their lips either wrapped around a freshly rolled joint or pressed against another partygoer. Jennifer spotted me through the haze of smoke and waved, walking over.

"My new place!" she shouted over the music. "You like it?"

"Pretty sure I don't!" I shouted back with a smile. "Somewhere we can talk?"

She tugged my sleeve and led me into the kitchen, where we could both hear ourselves think.

"Why," I said, "are you throwing a party at ten in the morning?"

She laughed and waved a hand, giggly. I was feeling a little fuzzy myself just passing through.

"Aw, sugar, that's whatcha call the 'new normal.' Starts whenever people wake up, ends when the last one drops.

After a while, you don't even notice it. I was gettin' too hands-off living out in the burbs."

"Considering we're under federal investigation," I said, "isn't hands-off a *good* thing?"

"Not when I can take the bull by the horns. This building? I own it. I've been working with the Cinco Calles for years, but now they're full partners. Gives 'em something to fight for."

"The guards, the lookouts, changing rooms from day to day," I said, figuring it out. "You turned this place into a fortress."

"You always were a quick one, sugar. You know how paranoid Nicky's being? Well, if he decides to take me out of the picture, he's gonna have the fight of his life. Not just with the Cincos, neither. Look out there. You see the big guy in the blue and black? He's with the Bishops. They're not scrappin' with the Cincos anymore, not since I sat 'em all down at a table together."

Something about that nagged at the back of my brain, and I scoured my memory until a bulb lit up.

"The Bishops? Don't they guard some of Nicky's warehouses?"

"Sure do," Jennifer said with a sly smile. "For now, anyway."

21.

"No," I said. "Absolutely not. Not under any circumstances. Jennifer, you are *not* going to war with Nicky Agnelli."

She had the grace to pretend to be hurt, but not enough to keep from smiling.

"What? Little ol' me? Thought never even crossed my mind. All I'm saying is if he wants to come at me, I won't make it easy for him. And when he tries, he might find out he doesn't have as many friends as he thinks he does."

I knew that tone of voice, and I knew I wasn't going to budge her. The best I could do was shake my head and say, "Just...be careful, okay? Don't push for a fight if you don't have to."

"Oh, I never push. I'm all about freedom of choice. So what brings you around?"

I took a deep breath.

"I need to get high," I told her. "I mean, *really* high."

She blinked. "This early in the morning? Like you don't have work to do? I can't be the responsible one in this friendship, Danny. I just won't do it."

"No, it's not like that. Listen, you remember when I told you about the smoke-faced men? Well, I was checking out a lead, trying to track down Lauren. I got dosed with some nasty shit that put me out of my head for a while, and *they* showed up. I'm getting the idea that you can only see them if you don't have both feet firmly on the floor of reality. I need something that'll really mess me up, but only for a little while."

She thought about it for a moment, then nodded. "Come with me. I've got just the thing."

We left the party behind, walking down to a seemingly random door on the second floor. "This one's the real McCoy," she said, jiggling her key in the lock. The room beyond was a cramped but clean apartment, furnished with Amish wood and gingham print, most of it furniture from her old place. A window unit rattled on full blast, filling the room with cool air, and the ceiling subdued the music from upstairs into a faint, almost hypnotic thumping.

She took me into her bedroom and clicked on a table lamp. "Take your shoes off and lay down," she said as she rummaged through a lacquered wooden jewelry box on her dresser. She held up a small baggie filled with tiny dried lumps and weighed it in her hand, glancing back at me and frowning.

"About two grams, I'm thinking."

"What are those?" I said. "Mushrooms?"

"Good ol' psilocybin, nature's gift to the shaman. Here, take these and don't just gulp them down. Chew 'em. They don't taste great, but they'll work faster that way."

I took the dried pieces dubiously and popped them into my mouth. They had an earthy, pungent flavor, like a mouthful of sour dirt. I started to have second thoughts about this plan the moment I swallowed. Just in time for the train to leave the station.

"Don't worry," she said. "I'll be your sitter. Gonna be right here the whole time."

I lay there for what felt like twenty minutes, just staring at the flowered wallpaper, before I shook my head.

"Are you sure you got the real stuff? I don't feel different at all."

That was when the room started to vibrate.

It was subtle at first. A tremor under the bed like a low-wattage earthquake, spurring images of great gears churning a hundred miles below Jennifer's bed. The room turned slowly, and the corners where the walls met the ceiling left neon trails in their wake.

Jennifer wouldn't stay still. She was sitting on the edge of the bed. Then she was by the door. Then she was over by the dresser—and suddenly I realized that I was only looking at life-sized photographs that someone had cut out of a fashion magazine.

"That's right," I mumbled. "Jennifer is modeling in Spain and sent her pictures back to watch me. It all makes sense now."

"The rain in Spain falls mainly in your brain," buzzed the smoke-faced man in the mortarboard and smock, perching on Jennifer's dresser.

"We've replaced this sorcerer's illusion with conditions of stark and terrible reality!" said his suited companion, now standing at my bedside. "Let's see if he notices."

"This isn't reality," I said.

Then we were in Nepal.

"We were not in the tomb," the professor said softly, almost fearfully, as we walked through the steaming jungle under the light of a hot-pink sun. "We did not give her the ring."

"You told me that back at the shelter," I said. "So who did?"

"*The Garden*," the professor whispered.

The pink sun tumbled from the sky like a shooting star, turning day to night in the space of a trembling breath. What rose in its place was a moon made of rotting meat, its vast surface pitted with crawling black mold, glowing in a starless sky.

Young Lauren Carmichael crept from the underbrush with a hooded lantern in her hand, moving swift and sure-footed. Night birds warbled in the dark. We floated behind Lauren as she approached the overgrown and vine-tangled entrance to the unearthed tomb.

"This is the part Eugene Planck didn't see," I said. "His memories showed them discovering the door, and how she had Solomon's ring the next day, but he wasn't here for this."

I expected to see Lauren take a machete to the tangled roots. Instead, they moved aside on their own. Vines untwisted and brambles pulled away, parting like the Red Sea for her slow and curious descent. We followed her down, drawn by the firefly glow of her lantern.

Green lichens clung to the ancient stone walls, and soon grass began to spring between the cracks in the floor. Somehow, deep beneath the soil and away from the sun's light, life thrived in the musty tunnel air. A strange flower rose up from a bed of grass, and I crouched to take a closer look.

It was made of skin.

The flower bent and wilted, its bloody petals glistening, and a nodule of flesh at its tip began to throb and stretch from within. It burst with a wet *splurt*, spitting yellow pus across the grass. I watched in horror as the blades of grass started to thicken, twist, and sprout tiny pustules of their own.

"Do you know another word for life abundant?" the professor's voice buzzed in my ear. "We did not build this place. We did not give her the ring."

"We can go no further!" the suited man cried. "You must be this tall to ride! You must have a body, and we refuse! We are against having bodies!"

"Against having bodies," I repeated as the world turned fluid and ran like wet paint at the edges. "Against bodies. You're anti..."

I blinked.

"You're antibodies."

We stood in a laboratory, invisible and bodiless amid huge stainless-steel vats and racks of elaborate industrial tools. Nedry and Clark were there, though they both looked younger, like they'd come fresh out of college, and they were in a shouting match with a man I'd never seen before. He looked too laid-back for the room, with his gray hair tied back in a ponytail and his open lab coat draped over ragged jeans and a tie-dye T-shirt. Their words were muffled, impossible to make sense of, as if they were talking underwater.

I felt us slide in time, like squeezing through a tunnel of vinyl coated in warm grease. Green droplets dribbled from a palmed plastic tube, blending into a cup of coffee. We slid through time again, five minutes into the future-past, and the coffee came with us. I shouted for the ponytailed man not to drink it, but my words spilled out in the shape of soap bubbles and popped helplessly on the floor.

"Hey, buddy," Clark said pleasantly, rubbing the man's shoulders. "You okay? You look sick."

The man frowned, three shades of color draining from his face in the space of a breath.

"I...do feel a little nauseous, yes. Must have been something I ate."

"You should go home," Clark said. "Nedry and I can handle the next round of trials. Go on. It's okay."

A train blasted through the laboratory wall, trailing streamers of light. In its wake we stood in a desolate subway station lined with dingy olive tiles. The crumpled front page of the *New York Post* blew past my shoes on a gust of cold wind. The ponytailed man checked his watch and walked into the men's room. We followed.

He was alone, splashing water on his face from the grime-smeared sink under the buzzing glow of a flickering light sconce. He looked at himself in the long row of mirrors, touching his pallid cheeks with shaky fingers.

Nedry casually strolled into the bathroom, stood at the sink next to him, and started washing his hands.

"Hey, Bob," he said.

"Nedry? What are you—"

The ponytailed man—Bob—froze. He looked from the reflection in the mirror to the actual sink on his right. Nobody was there.

Nedry's reflection turned off his faucet and shook droplets of water from his hands. The droplets spattered against the inside of the mirror, like rain on a windshield.

"Bad news, Bob. Word from the top. We have to downsize the team. Looks like you're the first casualty."

Bob's hands flew up, fingers hooked in a ritual gesture I knew well: the first step of a warding spell. He didn't have time to finish.

The mirror exploded.

Shards of broken glass sliced across his face and chest. One jagged chunk impaled his arm down to the bone, and he tumbled to the filthy floor. The door to the restroom swung open, and a man in a hoodie and dark glasses speed-walked in. As he got close, I recognized Clark's face. Clark dipped down, picked up a shard of glass from the ground— one with a long, sharp tip—and bent over Bob.

He drove the shard into Bob's chest, again and again, as Nedry watched with glee from a ragged chunk of mirror at the edge of the buckled frame. Nedry's head dipped out of sight, then reappeared again a second later.

"Security guard just walked past the mirror over the ticket gate," he said. "You've got twenty seconds of clear space between here and the loading platform. Go!"

Clark dropped the shard and dug in his pockets, pulling on heavy winter gloves instead of taking time to wash the blood from his hands. He strode back out as briskly as he'd come in, as if nothing had happened.

The smoke-faced men hovered on either side of the fallen victim, their dangling feet an inch above the spreading pool of blood and shattered glass.

"Find our father," they buzzed in unison.

22.

"What, him?" I said, nodding down at the body. "You want me to find a dead man?"

"He is not dead," the professor said. "Find his grave, and you will see."

I lay in Jennifer's bed. She handed me a slice of orange.

The orange burst between my teeth, and the juice rolled down my tongue like a first drink of water after a week in the desert. Jennifer's hand left little trails of light in its wake, but they sparked and faded fast.

"You steady there, sugar?" she asked. "Think you're coming out of it now. Eat up. Vitamin C makes for a smoother landing."

I didn't have to be told. The last traces of the psilocybin pumping through my veins turned the slice of orange into a symphony.

"You get what you needed?" she asked.

"Yeah," I croaked, learning to use my voice again. "No. Sort of. I'm not sure. What time is it?"

She glanced at her wrist. "Little after three. You've been out for a few hours."

I groaned. Longer than I'd wanted to spend in a drug-induced haze, but at least I had something resembling a lead. Assuming, of course, that the smoke-faced men weren't walking me into a trap just like they'd manipulated Lauren. But I had to check it out. Didn't have a whole lot in the way of alternatives.

I pushed myself up, willing my stubborn muscles back to life. "Need to get in touch with Pixie."

Jennifer gave her hair a little flip. "Yeah? Say hey for me, all right?"

"Jennifer," I said, catching her tone, "we already talked about this. Pix is straight edge. She's not going to work for a drug dealer."

"Work, nothin'. That girl is *fine*. You ever find out what team she's playing for, you let me know."

I called Pixie on my way downstairs. She told me she was on her way to St. Jude's to start prep work for the evening meal. I arranged to meet her there in twenty minutes and hoped I didn't get conscripted into peeling potatoes.

I walked out under the watchful gaze of the Cinco Calles, feeling eyes on the back of my neck. The kid on the street gave me a nod and gestured to my car. Untouched, like he promised. I started up the Barracuda's ignition and the radio came on, tuned to the hourly news. My ears perked up.

"—raid of a homeless shelter resulted in the rescue of nine people who were allegedly being kept in a makeshift prison cell. The prisoners, who were heavily drugged so they could not identify their abductors, have been taken to local hospitals. An official statement came from FBI Special Agent Harmony Black."

Harmony's voice drifted from my car speakers. "Thanks to the efforts of the Las Vegas Metropolitan Police, we were able to take decisive action. We believe that the prisoners were being forced to compete in what the perpetrators called a 'bum fight club,' streamed to a paying audience over the Internet. At this time we cannot release any names or details about the persons responsible—"

I flipped over to the blues station, swapping Agent Black for a crooning Billie Holiday.

"Couldn't even give me a thank-you call," I muttered as I put Jennifer's fortress in my rearview mirror. It was a good bit of spin, I had to admit, with an explanation just sleazy enough to be believable. The media had the attention of a gnat hopped up on raw sugar. A week from now, nobody would think to follow up on the story.

Pixie waited for me on the sidewalk outside St. Jude's, wearing an army surplus canvas backpack and pacing a groove in the concrete. I guessed she'd heard the news, too.

"So how much of that was total bullshit?" were the first words out of her mouth.

"Ninety-nine percent of it. Only true part is that they got nine people out, plus the two who left with me. Some of the others didn't make it. Anyway, job's not done."

"No kidding it isn't. I know thirty people who disappeared, and that's *just* our regulars. There's no telling how many people are still missing all over the city."

It's not our only clinic, Nedry had said back at the standoff.

"That's not all," Pixie said. "Remember how I broke down the whole Nevada Heritage Coalition thing for you? They cut ties. According to the state records, all of a sudden there's no connection between the NHC and the McMillan Trade Group at all. The paper trail's been destroyed, real names scrubbed from corporate charters and replaced with bogus ones. It's a total burn job."

"How?" I said. We walked into St. Jude's, swapping the arid heat outside for the muggy, wet heat inside.

"Senator Roth has a hacker who's as good as me," she said. "Or better. No. Just as good. Maybe a little less."

"Okay, I get the idea. I've got a lead, but I need help. Can you do some research for me?"

"Normally I'd make a comment about not being your personal Google," she said. "But for this I'll make an exception."

We set up camp at an empty table, and she slid her laptop out of her backpack.

"Search for articles on, what was it called, Ausar Biomedical? From about twenty years ago, just before the big scandal. I'm looking for pictures of their research staff. Especially anyone named Nedry, Clark, or Bob."

"Anyone named Bob?" Pixie said, arching an eyebrow. "Real specific there, Faust."

I shrugged. "It's what I've got to work with."

It took her less than three minutes to hit pay dirt, pulling up an archived *Time* magazine article. The grainy scanned photo showed the three men standing side by side—all smiles, with Nedry still wearing his mirrored glasses—in the laboratory the smoke-faced men had showed me.

"The future's so bright, they've got to wear shades," the caption read. "Pictured: Dr. Francis Nedry, Dr. Noah Clark and Dr. Bob Payton of Ausar Biomedical, celebrating the FDA's approval to begin human trials of the eagerly anticipated fertility drug Viridithol. Industry insiders have named Ausar as this year's hot stock to watch."

"Who are these guys?" Pixie said.

"The two on the left are serious bad news. It's Payton I'm interested in. He was stabbed to death in a subway bathroom, probably not long after this picture was taken. I think—"

I paused, straining to remember the vision. It all felt so far away now, slipping from my memory like strands of gossamer. I'd seen the newspaper blow by, past a pillar, under a slate-gray sign...

"The Canarsie Line," I said. "I think it's in New York."

Her fingers rattled the keyboard. She frowned.

"Correct on the location, but negative on the crime. I've got nothing even close to a men's-room stabbing here. You sure that's where he died?"

He is not dead, they'd told me. *Find his grave, and you will see.*

"Try this," I said. "Just look for an obituary or a burial notice for Payton. Forget the stabbing part."

"This is now officially weird." Pixie squinted at her screen. "You're certain he was murdered?"

"Watched it happen."

She turned, pushed her Buddy Holly glasses down on her nose, and stared at me over the rims.

"I wasn't *there* there," I said. "Forget it, it's complicated. Why, what did you find?"

"No police record of his death, but he does have an obituary. It ran in the *Oakland Tribune*. Guess he was from around there originally. Talks about how he got his PhD from UC Berkeley and moved back to New York to get in on the ground floor with Ausar."

"Does it say how he died?" I said, leaning in to read over her shoulder.

She shook her head. "Not a word. Just says he had no surviving family, no spouse or kids. He was interred at Sunset Rest in El Cerrito. What are you going to do, go dig him up?"

I didn't answer right away. She looked over at me.

"Tell me," she said, "you're not going to go dig him up."

"I don't think that'll be necessary," I said, turning the pieces over in my mind. "There's nothing buried there but an empty casket. The Ausar brain trust had a falling out just before the Viridithol scandal. Nedry and Clark tried to assassinate Bob Payton, but they didn't stick around to see the aftermath. I think he survived the stabbing. He knew he was in over his head, and he faked his death and went into hiding so they wouldn't take a second shot at him."

"What difference does it make?" Pixie said. "What does this have to do with my missing people?"

"It's all connected. Ausar Biomedical, Lauren Carmichael, Senator Roth, the missing people, all of it. Twenty years ago, Nedry, Clark, and Payton were messing with something they should have left alone. Now the experiments are starting again, bankrolled by Carmichael-Sterling and greased by Roth's political influence. They're all after the same thing."

"What?" Pixie said.

I thought back to the prison cell and that mutated, twisted creature that had been an innocent man before Nedry went to work on him. The vision of Lauren descending into the tomb, its ancient stones bristling with grass and flowers made of flesh.

"Something terrible," I said.

#

Two hundred bucks bought me a window seat on a jet to Oakland International. It was only an hour and a half away from Vegas, the kind of flight where you spend more time on the runway than you do in the air. I didn't bring luggage.

I rented a little red Altima and set the GPS for Berkeley. I made it just in time to catch the sun setting over the San Francisco Bay, turning the cloudy sky and the clear water into sheets of hammered gold. My stomach was grumbling, so I headed for the Gourmet Ghetto on Shattuck and Vine, on the north side of town. Besides, I needed less light in the sky before I could take care of business.

I ended up at La Fable, a cute little bistro on Walnut Street, and sat under an umbrella on the patio with a menu in one hand and a whiskey sour in the other. The Bourbon whiskey, laced with lemon juice and sugar, went down with a smooth heat and helped me think. The strains of a jazz quartet drifted up from the street as the lights of the city—and out in the distance, the sprawl of San Francisco—blazed against the falling night.

Lauren and the science boys at Ausar were on the same mission. The linking element was Senator Roth. I wondered if they'd discovered their common interests when she bribed him into sending the feds after Nicky and decided to hitch their wagons together. The one thing I knew for certain was that Bob Payton wanted nothing to do with it. He'd created the smoke-faced men as some sort of antibody, a cure against what his old colleagues were planning, though it hadn't done a hell of a lot of good. Given that they'd almost started the apocalypse, their idea of a cure was worse than the disease.

Payton could tell me what I wanted to know. And he would, once I got my hands on him. Down to every last detail.

I ordered the moules frites and switched to sparkling water for the rest of the meal. It was my old habit before a job from my days of working for Nicky: one stiff drink, then nothing but water. Just enough to get me limber but not sloppy.

The waitress brought me a plate of black-shelled mussels in a cream sauce, along with a side of fries. There's nothing like fresh seafood, so juicy and tender you can smell the ocean salt with every bite. I idly stirred a fry in the mussel sauce and glanced at my watch, pacing myself. I was going in blind tonight. I hated going in blind.

Once I decided it was late enough and I'd had enough of mussels and jazz, I paid my check. El Cerrito was thirteen minutes north of Berkeley, most of it a straight shot along SR-123. I drove five miles over the speed limit and took my time.

I'd never broken into a cemetery before. There's a first time for everything.

23.

Sunset Rest was a one-stop shop for the dead. Wrought-iron fences curled along rolling lawns studded with monuments in marble and basalt, salt-and-pepper memorials to the fallen. Its sprawling chapel arch overlooked a tranquil pond. Tiled outcroppings and concealed pumps created perpetual miniature waterfalls that burbled in the dark. The polished granite walls of the mausoleum leaned in over the chapel's shoulder, as if hungry for more bodies to stuff inside its endless niches.

Office hours ended at five, and the cemetery gates locked at sunset. Unless somebody was burning the midnight oil, I'd only have rent-a-cops to worry about. I parked the Altima on the street a block away and hopped the fence.

I moved low across the lawn, keeping it smooth and quiet. I didn't expect a lot of resistance—professional grave robbing, as a career, was about a hundred years past its sell-by date—but I figured they'd have a few uniforms on the grounds keeping a lookout for kids and vandals.

The strobe of a distant flashlight caught my eye, and I got down fast, crouching in the grass behind a chiseled marble plinth. I peeked around the edge. Just one guy, strolling along and oblivious to the world, swinging his flashlight in time with the music pumping through his earbuds.

Private security could be tricky. A lot of these guys used to be on the job, and they still had cop instincts under the starched uniforms and cheap shoes. Any hired guard had an inherent weakness, though, and that was boredom. When you're pulling a graveyard shift keeping watch over a place nobody in their right mind would want to break into, walking the same uneventful route for the fiftieth time that night, you become your own worst enemy pretty fast.

The guard strolled right past my hiding spot, singing under his breath. I gave him another ten feet and then darted past him behind his back. From there it was smooth sailing all the way to the chapel, where I skirted the edge of the burbling pond and let the tiny waterfalls cover the sound of my footsteps on the concrete walkway.

Finding the administrative office wasn't hard. I just circled the building and peeped in windows as I went until I found a room with a tiny desk and enough filing cabinets to please the world's most obsessive organizer. Getting in, that was the problem. The window was latched tight, and a tell-tale alarm cord ran from the base of the windowsill on the inside.

Another flashlight up ahead. This one sagged toward the ground. I got behind a tree and watched his movements, trying to work out his pattern. He headed for the chapel doors.

I crept along behind him, quieter this time. This guard was an older guy with a hangdog face and a comb-over, and he wasn't wearing any headphones to block out the sound of my approach. I hovered at the edge of the chapel's outside fluorescents, a shadow at the border of a blob of white light, and watched as he fumbled at his key ring and got the doors unlocked. He disappeared inside.

That was my way in, but it wasn't a clean approach. There weren't any windows up front. If he was standing in the foyer or anywhere within earshot of the front door, he'd spot me the second I came inside. I stayed still as a statue and silently counted down from fifteen. As soon as I hit zero I dashed across the lit walkway and up to the chapel door, turning the heavy brass handle and slipping through.

Faint safety lights painted the chapel gloom in shades of Christmas red. I kept my ears sharp and ducked behind a wooden pew, taking a few heartbeats to get my bearings. Clunky shoes slapped on ceramic tile on the left side of the chapel, on the far side of an open arch. I crouch-walked around the pews, keeping my head down.

A flashlight beam roved across the room, careful and slow. I froze.

The beam snapped away, and the shoes trudged toward the chapel doors. I didn't move until I heard the door click shut and the sound of keys rattling, locking me in.

Just a wolf alone in the henhouse.

I clicked on a small desk lamp in the administrative office and aimed its green plastic hood toward the filing cabinets. I wished I'd brought a penlight to minimize the chance of anyone outside noticing the glow from the window. I'd just have to work fast.

I ignored the computer on the desk. Probably password protected, and any place that put their records on a hard drive didn't need twelve overstuffed filing cabinets. I tossed the place as quickly as I could, moving from cabinet to cabinet, rolling out each drawer and running my fingertips along the labeled folders until I'd seen enough to move on. I found what I was looking for about halfway through: sales receipts.

Thanks to the obituary in the *Oakland Tribune*, I had a date for Bob Payton's funeral service. That helped me narrow down the records as I pulled a pair of fat green accounting ledgers from the cabinet and laid them out on the desk. The ink scribbles had faded over the years, but that didn't stop me from finding the person who had paid for Bob's final resting place. His name was Erik Krause, he'd paid in cash, and his address was a boat slip at the Berkeley Marina.

Twenty years was a long time to stay in one place, especially for a hunted man. Still, it was the best lead I had to go on. It'd have to do.

I left the way I'd come in: crouched behind the pews in the dark, waiting like a spider for the guard to trudge through on his endless rounds. I could have let myself out, but then he'd have noticed the door was unlocked when he came back around. It was cleaner to wait until he passed me by, his clunky footsteps fading into the pews, and then dart out the chapel door leaving everything the way I'd found it. I jogged across the graveyard and clambered over the fence. I had one more stop before heading home.

#

It was a quarter past midnight by the time I reached the marina, but I wasn't tired. Silent boats bobbed on the tranquil waters of the bay, their sails furled, skeletal masts pointing like fingers toward the starry night sky.

Yellow lamps lit the way along the weathered concrete walk. The stone was stained from decades of sea spray, and I tasted salt and mildew with every breath. Toward the end of the line, as I closed in on the slip, another kind of light caught my eye: thread-thin lines of raw magic twisted into a warding spell, pulsing emerald green in my second sight. They coated the dock like a spider's web. Or a net woven from razor wire.

The boat tied to the pier was more of a barge, a boxy thing with shuttered windows and more spells laid on the deck. Calligraphy decals on the back gave the boat's name: *Second Chance*.

I stood at the edge of the dock, alone in the dark, and held up one finger.

With a focused thought and a puff of breath, a luminous spark of power jumped from my fingertip and drifted away. It floated like a puffball on a summer breeze and brushed against the farthest edge of the warding spell. The threads of magic rippled, shivering like the taut strings of a violin all the way back to the boat. I stood and waited.

The man who emerged from the boat's cabin might have grown a snowy-white beard and changed his name, but the passage of time couldn't hide the sliver-thin scars that covered his haggard face and shaking hands. He wore a tattered bathrobe and slippers.

"Dr. Payton," I said, not moving. I kept my hands empty, palms slightly turned his way. "My name is Daniel Faust. I've come a long way to see you."

He looked like he was about to protest, insist he was Erik Krause, but then his shoulders sagged. He knew it was over.

"Are you here to kill me?" he asked.

"Probably not," I said.

"Come aboard, then." With a wave of his hand the warding threads slid back, making a clear path for me between their webs.

I climbed aboard the *Second Chance* and followed him into the cabin.

"Wasn't hard for me to find you," I said. "Other people could find you too."

"They've had twenty years to try. Either they believe I'm dead, or they know I'm just a broken old man. Why bother?"

The cabin was cramped but homey, with a little kitchenette and an old vinyl couch. A stuffed lizard stood watch over his laptop desk next to a small shelf of books. Occult grimoires stood shoulder to shoulder with texts on quantum engineering and advanced calculus, thrown together with no apparent rhyme or reason.

"So," he said, hobbling over to the kitchen nook, "if Ausar didn't send you, who did?"

Even though a tuft of tangled white hair dangled over his eyes, I could still see how his gaze narrowed as he turned to face me. His left hand dipped under the counter, reaching into a drawer. He kept his eyes fixed on me.

If you're reaching for something innocuous, like a new coffee filter or a spoon, you tend to look directly at it. If you've got a stranger in your home and you're reaching for a silenced pistol on the other hand, it's probably someplace you've taught yourself to reach by feel alone.

"Your creations sent me," I said. "The smoke-faced men."

His hand froze. It came back out of the drawer, empty.

"Coffee?" he asked.

"If it's not a bother."

"Not at all," he said and put on a fresh pot while we talked.

"I need to know what you were trying to do, you and Nedry and Clark. What you were *really* trying to do. They've got new patrons, and they're picking up where you left off twenty years ago."

Bob sighed and leaned against the counter. He rubbed his leathery forehead.

"The first thing you have to understand," he said, "is that ninety-nine percent of Ausar Biomedical was a perfectly legitimate company. Then there was us. The terrible trio, we called ourselves. We were recruited by a rogue faction on the board of directors and compartmentalized from the rest of the company, set to a special and very specific task."

He sat down at the little desk and powered on his computer, waving for me to pull over a vinyl-padded chair from the kitchenette. I sat at his shoulder as he typed. He showed me pictures, scanned in from old Polaroids, dusty and faded. An aerial photograph of a dig site. A cordon of security tape and men in dark glasses. A stairway carved into rocky ground, leading down into the dark.

"They found it in Mexico," he said. "A tomb where there shouldn't have been one, carved with glyphs matching nothing in Mexican history. No, not a tomb. A *tunnel*. Eventually we found a second, identical one in the French Alps."

The vision of Lauren descending into the darkness, in Nepal, flashed behind my eyes.

"They were filled with plant life," Bob said as his eyes went distant. "Impossible life, nothing anyone had ever seen before. We could only explore so far. Anyone who went past a certain point in the tunnel...was lost to us. The board of directors was aware of certain secrets. They needed specialists, and they found us. Nedry was an expert on quantum sorcery. Clark's expertise was occult biochemistry. As for me? Warding and containment.

"You must understand, Mr. Faust, that this is not the only world that exists. Like the petals of a snowflake, other dimensions weave and lace around our own, sometimes touching our planet, sometimes violently drilling through it. The tunnels were ancient relics, the doomed efforts of some long-dead sorcerer to create a permanent bridge between our world and another."

"What other world?"

He didn't answer at first. He got up, took a pair of mismatched mugs down from a cabinet, and poured two cups of coffee. He held one out to me. His hand trembled.

"The Garden of Eden."

24.

"We focused on theory at first," Bob said. He cradled his mug with both hands as he sat back down at the desk. "Using what we could learn from the tunnels' energy, we developed means of glimpsing into other worlds. Our efforts were slipshod and random, but what we saw...it was beyond imagining. Worlds of ice, and the things that wriggled and swam beneath that ice were the size of cities. Worlds of screaming glass. A world that was nothing but a windowless mansion of endless rooms, and in each dusty room lay an abandoned porcelain doll. Eventually, with a fusion of magic and technology, we built the means to see what waited on the other end of those tomb-tunnels."

"What did you find?" I said.

His hands tightened around his mug.

"A sword. Twenty feet long and blackened by fire, lying forsaken in an overgrown field. Beyond it, a garden, wild and dense. Not just with plants, no, with...hybrids. An impossible mingling of plant life and human flesh and organs.

The garden was abandoned, Mr. Faust. Left to its own devices, left to plummet into a Darwinian nightmare, and every creature springing from that poisoned soil either a predator or a parasite. We watched entire species rise and go extinct in the span of hours. We should have known. We should have known, right then and there, to dynamite the damn tunnels and leave it all alone. The garden wasn't *for* us."

"You're right," I said. "You should have."

"Life, though. Aah, that's the thing. We were in the business of saving lives, weren't we? And here we had a source of abundant life and unstoppable fertility."

I set down my mug.

"Viridithol," I said, my blood running cold as I pieced the story together. "You reckless, dumb sons of bitches. You put samples of plant life from *another fucking dimension* in a drug and *fed it to pregnant women*. And you were, what, *surprised* when the kids came out looking like that?"

"It was a tiny sample," he said, shaking his head. "Just...just the tiniest fraction, given to a small portion of the test group. We thought we had it under control. We were trying to help people."

"Well, I guess that makes up for everything then."

Bob stared into his coffee. "We never should have called it Eden. That was hubris. It made us think we were dealing with something benign, something positive, when the truth was right in front of our faces. Whatever the Garden had once been, now it was seething with corruption. Abundant life. It makes me laugh, in retrospect. Mr. Faust, did you know that there's a medical term for abundant life? For cellular life bursting out of control and running wild."

The smoke-faced men had asked me the same question. *What's another word for life abundant?*

I shook my head. "Don't know it."

"Of course you do," he said, taking a sip of coffee. "It's called cancer."

He turned to the laptop and pulled up a file of scanned pages. Florid handwriting filled every inch of each parchment sheet, in French.

"Everything changed when we found the journals," Bob said. "Have you ever heard of a man named Gilles de Rais?"

I just nodded. He didn't need to know how or why.

"Mountaineering in the Alps, de Rais discovered the second tunnel," Bob said. "He was already an accomplished sorcerer, insofar as we can gather, and he began having visions of the Garden. He felt it calling to him, promising him the power of a god."

"Is that before or after he started killing kids?" I said.

"The visions triggered the killings. He was convinced that he could steal a human's life force, drain their soul dry, and use that power to turn himself into the Garden's conduit and master. It was very trial and error, though. Several hundred victims worth of trial and error."

"Yeah, well," I said, "that and he really liked murdering people. None of that good old scientific detachment."

"Exactly," Bob said. My sarcasm was lost on him. "As we traced his steps, the results from the Viridithol test trials came in. I had misgivings about, well, all of it. I wanted out. Nedry and Clark and the board of directors wanted full steam ahead. That's when I created my little insurance policy."

"The smoke-faced men."

He nodded. "In our early work, we came across a world of absolute silence. An Earth stripped bare of resources, of life, of anything at all, crumbling under a cold and black sun. Lonely creatures walked the wastes, creatures born of entropy. The antithesis of life itself. I created an experimental bridge in my laboratory, coaxed two of them across, and showed them the samples from the Garden. They were on it like bloodhounds. I felt confident that they'd do their best to destroy any further attempts to breach the Garden's walls. The antimatter to the Garden's wild matter, you could say."

"Problem there," I said, "is you didn't keep track of them. The name Lauren Carmichael mean anything to you?"

He shook his head, brow furrowed. "No. Should it?"

"There weren't two tunnels. There were *three*. She found the third on a dig in Nepal. Your boys showed up to save the day. See, first they pushed Lauren into slaughtering all the witnesses, except for one."

Bob blinked. "I...didn't intend for them to hurt anyone. That wasn't the idea at all."

"Second, instead of taking Lauren out, they pretended they were on her side and spent the next two decades trying to con her into triggering the apocalypse. You said it yourself, Doc: they're creatures of entropy from a dead world. Did it occur to you, even for a second, that they might not stop at the end of your leash? That they might maybe, just *maybe*, want to turn this planet into a lump of charcoal so it'd feel more like home?"

He didn't have to answer. The shame on his face told me everything I needed to know.

"Your old buddies Nedry and Clark hooked up with a senator," I said. "They're getting funding from him and Lauren, along with cash laundered from Ausar's old offshore accounts. I don't know Senator Roth's angle, but Lauren was hot to get her hands on Gilles de Rais's work. She wants to follow in his footsteps. His plan, taking control of the Garden—you think it could have worked?"

Bob shook his head. "No, not at all. For one thing, de Rais was thinking too small. He killed his subjects one at a time, spread out over years. If you need an explosion of life energy to power a ritual, a single mass sacrifice is the only way to go. The ancient Greeks did it with cattle; they called it a *hecatomb*. De Rais's approach was like trying to fill a bucket by adding a single droplet of water once every week or two. It evaporates."

Now I knew what had happened to the missing homeless people, the ones that weren't being experimented on at the clinic. Lauren must have been warehousing them somewhere, collecting victims for her grand finale. At least that meant they were probably still alive. I just had to find them before the clock ran down.

"Then there's the attunement issue," Bob said. "You would need to bring your body and spirit in alignment with the Garden's...vibrations, for lack of a better word. Simply digesting samples from the tunnels wouldn't work. You saw what happened to the Viridithol babies, and we're talking about a much greater amount. It's a catch-22. In order to survive the ritual, you'd have to take so much of the Garden into your body that you'd inevitably mutate and die before the ritual even began."

There was an unspoken "but" at the end of his sentence. I stared at him, expectant, until he coughed it up.

"Clark had a theory. A brainstorm based on vaccination therapy. He thought we could give a fatal overdose of

Viridithol to a test subject, extract their blood, centrifuge and purify it, and use *that* as the active base for the final drug. There would still be mutation, that's unavoidable, but theoretically it could be managed and endured. These were all just ideas on a blackboard, of course. We were hardly going to start murdering people to test a theory."

"Got news for ya, Doc. That's exactly what they're doing."

Bob rose slowly from his chair. He walked over to the other side of the cabin, staring out the darkened porthole window. I could see his face, haunted, reflected in the glass.

"I only ever wanted to help," he said softly. "All my life, all my research, my work...and this is what they're doing with it. I knew we were going the wrong way. I pushed back as hard as I could, and they tried to murder me for it."

He wanted a shoulder to cry on. I was all out of shoulders.

"A lot of people are dead," I said. "And a lot more are going to die if we don't do something. What else did you learn from de Rais's journals?"

He turned back toward me and shook his head. His hand fluttered in the air, playing it off.

"He had one idea, not long before his execution. An obsession, really. He had finally caught on that his sacrifices weren't working, and he went all out in the other direction. He drew sketches of a great machine. Roped in everything he knew: geomancy, occult architecture, sacrificial currents, you name it. The idea was to create an amplification circuit that would harness a mass death and boost its power even further, sending it surging into his body at the moment he bridged this world and the Garden. He hadn't even *considered* the attunement problem, though. Would have killed him twenty times over."

"So he didn't actually build the thing," I said.

Bob wrinkled his nose and shook his head. "No, no, he couldn't possibly have. According to the sketches, it would have been enormous. Thirty-six stories tall, literally. Even if you had the money, how would you create a monstrosity like that without drawing attention?"

My heart sank as I pulled over his laptop. I opened his web browser, rattled out a quick address, and turned the computer so Bob could see the black monolith on the screen.

"If you're Lauren Carmichael," I said, "you disguise it as a luxury resort hotel and build it at the end of the Las Vegas Strip. You build it right in front of the entire world."

25.

Bob turned pale. His hands shook against his knees. The inside of my mouth was bone dry.

"She...she built it?" he whispered. "She actually *built* it?"

I nodded. "I don't think it's finished, but it has to be damn close. I got a look at the blueprints once—the real ones, not the ones they filed with the state. It was all zigzagging hallways and stairways to nowhere, rooms doubling back on other rooms. I didn't know why, at the time."

"The mystic circuitry," he said. "They'll inlay glyphs over every surface of the interior. The way de Rais conceived it, the *hecatomb*—the mass sacrifice—takes place at the bottom of the tower. The energy of the dead spills upward, caught in the net, amplified, and spun into a maelstrom of raw power."

He leaned in and tapped the screen. His fingernail rested on the Enclave's top floor.

"Here," he said, "at the very top, a golden throne at the heart of the pattern, the eye in a psychic storm. Timed perfectly, the user would merge himself with the Garden at the moment the surge hit."

"And would that *work?*" I asked him. "Is this just some fifteenth-century psycho's pipe dream, or does she actually have a chance of pulling it off?"

He stared at the picture on the screen. His lips moved wordlessly, as if laboring over a hard math problem.

"*Doctor,*" I said.

He turned slowly to face me. "*If* Nedry and Clark solved the attunement problem, and *if* this Lauren Carmichael is a good enough magician to work out the holes in de Rais's design—"

"Do Nedry and Clark have a copy of his journal?" I said.

He nodded. "Yes, why—"

"Then that means Lauren has it now, and yeah, she's good enough."

"The end result of the ritual," he said, "would make *her* the portal. A living bridge between worlds, with total mastery of the Garden's energies."

"She'd become a goddess," I said, the horror of Lauren's plot unfurling before me. I remembered what Tony Vance had told me just before I kicked him to his death. *The things we've done, Faust. Christ, the things we're GOING to do. If you knew the entire plan, the scope of it, you'd never sleep again.*

"Theological quibbles aside," Bob said, his face pale, "yes. She could spread the Garden with a wave of her hand, lay waste to the Earth and remake it however she pleased. I—I have to help, to stop her. Let me help."

I stood up sharply and pushed my chair back.

"You've done enough," I said.

Bob followed me to the cabin door, right on my heels.

"Please," he said, tears brimming in his eyes. "I never meant for any of this to happen. I just wanted to help people, to make the world a better place."

He put his hand on my arm. I bared my teeth, yanked my arm away, turned, and gave him a hard shove. Bob staggered back, slipped off his feet, and landed on the vinyl sofa. He grabbed at the slick fabric, trying not to hit the cabin floor.

"The only reason I'm not turning your make-believe funeral into a real one," I said, "is because you've got a job to do. The smoke-faced men. Get them under control. If you don't, and if I so much as *think* they're pulling another stunt, I'll take care of them myself. Then I'll be back here to put a bullet in your head."

He slumped over, face buried in his hands. His shoulders started to shake. I let myself out.

A brisk walk and the cool night air helped clear my head, but it didn't do much for the rage boiling in my gut. Lauren Carmichael, the lab rats at Ausar, Gilles de Rais—working alone, none of them could have succeeded. It took a perfect storm to bring that much greed and madness together, and now that storm was aimed straight for my city.

Then the entire world.

#

I drove straight back to Oakland International, but there weren't any flights home until morning, so I crashed on a row of hard plastic seats at an empty boarding gate. I slipped in and out of an uneasy sleep, lulled by the throbbing hum of a floor waxer.

A little after six in the morning, I went to the men's room and splashed cold water on my face. Then I stopped at the McDonald's kiosk, dug in my pocket for a few rumpled bills, and bought a greasy egg and muffin sandwich. By the time I shook off the last dregs of sleep and tossed away the crumpled wrapper, I'd come up with an idea.

I called Harmony Black and got her voicemail. "It's me," I said. "Call me back."

Fifteen minutes later, my phone buzzed against my hip.

"I know where the other missing people are," I told her. "They're being held hostage at the Enclave construction site. It's the only place that makes sense."

"What? That's ridiculous. Why would Lauren risk being connected to a kidnapping scheme by stashing these people in her own hotel?"

Because it's not really a hotel, I thought. *And because that's where she's going to kill them.* I didn't say it, though. The feds didn't need to know that much. Especially not this particular fed.

"If I can verify it," I said, "can you do what you did at the New Life shelter? Round up a posse and kick some doors in?"

I heard her sigh on the other end of the line.

"We had this little thing called 'evidence' at New Life. A business card and a sandwich laced with drugs bought me a search warrant. What do we have on Lauren Carmichael?"

"You know what she is—"

"*Provable*, Faust. I need something in my hand that I can take to a judge. Without that, I can't touch Carmichael or set foot on her company's property. Get me evidence that something dirty's going down at the Enclave. *Real* evidence, legally obtained, that'll stand up in court. Until then, we don't have anything to talk about."

She hung up on me. They called my flight's number over the PA system and I shuffled into line with the other red-eyed commuters, a flight of zombies headed east into the morning sun. I tried to nap again on the flight, but it was like sleeping in the terminal, just a shadowy imitation of the real thing that left me drowsier than when I started.

As soon as we touched down at McCarran, wheels slamming against the tarmac and jolting me out of my fugue, my phone was in my hand. I called for a family meeting.

Times change. Back in the old days we'd have our get-togethers at the Tiger's Garden, but the Garden had a strict "magicians only" policy, and my crew had gotten a little more diverse lately. Bentley and Corman volunteered their place, and that was how we all eventually ended up squeezed into their living room, surrounded by antique bric-a-brac and the shadow of an empty, gilded parrot cage.

When I arrived, Margaux and Pixie were already there, sitting side by side on the couch and huddled over Pixie's laptop. Bentley gave me a wave as he dragged a couple of folding chairs out from the kitchen nook. I jogged over to help.

"I think we can fit everyone in," Bentley said, fretting over the clutter. "Corman and Jennifer should be back in a few minutes. They went out to get refreshments. I was going to make lemonade, but they thought something a bit harder might be advisable."

"They're not wrong," I said.

He leaned in and lowered his voice. "That bad?"

I shrugged and gave him a gentle pat on the back. "Nothing we can't handle."

I hoped I wasn't lying.

"Danny," Margaux said, "where did you find this girl? She's amazing! She just showed me a way to send money back home without making a ripple. No fees, no fuss, no nothin'."

Pixie gave a modest wave. "Eh, it's easy sauce. And taking advantage of big banks is kind of a moral imperative."

"That's what I've always thought," I said.

Pixie shot me a look.

"Hey, Faust," she said. "I hope we're here to get some good news."

Oh, boy. She wasn't going to like this meeting at all.

Bentley scurried to answer a soft knock at the door. Caitlin stepped inside, cradling a bottle of red wine in the crook of her arm. She'd never been invited up above the bookstore into Bentley and Corman's apartment. Looking between them, I wasn't sure which one was more nervous.

"Caitlin," Bentley said, his tone as unreadable as his face.

"I brought a gift," she said quickly, offering him the bottle. "I know this isn't exactly a social occasion, but it's tradition among my people, and I appreciate being invited into your home."

He reached for the bottle, but his arm froze when she said 'among my people.' Then he caught himself, forced a smile, and took the wine from her outstretched hand.

"Thank you," he said stiffly. "I'll just put this in the kitchen."

Bentley and Caitlin had one thing in common, and that was me. They'd come to a detente, especially after she had saved my life, but he still wasn't thrilled with my choice of lovers and wasn't too good at hiding it.

Caitlin came over and curled her arm around mine. The doorknob rattled a minute later, and Corman and Jennifer came in with a case of Sam Adams. It took me a second to realize why Jennifer looked different.

Oh no, I thought. *She's wearing makeup.*

Jennifer plopped down next to Pixie on the couch, a lock of hair twisted around one anxious finger.

"Hey, sugar!" she said to Pixie. "Haven't seen you in a while. How've you been?"

"Beer me," I said to Corman.

He gave me a bemused look. "Since when do you drink beer?"

"Since now."

He tossed me a bottle and cracked open one for himself. Soon everyone was sitting down, filling the cramped living room anywhere they could find a spot, and all eyes were on me. I took a pull on the bottle, swallowing down the bitter hops, and tried to find a place to start.

Beginning at the beginning sounded like the best bet, so I walked them through it, from the New Life shelter to my sit-down with Bob Payton.

"So that's that," I said. "Once Carmichael gets all the victims she needs for the mass sacrifice and she's done 'attuning' herself, she'll be unstoppable. We don't know how close to finished she is, either. Let's assume time isn't on our side."

"This can't be real," Pixie said. "I mean, somebody tell me this isn't real."

"We don't lie to our own," Margaux said. She leaned back on the sofa and crossed her arms.

I looked out over a sea of grim faces. All but Pixie, who looked on the edge of a panic attack. She'd seen some things since I dragged her into my world, sure, but she didn't know how bad it could get. Not until now.

"No second chances this time," I said. "We stop Carmichael, for good, and put her in the ground where she belongs. Her and everyone with her. What we need right now is a plan."

26.

"The whole building's basically a machine, right?" Jennifer said. "Mystic circuitry and four-dimensional architecture, but a machine's a machine."

I nodded. "That's how Payton explained it to me."

"So we cowboy up. Crash the gate, guns blazing, and toss a bomb or two. Don't matter how big a machine is. Take out a few cogs, and it just stops workin'."

"Only problem there," I said, "is the small army of mercenaries that'll be standing between us and the front doors. I've seen these Xerxes guys in action, and they're no joke. Their boss knows his way around our world, too, so I'm betting they're bringing more than guns to the table. Brute force isn't going to work this time. We need finesse."

"Seems to me," Margaux said, "we know everybody's dirty business except for one person. The senator. What's his story? He's the glue binding this whole mess together. Without him, Lauren never would have met up with these Ausar boys."

"I-I might have something there," Pixie stammered. She was still reeling. "I was digging into his finances and...it's weird. It doesn't make any sense to me, but maybe it's something you guys...you know, something that you'd understand."

"What've you got?" I said.

She pulled up a spreadsheet on her laptop. Margaux leaned in to see, and Bentley walked around behind the sofa. He slipped his reading glasses on.

"Okay," Pixie said. "Alton Roth comes from oil money. Big Texas family, oilmen for three generations. He's the first of the family to go into politics. He's never met a lobbyist he didn't like. Pretty much takes money by the wheelbarrow to sell his influence. A lot of it off the books, if you know what I mean. *Business Insider* named him one of the wealthiest people in the Senate last year. So here's where it gets weird. That's all on paper. In terms of real cash? He's *broke*. Not only broke, but mortgaged up to the eyeballs on every piece of property he owns."

I frowned. "Where's the money going? Footing Clark and Nedry's research bills?"

"Only recently. About seven years ago, he was as rich as he looks on paper. Then all of a sudden he started spending money like it was going out of style. First, there was a longevity clinic in Tucson. Turned out the owner was a quack, and the feds shut it down. Then he was pouring cash into a cryogenic research think tank. Then he cut them off and started throwing money at this guru who claimed he could teach his followers how to live forever through meditation. For a smart guy, Roth isn't too smart, you know?"

Bentley rubbed his chin. "Desperation sometimes leads people down foolish roads."

"That's a guy who's afraid of the reaper," Corman said. "Is he sick?"

Pixie shook her head. "No sign of it that I can see. He's in his early fifties, gets regular checkups, big exercise-and-healthy-eating guy. He ran in the Tristate Marathon last year and finished, so he's not faking being fit."

"Then it's not death he's afraid of," Caitlin said. "It's what's waiting for him on the other side. This is a man who knows where he's going when he dies, and he doesn't like it. Doesn't suspect, or fear, or believe—he *knows*, as sure as he knows the sun will set. Suffice to say, I've seen this kind of behavior before."

"What's your take?" I said.

She paced the carpet, thinking. "I need a closer look at our dear senator. In person. I have my suspicions, but once I look in his eyes I'll know for sure."

"Where's he at?" I said. "D.C.?"

Pixie typed out a quick search and shook her head. "He's home this week, doing a round of fundraising. Looks like he's in Carson City. Only the third time he's visited his home office in the last five years."

"Carson City's a seven-hour drive," I said. "Road trip?"

"Road trip," Caitlin said.

"What can we do in the meantime?" Corman asked.

"I think our best lead is figuring out where Meadow Brand buys those mannequins she uses," Caitlin said. "I've been doing a bit of research, checking out woodworkers in Nevada and Seattle, but if someone could take the list and pick up where I left off—"

"Research?" Bentley said. "My forte. Done. Everyone can pitch in."

Pixie shut her laptop. "I'll keep following the money. Maybe they slipped up somewhere and left us something we can use."

"I could help with that," Jennifer offered, a little too eager.

Pixie blinked at her. "You've...done forensic accounting before?"

"I'm a fast learner."

"Okay," I said, "everybody stay in contact, and spread the word if you find anything. We're working on borrowed time. Let's act like it."

#

We took my car.

There were 420 miles of lonely Nevada desert between Vegas and Carson City, a long and winding drive along US-95 that never seemed to end. Occasionally we'd roll through the main street of a town so small you'd blink and miss it, or ride past a rusting gas station frozen in time since the 1950s. Mostly it was just me, Caitlin, a roaring engine, and a cloudless blue sky.

We listened to the radio for a while, until our favorite stations crackled out and died one by one, replaced by static or silence. Eventually, the only thing left was a show broadcasting from the middle of nowhere, a preacher with a Georgia twang spitting into the microphone about the end of days and the time of repentance. He ranted on for a couple minutes, and then Caitlin leaned in to click the radio off.

"That's quite enough of that," she said.

We rode in silence for a while.

Caitlin shifted in her seat, turning her gaze from the empty landscape.

"Has it been nine months yet?" she said.

"Huh?"

"You've been carrying a pregnant pause since we got in the car. I'm just wondering if you're due to give birth to the question you obviously want to ask me."

I smiled. "Am I that transparent?"

"To me, you are. What are you afraid to say?"

It wasn't fear as much as awkwardness, and it wasn't awkwardness as much as not being sure why I cared. But I did.

"That abandoned world Payton and his buddies found," I said. "Is it really the Garden of Eden?"

She blinked at me. "Daniel? Just how old do you think I am?"

"I know you weren't around *then*," I said. "I just..."

"Is it the Garden itself that troubles you? Or is it the confirmation of what you already believed: that this ship of worlds is sailing through maelstrom and blackest night, with no captain at the wheel?"

I didn't have an answer for that. I just drove. She reached across and rested her hand on my thigh.

"You know," she said, "I do understand what it feels like. Our creator left us too, though I have faith that he had a good reason."

"The worst-case scenario isn't finding out that what I already believe is true. Most people would call that reassuring. What's eating me is...the cavalry isn't coming to the rescue, Cait. There's no flight of angels—or anything else— waiting in the wings to pull us out of trouble if Lauren gets her way. We fight, and we win, or the world dies. That's a hell of a lot of responsibility."

She shook her head. I glanced over and realized she was smiling.

"What?"

"You humans. Always so eager to spite a gift. Daniel, do you have free will?"

"Of course."

"Then you are responsible—for this world and everything in it. That weight was put on your shoulders the moment you were born. People complain that the world is filled with misery, but how many of them lift a finger to do anything about it? Or better yet, they point their fingers at *us*. 'The devil made me do it.' Oh, please. We take advantage and have our fun where we can, but believe me, all the great atrocities in history? *You* people did that."

"This is an odd pep talk," I said.

"Not a pep talk. It's a dash of cold water I like to call reality. No. No one is coming to the rescue, and no one ever was. You should see that for what it is: a gift. What would your life be worth, if you didn't have to fight for it? How happy would you really be in a universe with no struggle, where all the edges were rounded off and some cosmic power stood ready to swoop in and save you from your own mistakes? *You are responsible.* So put your chin up, your shoulders back, keep your head, and get ready for a brawl. Nothing else to be done for it."

I chewed that over, driving in silence.

"Of course," she added, "I'm a demoness, not a theologian. Take everything I say with a pillar of salt."

"No. You're right. This is our fight. This is our problem to solve. So we'll solve it."

Caitlin leaned back in her seat and stretched, purring out a yawn.

"Mm-hmm," she said. "Responsibility is sexy."

We couldn't chase the sun fast enough, and nightfall beat us to the edge of Carson City. Down on Fifth Street, lights still burned behind half the windows of the Legislative Building, a block away from Roth's personal office, but we were well past visiting hours.

"Well," I said, "Roth's in town somewhere. I don't want to wait until morning to get this done. Any ideas?"

"Of course," Caitlin said, looking almost offended that I asked. She took out her phone, snug in a slim white case, and cut her way through three layers of bureaucracy like a hot knife through butter.

"Oh *hi!*" she said, putting on a Valley Girl accent and spinning up her voice on every other word. "It's Mandy, with Senator Zito's office? Yeah, I've got those papers on Amendment 77873-B that Senator Roth needs for—no, no, he needs them tonight. *Please?* You'd be so helping us *all* out. Oh *thank* you, you're *such* a *sweetheart!*"

She hung up the phone and shrugged, back to her normal voice. "He's dining at Adele's on North Carson. If we move fast, we might catch him."

"That was scary," I said.

She just winked.

If you look up "charming" in the dictionary, there's probably a picture of Adele's. The owners converted a Victorian house from the late 1800s into a restaurant and kept as much of the cozy charm as time and progress allowed. The air inside was rich and laden with mouthwatering aromas, but Caitlin and I were more interested in the guests. We spotted Alton Roth at a corner table, holding court with a couple of his State House cronies. Broad shoulders filled out his tailored suit, and his hooknose made me think of a well-fed raptor. His movements were big and expansive, equal parts charisma and muscle. Pixie was right. In his fifties or not, I could see him running marathons. And winning.

We finagled a seat a couple of tables away, and Caitlin took the chair facing Roth. She dipped into her handbag and took out her big dark glasses.

"Give me a moment," she said, slipping them on. Her face turned toward Roth slowly, and her breathing stilled. She looked like a diva from the golden age of Hollywood.

After a moment, she nodded to herself. "Oh, you little scamp," she murmured.

"What is it?"

She lowered her glasses, just enough to show me the burning molten-copper swirls of her eyes. Her real eyes.

"He's marked by one of my kind," she said. "That's why he's so afraid to die. He literally sold his soul."

27.

She slid her glasses back up and took a few steadying breaths. When she removed them and slipped them back into her bag, her irises were back to sharp emerald green. The change came just in time, as our waitress walked up behind her chair.

"We'll start with the sweet Thai chili prawns," Caitlin said after a cursory glance at the menu. "He will have the medallions of filet Diane, and I'll have the chicken marsala scaloppine. Wedge salads for both of us, please, and...a bottle of the Covey Run merlot, I think. Thank you."

The waitress looked at me and blinked. I just shrugged at her. Caitlin's Rules for Restaurants meant she ordered, you ate. I'd learned to live with it.

The waitress went off to put our order in, and I leaned closer to Caitlin.

"Literally sold his soul? Like, 'Devil Went Down to Georgia,' Robert Johnson at the crossroads—"

"Like Mephistopheles and your namesake, or the violinist Niccolò Paganini, or the Rolling Stones, yes, exactly." She paused. "Forget I said that last one."

"I didn't think that was a thing people actually did."

"Tell that to Robert Johnson. I've heard the man play—he's *really* good. But you're half-right. It's extraordinarily uncommon for two reasons. Firstly, if someone is, let's say, of a mindset where they'd be willing to buy their earthly desires with eternal damnation, they're probably already in our pocket. So why bother? Secondly, that's an *awful* lot of hard work. We're not genies. Promise someone wealth and power, and we either have to come through, or the contract's null and void. That sort of thing can keep a demon on the hook for decades."

I craned my neck to watch Roth dig into his lamb, nodding to his buddies and chewing a big forkful of tender meat like it was his last meal on Earth.

"But Roth managed it," I said.

"There is a sect, the Venerable Order of Bargainers. They're very, very old school, Daniel. They predate our civil war, the formation of the courts, all of it, and there aren't many of them still around. What they do is...it's not about results or efficiency. It's an art form, part of our cultural traditions. Everything they do—from the first approach, to weaving the deal, to following through on the hardest and most demanding conditions in order to keep a pact from unraveling—is measured in grace and style. I suppose they're the closest thing we have to rock stars. Well...except for the actual rock stars."

"It makes sense," I said. "He's got seller's remorse, and he knows he's headed for the express elevator downstairs when he dies. He hooks up with the boys from Ausar, hoping they can use their Garden research to make sure he *doesn't* die, ever. Somewhere along the way Lauren comes to him, paying him off to set the federal task force on Nicky's heels, and they start talking about common interests. Introductions happen all around, and it's a match made in hell."

The waitress brought over the bottle of merlot and our Thai chili prawns. The first bite had a perfect tang, leaving my tongue tingling. I took a sip of wine and thought things over.

"What Lauren's doing is incredibly dangerous," Caitlin said. "Roth wouldn't take that kind of risk, not with his soul in the balance. So he's funding the research and using his influence to grease the wheels in the hope that Lauren, newly minted nature goddess, will reward his loyalty with life eternal."

I tried not to snort into my wineglass. "That'll last about five minutes. Lauren's never been big on rewarding loyalty."

"We won't convince him of that," Caitlin said. She frowned, deep in thought.

I poked a prawn around the dish with my fork.

"What if we buy it back for him?"

Caitlin looked up. "His soul?"

"Sure. Why not? We get his contract annulled, he's got no reason to fear death anymore and no reason to work with Lauren and company. We can turn him."

"I doubt it. Remember, the Bargainers do what they do out of a sense of art and tradition. Rembrandt wouldn't splatter paint on his masterpiece just because you waved a handful of cash at him. Still...I suppose it can't hurt to ask. Wait here, I need to make a call."

"Who are you calling?" I said.

"Emma. She can look up who holds Roth's contract and where they are now. Hopefully not somewhere on the other side of the world."

The answer, as it turned out, was a bit closer than that. It was half an hour north, in Reno.

It was tempting to think of Reno as a low-rent Vegas, the kind of place where washed-up croupiers went to die. The town had a flavor and a pulse of its own, though, and the San Francisco tourist crowd kept things jumping. We rolled past the cherry neon arch reading "Reno: The Biggest Little City in the World," cruising for Fourth Street. The street itself—and the blues bar that bore the street's name up on its red marquee.

All cozy and smoky and dark, 4th Street Scarlet was miles away from a tourist trap, all cozy and smoky and dark. The cool licks of a saxophone wafted from the stage as we made our way inside, wrapping around my heart and giving it a squeeze.

"His use-name is *Cth'pollosu*," Caitlin had told me on the drive over, fresh from her call with Emma. "But these days he goes by Calypso. He's a big deal, Daniel. One of the greats, a legend even, and he's been around for a long, long time. Some say he walked with the Morning Star."

"You sound like you're about to meet George Clooney."

"I won't lie, he's up there. Just watch yourself. He's not stupid."

"Not worried," I said, taking her hand in mine. "I've got backup."

Calypso wasn't hard to find. He glowed in my second sight like a blood diamond, all hard edges and cold allure. He wore a tan linen suit that stood out against his skin. He was dark, dark like roasted coffee, and a wisp of white smoke curled up from the unfiltered cigarette held between his long, slender fingers.

"Hello, hello," he said as we walked up to his table. His voice was like burnt honey. "If it isn't the Wingtaker herself. Pleased to find myself in the presence of greatness."

"The feeling's mutual," she said. "I admire your work."

His easy gaze slid toward me. His eyes were unnaturally bright.

"And if this is Sitri's honored hound, the man beside her must be Daniel Faust. You've been making waves, son. I've heard things."

"Good things or bad?" I asked.

He chuckled, a low amused rasp. "Things. I'm a ramblin' man, you see. I hear things all over. Why don't you both take a load off? Join me for a spell."

As we pulled out chairs and sat down at his small table, he lifted his half-empty glass and waved toward a passing waitress.

"Grace, baby? Another whiskey on the rocks. Bring a couple for my new friends, too."

"We're here about one of your clients," Caitlin said. "Alton Roth."

Calypso took a long, slow drag of his cigarette. He exhaled a plume of smoke that drifted up toward the rafters, swirling in time with the music.

"Mm, Alton. Alton's a keeper. My most ambitious project in four hundred years. See, that boy's bound for greater things than the Senate."

"You know he's looking to wriggle out of the deal?" I said.

"They always do," he said with a lazy smile. "Oh, they always do. I understand Alton's looking to live forever. Had a few clients try that game over the years. Not one's ever pulled it off. Nah, immortality's a losing proposition. Only fame lasts forever."

"He might prove you wrong," I said.

Caitlin rested her hands on the table.

"This is a matter of infernal security," she said. "You're a Bargainer, and the terms of the Cold Peace give me no authority over you or your order. I am *asking* you to release Alton Roth's contract as a favor to me and to Prince Sitri. Your generosity will be repaid."

Calypso ashed his cigarette and took a sip of whiskey, shaking his head.

"I appreciate the tone of respect," he said, "and I appreciate the offer of recompense. But come on, Wingtaker. You aren't one of those come-lately upstarts with no love for your elders, our traditions, and our ways. You *honor* your history. So you know, well as anyone, that I can't let Roth off the hook. Every soul is a song, and I'm still writing his lyrics."

"There's no offer you'll consider?" I said.

He let out a long, slow chuckle and took another sip of whiskey. "I do so enjoy a man named Faust asking me about a deal. Makes me feel at one with history. Shame we can't talk business, son, but you're already damned. Spoiled product."

"He's also mine," Caitlin said with a hint of warning in her voice.

Calypso took a foil pack of smokes from his inside jacket pocket, some European brand I didn't recognize, and shook out a single cigarette.

"Point is, I've got big plans for that man, and I just can't go parting with him. Genuinely sorry if that steps on your toes."

I thought fast. Roth's contract was the one piece of leverage we had, the one wrench we could throw into Lauren's machine, but only if I could figure out how to use it.

I got an idea. A sketchy one—my best ideas usually were.

"What's your interest in Roth," I said, "outside the scope of his contract?"

"All I have to do is deliver what I promised him," Calypso said, "and all he has to do is die. In his proper hour, that is. I won't brook you interfering with my work."

"I wouldn't do that," Caitlin said.

"Oh, I know you wouldn't. Your boy here, though, he's on a hair trigger. You'd best school him before he does something foolish."

I held up my hand. "Let me rephrase. We need Roth to lean in a certain direction. It shouldn't interfere with whatever you've promised him. In fact, it might help. Is that a problem? If we just talk to the guy? Maybe play with his head a little bit?"

"Long as you mind your boundaries, I'm copacetic," Calypso said.

The waitress brought over a round of drinks. They sat before us, untouched.

"Let's talk a different kind of business, then," I said. "What would you want in exchange for a copy of his contract? Not the original, nothing binding, just a copy."

"Now you've got me curious," Calypso said, "but such things aren't for sale. Tell me something, sorcerer: are you a gambling man?"

"Now and then."

I didn't see where the cup came from. Calypso just waved his hand and there it was on the table, an old cup of battered and stitched leather. Beside it, five little dice carved from yellowed bone bathed in the smoky electric light.

"I can always spot a gambling man. No, I won't sell you the copy," Calypso said. "If you're willing to put a little something on the table, though, let's play for it instead."

28.

"Absolutely not." Caitlin bristled. "I forbid it."

Calypso looked pained. "Wingtaker, please. You're charged with upholding the law, and you *know* the law. The mortal has every right to bargain with me. No one can interfere with that."

"I can. He's mine."

He shook his head. "Not in the eyes of hell's law. No mark, no brand, no tokens? You can't speak for him."

"What's the game?" I said, wanting to get between them before things escalated.

"Liar's dice," Calypso said with a smile. "Individual-hand style. A simple little game of chance and skill."

"And what do you want me to put on the table?"

Calypso took a drag from his cigarette, studying me through the haze. I felt like he was peeling me back, layer by layer, measuring how badly I wanted the contract and what he could get in return.

"One year of your life."

I tried to look like the proposal didn't faze me. In any contest of wits, steady nerves are half the battle. If you don't have them, fake them.

"Front end or back end?" I asked.

"Back end. Memories aren't worth a thing to me. Now and then, though, I get a client who wants to live just a little longer. Five years, ten years, enough time to appreciate what they've got. Those years have to come from someplace. Every man has his time to go, and your candle will burn out exactly one year sooner than its appointed date."

"Daniel," Caitlin said warningly.

"Could we have a second?" I said to Calypso.

He slowly rose from his chair. "Take your time," he said. "Need to freshen up."

I waited until he was out of earshot—I hoped—and leaned in.

"Cait, I have a plan, but we're going to need that contract to swing Roth. It's worth the risk."

"A year of your life?"

"On the back end," I said. "And if Lauren wins, I'm gonna lose *all* the years left in my life, along with everybody else on Earth. Look...if you really don't want me to do this, I won't. But I believe it's worth taking a chance."

She reached out and put her hand over mine. She looked me in the eye.

"All right," she said, "here are the rules. He has to play fair, and so do you. That means following the *spirit* of the game. He can bluff, he can use wordplay, he can mislead within reason, but he can't use loaded dice or cast a spell to swing the outcome. He likes games where you have to read people's faces, because he's been doing it for a very, *very* long time. You've never played against anybody this good."

"Oh, I doubt that. You've never played Scrabble with Bentley. He has all the X, Y, and Z words in the dictionary memorized. Triple word score, every time."

She squeezed my hand. "*Please*, Daniel. Take this seriously."

I leaned in closer. I couldn't resist a kiss at her earlobe as I whispered, "See? I'm nervous as hell, and I made myself look flippant. Trust me, I can take this guy."

Calypso came back and slid into his chair, looking between us with an unspoken question on his lips.

"Let's do this," I said.

He smiled.

"Did your lady explain the rules?"

I nodded. "We play by the spirit of the game."

Now there were two identical leather cups on the table and two sets of dice, as if they'd always been there.

"Then let's play," Calypso said.

Individual-hand liar's dice is a stripped-down version of the real game. It's a two-player showdown based on a little luck and a lot of bluffing. I scooped up the bones and spilled them into the cup, keeping my palm pressed over its mouth as I gave it a shake. All the while my eyes were fixed on Calypso's face, roaming from his forehead to his lips, trying to get a read on his expressions.

They say that everybody has a tell. That's not true. Everybody has *lots* of tells. There are over forty muscles in the human face, working in concert with thousands of possible ways to put your feelings on display to the world. Add in little twitches, shrugs of the shoulder, or the curl of a finger, and the number of tells—and the number of possible interpretations—is too many to count.

Show me a stone poker face when you've been expressive all night, and I know you're hiding something. The right way to bluff isn't to throw up a wall, because it can't be done. What you want to do is mix your signals, throw up so many conflicting reads that your opponent can't possibly get a fix on what you're thinking. Baffle them with noise, not silence.

I slapped the cup onto the table mouth-down and listened to the dice rattle. We peeked under our cups at the same time, tilting the rims back. I had three twos, a one, and a five. Three of a kind, solid hand.

"Runt," I said, calling the lowest hand. Calypso stared me down long enough to turn the silence into a weapon. His quiet patience grated at my nerves. I willed my shoulders to unclench and thought of a dirty joke Corman had told me a couple of days ago. The amused smile that rose to my lips was smooth and genuine, just not related to the game at hand.

"Pair," he said.

Now I could call his bluff, raise my own bid, or roll my dice again. Sticking with my hand felt like the safest move. By the odds, he probably didn't have a runt—a no-combination roll—so he most likely wasn't bluffing.

"Two pair," I said.

"Three of a kind," he shot back, upping the bid without skipping a heartbeat. I blinked, rattled.

Now I was leaving safe harbor. If I upped the bid past the real hand under my cup and he called me on it, he won. Was he bluffing? It didn't feel right. He was confident. Not the kind of bluster you see from someone overplaying their hand, but the quiet confidence that comes from a winning hand.

I didn't like it. I needed to mix things up.

"Rolling again," I said. "All five dice."

The bones rattled in my cup and bounced on the table. I kept my face slack as I looked underneath. Now I had nothing but a lousy pair. I'd landed in the exact same boat I'd tried to jump out of, and it had just sprung a leak.

"Low straight," I said, upping the bid.

Calypso smiled like a wolf.

"Liar."

My stomach clenched. We both uncovered our dice at the same time. I sat there, exposed with my single pair. On his side of the table, a scattering of mismatched and worthless dice.

"You had a runt," I said.

"What do you know? Looks like I did, looks like I did."

Caitlin's hands clenched on the edge of the table, knuckles turning white.

"What now?" I asked him.

Calypso reached out across the table, like a gentleman.

"We shake hands on a game well-played."

I took his hand. He took my life.

It didn't hurt, not like a punch or a burn or a shock, nothing on the level my flesh could understand. It hurt like racing to meet a lover at the airport, only to get caught up in traffic and miss her flight. It hurt like discovering you've forgotten your mother's face, and you don't have any photographs left. It hurt like realizing a decade just slipped out from under you, and you don't have anything but missed opportunities and empty bottles to show for it.

He let go and gave me a firm nod.

"I appreciate a man who pays his debts," he said. "Respect."

"Again," I said.

Caitlin's eyes widened. "Daniel—"

"Again," I said, harder.

Calypso nodded and waved his hand slowly across the table, gesturing to the dice. We rolled and slapped our cups down at the same time.

Two sixes and three ones. Full house. Strong hand. He went first this time, bidding a runt. I upped it to a pair.

"Think I might just roll again," he said, scooping up his dice.

He didn't like his old hand, but that didn't mean his new one was any better. His cheeks tightened when he tipped back his cup. Just a little. Just enough for me to notice.

"Two pair," he said.

I pretended to mull it over. "Three of a kind."

"Low straight." His voice caught on the "low," the faintest edge of a nervous hitch.

My fingers curled against moist palms. Time to lay it on the line.

"Liar," I said.

We lifted our cups. He ran his fingertips over his bone dice, arranging them in a neat little row. One, two, three, four, five. A low straight. If I had pushed him for one more round, he would have been in the danger zone. So he made sure I didn't.

"Sorry, son," he said. "Guess this just isn't your night."

He extended his hand. I took it firmly in mine, without flinching. I paid my debt. The sense of loss washed over me like an early winter, when you've lived long enough to start wondering how many summers you've got left. I put my hands in my lap to keep anyone from seeing them tremble.

Calypso shook his head, looking almost regretful. "That's two years of your life gone, son. An old man can do a lot with two years if he puts his mind to it. Out of respect to your lady, I think we'd best—"

"Five years," I blurted.

They stared at me. I wasn't sure whether Calypso or Caitlin looked more shocked.

"Five years," I said. "Last game, last try. Five more years of my life against the contract. Except this time we play a different game."

Calypso quirked a smile. "Hell, son, I'll give you points for moxie. What's the game?"

I took the deck of cards from my hip pocket and set them down on the table.

"Three-card monte. I deal, you pick one card. You find the queen, you get five years of my life, and I go home a loser. You fail, I get the contract. Deal?"

I shot a glance at Caitlin and touched her knee under the table, gently. *Trust me.* She didn't look too confident, but she gave me a slight nod.

Calypso ashed his cigarette and took a sip of whiskey while he thought it over. Suddenly, he rapped his knuckles on the table and stood up.

"I'll be right back," he said, making his way over to the crowded bar.

Caitlin squeezed my hand under the table and whispered, "What are you *doing*? He just beat you twice without even trying. Is this some sort of pride thing? Calypso's a *legend*, Daniel. I won't think any less of you for walking away from the table."

I lifted her hand to my lips, and kissed the curve of her fingers. "Trust me. I think I've got him figured out. Besides, the monte isn't a game, it's a hustle."

"You think he doesn't know that?"

"Oh, he knows it," I said. "In fact, I'm counting on him knowing it."

I fiddled with my deck, idly shuffling, until Calypso returned. He held up a fresh pack of cards, still sealed in cellophane.

"We play," he said, peeling the translucent plastic open, "but not with your cards. With *these*."

My shoulders tensed. I forced myself to nod and smile. "Fine."

He handed me the open pack, and I shook the cards out into my palm. Smooth, glossy, never creased, and slick as grease. I fanned out the deck on the table, so they could both see every move I made. I slid out the queen of hearts and held it up.

"Behold, the lady fair," I said. "This is the money card. Keep your eye on her, she's more slippery than she looks."

The jack of spades and the jack of clubs joined the queen of hearts, and the other cards went back in the pack, set off to the side. I flipped the blue-backed cards facedown, then picked up two in my left hand and one in my right.

In any game of three-card monte, the opening throw is the most crucial. A good operator learns how to make a deal from the top of two cards look like a deal from the bottom, and vice versa. Before you even start shuffling the cards around, the mark is already looking in the wrong place. Get that right and the game is yours.

The three cards hit the table. A perfect bottom deal, undetectable and designed to throw Calypso off the trail.

His unblinking gaze darted straight to the middle card. Straight to the queen.

29.

I took a deep breath and laid my fingertips on the outer cards, swapping them, jumping to the middle card and sliding it around to the left, keeping them in constant motion. As I did, an old patter line spilled from my lips, words dancing to the beat of the cards.

"It's a little game from Kathmandu, the black for me, the red for you. One gets you five, and five gets you ten. I don't get mad when I lose, I get happy when I win. Hey, diddle diddle, the queen's in the middle. Now, *sir*—"

I pulled my hands back. The three cards lay on the table between us, facedown and anonymous, waiting for Calypso's choice.

"Tell me," I said, "can you spot the queen? Where's that slippery lady hiding out now?"

Calypso lifted his chin. He smiled, almost condescending, as his finger hovered over each card...then lifted to point at my arm.

"The queen," he said, "is up your right sleeve, tucked into your watchband."

I'd been holding my breath while he chose. I let it all out in one sigh, deflating.

"I'll be taking my five years now," he said.

I reached out and flipped over the middle card. Showing him the queen of hearts.

"Don't think so," I said. "Weird choice, too. I mean, I *told* you the queen was in the middle. Weren't you listening?"

Caitlin flashed a sly smile, like she knew it all along, but I could see the relief in her eyes. Calypso just stared, brow furrowed, as he tried to figure out what he'd missed.

"Pull up your sleeve," he said, wagging his finger. "I can *see* the corner of a card poking out there."

"What, this?" I said.

I tugged out the hidden card and held it up. It was the six of diamonds. I turned it around to show him the twined red dragons on the back, not the blue back from the deck he'd chosen.

"This is one of *my* cards," I said. "I slipped it up my sleeve while you were over at the bar, before the game even started. Then I let you see it while I was shuffling. Your assumptions did the rest of the work for me."

Calypso quirked an eyebrow. Then he laughed, a deep and hearty rumble, lifting his glass and tossing back a swig of whiskey.

"Spirit of the game," I said. "We both know that three-card monte is a grift. Therefore cheating *is* in the spirit of the game. You assumed I chose the monte because I thought I could pull one over on you with some simple carny tricks. I chose it because I knew I *couldn't*. I did the one thing you didn't expect."

I tapped the queen.

"I played fair."

"Well," Calypso said, reaching into his suit coat. "That was nicely done, son. Like you said, I don't get mad when I lose. I get happy when I win. This is yours, fair and square."

He took a furled sheaf of papers from inside his coat, rolled up and bound with a black silk ribbon, and handed it over to me. I raised my glass to him with my free hand.

"Cheers," I said. "And don't worry, I won't tell anyone about this."

He laughed again, looking incredulous. "You won't? Why you'd better, or I'm gonna have to do all the work."

It was my turn to be baffled.

"Wait," I said, "you *want* people to know you lost a bet? I thought the whole point with you guys is that you never lose."

Calypso looked over at Caitlin. "M'lady fair, you need to school this boy."

"Can't say I don't try," she said, sipping her whiskey.

"I deal in stories," Calypso said. "Stories of temptation and ruin, of damnation and repentance, risk and reward. Let me lay one on you. Once upon a time, there was a boy named Johnny. He was a fiddle player, swore he was the best there'd ever been."

"Yeah," I said. "'Devil Went Down to Georgia.' I've heard the song. Everybody has."

Calypso snorted. "Don't interrupt a storyteller. For the record, the real deal went down in Tennessee, back in the nineteen twenties. Johnny wagered his soul against a fiddle of gold, betting he could outplay the devil himself. Well, a dark and handsome stranger who he thought was the devil, anyway."

"In the song, Johnny wins," I said.

"And that's just how it happened. Except for one little detail."

Calypso beckoned us closer. Caitlin and I leaned against the table to listen as he dropped his voice low.

"That boy," he said with a grin, "couldn't fiddle for *shit*. Sounded like beating a sackful of cats with a hickory stick."

"You...let him win?" I said.

"Mm-hmm. I'd been in a slump. Then there's good old Johnny, holding aloft his golden fiddle—which he never did learn to play worth a lick—and bragging to everyone from Appalachia to the Florida shore that he beat the devil and won a prize. Put a lot of bad ideas in people's heads. Bad for them, anyway. Good for my business. And as for good old Johnny, well...pride's a terrible sin."

"Art," Caitlin told me. She left it at that.

"You beat me fair and square today," Calypso said, "and that's something that has to happen once in a while, just every once in a while, to spice up the story. It's the reward to the risk, the pot of gold everyone who buys a lottery ticket dreams about even though they'll never, ever win. Every once in a while, some clever son of a gun has to beat the devil. That's what makes everyone else think *they* can do it, too."

Calypso finished his drink and laced his fingers together, cracking his knuckles.

"Besides," he said, "I'm walking away with two years of your life tucked in my back pocket. That's not bad for a lazy night. Best of luck to both of you, and I hope that paper helps you out some. Remember, you can play with Roth all you want, just make sure he lives through it. Don't step on my toes, and I won't step on yours."

"He's not the person we're after," I said. "He's just going to help us get to her."

Calypso reached down and tugged up the strap of a big black guitar case. He slung it over his shoulder and stood, pushing his chair back.

"Now, I know you're on a tight schedule," he told us, "but I'm just about to go up on stage and do a little set. Keeps me from getting rusty. If you've got any love in your heart for the Delta blues, I'd be honored to have you stay a while."

"We'd love to!" Caitlin gushed, squeezing my knee hard enough to make my leg ache. She beamed like a teenager in the sixties who had just been offered front-row tickets to a Beatles concert.

"Sure," I said, nodding slowly. "Sounds good."

I could have used another drink, and besides, I got the feeling I didn't really have a choice in the matter.

#

I had to admit, it was worth the time we lost. Calypso's hands played that guitar like it was a lover's body, like they only had one night left in the world together and every second, every aching, wailing note, had to make up for a lost lifetime. This was the real blues, down-home raw and ragged, drenched with sweat and sex and the bloodied edge of a switchblade. Out on the dark and silent street, his music still echoed in the back of my mind, floating and fading like a dream that slips away on waking.

Caitlin's arm was wrapped in mine, and she wobbled against me a little, higher than a kite even though she'd only drunk two fingers of whiskey. I was feeling it too. I felt confused in all the right ways, basking in the afterglow.

"Now you get it," she said.

"Rock star," I said. "Right. I hate to say it, but we should find a motel or something. It's another seven hours back home, and between the lack of sleep and the booze and the...*that*, I'm in no shape to drive."

"I am," she said. "And I don't need to sleep. I'll drive us back, and you can nap."

I gave her a dubious look. Maybe because she was a little too giddy. Maybe because I was a little protective of my car. Still, she held out her open palm in a way that brooked no argument.

"Keys," she said.

While she adjusted the driver's seat, I tugged the ribbon on the copy of Roth's contract. The dense text read just like the real thing, down to the tiniest detail, but it was magically inert. I traced my finger over tight lines of perfect calligraphy, feeling like a medieval monk. The streetlight outside the car window cast a pale glow, giving me enough light to read by if I squinted.

I slid past lines of preamble and jargon, down to the meat of the contract. My finger froze on the page. "Holy shit."

"What?" Caitlin said, glancing over as she revved the Barracuda's engine.

"Calypso wasn't kidding when he said Roth was bound for greater things, or that this was his most ambitious project in centuries. Cait...Roth didn't sell his soul for the Senate. He wants to be the president."

"Ambitious is right. Still, wouldn't be the first time we've put a man in the Oval Office."

I looked over at her.

"No, not *that* one," she said. "And not that one, either."

"Since when can you read minds?"

She smiled and pulled out of the parking spot, gliding onto the open road and aiming for the highway on-ramp.

"I can't," she said. "I can just read *you*."

"Can Calypso actually pull it off?"

"He wouldn't have taken the contract if he didn't think he could. The more pressing question is what this means for us. He was deadly serious, Daniel. We can't do anything that puts Roth in mortal danger or jeopardizes his chances of success."

"In other words," I said, "we can't expose him. If he gets implicated along with Carmichael and Ausar or worse yet, arrested—"

"Bye-bye, White House," Caitlin said, finishing my thought.

"We can still use him," I said. I rolled up the contract and tied the ribbon around it. "And we can still use this. I've got an idea."

We rolled along down US-95. Caitlin found a blues station broadcasting out of Reno, but the tinny recording was just a ghost of a live show. She twirled the old radio's dial until it landed on dance music. Thumping, pulsing bass carried us out into the desert night.

"What's the plan?" she said.

"Roth thinks Lauren is his best hope," I told her. "Let's disabuse him of that notion."

30.

I fell into a fitful sleep around the time the last radio station died, leaving us in the long dark silence between cities. I woke to soft sunlight and dusty streets, home again.

"You should have woken me up. I would have taken a turn driving," I said, wincing as I shifted in my seat. A jolt of pain shot up my neck, punishing me for sleeping slumped against the passenger door.

"You needed your rest," Caitlin said. "Besides, I've never driven a car with a hemi before."

I eyed the dashboard clock. We'd made great time on our way back. Suspiciously great time.

"Cait? Exactly how fast were you driving?"

"I drove five miles under the speed limit, stayed in the slow lane, and made sure to properly signal at all posted turns," she said. "Honest."

Now I was glad I'd slept through the ride home. My blood pressure was high enough already. I had a message from Bentley waiting on my phone, and I called him back.

"I have good news!" he said. I hadn't heard him sounding that chipper in a while.

"So do I," I said, "but let's hear yours first."

"I think we've found the place. The source of Meadow Brand's minions. There's a furniture workshop here in town, Y&M Custom Woodworking, and they handle all kinds of special requests. Well, I gave them a call and indicated I was in the market for a human-sized armature doll."

"Let me guess," I said. "They've already got 'em in stock."

"More or less. The gentleman I spoke to said that he'd already fulfilled several requests for that very item lately, and he invited me to stop in and discuss the particulars."

I smiled. "Fantastic. Pick up anything hinky about the guy? Like he might know what he's doing or who he's really working for?"

"Not at all. He seemed a little befuddled by the request and asked if there was some sort of big art project in the offing. Brand is keeping him in the dark."

Even better. I got the address and passed it on to Caitlin, who pulled a U-turn at the next stoplight.

"What do you think?" she said. "Find out when she's making her next pickup, then ambush her? Deny Lauren an ally?"

"I've been looking forward to putting a bullet between Meadow's eyes, and no one can say she doesn't have it coming. Lauren's ally, though? I'm not so sure. Last time we faced off, Lauren almost locked her out of her safe room while Sullivan and his Choirboys were tearing up the joint. I've gotten the idea that Lauren uses Meadow like a junkyard dog. She's rabid, vicious, and pretty much disposable the second Lauren doesn't need her anymore."

"The question then becomes does Lauren still need her?" Caitlin said. "And if not, how can we turn that to our advantage?"

Y&M was tucked away on a backstreet, inside what used to be an auto repair shop. I could still read the old lettering reading "Tire and Battery" under the new coat of paint on the sign out front. They had the old garage bay doors open, letting natural light stream into the grease-stained concrete hull where a couple of guys in T-shirts and jeans labored over a screaming table saw. They powered down the saw as we walked across the tiny parking lot.

"Mornin'!" one called out as his partner took the freshly sawed chunks of pine over to a worktable. He had a bright smile and a chestnut-colored mustache.

"Hey there," I said. "This your place?"

"Y&M," he said, nodding to the sign. "He's Young, I'm Messner. In the market for new cabinets? We just finished some real beauties that need a good home."

"Something a little more offbeat. Friend of mine called over earlier. Looking for armature puppets. Big ones."

Messner rubbed his mustache, looking between Caitlin and me.

"Yeah," he said. "Hey, I don't mean to be nosy, but you're the second person who's asked about commissioning those things. I sure don't mind the money, but mind telling me what the darn things are for? Young's guessing it's some kind of art installation."

"She didn't—" I said, then looked to Caitlin. "She didn't tell him. Can you believe that?"

Caitlin caught my drift and shook her head. "Oh, that's Meadow for you. She'd forget her head if it wasn't screwed on."

"I'm Peter Greyson," I said. It was an alias I'd used before. "Regional manager for Del Rey Fashion. This is Zoe, our director of marketing."

"Charmed," she said.

"Our flagship stores are in Florida," I said. "Think Abercrombie and Fitch meets Miami chic. We're getting ready to make a big splash on the West Coast. Those life-sized armature dolls are sort of a store trademark. We use 'em instead of plastic mannequins for setting up clothing displays. Looks a little classier, you know?"

Messner put his hands on his hips. "You hear that, Young? Y'owe me five bucks. Art installation, my ass."

Young pulled on a pair of plastic safety goggles, flipped Messner the bird, and turned back to his workbench.

"Now, this part's a little embarrassing," I said. "See, the reason you got multiple calls, and we had to track you down like we didn't know you were already building the puppets for us—"

Caitlin folded her arms and glared. "Oh, just *say* it, Peter. We fired the bitch. We trusted that woman to set up our entire Nevada retail hub, only to find out she's done nothing for months. We haven't broken ground on a single store."

I put on an apologetic, sheepish smile. "Right. Ms. Brand's basically dropped out of sight entirely, and we're still trying to recoup some of our lost assets. Did she make any arrangements to pick up the next batch of puppets?"

"Nope," Messner said. "In fact, we've been calling her, but she hasn't called back. Hasn't been around for a couple of weeks. So, uh, does that mean you're gonna pay for this batch? Because the order's just kinda sitting here, and there isn't a whole lot of demand..."

He trailed off with a hopeful lilt in his voice.

"Of course," Caitlin said primly. "That's why we're here. Will cash be acceptable?"

Messner's eyes lit up. "Cash is always welcome here, miss."

She stepped a little closer, holding him in her gaze.

"And you wouldn't mind helping us wrap up our paper-work, would you?" she said. "Having copies of Meadow's receipts would go a long way toward unraveling the mess she left for us. I'd consider it a favor."

Messner nodded and waved us into the shop. "Of course! Long as you're taking this last order off my hands. You're helping me out, I'll help you out."

The mannequins, four of them in all, were wrapped up in plastic sheeting and stacked like corpses in a shadowy back corner of the garage. Their blank, featureless faces stared out from under their glossy shrouds. I noticed their left hands were all missing. Meadow must do that part herself, I figured, equipping her murderous minions with their knives and rusty awls while bringing them to life.

"That's, uh, twelve hundred for the lot," Messner said.

Caitlin opened her purse and counted out a string of hundred-dollar bills. While Messner went to put together all of the paperwork on Meadow's past purchases, I called Pixie.

#

We wrestled two of the puppets into the backseat of the Barracuda and the other two into the trunk. "This isn't creepy or anything," I said as I shut the lid.

"If anyone looks in the backseat, we'll just tell them we're exploring an exciting new fetish," Caitlin said.

"You don't think that Meadow—" I caught myself as I slipped behind the steering wheel. "Never mind. That's on my list of mental images to never have again."

Pixie met us at the Scrivener's Nook. She pulled up out front in the Wardriver, an old white Ford panel van that rattled and wheezed when she killed the engine. It looked like a clunker, but that was just for show. Inside, the Wardriver sported enough electronics and surveillance gear to make an FBI agent drool. A bumper sticker slapped up on a control panel, just under a row of closed-circuit screens showing the street outside the van from every possible angle, read "This Machine Kills Fascists."

I pocketed my phone as Caitlin and I climbed in back. "Our first stop is Sapphire Skytours. Pix, can you scan this contract? We're going to need to email it to somebody."

"Whoa," Pixie said, reading it over. "So this is legit? Roth really sold his soul? Wait...*no*. Uh-uh. No fucking way, Faust. *President*? Roth is a thug. Do you even read the news? Just last week he voted in favor of—"

I held up my hand. "We're not going to help him, Pix. We're just not going to stop him. Not today. It's a question of priorities. Lauren's going to become a world-devouring goddess sometime in the next few days. Roth is just going to stink up the Senate for another decade or two and pass some bills you don't like. Let's aim higher, huh?"

"I don't see why we can't fix both problems," she said.

"Because," Caitlin said, "the other signatory on that contract is a very old and very powerful creature who isn't fond of being meddled with. We can use Roth with the understanding that we do nothing to endanger him, physically or professionally. Whatever you might be considering right now, I can promise you two things. One, it won't work. Two, you will regret it. Now bottle your hatred and store it in your heart's pantry for a thirstier day."

"I don't...I don't *hate* him," Pixie said, suddenly deflated. She sat in the driver's seat, not looking back at us. "I don't *hate* anybody."

"I don't judge," Caitlin said with a faint smile.

The faded billboard outside Sapphire Skytours, spelling out the name in big puffy cloud letters, screamed "tourist trap." The place was just a small lot and a couple of out-buildings, with a Big-Bird-yellow, six-seater Bell 407 sitting in the middle of it all like a museum piece. The sky was clear as springwater, but nobody was flying.

We parked and walked over to the management office. The trailer sat up on cinder blocks, and an air conditioner bolted to one fat end whirred like a chainsaw, working over-time against the midday heat. I didn't bother knocking on the door.

Nicky sat behind the manager's desk with his Italian loafers up and the stem of a frosted margarita glass in his hand. Juliette leaned against one wall of the trailer and flipped through a celebrity gossip mag while Justine loaded a blender for the next round of drinks.

"Oh, hey," Nicky said. "Just come right in. Don't knock or anything. Make yourselves at home."

"I'll get more glasses!" Justine said.

Nicky shook his head. "That was sarcasm, babe."

Juliette squealed and threw her magazine on the floor. She ran over to Pixie like a puppy on a sugar high. "Sis! She's back she's back she's back!"

I stifled a groan. This could get ugly.

31.

Justine quickly joined her sister. The twins circled Pixie like piranha eager for a bleeding calf.

"We were thinking, after the last time we met," Juliette said.

"We were thinking about *you*," Justine said. "And about our duty to help the less fortunate. Which you clearly are, dressed like that. It's all right. We're here now, and your days of shopping in thrift stores—because you're trying to be ironic, or you're poor, or both—are over."

"We're thinking *makeover!*" Juliette squealed.

Pixie cocked her left hand into a fist.

"I'm going to give each of you a different black eye," she said, cool and calm, "so I can tell you apart."

I looked at Nicky. Nicky sighed and looked at the twins.

"Girls?" he said. "It's a nice day outside. Why don't you go get some flight time?"

"*Flight time!*" they cheered simultaneously. A moment later they were gone, leaving the trailer door swinging in their wake.

I just blinked, staring at the door.

"Nicky?" I said. "That's a euphemism, right? You don't actually let them—"

Outside the trailer window, the rotors of the Bell helicopter started to spin.

Nicky sipped his margarita. "I know, weird, right? Turns out they're actually really good pilots. I bought this place so I could launder money through it, but you should see the reviews we've been getting on Yelp. So I'm guessing you didn't come out here for cocktail hour. What's up?"

"Your house in Eldorado," I said, memories of his torture basement fresh on my mind. "Is it clean?"

"Clean as the day it was built, long as nobody goes digging up the backyard. Why? You got someone you wanna take out there?"

"Senator Roth," Caitlin said.

Nicky arched an eyebrow. "I'd like to take a crack at the guy myself, but ain't that a little imprudent?"

"He'll survive," I said. "We've got a plan to get him out of the picture and pave the way for a shot at Lauren. Thing is I need a nice, remote, quiet place to get the job done. A place where nobody's around to call in a gunshot or two."

"Fine," Nicky said.

He rummaged in the desk drawer and took out a small ring of keys.

"Also I need to break a couple of windows," I said. "And maybe stain the carpets with blood."

He set the keys down on the desk with his hand over them.

"It's for verisimilitude," I told him.

Nicky sighed, looked at the keys, and tossed them over to me.

"I don't know who this Verisimilitude guy is," he dead-panned, "but he's gonna pay for anything he breaks. I'm planning on flipping that entire development once the housing market picks up again."

"Even with bodies in the backyard?"

He shrugged. "It ain't my name on the deed."

Bentley and Corman met us in Eldorado. They pulled up behind the Wardriver in Bentley's sleek silver Caddy while I was busy dragging wooden mannequins into the backyard of Nicky's kill-house. They were heavier than they looked. I still hadn't figured out how Meadow Brand's animation trick worked, but I could have used a little of that magic.

I laid the mannequins out on the grass. We had made a couple of stops on the way over. One was to pick up my gun. I leveled the heavy barrel of the Taurus Judge, taking careful aim.

"Shooting!" I shouted over my shoulder. "Stay out of the yard for a second."

Two gunshots crackled through the sky, scattering a flight of birds from the kill-house roof and sending them winging over the deserted development.

"Wow," Pixie said, walking past me with a cardboard box of electronic odds and ends in her arms, heading inside with Bentley and Corman in tow. "Good shot, G.I. Joe. Those dolls won't mess with *you* again."

Now I had to worry about splinters along with my aching back. I'd shot each puppet square in the chest, and now they looked like trees that had met the business end of a lumberjack's ax. I lugged them through the kitchen door one by one.

"We brought everything you asked for," Bentley said. He laid out a pair of battered tackle boxes on the kitchen counter next to Pixie's overflowing carton of odds and ends. "It's exciting to be doing a little acting again!"

"It's not exactly Shakespeare," I said.

Corman waved a hand and poked his head in the refrigerator. "Eh, close enough. He means it's exciting to be pulling a grift again."

"He *knows* what I meant, Cormie," Bentley said.

Corman shut the fridge in disgust. "Seriously, Nicky doesn't even keep snacks in the house? And no beer? He really is half demon."

Caitlin waved to me from the living room. She took my arm and led me up a short hallway into a guest bedroom at the end. It was unfurnished, like the rest of the house, but sunlight streamed through a big picture window and painted the beige carpet in squares of gold.

"What do you think?" she said. "Outside access, the hall's visible from the living room, and there's a small closet off to the side."

I nodded, looking around, counting the paces from the door to the closet.

"I think," I said, "you'd make one hell of a magician's assistant."

"Bugger that," she said, taking my arm again. "You can wear the sequins. I want to wear the top hat."

It pays to have a mixed bag of tricks. When they're expecting a gun, whip out a little sorcery. When they're expecting the supernatural, think like Harry Houdini instead. We had a few surprises in store for Alton Roth. That was, if he took the bait. Back in the kitchen, Pixie handed me the key to the van.

"Console's all set up. A monkey could operate it," she said. Then she looked over to Caitlin. "He might need your help."

We idled the Wardriver's engine to get the air-conditioning running. The computers were liquid cooled, but we weren't, and the van's shell didn't take long to turn into a sauna on a hot afternoon. Caitlin and I sat side by side in front of the bank of controls, double-checked everything one last time, and put on twin headsets.

A dial tone reverberated in my ears. I lowered the volume a little, running my fingertip over a slider on one side of the headset, and made the call.

"Senator Roth's office," said the nasal voice on the other end of the line. "How may I direct your call?"

"I need to speak to the senator, please," I said.

"I'm sorry, sir, but the senator is in meetings all day. I'd be happy to leave a message for him, or you could schedule an appointment—"

"He'll want to take this call. Tell him the word 'Calypso.' He'll understand."

We waited patiently. I imagined one flunky flagging down another flunky to pass a hurried message to a third, running through the halls of government power like relay racers. After four minutes of vaguely inspirational, vaguely patriotic hold music, Roth picked up on the other end. His voice was a hushed murmur just on the edge of panic.

"Calypso? Is that you?"

"Nope," I said, leaning back in my chair. "But I'll give you three guesses."

He got it in one try. "Faust. Lauren warned me about you."

"Of course she did. She wanted to make sure you wouldn't trust me, when the time came to take action. Truth is, we have a mutual friend. Calypso hired me to protect you."

"I...I don't know what that is, or who that is," he said hurriedly. "Or who you are. This is a crank call and I'm hanging up."

"Before you do, check your email," I said. Caitlin rattled off a quick message on the Wardriver's console, sending him the scan of his infernal contract. On the other end of the line, I could hear Roth's mouse clicking.

"That's proof," I said. "Proof we're on the same side. I could never have gotten my hands on that contract without Calypso's permission. If I hurt you or exposed you, that'd bust your deal, and that's the *last* thing he wants. Therefore, I must be trying to help you. Think it over, Senator. Simple logic."

"All right," he said, reluctant. "If that's true, then what do you want?"

"To save your life. Lauren's going to betray you."

"Ridiculous. Lauren's a traitor? Why? She's literally getting everything she wants. I'm showering her with money and support. She gets to—" He paused, catching himself.

"To become a goddess," I said. "We know about the Enclave. We know everything. What *you* don't know is that Lauren doesn't like to share. You think she's going to reward you with eternal life for your loyalty? Guess again. That makes you competition, and she doesn't like competition. She's planning on having you killed. We can prove it."

"How?" he said.

As he spoke, another monitor running a speech-to-text program displayed a running transcript. Reminding me what words he'd spoken, and what I still needed to get on tape for the second half of the plan.

"Not here, not on the phone. Let's meet tonight, just you and me. I'm sending you an address in Eldorado."

"You want me to meet," he said, "alone? With a murderer who's trying to destroy my life's work and my best chance of salvation."

"And what happens if I kill you tonight, Roth? Oh, that's right, contract's null and void, and you don't have to burn in hell. Want more proof that I'm looking out for you? Try this on for size. I've got a document, in your handwriting and with your verifiable signature, literally selling your soul for political power. What happens if I email this to every media outlet in the country? If I was really out to get you, I'd have already *done* it."

He didn't answer right away.

"All right," he said, chewing it over. "I'll come."

"You'll come alone?"

"Yes!" he snapped. "I'll come alone!"

Caitlin tapped the transcript of his words on the screen and gave me a thumbs-up before sending another email. Pixie had set the system up for us in advance, making sure anything we sent would bounce off proxy servers from here to Beijing and land in Roth's inbox with nothing but a generic user name and a dead trail behind it.

"Did you get the email?" I said. "Confirm the address, please."

"Uh, 14082 Sauk Trail, room six," he said. I heard him typing in the background. "Wait a second, that's not in

Eldorado at all. Google Maps says it's a motel off I-15 about ten miles outside Vegas."

Another thumbs-up from Caitlin.

"Sorry, sorry," I said. "Ignore that. That's for a different meeting. Sending you the right one now."

"I can't believe Lauren's trying to kill me. After all I've done for her! You'd better be right about this, Faust."

"Trust me," I told him. "I'm your best friend in the world right now, Roth. I've got no reason to lie."

32.

With Roth on his way, it was time to get the hard work done. Caitlin and I helped set up a cluster of remote cameras in the house, little gray plastic orbs smaller than a cue ball, fixing them in place with ceiling brackets. Pixie linked them up with the screens in the Wardriver, calling in to give us directions.

"Little to the left," she told me. "No, your *other* left. Right there, perfect. I can see all the way down the hall."

Caitlin and I shared a stepstool, our bodies pressed dangerously close. She held the camera in place while I slipped the bracket under it, screwing it in tight with an electric screwdriver. I jumped down and ran into the living room to check the sight lines. It was perfect. The cameras were already unobtrusive, but thanks to a low-hanging bit of molding, this one was literally impossible to see from where Roth would be standing.

Bentley and Corman practiced their moves like they had been born on the stage, coordinating with Caitlin and Pixie.

I stopped Corman near the basement door, nodding at the stairs.

"You sure about this? That's a pretty steep climb," I said.

"Kiddo," he said, "did you just imply I'm too old to run up and down a goddamn flight of stairs?"

"Not in the slightest."

He nodded grimly. "Good. Because I'm also not too old to smack you upside the head. You just worry about getting Roth on his mark, so he gets a nice clear view. We do this right, he'll be pissing his pants."

The guns were the last ingredient. A black nine-millimeter Glock for me, a pair of big chromed .45s for Bentley and Corman. I checked my load; then I checked it twice. Then a third time, just for safety. If everything went right, nobody would get hurt tonight. Problem was, it'd be real easy for everything to go wrong.

#

Night fell over the abandoned development. Pixie and Caitlin took the Wardriver, pulling it into a half-built garage across the street. Bentley and Corman took their marks. I took a slow, deep breath and waited.

Tires rumbled over fresh asphalt. I ran out the back door and into the dark, standing in the oncoming headlights and waving my arms.

The headlights died along with the engine. I had to squint for a second, getting my night vision back, as Roth clambered out of a compact rental car. I ran over and grabbed his arm, pulling him toward the back door.

"Are you crazy?" I said, moving my hand from his arm to his back, giving him a little push. "Are you *trying* to get killed? Listen to me—"

He tried to pull away, and I turned him around, grabbing his other arm, my hand slipping and brushing his waist. The light from the open kitchen door spilled out onto the cold grass. I put my hands on his shoulders, holding him in place.

"Listen to me," I said. "Did you come alone?"

His eyes bulged, not sure what to make of the crazy man pawing at him. "Yes! I said I would!"

"Well, that's a big fucking problem," I said, pulling him inside and slamming the door shut behind us.

I wasn't just trying to make him uncomfortable. The groping had been an impromptu pat down, feeling for suspicious bulges or the seam of a shoulder holster. The last thing I wanted was another gun in the house, one I didn't control.

"Wait," he said, "it's a problem that I came alone? Why?"

I led him into the living room. A walkie-talkie sat on the sill of a picture window, leaning against the drawn blinds. I snatched it up.

"Roth's here with me," I snapped into the handset. "You're sure you saw what you saw?"

Caitlin's voice echoed over the static. "Positive. I shadowed him for the last fifty miles. He had a second tail."

"You hear that?" I said, turning on Roth. "You damn amateur! You had *two* tails, and you didn't spot either one of them. My operative and *hers*."

I thought Roth was going to have a heart attack. Good. That was the entire point. Pour on the pressure, don't give him a moment to think. The most important key to any short con is that you *never* give a mark time to think.

"Hers?" he said.

"Lauren! Which means she sent Meadow Brand. Which means she's coming here to kill both of us *right now!*"

"W-we have to go!" Roth stammered. "We have to run—"

"There's a van blocking the development exit," Caitlin said over the walkie-talkie. "Looks...yes, looks empty. The occupants are already on the move."

I shook my head. "We can't go outside. Out there in the dark, on foot? It's a shooting gallery. No, we stay here. We hunker down. We wait it out until sunrise. Come here, get away from the window."

I got him into the middle of the empty living room, right where I needed him. Guaranteeing him a front-row ticket to the show.

"I can get us through this," I said, "but you have to trust me. You do trust me, yes?"

"Yes," he parroted, instinctively echoing the cues in my voice. He took a Blackberry from his pocket, working the tiny buttons with shaking fingers.

"I'll—I'll call for help," he said. "Caine can send his men—"

I yanked the phone from his hands, hung up, and shoved it back at him.

"And they'll get here just in time to scoop our dead bodies off the carpet. Forget it. Stick with me, stay close, do *exactly* what I tell you, and you can call for a ride once we're free and clear."

Right on cue, glass exploded in the back bedroom. Another clatter rang up from the basement as a casement window smashed open. I pulled my gun.

"Relax," I told Roth. "This is what I do."

Bentley jumped out from the side bedroom, spinning, raising his .45 to fire. I shot him twice. His chest erupted in billows of scarlet blood, and he staggered back, his arm jerking up and a return bullet going wide, screaming over our heads and punching into the freshly painted wall. Bentley fell back, clutching his chest, and staggered into the bedroom.

Behind us, the door to the basement slammed open. Corman emerged from the darkness and fired, his shot winging close enough to ruffle my sleeve. I fired three shots and gunned the old man down, sending him reeling toward the open doorway. We heard the grisly thumping as his corpse rolled down the steep staircase all the way to the concrete floor.

All was silent. The air smelled like blood and gun smoke. Roth's mouth hung open, his jaw trembling. I held up a finger for silence and led him up the hall, over to the guest bedroom.

A wooden mannequin lay on the ground, broken and lifeless, its chest splintered exactly where I'd shot Bentley. It was frozen in a crawl, one arm stretched toward the broken window, as if it had succumbed to its wounds while trying to escape.

"Meadow Brand," I snarled. "She uses illusions to disguise her puppets as humans. That's how she gets them close to her targets."

"I-I know," Roth whispered. "I've seen her do it."

We jogged to the basement door. Down at the bottom of the stairs, silhouetted in the light of a slowly swaying bulb, a second mannequin lay shot and dead.

"Come on," I said. "She has to be close to control these things, but she won't stick around for long."

He froze as we approached the kitchen door. "Wait, how do you know that's all of them?"

"You know how Brand operates," I told him. In fact, I was counting on him knowing it. "She always goes for the over-kill, and she doesn't send two puppets when she can send ten. If she had more to throw at us, she already would have."

Roth nodded, getting it. We ran out to the driveway just in time to see the Wardriver speeding away with a screech of tires.

"There she is!" I shouted. I dropped to one knee, brought my gun up in both hands, and shot at the van, pulling the trigger until the hammer clicked down on an empty cham-ber. I cursed and stood back up, shoving the worthless gun back under my jacket.

Roth watched me, eyes wide as his brain tried to catch up with his eyes and ears.

"You...you saved my life," he said.

"Told you I would." I nodded at his rental car. "Come on. Let's get out of here before she sends reinforcements. We need to talk."

The key to stage magic is playing on assumptions. You don't need elaborate stages and thousand-dollar props to perform a good trick—you just need an audience ready and primed to be fooled. I had figured that Roth knew all about Meadow Brand through his partnership with Lauren, and that he'd have seen her mannequins in action along with how she used illusions to disguise them—for a little while, at least—as dead-eyed human beings.

That was all I needed.

My gun? Loaded with blanks. Made for a nice loud bang and a smoky sizzle, but the "blood" from Bentley's and Corman's wounds came courtesy of squibs and dye packs hidden under their shirts. Back in the Wardriver, Caitlin and Pixie used the hidden cameras we'd placed to keep track of the action, setting off the squibs in time with my shots.

We'd placed the "dead" puppets in the guest bedroom and the basement before Roth even arrived. Meanwhile, Bentley hid in a side closet, and Corman—dragging a garbage bag of junk down the stairs to simulate the sound of a tumbling body—just ducked around the corner and out of sight. It was so simple it was almost complicated.

Roth was so rattled he didn't even notice the one giveaway: the broken windows were both smashed open from *inside* the house.

As we pulled out of the development and onto the main road, I saw the van parked on an unlit cross street. Once we were out of sight, they'd double back to pick up Bentley and Corman and yank out the cameras. As for the broken glass, the red-dye-stained carpet, and the bullets in the walls, I figured Nicky could send me a bill. I'd be sure to get right on that.

We drove for ten minutes in a direction close to random. I wasn't sure if Roth kept turning to throw off an imagined tail, or if he was just too scared to plot a course, and I didn't care either way. I owned him now. I spotted an all-night diner and pointed for him to pull in under the yellow neon sign.

"Here's good," I said. "Time for us to have a little chat about your former partners, and what we're going to do about them."

33.

Waylon Jennings crooned from the speakers of a jukebox as we slipped into a booth lined with yellow vinyl and hard plastic. The diner smelled like fresh hash browns and black coffee from a day-old pot.

"Two eggs, scrambled," I told the sleepy-eyed waitress. "Side of white toast, and a Coke."

"Nothing for me," Roth said.

I slid the laminated menu in front of him.

"Eat something," I said. "It'll help your stomach settle."

"Really," he said, "I can't."

I sighed, picked up both menus, and handed them to the waitress. "He'll have what I'm having, but a cup of decaf instead of the soda."

Once she disappeared, I studied Roth from across the Formica table.

"How long did you think it'd be, before Calypso noticed you were trying to live forever?" I said.

Roth looked pained. He shook his head. "It's not a violation of my contract. I checked. I read it a hundred times. I'm not in default, he can't collect."

"If he could," I said, "we wouldn't be having this conversation right now. Relax. He's not mad. Thinks it's kinda funny, truth be told."

Roth slumped back in the booth and closed his eyes. "Funny? None of this is funny. I never should have signed that damn contract, never should have heard him out—"

"But you did," I told him, "and that's ancient history now. Done. Writ in stone. All you can change is how long you get to live now, and how much luxury you get to ride in. See, we've got a bigger problem."

"Lauren wants to kill me."

"Bigger than that. You're not in violation now, but you're going to be. Real soon."

He sat up straight. "How do you figure?"

"Lauren. She's becoming a goddess, with your help. Once she does, once she starts flexing her muscle over the entire planet, do you really think there's going to *be* a United States for you to lead? That means you've deliberately made a clause of the contract unfulfillable, which means you broke the deal, which means your soul is forfeit, and you go straight to hell."

I didn't know if that was true, based on what little time I'd had to skim the fine print. It didn't matter, though. All that mattered was that he believed me. From the fresh panic in his eyes, I'd hit a home run.

"She promised me," he said. "She promised me she could get me out of this jam if I helped her."

"I don't care. Neither will Calypso. The best thing you can do right now, the *only* thing you can do, is help me stop

Lauren. She goes down, everything goes back to normal, which means you're alive and well and on your happy way to the White House, *Mr. President.* No harm, no foul, and we can all forget about this mess."

The waitress came back with our plates. I sprinkled a little salt and pepper over the scrambled eggs and unwrapped a red plastic straw. Roth stared at his food like he didn't know what it was for.

"What can I do?" he said. His hands lay dead in his lap, limp and helpless as the rest of him.

"Start from the beginning. How did you get mixed up with the lab rats from Ausar?"

He shook his head and let out a bitter little chuckle.

"You mean, how did they get involved with us," he said. "I was on the Ausar board of directors. I'd originally wanted to use the company to push longevity research. Then we found the tunnel in Mexico, and it was off to the races."

"Who else was on the board? Were you all clued-in?"

"Clued-in?" he said, tilting his head. "Oh! You mean did we all know what we were dealing with? No. Just a few of us. Everyone else was kept at arm's length. Nedry, Clark, and Payton were assigned to a black-books account and given facilities off the main corporate campus. Everyone knew they were working on the Viridithol project, but the actual details were kept quiet, and all the published papers were filled with garbage data. It was a very tight operation. Very smooth."

"Until you started feeding plant cuttings from another dimension to pregnant women," I said.

He reached for a packet of sugar and dumped it into his coffee. He wouldn't meet my eyes.

"That wasn't my fault," he said. "The researchers promised me they had it all under control. Not long after, Payton got cold feet and grew a conscience. He would have exposed us. Exposed everything."

I swirled my straw in my glass of Coke. Ice cubes bobbed up and down in the drink like tiny icebergs.

"It wasn't their idea, was it?" I said. "Nedry and Clark. *You* were the one who ordered Payton's murder."

"You would have done the same thing in my shoes. Come on, this wasn't about the deformed kids. He was going to tell the entire world that we'd found a gateway to the fucking Garden of Eden and draw the media a map to get there! You know, don't you? You've seen the horrible shit that's on the other side of that tunnel. You can imagine how many innocent people would have died trying to 're-turn to Eden.' Yes, I had him killed, and if I could do it all over again, I wouldn't change my mind. Bob Payton *had* to die."

I was tempted, for one perverse heartbeat, to tell him I'd spoken to a very alive and well Payton two nights ago. I kept it to myself, though. Payton could live until I was sure he'd sent the smoke-faced men back where they came from. After that, his survival would be highly negotiable.

"After the Viridithol scandal," Roth said, "the whole thing collapsed. We'd had the foresight to stash as many assets offshore as we could before the government came and kicked in the door. That was the end of the story, until I met Lauren Carmichael."

I scooped up a forkful of scrambled eggs. Greasy, salty, cheap, and perfect. Just what you want to settle a rumbling stomach, late at night after a gunfight.

"Let me guess," I said. "She came to you looking for help with bringing the feds down on Nicky Agnelli. You wanted to know why. You started digging and discovered you had common interests. Namely, she was trying to build Gilles de Rais's machine, while you, Nedry, and Clark already had access to his notes and could finish the puzzle. The peanut butter to Lauren's chocolate."

Roth sipped his coffee and nodded. "It's funny. She was so suspicious at first, thinking I wanted to usurp her position and be the one to activate the machine. I finally convinced her that I don't want to be a god. I just don't want to die. Besides, I'm more than happy to let her take all the risks. There's also the...changes."

"Changes?"

He glanced away for a moment, staring out the plate-glass window at the desolate parking lot.

"She's been taking Nedry and Clark's serum for weeks. Viridithol-2, created through an extract from white blood cells oversaturated with the original drug. It's not killing her, but...she's nothing I'd call human, Mr. Faust. Not anymore."

"She's attuning herself," I said. "Making her spirit and flesh friendlier to the Garden's energy, getting ready for the final step. How long do we have?"

"Days? Hours? The mutation is exponential. She's waiting like an expectant mother, waiting for the power coursing through her veins to tell her she's ready. The Enclave is finished. I'm almost certain they have all the sacrifices prepared and ready, and Nedry and Clark have been working around the clock. I'm not involved. I can't be. My job now was just to sit back, keep paying the bills, and wait. Given that she tried to murder me tonight...I guess all the bills are paid."

"Where do I find her?"

He nodded vaguely toward the distant lights of the Strip, a grimy scarlet smear against the diner window.

"The Enclave, behind more defenses than Fort Knox. You won't get to her. You wouldn't want to, even if you could."

"You let me worry about that," I said. "Nedry and Clark are there with her?"

"At all times."

"What about Meadow Brand?"

He shook his head. "I thought she was out hunting *you*. Lauren was furious—I guess you set a demon loose in her house or something? She said that killing you is now Brand's full-time job. I haven't seen Brand since, but she's supposed to have a part to play in the big ceremony. If you ask me? Before tonight, if I believed Lauren was going to stab anybody in the back, it'd be her. The woman is a raging psychopath. I think Lauren invited her to the final ritual just to keep an eye on her and make sure she didn't ruin anything."

"That might still be on the agenda."

"She'll be impossible to find now," Roth said. "She took a shot at both of us, and we're still alive. Brand isn't stupid. She'll hide."

"Even so, I have to try and track her down. You don't have any way of getting in touch?"

He took out his Blackberry and scrolled through his contacts list.

"Just an emergency phone number," he said. "She screens her calls, though. Won't pick up for anyone but me or Lauren."

Meadow's number was the same one we'd taken off her invoices from Y&M Woodworking. I pretended to copy it down anyway. It was Roth's number I was saving.

"Last question," I said. "Xerxes. Who do they answer to?"

"Angus Caine is *my* man. I write the paychecks, I give the orders. Don't ask me to send them up against Lauren, though. I'd be throwing their lives away."

"I've fought Lauren before," I said.

"That's right. *Before.* Before the treatments. You haven't seen her lately. No, even if I asked, Caine's too protective of his troops. He'd never allow it."

"That's all right," I said. "I don't need them to. I am going to ask you to do one more thing for me, but not just yet."

This was the hard part. Cutting him loose. I had to get rid of Roth in a way that would take him out of the fight, keep him loyal, and guarantee he kept believing his former partners were trying to murder him. I bit off a chunk of toast and chewed it over.

34.

"You've got to leave town," I told Roth. "Tonight. By now, Lauren knows that you know she's gunning for you. She'll take steps to defend herself, and that includes sending Meadow out for another go. Next time I won't be there to save you."

"I should confront her," Roth said. "Not in person, I'm not stupid. I mean I should call her. Demand some answers."

"What, because your pride is stinging? Fuck pride. You survived the attack, and that's all that matters. Calling Lauren is the *last* thing you should do. She'll deny everything, blame it all on Meadow going rogue, and do everything in her power to track you down and finish you off. Don't give her an inch."

The best kind of lie, as always, is the one nestled inside a wrapper of truth. If he did make the mistake of calling her, Lauren would definitely deny everything. She'd deny it because she was innocent. Either way, the story would hold.

"What if she calls me?" Roth asked.

"Let it go to voicemail, and that goes double for Meadow Brand. You won't be waiting long. If I can't shut Lauren down in the next couple of days, this'll all be a moot point. Right now I want you to go home, get your family, and take off. Is there a place you can go, somewhere Lauren doesn't know about?"

His fingers rapped the edge of his coffee mug as he tried to think.

"The ranch outside Dallas. Belongs to my wife's family. We go there every summer. It's secluded."

"Good," I said. "The farther off the grid you are, the better. Just be ready. Like I said, I'm going to need one last thing from you before this is done."

He left me with the tab and a half-eaten plate of scrambled eggs. I watched him leave, staring listlessly out the window until his taillights turned a corner and slipped out of sight. If he didn't realize he'd been played, if he didn't talk to Lauren or Meadow and find out the truth, if this whole scam held together just a little bit longer, we might be all right.

That was too many *ifs* for me. I needed to work faster. What I really needed right now, though, was at least six hours of sleep somewhere besides a plane or a car seat. Lethargy was catching up fast. I couldn't afford that.

I called Caitlin. "How did it go? Everybody make it home okay?"

"Fine," she said. "Everyone's fine. Did you get what you needed?"

She sounded more tired than I felt. There was something off in her voice, something distracted and moody.

"I think so. He'll back our play, if he doesn't wise up. You okay? What's wrong?"

"Emma's here...we should talk, Daniel. Can you come over? I can't leave right now."

"Yeah, sure," I said. I tossed a twenty on the table and called for a taxi.

The glass doors of the Taipei Tower slid open at my approach. I crossed the expanse of cherry chrysanthemum carpet to the chromed doors of the VIP elevator. As usual, it was already keyed for the penthouse level and waiting to sweep me to the top.

Caitlin met me at her door. I'd seen that hardness in her eyes before. It was the look she got when she was working.

"Come in," she said. No embrace, no kiss.

Emma sat on Caitlin's black leather couch with a box of tissues in her lap. Her red, puffy eyes told me a little more of the story. I wasn't prepared for the anger in her voice when she saw me.

"He shouldn't be here!" she snapped. "This isn't about him. He isn't *relevant*—"

"He is entirely relevant, and you know it," Caitlin said. Her voice was calm and cold, layered over unbending steel.

"Look," I said, "if you want me to come back later—"

Now Emma's eyes were molten copper, and she shouted at me from a mouth that had too many teeth in it. "*I do!*"

"Emma!" Caitlin snapped. She strode across the floor, getting between us. "You will calm down, *now*, and remember that you are a guest in my home. Don't *make* me tell you twice."

Emma lolled her head back on the couch and pressed the heels of her palms to her human-again eyes, rubbing them.

"I'm sorry," she said, her voice weak. "I'm sorry, Daniel. I just...I don't want anyone seeing me like this."

I held up my open hands. "It's okay. What's wrong? Can I help?"

Emma plucked a tissue from the box and blew her nose. She looked over at Caitlin. "Well? Go ahead. You wanted to tell him, tell him."

Caitlin clasped her hands behind her back and paced the hardwood floor, poised like a general as she considered her words.

"There are agreements in place between our courts," she said, "treaties of old made in the interest of mutual survival. One of these agreements is called Case Exodus. It's a plan of last resort, in a situation where the Earth is...compromised beyond recovery by an occupying force. In such a case, our greatest concern is the protection of hell itself."

She stopped pacing and turned toward me.

"Orders came down tonight from the prince's council. Lauren's ascension, and the union of this world and the Garden, would constitute such a threat. If she succeeds, Case Exodus will be executed."

"Wait," I said, "what exactly does that mean? What happens?"

"Severance," Caitlin said. "Every gate and conduit leading off of Earth, either to hell or to any other realm we know of—we seal them. Blow them up. Shut them down. Whatever we have to do to completely sever any escape from the planet. Whatever it takes to stop the contagion from spreading further. Earth will be thrown under eternal quarantine."

"We salt the soil on our way out," Emma said. "Spark as many incidents as possible in what little time we have to reap as many damned souls as we can."

"Incidents?" I asked.

Emma shrugged. "Massacres, power plant accidents, plane crashes, whatever we can manage. Then there's the..."

She paused and looked questioningly at Caitlin. Caitlin sighed and looked back to me.

"The Court of Tarnished Memories," she said, "has control of at least one nuclear weapon."

I shook my head. "What you're telling me is if Lauren gets the ball, you're going to break all the toys and go home."

"To stop her from invading *our* realm?" Caitlin said. "Yes, without hesitation. You know her. She won't be satisfied with ruling the Earth. She won't be satisfied *at all*. Some hungers can never be fulfilled. Once she ascends, quarantine will be the only way to keep her in check."

No pressure or anything.

"So how about a little help, then?" I said. "If everybody knows it's five minutes to doomsday, why aren't the other courts sending the cavalry? Every prince has a hound, right? So why are you the only one here?"

"Duplicity is in our nature." Caitlin paced the floor. "It could be doomsday, or it could be my prince playing an elaborate trick, trying to lure the other princes' elite forces into an ambush. It's a game of odds. It's far more likely to be a trick than a genuine crisis, so they'd rather play it safe, keep their distance, and save their own skins."

"Then I guess that means we're on our own," I said. "Now, what aren't you telling me?"

"What—what do you mean?" Emma said.

I nodded to the box of tissues. "I can understand being pissed off about losing your favorite sandbox, but let's get real. I know you, Emma. This is a business decision when you get right down to it, and you don't cry over business. You fight, and you thrive. So what's wrong?"

She looked over at Caitlin with wet eyes. Caitlin gave the slightest shake of her head. No help there. It had to be something personal, something Emma was worried she'd lose and couldn't replace...

"Melanie," I said. "You don't think Melanie's damned."

The kid had demon blood but a human soul. And a good heart. Like she'd made crystal clear when she stood up to Sullivan and told him off, she had just as much power over her fate as anyone else. Maybe the power to find her own road into the afterlife, too.

Truth was, we didn't know what was out there in the great beyond. Hell was real, but heaven? You tell me. All I knew was that when some people shuffled off, decent people, there was no finding them again.

"I don't know," Emma said. She tugged another tissue from the box and crumpled it in her clenched fist. "I thought...I thought maybe I could get her to cross that line. It wouldn't take much. A random killing, a mortal sin or two—"

"But she wouldn't do it, and you know that," I said.

"She wouldn't, not if I asked her to," Emma said. She took a deep breath. "You know, Daniel...she listens to you."

She could have punched me in the gut, and it would have hurt less. I turned my back. I had to walk away, just a few steps, to keep my temper from boiling over.

I kept my voice soft. "I took the rap for killing Ben, and I didn't mind, because it was for a good cause. I've done a lot of shitty things in my time, and I've done them for worse reasons. But this...you want me to talk Melanie into sending herself to hell?"

I turned to face her.

"No, Emma. I won't do that. Because I've still got some fucking self-respect left."

She rose from the couch. The box of tissues fell to the floor. She walked toward me, slowly, hands balled into fists and fresh tears welling in her eyes.

"Then let me help. With stopping Lauren."

"No," I told her. "You want to take a chance at turning your daughter into an orphan? Leave this to me. You go home. Go home, be with Melanie, and *stay* with her."

"Then you do something else for me," she whispered hoarsely, forcing the words out. "You do whatever it takes, and you *kill Lauren Carmichael.* I can't lose Melanie. Not for eternity. Please, don't let her take my baby from me."

"I promise," I said.

That much I could do.

Emma turned, flustered. "I should go. I have to prepare, have to get notifications out—"

Caitlin reached out and clasped Emma's shoulder. Her eyes were hard as emeralds and her lips a tight, bloodless line. I realized, looking at Emma's face, that this was the Caitlin she needed right now. Not her friend, but the prince's hound, in complete control. A bastion of cruel authority to hold back the storm.

"Hell prevails," Caitlin said.

Emma took Caitlin's free hand and raised it to her lips, kissing the curve of her pale fingers. Caitlin stared impassively, nodded once, and saw her to the door.

I hoped that when she turned around again, her mask of ice would thaw. If anything, after she clicked the lock and met my eyes, she was colder than before.

"I had to make a difficult decision tonight," she said.

"So basically just like every other night?" I asked, trying to find a smile.

"Don't be flip. Not now. Daniel, do you understand what the scope of Lauren's power will encompass, should she master the Garden? She will rule over life and death itself."

"Right. She's going to kill everybody. We know that."

"You think?" she said. "Will she be that merciful to her enemies? After all you've done to stand in her way, what do you think she'd do to you, given her whims?"

I suddenly thought back to the New Life clinic. That poor mutated bastard, bloated with black tumors and cannibalized by cancer, dying in unimaginable agony.

Except I wouldn't die, I thought. *She would NEVER let me die.*

The sudden chill in the room must have shown on my face. Caitlin nodded.

"There are more hells than mine," she said.

35.

"I'm not backing down," I told Caitlin.

"I know," she said and took my hand.

She led me into the bedroom. I wasn't sure what she had in mind, until she pulled back her gray silk pillow. A dagger lay underneath. It was a short, nasty little blade with a jagged edge and a handle of bone.

"I thought about killing you tonight," she said.

I took a step back, toward the open door. "What? Why?"

She crossed the distance between us and took hold of my shirt collar.

"Because I keep what is mine, and you are mine. Because I don't want to take any chance of losing you to Lauren's revenge, cut off forever between two severed worlds. Because," she said through gritted teeth, "I love you."

She let go, shoving me back, and turned away. The anger in her words grew, her voice breaking as she tried to hold it in.

"And that's why I can't do it. Because if...if that's what I feel for you, if it's really love, then I have to trust you. And I have to trust your choices. And these are feelings...these are feelings I was not created to *deal* with, and it is not fucking *fair!*"

"Hey," I said.

She turned around. Her bottom lip quivered, trapped between pearly teeth.

"I think you're doing a pretty good job," I said.

She gave a tiny shrug and stared at the carpet.

"Thanks for not killing me."

Her gaze lifted to meet mine. Maybe she'd expected me to reject her when she told me what she was feeling. Maybe part of her had wanted me to. I tried to make sure she didn't see anything in my eyes but understanding. What I saw in hers was a spark of hope.

"Don't mention it," she said, sounding tired.

"Besides," I said, "I promised Emma, so you know, now I have to win. That woman holds grudges like crazy. Do *not* want to get on her bad side."

Caitlin sat down on the edge of the bed. She tugged my hand, pulling me to sit beside her.

"I can't be there when you face Lauren," she said. "My prince's orders. Thanks to Case Exodus, my job is to watch from a distance, sound the call to action if you fail, and leave this world. Immediately and forever."

I reached up and stroked the curve of her cheek. She gave me a little smile.

"Be prepared for a boring night," I said, "because I'm not going to lose."

"You have to promise me one thing," Caitlin said.

"Name it."

"Whatever happens, no matter what...don't let her take you alive."

I couldn't hold back a shiver, thinking of that thing at the clinic. Wondering what worse nightmares Lauren could conjure up with the power of a goddess at her fingertips.

"Don't even worry about it," I said. "I've gotta get some sleep. Okay if I crash here tonight?"

She reached over and untucked my shirt, undoing the buttons one by one.

"You say that like you have a choice."

#

I woke up on an airplane.

The lighting was all wrong, like I was a bug inside a chunk of amber, and there was nothing outside the porthole window but smoke. The smoke roiled in thick black clouds.

"I'm sorry about this," Bob Payton said, sitting next to me.

I squinted, trying to focus. It was a full flight, but everyone around us was sound asleep.

Asleep. Dreaming. You're dreaming.

"I didn't have any other way to reach you," he said. "You have to come to New York, right away."

I tugged at my seat belt. It didn't budge. There was no reason for the latch not to work. It just didn't want to.

"I don't have time for this," I told him.

He leaned in and grabbed my arm. His eyes were manic.

"I caught one. One of the smoke-faced men. Trapped it."

"What part of 'no time' are you not understanding?" I said. "There are bigger problems to deal with—"

"That's the point! I did more than trap it. I can *weaponize it.*"

That caught my attention.

"Against Lauren?" I said.

"Against the Garden and anything touched by it. Unchecked life meets concentrated occult entropy. Boom. Or more likely, a faint hissing sound as it just...boils away. Come to New York."

"Why New York?" I said. "What's there?"

"Our laboratory, the off-site facility Ausar set up for Nedry, Clark, and me during the Viridithol experiments. I needed some of my old equipment. The old girl's in lousy shape, and I had to bring in a portable generator for power, but it's good enough for my work."

"I'm up against the wall here," I told him. "Flying across the country and back is going to cost time I can't afford to waste. You are absolutely, completely, one hundred percent certain you can do this?"

He took a deep breath and nodded. The mania in his eyes faded to steely determination.

"I want to make amends," he said. "This is how. Just come as soon as you can."

The smoke cleared outside the window, ripping apart to show the skyline of New York City directly below us. Then the plane's nose wobbled, tilting like the first car of a roller coaster at the top of its peak, and veered straight down. The plane plummeted from the sky.

I clutched the armrests, gravity forcing me back into the seat, my heart pounding as we went into free fall. A crowded city street lined with cars came racing up to greet us with the speed of a cannonball. I didn't have the breath to scream or time to think. At the last second, I caught a blurry glimpse of a street sign and a string of numbers. An address.

Then I slammed into the ground at four hundred miles an hour.

I shot bolt upright in bed. My skin was clammy, slick with cold sweat. The scarlet letters of the bedside clock read 3:18. I stumbled into the hallway. Caitlin was already awake, sitting at the glass kitchen table and puttering on her laptop. She glanced over, her eyebrows lifting.

"Go back to bed," she said. "You need more sleep."

"No time. Bob Payton dreamwalked to find me. He might have something. I'll explain in a minute, have to get cleaned up."

No sooner had I cranked up the twin heads in Caitlin's shower, filling the chamber with billowing steam, than the frosted glass door swung open and she joined me inside.

"If things are that urgent," she said, holding up a loofah, "you can tell me now. Turn around."

"He snagged one of the smoke-faced men. Says he can turn it into some kind of weapon."

Caitlin's hand slid over my back, followed by the plush, wet touch of the soapy sponge, milking away the tension in my shoulders.

"Can he do it?" she asked.

"He thinks he can. Look, he knows I wouldn't have any qualms about killing him. He's putting his neck on the chopping block, reaching out to me like this. If he didn't think he could deliver, he wouldn't have done it."

"How long will you be gone?"

"If all goes well, I'll be back by sundown," I said. "I know Pixie needed a little time with the recordings we made of Roth's voice, to get the next part of the plan ready. I also need somebody to rent the motel room for that part, and basically to make sure everybody's on call when and where I need them. I know you're busy planning for Case Exodus, so I hate to ask—"

"Yes, I'll keep everyone on task while you're gone," she said, purring in my ear. "I'm *very* good at cracking the whip."

That was how I ended up back at the airport before dawn, drinking black coffee from a recycled paper cup and listening to the come-play-me chimes from a bank of slot machines in the concourse. Vegas's farewell to the tourist traffic, suctioning out the last of their pocket change before kicking them back home. Every minute I spent here was a minute lost forever. I blew on my coffee and tried not to pace.

Five hours and five minutes to JFK International. That was 305 minutes for Lauren to get closer to the prize, while I sat crammed into an economy-class seat somewhere over the endless American heartland. All I could get was a window seat, and every bump of turbulence brought back the memory of my dreaming death-dive. They showed a movie on the flight, some romantic comedy I remembered seeing commercials for a few months back and promptly forgetting, and I dozed my way through it. Snatches of canned dialogue and laugh lines washed over the cheap plastic headphones and slipped through my groggy thoughts, none of it making much sense.

We touched down on the tarmac with a heavy thump and a mechanical howl as the jet braked hard and fast. JFK was like a microcosm of New York itself: hard and brusque and impatient, under skies that looked like chunks of broken slate. I skipped the crowds at the baggage claim and headed outside, bracing myself against a sudden gust of cold wind. The weather was somewhere in the mid fifties, with rain on the horizon, and I hadn't even thought to bring a jacket. The air outside tasted like burnt diesel.

I didn't have to wait long for a cab. I gave the cabbie the address I'd seen in Bob's dream, and he looked back at me through a sheet of knife-scarred Plexiglas.

"Yonkers, huh?" he said in a thick Jersey accent. "Y'know that's a seventy, eighty-buck ride, right? Lot cheaper to take the airtrain up to Jamaica Station, then hop the blue line."

"I'm in a hurry," I said.

"Suit yourself," he told me and gave the meter box a fat-fingered slap to start it running.

The address turned out to be in Northwest Yonkers, in a long and lonely stretch of decommissioned factories with their dirty noses pressed to the Hudson River. The taxi rumbled over broken train tracks and splashed through mud puddles on the torn-up remnants of old parking lots.

"You, ah, sure you got the right address?" the cabbie asked.

I was sure. It wasn't what I saw—it was what I felt: an electric tingle in the air that had nothing to do with the black thunderclouds on the horizon. There was magic here, old and rich and powerful, setting my teeth on edge. The numbers that flashed before my dream-eyes hung on a red brick wall, under a concrete plaque reading "MacKenzie and Sons Shipping, Est. 1891."

"This is the place," I said. "Right here's fine."

He stopped the cab, and I counted off bills from my wallet.

"You know," he told me, "you can get out here, but coming back's another story. You ain't gonna find a cab within a mile of this place, especially after sundown."

I slipped the fare through a slot in the plastic window, plus an extra twenty.

"Don't worry, I've got an exit strategy," I told him. I got out, and the cold wind ruffled my hair as the taxi drove away.

A big orange CONDEMNED sticker covered the wire-grid window on the warehouse door. A padlock lay on the broken concrete at my feet, snipped open with a pair of bolt cutters. Bob had let himself in.

I let myself in, too.

36.

Klieg lights dangled from the warehouse scaffolding, their power lines running to a portable generator that chugged and coughed like a heavy smoker running a marathon. Harsh white beams rained down on the warehouse floor, casting stark illumination against rusted vats and shelves lined with broken equipment and cobwebs.

Bob Payton had traded his tattered bathrobe for a lab coat and shaved his frosty beard. His cheeks were a mess of uneven stubble and old scars. He looked to the door and waved me over, toward a table where he'd set up a teapot on a hotplate.

"You're here. Good. Right on time. Here, drink this."

He sloshed three fingers of pale herbal tea into a dirty coffee mug and held it out to me. It smelled like sweaty socks and mint.

"What is it?" I said, wrinkling my nose.

"Green tea mixed with ground datura seeds."

I shook my head. "I can't get messed up right now. No time."

"A very, very light dosage," he said. "Please. You'll need it to see what I've done."

He had a point. I held my nose and gulped it down in two swallows. It had an aftertaste like cold medicine, bitter and filmy on my teeth. Bob flitted away like a bird, jittery and fast, huddling over a workbench.

"Aren't you going to drink any?" I said.

"What? No. For one thing, taking datura orally is incredibly dangerous. You should never do it. It can wreck your stomach lining."

"But—I just—"

He looked back and pointed at his dilated eyes. The back of his hand was coated in ink, scrawled with occult glyphs that ran under the sleeve of his coat.

"Second, there's not enough in there to touch me," he said. "Like I said, very light dose. I have to ingest very large quantities of hallucinogens to get where I'm going. And I have been. For two days straight. Haven't slept a wink."

"For somebody who's tripping balls right now," I said, "you are remarkably lucid."

"I went to college in Berkeley in the sixties. Trust me, I can swallow down a fistful of Quaaludes and lead a discussion on the themes of Sartre. Angle that standing light my way, would you please?"

I tilted the lamp toward his bench. Bob had a vanity mirror propped up against the wall and a fountain pen in his hand. He leaned his head back, dipped the brassy nub of the pen in a vial of black ink, and carefully traced more glyphs along the skin of his throat. I couldn't place the symbols.

They looked a little like Sanskrit, but that was out of my wheelhouse.

"Seals of protection," he explained. "Like I said, warding and containment is my specialty. I know how to keep my skin intact when dealing with creatures not of our world."

"I thought the smoke-faced men were buddies of yours. They called you their father."

In the mirror, he gave a pained smile. "That was before."

I gazed across the room. In the center of a block of bare concrete, white chalk marked the curves of a binding seal, a pentacle inside two concentric circles lined with writings in ancient Hebrew. Five white candles, halfway burned down, stood at the points of the star. There wasn't anything inside the circle, at least nothing I could see.

The side effects of the tea crept up behind me, in the shape of a slowly growing headache and a sudden wave of nausea that made my guts clench.

"You're feeling it," Bob said, looking back at me through the mirror as he dipped his pen in the inkwell. "Sorry. This isn't exactly a recreational drug. Shamanic experiences are rarely joyrides."

"What I'm feeling," I said, "is hungover and pissed off. This isn't even worki—"

I watched as the tip of Bob's pen touched his throat and left a squiggling black worm in its wake. The glyphs on his skin were alive, subtle but squirming, wanting to break free of the flesh and fly. I watched him in rapt silence, my eyes tracing the faint trails of light that ebbed from the motions of his fingertips.

"Still with me?" he said.

Strange question, my brain said. *How could anyone be with anyone? We're born alone. We die alone. It's better that way. You disappoint fewer people.*

Still, the air between us rippled, and I thought I could pick out the currents of our breaths flowing between our bodies. How many other people's breaths did I have in my lungs? How many of their molecules were in my body? Weren't we all together, basically?

I lolled my head to the left. My blood ran cold, and my college-freshman philosophy ran dry. The binding circle wasn't empty anymore. The creature trapped inside had given up all pretense of playing at a human form. It was a tornado of black smoke, churning and furious, lashing out like a bullwhip at the invisible barriers that caged it. I could feel its emotions, vibrating like discordant music on a half-tuned radio station. Hunger and hate. The urge to consume and consume, until nothing remained but ashes.

"You can see him now," Bob said. "Good. Let me show you something."

He held up a test tube, corked on the end, filled with a luminous green goo.

"Concentrated Viridithol," he said.

He walked over to the binding circle. I was sitting down on the floor. I couldn't remember sitting down, but it made sense. My legs were woozy, and my head wouldn't stop pounding.

"Have to be careful with my aim," Bob said, gesturing at the candles. "This stuff is flammable as hell. Wouldn't do to break the wards right now. That'd be bad for both of us."

He threw the flask down. It hit the heart of the circle and cracked, splattering tiny glass shards and rivulets of goo across the concrete. The tornado of smoke hit it like a freight train, blasting down and gusting out over the spill. When the smoke lifted, nothing was left but broken glass. There was no trace that the toxic drug had ever been there, not even a single spilled droplet.

Something was different about the smoke, too. It was a tiny bit lighter, a tiny bit slower. *It's sick*, I thought.

"I could kill it right now," Bob said, walking back to his ink and mirror. "Just drag over the drum and splash in the toxins, a cupful at a time. I was tempted. So tempted. Problem is, to my shame, I could only catch one of the creatures. The other one's running. He knows that 'father' has turned on his loving sons."

He turned and gave me a sad-eyed smile.

"To my shame," he said. "I've been saying that a lot lately."

The outline of Bob's body vibrated like a delicate crystal bell. He moved his hands when he spoke, and they left streamers of light in their wake.

I decided I wanted to get up. My legs wouldn't listen. They went all noodly on me. Treacherous legs.

"I'm afraid I told you a little white lie, Mr. Faust. There was perhaps a bit more in that tea than I let on. Enough to keep you incapacitated for the next four or five hours. Long enough to finish my work."

He walked to the back of the derelict lab. Rusty wheels squealed as he came back with a rolling cart. I watched helplessly as he checked the tools he'd prepared ahead of time.

A hacksaw. A blowtorch.

"You're right, you know," he said. "It's my fault. So much of it. The Viridithol trials? I knew what we were doing was wrong. All these years, I told myself it was an accident. That we didn't know anyone would get hurt. That's no absolution. Those mutated children, those dead mothers...we did that. *I* did that."

I tried to talk. My lips wanted to go the wrong way, and I felt myself drool a little.

"Bob," I slurred, "what're you doing?"

"Now the poisoned fruit of what we did has blossomed on the vine. Your sins always come back to haunt you, Mr. Faust. I've learned that much. No matter how far or fast you run, your sins *always* come back. So I'm done running. These people have to be stopped, and I will stop them. I told you the truth. I've found a way to turn this creature of entropy into a weapon."

He picked up the hacksaw, staring glassy-eyed as he ran a fingertip over the blade's jagged teeth.

"To do that, though, the creature needs a stable vessel. That means I need to commit one last sin. I hope you can forgive me."

My body was numb. I tried to get up again, to at least push back with my feet and squirm away from him, but the best I could do was flop around on the cold concrete floor.

"The process is simple," he said, "if...unpleasant for the vessel. It's essentially like an involuntary demonic possession. You are familiar with demonic possession, Mr. Faust?"

A wave of raw panic slapped me across the face and shoved my head under icy water. I felt myself plummet into a black abyss dragging me back to my teenage years. Yeah, I was familiar with demonic possession. The drug coursing through my veins hauling me through flashes of stark memory, forcing me to feel it all over again. Creatures of toxic waste burrowed like maggots in my brain, pissing behind my eyeballs, scratching bone, and carving filthy graffiti inside my skull.

Bob came closer. This time, I managed to kick. I swung my feet out, stomping air, fighting him with everything I had. He stepped back with ease and held up his hands.

"See?" he said. "This is why I had to drug you. I knew you'd try to stop me, but this has to be done. It *has* to. I hope you're understanding my words. I'm explaining this so that you'll grasp what's happening here."

Bob walked out of sight. I lay there, watching the tornado of smoke.

He came back and crouched before me. Something shone like a diamond in his hand, jangling in front of my eyes.

"Still with me?" he said. "These are the keys to my car. It's parked around back."

He set the keys on the tray, next to the other tools. I squinted.

"Why?" I managed to say. "Why're you tellin' me?"

He walked toward the binding circle and turned back to face me.

"So that you can get back home, when your part of the work is done," he said.

Tears glistened in his eyes. They took on halos of light in my confused vision, glimmering like drops of silver.

Now I understood.

"In the end," Bob said, "we all get what we deserve."

Then he stepped into the circle.

37.

The smoke screamed.

One of the Klieg lights dangling from the rafters exploded, showering glass and sparks onto the concrete below. Bob's body hung a foot above the ground, mouth wide, eyes bulging, wrapped and bound in tendrils of raw hate. Now he was screaming too, in ear-piercing harmony.

The smoke dove down his throat. The screaming stopped.

The smoke buried itself inside him, pouring in through his mouth, his nostrils, the corners of his eyes, anywhere it could tear open a foothold. As the last wisp of gray entered him, he collapsed to the floor.

Then he sat bolt upright.

His skin bulged and swelled, as if the smoke had been lured inside and now it wanted back out again. The glyphs inked onto his body glistened.

Warding and containment is my specialty, Bob had said. *I know how to keep my skin intact.* It was his final spell: turning himself into a living trap.

He seemed to move in stop motion. Fast, jittery, jumping from point to point and skipping the spaces in between. He reached into his pocket and pulled out a long, shiny needle and a spool. Sparks of enchantment flew from his fingers as he threaded the black mortician's thread through the needle's eye. I could smell the warding spell he'd prepared, taste it, like copper pennies on my tongue.

He slid the needle through his lips.

I watched, frozen and limp, as Bob sealed himself up. He finished his lips, then moved on to his eyelids, stitching them shut in tight little rows of thread.

All the while, the smoke raged inside him. I heard Bob's ribs crack and splinter as it pounded him from within, saw the blood leaking from under his fingernails and his stitched-shut eyelids. He didn't make a single sound. He was beyond pain now. Beyond anything but the task at hand.

The color drained from his skin, then the moisture. Bob convulsed, his muscles cramping and seizing. He looked more desiccated with every fevered beat of my heart.

When the rite was done, the thing that remained on the floor, curled into a fetal position at the heart of the binding circle, looked like an unwrapped mummy.

I think I passed out. Wasn't sure. The drugs in my system turned time into a question with no answers. All I remembered was the pounding headache and the dry cottony feeling in my mouth when I could finally move again. My vision was still a little blurry, but the trails of light were gone.

I pushed myself up and used the edge of a bench for support, getting my legs back. Once I was good to walk, I hobbled over to the circle. The hacksaw and blowtorch waited on the rolling cart. I knew what my part of the job was now.

Bob had also left a pair of plastic water bottles, along with a yellow sticky note that read "Drink me." I cracked them open and guzzled them down one after the other, fighting off the dehydration. I had dirty, thirsty work ahead.

An hour later I was on the move, pulling away from the abandoned laboratory in Bob's little yellow hatchback. It was a rental, but I didn't bother returning it. Didn't want to risk being seen driving it, especially not on a security camera. Bob Payton was on his way to becoming a missing person in some police station's database.

He would be missing forever.

I made one stop on my way back to JFK, a FedEx store where I arranged overnight delivery for a package to a Vegas mail drop. Then it was straight to the airport and onto the first nonstop flight I could book. Back to the West, away from the thundering slate sky and into a world of trouble.

#

The Wardriver sat in a parking garage two blocks off the Strip, just another hunk of junk rusting in the dark. Someone would have to get close to notice the faint green light leaking from the tinted windows, or pick up the muffled hum of the modified engine running in stealth mode as it fed power from the battery to the electronics suite in the back.

"I took all the recordings we could get," Pixie said, "from the phone call with Roth and what I could pick up inside the house. I was missing a few phonemes, but that's the nice thing about government stooges. They're always on television, running their mouths. Lots of raw sound to work with."

I leaned in behind her while she demonstrated the program running on the biggest screen.

"Soundboard," Pixie explained. "You click it, he says it."

She scrolled her mouse over a bubble of text and clicked. From tinny speakers mounted over the console, Alton Roth's voice said, "Meadow?"

"Pitch is the problem," Pixie said. "People don't talk in monotones. A statement can turn into a question, and vice versa, with just a lift or a drop in your voice. I've played with these clips as much as I can, but at the end of the day, that's all you've got: clips. The longer you push it, the more obvious it's going to be. Don't get into a conversation with her. Get in and get out."

"No worries there," I said.

"I went through and pieced together a bunch of clips I think you'll need. I cleaned them up as best as I could and played with the pitch. I'll feed some static into the line, so he'll be hard to hear. That'll help."

I nodded. "And it'll look like the call's coming from Roth?"

"Sure, assuming you copied his number down right when you checked out his phone. You...can handle writing down ten digits in a row, right?"

"Dunno," I said. "I'm pretty bad at math. Guess we'll find out."

I took her chair, and she handed me a headset. She sat down in the chair next to me, fiddling with dials and mixers with a consternated look on her face.

"Okay," she said, "the sound mix is as good as I can get it. You ready to do this?"

I gave her a thumbs-up. I wished I felt as confident as I looked. Our best and probably last chance at getting a noose around Meadow Brand's throat, and it was basically a high-tech version of a prank call on a wacky morning radio show. I didn't like our odds.

"Dialing," Pixie said. I scanned the words on the monitor, reading fast and trying to memorize the lay of the land. When Meadow spoke, I'd have seconds to react, picking the right response from a list of dozens. With no guarantee that there *was* a right response.

Meadow's voice echoed over my headset. My hand clenched the mouse, a reflex spasm of hate.

"What?" she said, irritated.

I clicked fast.

"Meadow," Roth's voice said, then a short pause. "It's Alton Roth."

"Yeah, I know. I have caller ID just like everyone else on the planet, chucklehead. What are you doing, calling from inside a wind tunnel? I can barely hear you. What do you want?"

"Lauren's a traitor," Roth said. Pixie had taken the original question Roth had asked me and pitch-shifted it, turning it into a flat accusation.

"What the fuck did you just say?"

Meadow's voice sounded more angry than surprised. After the fight at Lauren's house, I think she was long past any lingering feelings of loyalty to her mistress.

"Lauren's trying to kill me. After all I've done for her!" Roth said. I fumbled, nearly missing the next click. "You're next."

Meadow whistled, long and low.

"Gotta say I saw that coming," she said. "I figured she was going to do it at the ceremony, though. You know, stab us both in the back right before killing herself with this stupid plan of hers. I was just holding out for one last paycheck before I blew town. Well, that's it for me then! I'm packing my shit and heading for Costa Rica. You should probably do the same thing."

"Meet with me."

"Huh?" Meadow said. "Why would I wanna do that?"

I blanked.

Scanning the screen, I searched for something that would answer her question. Pixie cranked up the static, then leaned in and tapped her finger frantically on the glass. I clicked where she pointed.

"Money," Roth said at the tail end of the static burst.

Meadow thought it over.

"All right, fine, I can't hear shit on this line anyway. You get five minutes of my time. Not tonight. I'm busy making travel arrangements. Tomorrow morning, on my way out of town. Where at?"

"Uh, 14082 Sauk Trail, room six," Roth said, parroting the address I'd "accidentally" given him when we talked over the tapped line. "It's a motel off I-15, about ten miles outside Vegas. I'll come alone!"

"You'd better," she said. "I'll be there at nine. If I don't like what you have to say, I'll be gone at 9:01."

"Thank you," Roth told her.

"Yeah, whatever," Meadow muttered. "Freak."

She hung up. I leaned back in my chair and let out a breath I didn't realize I'd been holding.

"Nice save," I said.

Pixie looked as exhausted as I suddenly felt. "You're welcome. So, uh...you think she fell for it?"

"I think maybe, just maybe, things are going right for a change."

"Then why aren't you smiling?" Pixie said.

"I get nervous when things are going right," I said.

I should have felt good. We had a way in, we had a weapon, and if she showed up to the meeting, we'd have Meadow Brand too. That was three more cards than I'd expected to have up my sleeve.

Even still, every passing minute felt like the countdown to doomsday. Roth's comments about Lauren left me rattled. What had she done to herself? How close was she to taking the final leap, bridging two worlds and crushing both of them between her greedy fingers?

Was it even possible to stop her now?

That night, I dreamed about Bob Payton. He perched on the edge of Bentley and Corman's couch, looming over me like a mummified bird and trying to talk through stitched-shut lips.

I woke up a couple of hours before dawn. I didn't want to go back to sleep, but I didn't want to get up just yet. I felt bad enough that Bentley and Corman were letting me crash at their place—I didn't need to wake them up early too. I lay in the gloom and stared at the ceiling, listening to the occasional rumble of a lonely truck on the street outside.

We all get what we deserve, Bob had told me.

What did I deserve?

The more I thought about it, the more I realized I didn't care. He was wrong, anyway. Life was a lot of things, but "fair" and "just" weren't on that list. Every single day good men got kicked in the teeth, while the evil bought mansions in Malibu and slept like babies in their feather beds. I'd learned early on that the only real law was the law of the jungle. Protect your own with everything you've got, wake up every morning ready for a fight, and never expect anyone to hand you anything for free. That included justice.

Lauren Carmichael had skated a long time on money and power. Justice wasn't something she lost any sleep worrying about. She knew the law of the jungle too, and she thought she was the hungriest beast around. Only she'd forgotten one thing: there was always somebody hungrier. Always.

I made a promise to myself in the dark. No matter what it took, even if I had to lay my life on the line, Lauren was finally going to pay for all the wreckage she'd left in her wake.

If I was bound for hell, I'd drag her down with me.

38.

The SandVue Motel was a relic of the sixties, an oasis of aquamarine-painted concrete and white lattice rails out on a hot stretch of empty desert highway. Big magnetic letters on the roadside sign read "Welc me convention-goers we h ve cable TV swimming pool." Every room had a window, and every window had a chintz curtain pulled tight across it. This was the kind of place people went when they didn't want anyone knowing their business.

We'd rented two rooms: six, where Meadow hopefully thought she was coming to meet Alton Roth, and the one right next door. The rooms were sparse—a chipboard dresser, a bed that looked like it belonged in a county jail, and a big old TV with a dust-caked screen—but we weren't planning on staying long.

Caitlin, Jennifer and I were on the scene. Margaux was playing lookout, to give us the heads-up when Meadow pulled in. She'd gone over to the manager's office on the far side of the motel, pretended she had a busted engine, and asked if she could stay out of the heat while she waited for the tow truck. The pimple-faced kid behind the desk couldn't have cared less. Simple story, but it gave Margaux the perfect excuse to stand at the window and watch the parking lot like a hawk.

Caitlin brought the hardware, everything we'd need to keep Meadow pacified while we transported her. She carried it in a black plastic garbage bag and emptied it all out on the bedspread: handcuffs, a coil of stout yellow rope, a cotton head sack, and one other thing.

Jennifer held up the bright pink rubber ball, buckled to a pair of black leather straps, and arched an eyebrow. "A ball gag? Really?"

Caitlin shrugged. "It's all I had in my dresser. Short notice."

"Let's run through it one more time," I said. "Three rings and a hang-up from Margaux means Meadow's pulling in. Caitlin and I get ready just inside the door. Jennifer, you'll come out from room five, run up behind her, and give her the bum-rush. We'll open the door and help pull her in."

"Not the most elegant of plans," Caitlin said. "But it should work nicely."

I nodded. "We take her down fast, before she even knows what's hitting her. Toss her in the trunk of my car, bring her to the Scrivener's Nook. Bentley and Corman should have the back room set up by now."

Jennifer wandered over to the window, pulling back the edge of the curtain. A shaft of sun pierced through the dusty gloom.

"Still not sure about this plan, sugar. Not the smash-and-grab. The part after that."

"I don't like it any more than you do," I said, "but we don't have a lot of options. Now remember: she relies on her puppets to do her dirty work, but that doesn't mean she can't scrap. She'll fight like hell."

"No guarantees she won't get a little more banged up than strictly necessary," Jennifer said.

That was what worried me. Every member of my family had a personal reason to want Meadow Brand in the ground. I hadn't put Bentley and Corman on the sidelines because I was worried about their safety. Given that one of Meadow's victims was an old friend of theirs, I was more afraid they'd "accidentally" kill her before we got what we needed.

As for Spengler's death, well, we all owed her for Spengler.

After the setup, we had nothing but time on our hands. Time to sit in the dark, bracing for a fight, watching the minutes crawl past like an hourglass filled with molasses. My watch said 8:42. I could have sworn it said 8:41 ten minutes ago.

I figured I had time, so I stepped into the bathroom for a minute. When I came back out, rubbing a cheap washcloth between my damp hands, Caitlin and Jennifer were sitting dangerously close on the edge of the bed and talking in hushed tones. They both looked over and giggled at the same time.

"What?" I said.

"Just talkin'," Jennifer said.

"What? About me?"

Caitlin rolled her eyes. "Yes, pet. When two women have a conversation, it's only natural to assume they're talking about *you*. That's a perfectly reasonable conclusion to jump to."

"If you really *want*, we could talk about ya," Jennifer said, grinning. "Hey, Cait, does he still do that thing in bed where he gets that whole-body shiver and his leg twitches when you bite his neck? That always worked for me."

Caitlin nodded solemnly. "Every time. But if I *really* want to get him going, I simply need to curl my finger, just like this, and slide it—"

I threw up my hands. "Okay, okay! Point taken! Stop. Please. Really. Sorry I asked."

"We were talkin' about Pix," Jennifer said.

I valiantly resisted the urge to bury my face in my palm.

"Jen," I said, "we don't even know if Pixie is into girls. Or sex. With anyone. She might be, I don't know, robosexual."

They both stared at me.

"You know, because...computers," I said.

My phone vibrated in my pocket. I quickly tugged it out halfway and shot a glance at the screen. Mama Margaux.

I snapped my fingers and pointed to the connecting door. Jen nodded, darting through to room five and out of sight. Caitlin bounced off the bed and ran to the edge of the curtains, peeking out as far as she dared. I moved up behind the door. Outside, I heard a car door slam.

My heart pounded, pushing a straight shot of adrenaline to every nerve in my body. This was it, the dizzy-sick drizzle drip of time right before a brawl breaks out, the moment when every animal has to choose between fight or flight.

My phone kept buzzing. Margaux wasn't signaling—she was calling. She wouldn't do that unless it was an emergency, but with Meadow coming up the walk I didn't have time to talk. Caitlin looked over from the edge of the curtains and gave a sharp nod, letting me know Meadow was outside.

With seconds left I grabbed my phone and caught the call. "What?" I whispered.

"Something's wrong, Danny." Margaux hissed in my ear. "It looks like her, but it's not her. There's nothin' *inside* there!"

I dropped the phone and freed up my hands. Right now, Jen would be coming up from behind, putting herself in danger. Couldn't risk it. I flung open the door, reached out, and grabbed Meadow Brand's hand.

I had just enough time to recognize her dead eyes and slack expression, and the way her moves couldn't quite mimic a real human's. A second later I yanked my hand back, jolted by a lance of pain as a serrated knife slashed across my palm. The illusion ripped away in the space between breaths, and the wooden mannequin on the threshold raised its knife hand to stab me dead.

I caught its wrist and grappled the creature, trying to force it into the room. Tires squealed as a Jeep Cherokee spun out from its hiding spot behind the building and came to a stop in the parking lot.

Meadow Brand grinned from the driver's seat, her scar twisting along her face. She gave me a gleeful wave and drove off, launching over a speed bump and out onto the street.

Jennifer ran up, trying to grab the mannequin from behind, but I waved her off. "Go, *go! Catch her!*" I shouted. I didn't have to tell her twice.

Caitlin stepped back to open up some space in the cramped motel room. "Here, throw it!"

I ducked back from another frenzied swing of the puppet's knife, grabbed its shoulders, and shoved, sending it staggering off-balance right toward Caitlin. She spun on her heel and lashed out with a roundhouse kick straight to the creature's abdomen, crunching home with more force than any human could muster. Wood splintered, and the mannequin wobbled on its bent inner core. Before it could recover, Caitlin grabbed it under one arm, turned, and used her momentum to ram it headlong into the television set.

The screen shattered, and the mannequin collapsed with its head still buried inside the set and its arms limp at its sides. I scooped my phone off the floor and ran over to grab the damp bathroom washcloth, pressing it hard against my cut hand. Cherry stains seeped out through the dingy cotton.

"Looks worse than it is," I told Caitlin. I tossed her the car keys. "You drive. I'll shoot."

The Barracuda squealed out of the parking lot, kicking up asphalt and dust. While Caitlin gripped the wheel I dug my gun out of the glove compartment and checked the load. The washcloth had soaked through to useless, and I tossed it to the floor mat. Getting bloodstains on my slacks was the least of my concerns.

Jennifer called in. I set the pistol in my lap and picked up.

"She's too damn fast!" Jennifer shouted. "I'm chasing her up the interstate, but I'm gonna lose her any second now!"

"We're on our way. Turn around, go pick up Margaux at the motel, and meet us back at the Scrivener's Nook."

I hung up and looked over at Caitlin.

"Drive fast," I said.

She wriggled in the driver's seat, getting comfortable, and smiled. "With pleasure."

The hemi roared as we barreled up I-15 with the needle kissing the red. The speedometer rose past ninety, then a hundred, then a hundred and ten. We saw Jennifer's blue Prius dart by in the opposite direction, and we knew we were getting close. This time of day, this stretch of road, there wasn't much to dodge but the occasional camper or dirt-encrusted pickup. Just open air and a razor-straight road for the next fifty miles.

There she was, just up ahead, pushing the Jeep as hard as it could go. Caitlin pushed harder. As we slowly closed the gap, I rolled down my window.

"Get us close and on her left," I said. "I'll try to take out a tire."

Easier said than done, especially when you're bleeding like a stuck pig and chewing up road faster than you can see. My left was my gun hand and that one was useless, so I clutched the Judge in my right and leaned out the window. My first shot went high, and the bullet tore into the Jeep's back fender.

I didn't see the access road up ahead. Meadow did. The Jeep's brake lights flared, and suddenly she was gone, bouncing along a nameless road leading off into the desert. We overshot the turn. Caitlin slammed the brakes and spun the wheel, sending us into a skid, whipping the car's tail around and pointing us the wrong way on the interstate. I didn't have a second to catch my breath before she stomped the gas pedal and shot off in pursuit.

Meadow had a head start. Worse, she had home-court advantage. Muscle cars were built for smooth straight runs, but now we were chasing her along a road that wasn't much more than a suggestion. The run was coated in sand, loose rocks, and neglect. Her Jeep was made for this kind of terrain, while we jolted from pothole to pothole, our suspension taking a pounding.

The road rose up ahead, angling toward the red rocks in the distance. I saw it curve, sinuous and serpentine. She'd lose us on the curves. As we closed the gap again, taking advantage of the final straightaway, I knew I'd only have one last chance to take her down.

39.

"Little closer," I murmured as I leaned out the window. The arid wind whipped through my hair and burned my cheeks. I held the fat pistol out as steady as I could, fighting every bounce and jolt of the tires.

Caitlin saw the curves coming, too. "Running out of road, pet!"

"Little closer!"

Inch by inch we closed the distance, rolling up on Meadow's left side. I could taste the dust kicking off the Jeep's fat tires. Two hundred feet left before the first big turn. We were coming on fast, too fast, and I had just enough time to squeeze the trigger.

Her back tire exploded as Meadow spun the wheel. The Jeep launched off the road, flipping over, rolling end over end across the rocky sands. Caitlin punched the brakes, throwing me back in my seat as she fought to keep the Barracuda steady. The car went into a fishtailing spin, then evened out, and finally the wheels ground to a stomach-lurching halt.

I sat there a second, gasping for breath, waiting for my brain to catch up with my pounding heart. Meadow's Jeep lay fifty feet away, a capsized wreck of twisted metal and spilled gasoline.

"Nice shot," Caitlin said, breathless.

"Nice driving," I said.

She held out a shaky fist. I weakly bumped my knuckles against hers.

In the debris, something moved.

A battered door swung open, tortured hinges shrieking, and Meadow Brand climbed out on top of the wreckage. Her blouse was torn and a gash in her forehead spilled blood down her face, clotting one eye shut. She punched her fist against the twisted metal.

"That's right," she wheezed. "King of the hill. King of the motherfuckin' hill."

She tried to climb down from the wreck, lost her grip, and tumbled off, landing hard on the sand. Then she pushed herself back to her feet.

"Aw, shit, she's still breathing," I said.

"I thought we wanted her alive?" Caitlin said.

"We *need* her alive," I said. "Still, I'll admit to a certain level of disappointment here."

Meadow stumbled blindly, dazed, throwing punches at the air.

"Yeah," I said, opening the car door. "We should probably give her a ride."

I walked straight toward her while Caitlin circled around, careful not to get too close. Meadow spotted me and snarled like a rabid ferret. I didn't see where the buck knife came from, but I couldn't miss the gleam of the blade when she snapped it open.

"C'mere," she growled, waving the knife in front of her. "I'm gonna gut you."

She lunged faster than I thought she could move, and I jumped back as the knife slashed toward my face, slicing air. She pulled her arm back for another try, and that was when Caitlin stepped up behind her, curling her arm around Meadow's throat.

"Stop fighting," Caitlin whispered as Meadow flailed, her movements slowing as Caitlin squeezed off her airflow. Finally, she went limp. Caitlin let go, spilling Meadow's unconscious body to the ground.

We stood over her for a moment. I shook my head.

"Well, this whole thing could have gone smoother," I said.

Caitlin shrugged. "We got what we came for. Same end result."

"That's true," I said. "Let's throw her in the trunk."

"How's your hand?"

I gave it a look and grimaced. The cut had congealed, my palm thick with lumpy blood and black dirt, and it throbbed like I was holding it under a tattoo needle.

"Ugly. You mind driving us back?"

Caitlin got her hands under Meadow's arms and scooped her up, dragging her toward the car.

"That," she said, "is the silliest question I've ever heard. I may never give your keys back."

#

While we were off-roading in the desert for fun and profit, Bentley and Corman had prepared the storage room in the Scrivener's Nook to receive our special guest. They'd taken out anything remotely dangerous—like their special shelf of restricted books, for close friends only—and cleared a ten-foot circle of bare floor around an old metal office chair.

We pulled up around back. Jennifer and Margaux played lookout while Caitlin and I opened the trunk and hauled out Meadow—cuffed, trussed up like a Thanksgiving turkey, and her head bagged—to drag her inside. Bentley had the honor of shackling her to the chair. Trust a former escape artist to know how to tie somebody up properly.

We worked in silence and left her in the dark.

Out in the store, Corman checked to make sure the front door was locked and the closed sign was facing the sidewalk. We couldn't afford any interruptions.

"What are we waitin' for?" Jennifer said. "Let's get started on her right now."

I shook my head. "I want her to stew for a while. Let her sit there and wonder why she isn't dead yet. I'm sure she'll come up with all *kinds* of nasty reasons. I want her good and scared before we start talking to her."

"Let her torture herself," Caitlin said. "One of my favorite tactics. I approve. Corman, do you have a first-aid kit?"

Bentley caught sight of my hand and *tsked* his way across the store. "Daniel, that's going to get infected. Come on, let's wash that up. Cormie, grab the Neosporin and a bandage roll."

Cleaning the wound out and rubbing in antibiotic cream stung like hell all over again, but I felt better with a clean cotton bandage wrapped around my hand. At least I'd have a scar with a good story behind it.

The six of us lingered a while out front, keeping our voices down. Bound, hooded, confused in the dark—I had to think Meadow was having a hard time of it, imagining every horrifying thing we could do to her.

I heard something through the storage-room door. I thought I'd imagined it at first, but as the sound grew louder, more grating, I realized what it was.

Meadow was trying to sing through her gag. Specifically, she was singing "In-A-Gadda-Da-Vida" by Iron Butterfly.

"So much for terror," I said, letting out a heavy sigh. "Okay, everybody, let's do this."

Jennifer and I went first. Meadow knew both of us and knew how badly we wanted her dead. Bentley, Corman, and Mama Margaux followed us, spreading out around the storage room while Caitlin stood off in the shadows with her arms crossed and a curious look on her face.

Jennifer yanked the sack off Meadow's head, exposing her eyes to the glare of the light dangling directly over her. Her face was a mess of caked-in dirt and congealed cuts, one eye swollen over from the crash. Drool ran down her chin. Somehow, she still managed to look defiant.

I unbuckled the bright pink gag and pulled it out of her mouth. Meadow spat on the floor, wincing.

"A ball gag?" she said, looking from me to Jennifer. "Really? Do you wanna kill me or do you wanna shoot some bondage porn? Or maybe both. Yeah, probably both. You look like a couple of necrophiliacs."

"You wanna take this seriously," Jennifer said, her expression darkening by the second.

"I take it *very* seriously," Meadow said. "Necrophilia is a serious crime, and you should be ashamed—"

Jennifer punched her in the face.

I didn't even see it coming. One second Jennifer's fist dangled limply at her side, and the next Meadow's head snapped back and fresh blood ran from her split lip. Meadow grinned viciously, showing her scarlet-stained teeth.

"*Whoo!*" she shouted. Her chains rattled as she nodded her head and bounced in the steel chair. "*That* is what I'm talking about! *That* is a morning pick-me-up! Aw, but honey, you were just joking with that punch, right? Because if you think you're gonna get me to talk, and that's the best you can manage? Well you'd better order an extra-large pizza because we are gonna be here *all! Fucking! Night!*"

"I can do worse," Jennifer said softly. "I can do a lot worse."

Meadow bounced giddily. The chair legs thumped in time with the clacking of her chains.

"All right!" she said. "Let's get this party started! What've you got? Waterboarding? Little waterboarding action? Gonna pull my fingernails out? Yank my teeth out with pliers? Here, here, do me a favor, get this one in the back of my mouth. It's got a cavity. Drastic, I know, but you know how much health insurance costs these days? Girl's gotta do what a girl's gotta do."

"Like killin' Spengler and Sophia? That something you had to do?" Jennifer said. She took a step closer, and I reached out, putting my hand on her shoulder. Reminding her what we were here for. Vengeance had to wait.

"Who?" Meadow said. "You're gonna have to help me out here, hon. I kill a lot of people. It's kinda what I do for a living."

Bentley turned and stormed out of the room. Corman and Margaux weren't far behind, running to check on him. I forced my anger down, swallowed it, bottled it up deep inside where it couldn't push me into doing something reckless.

"You're serious?" Jennifer said. "You don't even remember their names."

"Aw, you look confused, sort of like a puppy that just got kicked in the head. I'm going to help you understand, because I'm nice that way. So, *story time!* Story time with Aunt Meadow! Gather around, kids, nice and close. One of you can sit on my lap. What, no takers? Fine, have it your way."

"I don't think we need to hear—" I started to say.

"You do," Meadow said, suddenly serious as the grave. "You really do, because you don't seem to know who you're dealing with. Story time. Last week I was grocery shopping, picking up a few things, and a stock boy of, hmm, maybe nineteen or twenty? He started hitting on me. I was surprised. I mean, I don't get a lot of action ever since someone *carved my fucking face up!*"

I almost took a step back under the heat of her sudden, furious glare. Then her expression softened, and she smiled and continued her tale.

"I figured he took me for an easy lay. Single woman, a little overweight, huge fucking facial scar, probably not starring on *The Bachelorette*. Well, I came back after his shift ended, and I let him take me to his dingy little shithole apartment, with his dingy little electric guitar from his dingy little garage band, and I pretended to listen as he told me all his aspirations and dreams."

"There a point to this?" Jennifer asked.

"Oh boy, is there ever. We ended up in his adorably embarrassing twin bed. And he was bad. I mean, really, excruciatingly bad in the way that only inexperienced young men can be. And I'm lying there while he's huffing and puffing away, and I'm saying to myself, 'Self? How can I find the fun in this situation? How can I turn this into *me* time?' So I got on top of him, rode him until he came, and—while he's climaxing, while he's still buried deep inside of me—I took my knife and I stabbed him, oh, seven or eight times."

I didn't say a word. I didn't have anything to say. The twinkle in her eyes made my stomach churn. *She's proud of herself,* I thought. Jennifer shook her head, mute.

"Two kinds of people in this world," Meadow said. "Sheep and wolves. I'm a wolf. I do what wolves do. Do you think I'm going to find some wellspring of remorse for your dead friends? I won't. Do you think I'm going to piss myself because you're going to torture me? I'm not. Sure, you can make me scream until my vocal cords snap, but you have no *idea* how to *hurt* me.

"Moral of the story, kids? Go ahead and put a bullet in my brain. Right now. Between the eyes. Do it. Because whatever you're hoping to gain by keeping me prisoner, you can't have it. The only rational thing you can do right now, the only sensible, sane thing, for you and for all of humanity, is to kill me here and now. If you don't, you'll regret it. That's a promise."

"Deal," Jennifer said and pressed the barrel of her chromed .357 to Meadow's forehead.

40.

"*No!*" I shouted, grabbing Jennifer's wrist and yanking the gun upward before she could pull the trigger. I dragged her back a few steps and shook her shoulder hard with my bandaged hand.

"What the hell do you think you're doing?" I said. "We have a *plan.*"

"You heard the bitch," Jennifer seethed, looking between Meadow and me. "We're wasting our time here. Let's just put her in the ground and be done with it."

I leaned in and whispered in her ear. She nodded slowly, grudgingly, and put her gun away.

All part of the plan.

"Trouble in paradise?" Meadow said.

"We're not here to torture you," I said. "And we're not here to kill you."

"Well golly gee willikers, now you've got me all kinds of curious."

"We're here to hire you," I said.

Meadow blinked. Then she squinted, as if she didn't think she'd quite heard me right.

"Lauren's gravy train is coming to its last stop," I said, "and trust me, you want to jump off before it gets there."

She snorted. "Damn right. That's a little too much crazy even for me. Don't get me wrong, I don't think she's got a snowball's chance in hell of pulling this off. When she messes it up and dies, though, eventually a hundred dead bums are gonna lead right back to her front door, which means they'll eventually lead to *me*. No, I'm taking my cash and going somewhere with sunny skies, frosty drinks, and no extradition treaty with the US."

"Guess again," I told her. "Lauren's going to win. Once she ascends, there won't be anywhere on this planet you can hide. There won't be much of a planet left at all. I hate to say it—believe me, you have no idea how much I hate to say it—but we need your help."

I walked behind her. Most people would tense up a little, losing sight of their interrogator like that, but she was cool as a cucumber. I uncuffed her. She rubbed the red lines around her wrists, looking dubious.

"A hundred and twenty-five thousand dollars," I told her.

"Bullshit," she said.

"A hundred and twenty-five thousand, in the currency of your choice, deposited to the bank of your choice, once Lauren is dead."

"Bull. Shit. You're piss broke, Faust. You don't *have* that kind of money."

"No," Caitlin said, "but I do."

She strode slowly across the room, stepping out where Meadow could see her. Meadow's eyes widened. It was the closest thing to fear I'd ever seen on her face.

"You're that succubus," Meadow said, "the one Lauren bound. Why are you still here? Faust, why is she still here?"

Caitlin nodded. "Right. Nicky Agnelli told you he found some random bottom-feeder to enslave, didn't he? Never trust a career criminal, they're always working an angle of their own. Let me properly introduce myself. I am *Caitlleanabruaudi*, the Wingtaker. Hound of the Court of Jade Tears."

"Hey," Meadow said, "what happened back there, that was all Lauren. Her plan, her magic. I was just along for the ride. Nothing personal."

"Just along for the ride," Caitlin mused, looming over her. "Much like Carl Holt and Artie Kaufman. Would you like to know what's happening to them, in hell, right at this very moment?"

She leaned close and whispered in Meadow's ear.

Now I knew what Meadow looked like when she was afraid.

Caitlin stepped back and folded her arms. "Almost every single person involved in my abduction has been delivered to their doom, or soon will be. You're a very lucky woman, Meadow Brand. You're in the right place at the right time to make history. The one human to ever tempt my wrath and escape."

Jennifer and I might as well have been invisible now. Meadow only had eyes for Caitlin. She rubbed her hands, trying to hide the way they shook.

"What do you want from me?" Meadow asked.

Caitlin nodded my way. "As Daniel said, we want to hire your services. I will guarantee the sum. You will help facilitate our plan. Once Lauren is dead, I'll wire the money to the account of your choosing, in the currency of your choosing."

"Then what?" Meadow said, uncertain.

"Then you're free to leave. Which you will. Make no mistake, Meadow Brand, your sins are not forgiven. I want you gone. Where you go is up to you, but you will never set foot in my territory again."

"You lost your Vegas privileges," I added.

Meadow thought it over. A bit of her old cockiness came back as she shook her head, glancing between us.

"No way," she said. "Hundred and twenty-five grand? Might as well offer me a million. You won't pay. I've been in this game long enough to know that 'payment after the job is done' is just another way of saying, 'We'll kill you and keep the money.' I want the payment up front. All of it."

"So you can stab us in the back and skip town with the cash," I said. "Not happening."

"You gotta admit, we're a little more trustworthy than you are," Jennifer said.

Meadow barked out a laugh. "A witch, a sorcerer, and a fucking *demon from hell* say I'm not trustworthy."

"You're a psychopath," I said.

She shrugged. "I've been told that means that I *know* the difference between right and wrong, I just don't *care*. Hey, that description sound like anybody you know, Faust?"

"You're not getting the money up front," I said.

"Then I guess you're not getting my help. What a predicament."

I reached into my pocket and took out a USB stick. A black little rectangle, sheathed in transparent plastic tinted the color of smoke.

"How about I put up some collateral?"

"I'm listening," Meadow said.

"On this stick is a scanned document. That document, handwritten by me, confesses to two outstanding murders. Full details, full disclosure. You give this to the cops, I go to prison, period. Once you walk out of here, take it to your favorite lawyer. Instruct him that if anything happens to you—like you die or disappear for any reason—he should turn it over to Special Agent Harmony Black of the FBI. She's leading the Agnelli task force, and she's already got a hard-on for me."

"Risky." Meadow eyed the USB stick and licked her chapped lips. "What's to stop me from just going straight to the feds the second I walk out this door? You ruined my *face*, Faust. You think I don't want payback?"

"I'm gambling that you want the cash more than you want revenge. Like you said yourself, eventually a light is going to shine down on all of Lauren Carmichael's dirty deeds. You won't get away clean. You need to be thinking about your retirement options, somewhere far away from Uncle Sam's reach. Hundred and twenty-five Gs will go a long way toward buying your very own tropical cabana."

"You mean three hundred," Meadow said.

That was when I knew we had her.

"You're asking a lot," Caitlin said.

"No," Meadow said, "you are. Just asking me to set foot in that tower again is worth a hundred easy, let alone taking the risk of crossing Lauren. I can get you in. I can tell you everything you need to know. Nobody else can. I want three hundred thousand dollars. I'm betting the First Bank of Hell is good for it."

"One hundred and seventy-five," Caitlin said.

"Two seventy-five."

"Two hundred and ten thousand dollars."

"Two thirty," Meadow said.

Caitlin nodded. "Agreed. But you do everything you're told, when you're told to do it, or the deal is off. Until Lauren is dead, we *own* you. Understood?"

"I just live to make people happy," Meadow said. "Where do we start?"

She held out her hand. I gave her the USB stick. She clutched it tight.

"We start with Lauren," I said. "When's the attunement ritual?"

"Any time now. She's been pent up in the Enclave with her little mad scientist nerd buddies, getting ready for the big day. The killing cells below are all stocked with only the finest and ripest of unbathed street trash, just waiting for the sacrificial knife. Figuratively speaking. I mean, knives? You know how long that would take?"

"Are there any traps?" I said. "Anything that would kill the hostages if an alarm sounds, like the tanks of lye at the New Life building?"

Meadow smiled. "Did you like that one? My idea. I would have *loved* to see that thing go off. But no, Lauren wouldn't let me touch shit at the Enclave. Something about misaligning the 'perfect occult circuitry' of the walls. Besides, with all the work it took to snatch that many people off the streets, can you imagine if they all got smeared by accident and we had to start over? Timing is kind of a thing here."

"So how does the sacrifice work?" Jen asked.

"Funneling glyphs set into the cell floors in mosaic tile," Meadow said. "Huge ones. Those Xerxes assholes are gonna do the job when Lauren sends the command down. They'll just open up with assault rifles and shoot through the cell bars, gun 'em all down. Corpses drop, souls fly up to the penthouse. Crude, and not much fun, but all Lauren needs is one big-ass harvest of life energy. That'll do it."

"Lauren's in the penthouse?" I said.

Meadow nodded. "Top floor is *all* penthouse. It's this big open space tiled with invocation patterns on the floor, windows all around. Nedry and Clark have a space set off to the side for all their science-geek shit, but they spend most of their time downstairs near the cells. They don't want to be near Queen Bitch any more than the rest of us do."

"I'm going to need a floor plan," I said. "Hand drawn is fine, whatever you can remember. How about those mannequins of yours? You have any left?"

"I keep a few in a storage locker, in case of a rainy day. And no, I'm not telling you how they work. That secret isn't for sale."

I shook my head. "No need. Just get ready and do whatever it is you do to make 'em jump up and boogie. Oh, and I'm going to need you to do one other thing before we go in."

I told Meadow my plan—the part she needed to know about, anyway—and she nearly tried to walk out right then and there. It took twenty minutes of arguing and Caitlin bumping the payment back up to two hundred and fifty grand, but finally Meadow came around.

She held on to my collateral as she sauntered out the door, brandishing the USB stick like a schoolkid with a permanent hall pass. Out front, Bentley, Corman, and Margaux stood close and talked in low tones. They glared daggers at Meadow as she strolled by, and she responded with a sneering wave.

A bottle of Bombay Sapphire gin, Bentley's brand, sat on the counter next to a couple of empty glasses. Some people drink to celebrate, some drink to numb the pain. There wasn't a celebratory face in the room.

"Ta for now, kids," Meadow said. "I'll call as soon as Her Highness summons me to her royal court. You miss the call, it's not my problem."

"Yeah, it is," I said, following her out of the back room. "You've got your instructions. Follow them."

"Long as I get paid," she said.

She let herself out. The door swung shut, and the bookstore fell into a hard silence. I felt the weight of every eye in the room.

41.

"I don't like it any more than you do," I said. I didn't have to direct my words at anybody in particular. Everyone in the room was thinking the same thing.

"I just hope you know what you're doing," Corman said.

"Hey, don't I always?" I said. Nobody wanted to touch that, so I let it drop and moved on. "Jen, how are we looking on the explosives end of things?"

"Boom boom check," she said. "Already got Winslow sourcing it for us. Speaking of, he wants to know when you're gonna pay him for the car and the piece. He's gettin' a little itchy."

"Least of my worries right now. Okay, everybody, Lauren could make her move at any time. The second she does, things are going to happen very, very fast. Be ready for it."

The party broke up after that. There wasn't anything left to say, and putting Meadow Brand on the payroll had left a bad taste in everybody's mouths. Bentley followed me to the door.

"Daniel—" he started to say.

"I know." I reached out, gently, and touched his arm. "I'm sorry. We were all close to Spengler, but Sophia was special to you and Corman. You've got more reason than anyone to want Meadow dead for what she's done. I wish there was another way. I just need you to trust me right now."

"There are times when I disagree with you," he said, "and times when I worry about you, but I *always* trust you. Just tell me one thing and make an old man happy."

"What's that?" I said.

His pale eyes were grave.

"In the end," he said, "will all debts be paid?"

I squeezed his shoulder and gave him a nod.

I should have felt more confident than I did. With Senator Roth and Meadow Brand in my hip pocket, I'd turned two of Lauren's strongest allies into turncoats. I had the inside line on her movements and a plan in play to cut her off at the knees.

Still, I couldn't shake this creeping feeling of doom, like everything was about to go horribly wrong.

\#

The next morning I woke up in a suite at the Medici, swamped under too many covers and too many pillows and nursing a tequila hangover. I vaguely remembered feeling like I'd relied on Bentley and Corman's hospitality a little too often lately. Caitlin's bed was out—she was slated to make contingency plans and drive all night, getting ready for Case Exodus. I was better off alone for the night, anyway. After bringing in Meadow Brand, I wasn't sure if anyone wanted me around.

Somewhere along the line I'd ended up on the Strip, barhopping from casino to casino and soaking up the night all alone. Details got a little hazy from there. Getting drunk and splurging what little cash I had left on a fancy hotel room was half bad move, half comfortable old habit.

My phone vibrated on the end table, demanding my attention. Its purple face glowed. I picked it up and mumbled something close to a greeting.

"Showtime, twinkle-toes," Meadow Brand said. "Hope you packed your tap shoes."

I shot upright, tossing the sheets aside. A bucket of ice water and a pot of double espresso wouldn't have woken me up as fast.

"When?"

"Tonight," she said. "I'm supposed to show up around seven. Fireworks kick off at nine, followed shortly thereafter by the end of the world. The *Washington Post* is calling it, 'Do not miss, a real humdinger of a show.'"

"I need to make some phone calls and line up all the dominoes. Come meet me at the Medici as soon as you can."

"Love their buffet," she said. "What room?"

I looked around the suite, helpless. "I'm...not sure. Just call from the lobby when you get here. I'll come down."

I made four calls in quick succession. Jennifer, Senator Roth, Nicky Agnelli, and Special Agent Harmony Black. Everybody had a part to play, some more willing than others, some more clued-in than others. Caitlin was the last name on my list.

"It's going down tonight," I said when she picked up. "Nine o'clock."

I could hear her breathe.

"I'm out at the Silk Ranch," she said, pensive. "It's hours back to the city and I've still got work to do here, but if I leave right now—"

"No," I told her. "Like you said, you've got work to do. We both do. It's okay. Keep at it."

"I wanted to see you before you went in there," she said. "I wanted..."

Her voice trailed off, but I knew where she was headed.

"If you were about to say 'just in case,'" I told her, "forget it. You're stuck with me, remember? Lauren won't take me alive. Which means win or lose, I'm gonna see you tonight."

It almost sounded good, putting it that way. Then I remembered that one of those two outcomes ended with the Earth burning, humanity extinct, and me in hell.

"Hey," I said, "tell you what. You know that little pizza place you like, the one at the Metropolitan?"

"What about it?" she said.

"How do you feel about a late dinner? Say, midnight, tonight. I'll meet you there."

"Are you asking me out on a date right now?" she said, her voice tinged with amusement.

"Damn right."

"Then I'll see you there, at the stroke of midnight. Don't stand me up."

"I wouldn't dream of it."

By six o'clock I'd spent the day running from one side of town to the other. I'd done everything I could do to prepare. I had a couple of hours before the fight of my life and nothing but time on my hands.

I ended up at Tiki Pete's, a shabby little strip-mall restaurant a few blocks away from all the action. I felt a weird flash of nostalgia as I walked through the door. Once I sat down in a vinyl-cushioned booth, glanced over the laminated menu, and ordered a mai tai, I realized why. This was where I'd met with Jud Pankow, the old farmer from Minnesota who wanted help getting payback for his granddaughter's murder. That was the job that led me to Caitlin, and then to Lauren Carmichael.

Everything comes full circle eventually.

I looked up as Jennifer walked into the restaurant. I'd asked her to meet me here. She dropped into the booth, sitting across from me and looking philosophical. She wore a light linen jacket, a little more stylish than her usual look, and as she settled in I caught the bulge of her shoulder holster underneath.

"How's the food here?" she said.

"Edible."

The waitress brought my cocktail. Jennifer gave me a look.

"Just one before a job," I said. "Something to unwind my nerves a little."

She ordered a Manhattan for herself.

"You see Caitlin today?" she asked.

"Talked to her. I'll see her after. When we come home safe and sound."

"Well, your words are confident," she said, looking at me over her menu. "The voice saying 'em, though? Not so much."

"I don't know, Jen. Lot of moving parts in play, lots of plates to keep spinning. I keep feeling like we're missing something, like we're headed right off the rails and I can't see the crash coming."

"Reckon that's better than thinking everything is hunky-dory and getting spanked by surprise," she said. "So we'll have to think on our feet, so what? We're good at that."

"We're okay at that."

"*You're* okay at that," she said, quirking a smile, "I'm *great* at it. Just talked to Mama Margaux, by the way. She's taking Bentley and Corman to the Tiger's Garden. They aren't happy about it, but they understand."

I didn't want them on the scene for this job, not when Meadow Brand was the key to my entire plan. I knew she'd antagonize them until somebody snapped. Couldn't risk it.

I also couldn't risk *them*. Not with so much at stake tonight. Knowing they were someplace safe—in the case of the Tiger's Garden, a place only vaguely connected to the world, with a chance of escaping Lauren's attention if she beat us—was one tiny bit of weight off my shoulders.

The waitress came back, and I had to make up my mind. Last meal for a potentially condemned man.

"Pineapple chicken," I said. "And shrimp toast for an appetizer, please."

"Beef lo mein and an order of crab rangoon," Jennifer said.

I sipped my mai tai while the sun slid down behind the plate-glass window, slipping out of sight and staining the sky neon pink. The food came out fast. It was a little too soggy, a little too greasy, like something you might reheat in a microwave. But it filled me up and kept me from getting too much of a buzz off the cocktail, so that was something.

"Proof that we're gonna survive tonight," I said.

"Hmm?" She tilted her head.

I speared a triangle of shrimp toast with my fork and held it up. "We're in one of the biggest food capitals of the world. Gourmet restaurants, celebrity chefs...what I'm saying is, this *cannot* be our last meal. That'd just be embarrassing."

"It does have a certain death-row, Styrofoam-carryout ambiance to it, though, don't it?"

"Crap," I said. "Good point."

I ate my fill and left the rest. My watch said 6:51.

"Meadow should be on the move right about now," I said. "Getting ready for her part."

"You think we can trust her?"

"I think we can trust her greed," I said. "She'll feel safe with that blackmail material to hold over my head, and we know she's been expecting a double cross from Lauren, so she's got no reason to betray us. Basically, doing exactly what we tell her is the smartest move she can make tonight."

"She is nuts, though," Jennifer said.

"There is that."

The minutes dragged on. 7:04. 7:07. We could linger a little bit longer, but we really didn't have an excuse.

"All right," I said, tossing some cash on the table. "Feel like fighting a goddess?"

"Goddess, nothin'," Jennifer said. "Strictly a wannabe in my book."

We took a taxi almost to the far end of the Strip, got off two casinos down, and walked the rest of the way. The chain-link construction fence still ringed the Enclave's lot. Last time I was here, the Enclave had been a skeleton of drywall and steel bones. Now it was a black, mirrored monolith. It made me think of a giant basalt tombstone.

"Roth told me there's normally about thirty mercenaries in there," I said. "All Xerxes vets, trained and blooded. They've got assault rifles, flashbangs, and there's usually a sniper with a fifty-caliber rifle perched on top of the foreman's trailer to get a perfect view of the lot."

"Sounds scary," Jennifer said.

"Yeah," I told her, "but they haven't met us yet. Let's go say hi."

A gate blocked the entrance to the lot. Normally at night, once the construction crews had all gone home, it'd be sealed with a length of chain and a padlock. Not tonight, though. I swung open the gate. Jennifer and I walked in together, side by side.

42.

The lot outside the Enclave was silent, strewn with construction equipment dozing in the dark. I'd gotten about ten feet from the gate when I saw the glowing dot blossom on my chest.

I held very still and kept my hands in full view. Jennifer paused, looking to see why I'd stopped walking, and froze right along with me.

The tower's tinted glass doors took a slow spin. A burly man in fatigues, an assault rifle slung over one shoulder, emerged alone from the building. He stopped about five feet away and gave me the stink eye. I recognized him. He'd been one of the mercs guarding the New Life building. One of the ones who'd walked out alive.

He stood in stony silence, staring me down. I tried to keep my heart from pounding. Either my first gambit was about to pay off, or I'd guessed wrong and gotten me and Jennifer killed.

"Sir," he spat, treating the word like venom on his tongue. He snapped a salute.

#

"Did I mishear you at the diner?" I had asked Roth earlier that day. I paced the hotel room carpet, drinking a bottled water courtesy of the minibar, and listened to him whine over the phone.

"I might have exaggerated—" he started to say. I didn't let him finish.

"You said, and I quote, 'Angus Caine is *my* man. I write the paychecks, I give the orders.' That sound familiar to you?"

"I also said I wouldn't send them against Lauren. They'll be slaughtered!"

"Take the rocks out of your ears. I'm not asking you to."

"You might as well be!" Roth said. "If Lauren gets wind of this, it'll mean the same—"

"I talked to Calypso this morning," I said.

That was a lie, but it shut Roth up.

"He thought I should remind you," I said, "just how close you are to breaching the terms of your contract. Do you want to do that? Should I hang up and call him, right now, and tell him, 'Hey, Senator Roth says to fuck off?'"

"No! Don't do that. I'm cooperating!"

I sat down on the edge of the bed and rolled my neck, working out some tension.

"I realize you're a politician, so this is a new concept for you. 'Cooperating' means actually doing what you're supposed to, not just saying you will and then weaseling out."

"I will *try* to contact Caine," he said, "but I can't guarantee—"

"That's it, hanging up. See ya in hell, Alton."

"*Wait!* Wait, wait, *wait!* I'll do it. I'll call Caine right now and give the order." He fell silent for a moment, and I listened to his ragged breath. "You son of a bitch. If those soldiers die because of this, it's on your head."

My teeth clenched. I thought back to the New Life building, where Angus Caine and his men had stood guard while innocent captives were being tortured to death in the laboratory.

"They aren't soldiers," I seethed, my voice rising. "They're thugs with guns. And I'm not a television camera, so save your crocodile tears and your sanctimony, shut the fuck up, and *do as you're told!*"

#

From the naked hate in the mercenary's eyes, I knew Roth had done his part. The merc waved his hand, and the laser light on my chest faded away.

"Orders came down from Major Caine this morning," he said. "We've spent most of the day quietly moving our troops off-site, a few at a time. There's just a skeleton crew left, working in areas that show up on Ms. Carmichael's security cameras. She doesn't suspect a thing."

"And if she sets off an alarm?" I said.

"That's the cue for the final evacuation. Xerxes is officially off-mission. She's on her own. I've been instructed to escort you directly to the penthouse elevator. No further."

He turned on his heel and marched toward the tower. Jennifer and I followed.

The Enclave's lobby was beautiful, silent and cold, like a museum with all of the art taken away. The hotel itself was never real, but they'd had to build the ground floor to pass casual scrutiny for investors and the media. A span of black-and-white checkered tiles stretched out under a dangling crystal chandelier, all the way to a long cedar check-in desk where new computers sat sheathed in shrouds of protective plastic.

"Where are Nedry and Clark?" I asked the merc.

"Dr. Nedry's upstairs with Ms. Carmichael. The other is down in the cellblock. They've been kept out of the loop."

"Nedry's the one with the thing for mirrors," I told Jennifer. "If he gets loose, keep away from reflective surfaces."

She pulled back her jacket and showed me her chromed .357. "How 'bout this one?"

The elevator doors were brushed steel coated in scarlet lacquer, like the skin of a candied apple. Our reflections were black, smoky blurs in the metal.

"You're gonna die up there," the merc told me.

"Thanks for the heads-up."

"I wish I could be there to see it," he said. "You killed a buddy of mine, back at the shelter."

"Yeah? What about the other three guys I killed? You didn't like them as much?"

That shut him up, at least.

The elevator door whispered open. Jennifer and I stepped into the cage, bathed in cherry light. The merc leaned in, swiped his keycard, and hit the button for the penthouse floor.

"Bon voyage, asshole," he said with a wave as the door closed tight.

The elevator hummed as it slowly carried us to the top of the tower. Point of no return.

"You ready for this?" Jennifer asked me.

"Nope. You?"

"Nope. Figured we'd wing it."

"Yeah." I stretched my arms behind my back and cracked my knuckles. "Just another day at the office."

The penthouse floor was a box of glass on three sides. No rooms, no doors, just support pillars set into a white marble floor. Mystic patterns chiseled into the marble glowed faintly in my second sight, like the wiring on a circuit board. Walls of glass looked out onto the world below, the flashing lights of the Vegas Strip on one side and the black desert night on the other.

In between, taking up one entire wall, were the plants.

Thick ropy vines choked the far end of the penthouse, pushing through floors and ceilings, winding through Amazonian bushes and big, leafy fronds. The foliage burst with color, sprouting blossoms in vivid purples and pinks. A lush aroma filled the air, the earthy scent of a greenhouse under hot lights.

What I didn't see was any water or soil. The plants didn't need any. The whole scene felt skewed, wrong, like finding a teapot on Mars.

We strode out of the elevator and onto the chiseled marble. It thrummed against the soles of my feet. Off to the left, a bank of security monitors showed the views from cameras all over the tower in grainy black and white. I saw a couple of Xerxes guards walking up and down between prison cells stuffed full of drugged hostages.

Nedry didn't notice us at first. He stood behind a bank of computer terminals in the corner of the penthouse off to our right, next to the fire-exit door. Cables ran to a polished chrome vat about eight feet high, and transparent hoses snaked across the penthouse floor, disappearing into the greenery. Viscous, faintly glowing fluid, like radioactive lime juice, trickled through the hoses.

"Tolerances are fine. Variances are all holding in the expected range," he said, talking to Clark on his monitor. A webcam clipped to the edge of the screen kept watch.

"Hey, buddy?" Clark said. His voice crackled out over a cheap pair of speakers. "Don't mean to interrupt—"

"We're ready for final integration," Nedry said. "How are things looking down there?"

"Uhh, buddy?" Clark said. On the screen, he twirled his finger in a *look-behind-you* gesture.

Nedry turned around. His bushy eyebrows shot up behind his mirrored glasses. "Oh. Shit."

"Those are some terrible last words." Jennifer pulled her gun. "You wanna try again? I'll give ya a do-over."

"Lauren," I said flatly. "Where is she? Cooperate and you might, emphasis on *might*, walk out of here alive."

Nedry shook his head wildly. "You can't interrupt her now! She's so close. You'll ruin everything!"

"That's the general idea," I said.

Then we heard Lauren's voice. It seemed to come from everywhere and nowhere at once. A whisper carried on a plague wind.

"It's all right, Doctor. I will deal with this personally."

The vines twitched and began to unspool, taking on animated life. Bushes parted, brambles and fronds peeling back. In the midst of the wild growth, seated on a throne of stainless steel, sat the thing that used to be Lauren Carmichael.

She was the green. Roots burrowed into the necrotic flesh of her bare feet and withered hands, and brambles wrapped around her brow in a crown of thorns. Her flowing hair was a cascade of tangled grass, and flowers and thorns sprouted from her naked body. One of her eyes was inhumanly bright and blue. The other was gone, and a crimson rose bloomed inside the empty socket.

"No," I whispered, shaking my head. "What did you do, Lauren? What did you *do?*"

The abundant growth that choked one entire wall of the penthouse quivered, expanding then contracting, as if taking a deep breath. It was *all* Lauren, all connected to her, growing from the soil of her body and blood. She slowly pulled away from her throne and stood. Behind her, hypodermic needles tipped in droplets of green fluid protruded from the back and seat of the chair. My eye followed the tubes on the floor. Nedry had been pumping Viridithol-2 straight into her body from the vat in the corner of the room.

Vines constricted, lifting up her arms in triumph, hoisting her into the air. She dangled there, looking down upon us.

"You want me to start shootin'?" Jennifer breathed.

"Not yet."

"No," the transformed woman said to us. She slowly shook her head. "I am not Lauren. Not anymore. That name is not grand enough to contain what I have become. It is time for something more fitting."

The vines gently set her down. She walked toward us. Where her feet touched the floor, the marble buckled and broke open. Wildflowers in a riot of colors sprung up in her wake, sprouting from the stone and filling her footprints with spontaneous life.

She stopped halfway across the room, standing in the center of the penthouse floor.

"Lauren Carmichael is gone," she said with a faint smile. "Call me...Eve."

43.

"It's over," I said. "Eve, Lauren, whatever the hell you want to call yourself. It's over. All of this."

Lauren stared into my eyes as she lolled her head to one side, too far for a human neck to bend without breaking.

"Bold words, but I can hear your heartbeat. I can taste your fear on every petal of my body. All this aggression, and for what? You should be welcoming me. Celebrating."

"Call me crazy," I said, "but I'm not seeing anything to celebrate here."

"No? This world is choked with evil, Mr. Faust. Drowning in it. It's everywhere you see. But where is the grace? Where is the touch of a loving creator? *I will be that creator.* I will begin with a purge. A small one, just enough to lower the planet's population to more reasonable levels, room for my garden to grow."

"You're talkin' about genocide," Jennifer said.

"No, child. Genocides are targeted. They are actions of hate. My purge will be as indiscriminate as a plague, taking life without pattern or malice. Meanwhile, I will topple the institutions that helped drive this world into ruin. Every government, every church, and every bank, every dividing line that ever separated human from human will wither under my hand. Imagine it! No more wars, no hatred, no famine or fear. No child will ever go to bed with an empty stomach. No one will lack a roof over their heads."

"Sweet deal," I said flatly. "And it only costs a few billion lives and humanity's freedom. Forever."

"I am a merciful goddess," Lauren said. "Let me prove it to you. Kneel down. Kneel down and worship me, and I will spare your lives. I will fill you with what I am, and send you forth as my first ambassadors to the world."

I looked over at Jennifer, deadpan. "What do you think? Wanna go for it?"

"Sweetie, I like to think my taste in goddesses is a little more upscale. She ain't a stitch on Bast or Hecate."

"Yeah." I folded my arms across my chest. "I've just never been much for going to church, myself. Sorry, Lauren, we'll pass. We're shutting this little freak show down, right here and now."

Lauren giggled. An uneasy feeling crept up my spine.

"Yes," she said. "Of course. I forgot. Because you turned Alton Roth against me, and he's been spending the better part of the day slowly pulling my soldiers out from under me."

Now the uneasy feeling turned into a hand of ice.

The fire-escape door banged open, and mercenaries filled the room. Angus Caine strode out ahead of his men, eight or nine of them. Enough for a firing squad. The mercs leveled their rifles. I raised my open hands. Jennifer did the same, keeping the barrel of her revolver pointed toward the ceiling. The grizzled man curled his lips into a nasty smile.

"Like I told you, boy," he said. "Maybe not today, maybe not tomorrow, but I'd have you. I'd have your heart on a fuckin' plate."

"Roth's deception was...charmingly incompetent," Lauren explained. "It wasn't hard to discern his plan. He failed to learn from history. For instance, consider the mercenary *condottieri* of Renaissance Italy. They were powerful tools for warring city-states, but dangerous ones. It wasn't uncommon for them to switch sides, literally in the middle of a battle. Sometimes more than once."

"The lady made us a better offer," Angus said. "So we decided to stick around and finish the job we were paid for."

"That wasn't my entire plan," I said.

"No," Lauren agreed. She pointed toward the bank of security monitors. One in the corner flickered to a new broadcast. "I believe this was."

They'd captured Meadow Brand.

One mercenary held her with her arms pinned behind her back, another keeping his rifle trained at her head as she struggled to pull free. A third looked up into the camera, holding up a detonator. When he spoke, his voice echoed from the walkie-talkie on Angus's hip.

"Sir! We found the target on the fifth floor, planting C-4 charges. All explosives have been recovered and disarmed."

The vines hoisted Lauren back into the air. She hovered, her thorny feet dangling a yard above the marble floor, and smiled serenely down at us.

"You tried to send away my men," she said, "to prevent the sacrifice. You tried to use the treacherous Ms. Brand to destroy the harnessing pattern. And you failed at both gambits. Utterly."

I bit my bottom lip, almost hard enough to taste blood. My gaze turned to the security monitors. This was it. All chips in on the last hand of the night.

"How delightful," Lauren said. "The great Daniel Faust, the trickster magician, caught with an empty sleeve. I wish you could see the look on your face right now, I really do. I'll savor its memory."

Movement on one camera, the view of the outside lot, caught my eye.

I smiled.

"Hey, 'Eve,'" I said. "Think you've got some uninvited guests."

Now they were on three monitors. Teams of men in uniform black, huddled down behind riot shields, forcing their way into the Enclave lobby. A tear-gas grenade exploded on one camera, blanketing the lens in white smoke. On the parking lot view, a swarm of police cruisers ringed the building.

"Oh, hey," I said. "Looks like the whole Vegas Metro SWAT division is here. Plus the FBI, Homeland Security, and probably the IRS for good measure."

Lauren shook her head wildly. Her plants quivered. "What? *How?* They have no reason to be here, no evidence against me! They have no *right!*"

"Yeah," I said, "funny story about that..."

#

On my list of things to do earlier that afternoon, one had involved sitting in a small, windowless interrogation room, drinking stale coffee across from Harmony Black. Meadow sat to my left, looking pained.

"Obviously," Harmony said, setting a tape recorder on the steel table, "any references to magic aren't going to fly. Just don't talk about those parts."

"No shit, Sherlock," Meadow snapped. "I know the rules. Do we have a deal or not?"

Harmony took a deep, centering breath and slid a manila folder across the table, pushing it in front of her.

"It's all there. The DA just signed off on it. You will receive full immunity and placement in witness protection, in exchange for testimony leading to Lauren Carmichael's conviction."

Meadow yanked the folder open and snatched up the papers inside, speed-reading them.

"Can't believe you talked me into this," Meadow grumbled at me.

"That makes two of us," Harmony said, shooting me a hard look. "And I'm still not happy about keeping Roth's name out of this. He should go down with Lauren."

I sipped my lukewarm coffee. "I don't disagree. Just not like this. Look, once you get your hooks into Carmichael-Sterling, the odds are pretty good you'll find something leading to his front door. I just can't be involved in that part."

"Why not?"

"Reasons," I said, and set my cup down.

Meadow tapped her fingernails against the papers. "All right. Let's get this over with. What do you want to know?"

Harmony pressed the red button and moved the recorder to the middle of the table.

"Everything. Let's start at the beginning. What is your relation to the Carmichael-Sterling Group?"

"On paper? Director of public relations. That was just to keep the money clean. I kill people. For Lauren Carmichael. First time was...hmm, remember back in '08, Ken Sterling's murder-suicide? The one that gave Lauren full control of the company? That was me. Took a Jet Ski and boarded Sterling's yacht. I shot him and his wife in bed. The kid ran. Found him hiding in a closet. I didn't bother dragging him out. I just shot through the door. That's a detail they didn't release to the newspapers, so there ya go."

"Jesus," Harmony breathed. "You can prove Lauren hired you?"

"Always figured she'd turn on me eventually, so I documented everything as an insurance policy. Oh, her dead husband and son? Not a home invasion. Lauren did the job. I was her getaway driver on that one, and I furnished the alibi. I've got a recording of her talking about it. What do you want next, the details on the city inspectors we bribed to get the Enclave's permits rushed through, or the honest one whose throat I slit when he wouldn't play ball? Or we can talk about some tortured and dead bums, and yes, I do know where the bodies are buried."

An hour later, she was finally finished. Harmony shut off the tape recorder. She stood on shaky legs, her cheeks pale, and gestured for me to follow her. Meadow sat placidly at the interrogation-room table as we stepped out into the hall.

"Jesus, Faust," Harmony hissed. "I thought she was just going to confess to some kidnappings. I just gave blanket immunity to a fucking *serial killer!*"

"So redact half of it. Lose chunks of the tape. It'll still be plenty of ammo against Lauren, and it won't hurt your career."

"That isn't remotely the fucking *point*! That woman is a goddamn monster, and now I have to let her walk!"

I got close to her, close enough to smell the scent of faded flowers on her skin, and whispered, "I need you to trust me. If it was for anything else, any other reason, I wouldn't blame you for laughing in my face, but this is just too big. We have to work together. There's no other way."

Harmony stared at the two-way mirror. Behind the glass, Meadow leaned back and put her feet up on the interrogation-room table. It looked like she was whistling.

"You bring her back here," Harmony said, not looking at me. "You make sure she testifies. I want her in a courtroom. I want to be certain the charges against Carmichael stick."

"Lauren won't get away. So does this give you enough probable cause to raid the Enclave and get those hostages out?"

She nodded. Her eyes narrowed. "My next stop is a friendly judge with a pen and a search warrant. We'll hit the place tonight. Don't be anywhere nearby when it happens. Or better yet, do. I'd love to arrest you right alongside Lauren."

#

"Those aren't some third-world scrubs with broken AKs, like you're used to fighting," I told Angus Caine. "Those are the toughest cops in Vegas, and they're rolling out all the party favors. Seems to me you've got two choices: one, you can get in a gunfight with the United States government—

because that *always* ends well—or you can run downstairs, get as many of your boys out through the emergency exits as you can, and order the rest to surrender. Your call, but bail money's a lot cheaper than a tombstone."

Angus's lips curled into a furious snarl. "You little gob of *shite*—"

"Yeah, I get that a lot. Oh, hey, Lauren, speaking of not learning from history? Check out that screen in the corner."

The mercenaries on five were still struggling with Meadow, waiting for their orders. They hadn't twigged that something was a little off about her. The way she kept making the same movements, over and over again, or how her eyes were expressionless.

"Don't you remember this trick?" I said. "It's the one you used on me, when you murdered our buddy Spengler."

Suddenly it wasn't Meadow anymore. The puppet's head lolled back, opening a hinged mouth to expose a painted sigil that glistened with malevolent energy. The mercenaries had only a second to react before white-hot light flashed from the sigil's heart. The camera went dead.

Meadow—the real Meadow—stepped into view on a totally different screen. She held up her detonator box in one hand, and stuck up her middle finger with the other.

"I reckon that's her resignation," Jennifer said.

The marble shook under our feet. One after another, explosions boomed from the floors below, blasting out windows and spewing glass and fire into the night.

"She wasn't planting the explosives on the fifth floor," I said. "She was planting them on the third, the seventh, the thirteenth, and the twenty-third."

44.

"Just a little C-4 in strategic spots," I said as the rumbling subsided. "Not enough to bring the building down or cut off the exits, but it should do a pretty good job of disrupting the mystic circuitry. Sorry, Lauren. The Enclave *was* a massive energy funnel, but now it's just another slab of overpriced real estate."

"No sacrifice, and no way to reap the power," Jennifer said, nodding. "You're finished. Look on the bright side. Maybe you'll find a nice greenhouse with cheap rent."

Caine took a step back and drew his sidearm.

"Move out, lads! We're leaving. But not before I take care of unfinished business."

A helicopter's spotlight dropped into view, hovering outside the penthouse windows. The blinding beam flooded the room with brilliant white light. Then the helicopter swung around, turning its open side door to face us. Not a police helicopter. Nicky Agnelli's big yellow Bell 407, its tail registry blotted out under a fresh coat of paint.

I had just enough time to grab Jennifer's arm and yank her to the floor before Juliette opened fire.

She sat at the edge of the open door, cradling a long-barreled monster of a machine gun while her sister flew the helicopter. The windows exploded in a hurricane of glass, and lead sprayed across the room like a swarm of angry hornets. Bullets punched into the Viridithol tank, rupturing holes and sending streams of the toxic venom squirting across the marble floor. Two of the mercenaries dropped, and the others scattered, falling back toward the emergency exit.

Angus threw up a panicked arm and raised his gun with the other hand, but Jennifer was faster on the draw. Her bullet slammed into his shoulder, shredding camo and bursting out the other side. His face contorted as he dropped his gun and ran, leading a stumbling retreat. Nedry just lay flat on the ground with his hands over his head, shrieking like a two-year-old.

The gun's belt ran dry, and the shooting stopped. If Lauren had even been hit, she didn't show it. The vines lowered her to the ground, and she bellowed with a fury I'd never heard before. The foliage rustled, and her vengeance slithered forth.

Snakes. A living carpet of them, hundreds, short and long and tiny and fat, and every one of them venomous, every one of them heading straight toward Jennifer and me.

Nedry caught sight of the snakes and jumped to his feet, screaming, "*Fuck* this job! Lauren, I *quit!*"

He threw himself at the ruptured tank. His open palm hit the mirror-polished surface and pushed right on through. His body flattened and became an image on the other side, a reflection with no source.

Jennifer ran to the shattered windows while I searched for a way to stop the writhing hordes. The tank caught my eye. Viridithol pooled on the marble floor, catching in the chiseled glyphs and running along them in channels, coloring them bile green.

Have to be careful with my aim, I remembered Bob Payton saying as he walked around his candle-lit circle. *This stuff is flammable as hell.*

I conjured a spark of raw power to my fingertip and flicked it through the air. It sailed, slow and serene, gliding like a fireplace ember to land in the pooled serum.

It ignited like gasoline.

I wasn't sure if the snakes were screaming, or if Lauren was, but the air filled with a shrill cacophony as her pets broiled under a wall of fire. Juliette clung to the helicopter door, leaning out, and swung a white vinyl bowling-ball bag through the air. Jennifer caught it and tossed it my way. As the helicopter launched straight up, vanishing from sight, I saw Lauren lift her hand and point at me through the crackling flames.

"You die here, Faust! I'm taking you with me!"

The elevator doors chimed pleasantly and slid open. Meadow Brand stepped out and raised her hands like a showgirl at the front of a chorus line. A pack of animated mannequins charged out around her, storming though the fire, heading straight for Lauren.

"Ta-daa," Meadow sang.

I unzipped the bowling-ball bag. Bob Payton's severed head rested inside, the pallid skin of his neck ringed with binding seals and the stump cauterized with a blowtorch. I grabbed the head by the hair and held it aloft, unleashing the spell I'd been fueling under my breath, the trigger for the ritual I'd carried out over Payton's corpse back in New York.

The stitches over its eyes and mouth tore apart as the head woke up.

Payton's dead eyes blazed with black light, and he bellowed with a voice like thunder, the concentrated entropy desperate to feast.

The mannequins' wooden shells ignited as they charged through the flames, and they threw themselves onto Lauren like they were trying to hug their long-lost mother. Others ran headlong into the greenery behind her, setting leaves and bushes alight. Her vines lashed through the air, catching one stray mannequin and smashing it to kindling, but she couldn't shake them all off.

I threw Payton's head. It sailed across the room, landing at the foot of Lauren's steel throne, and burst open. A vortex of snarling purple light whipped around her, wilting flowers, melting brambles to rancid goo. The rose in Lauren's eye socket withered and turned black. She screamed, stumbling backward, thrashing against the burning mannequins.

"Jen?" I said.

"Yeah?"

"*Now* shoot her."

Jennifer took aim and snapped off five shots. One at the glass window behind Lauren, and four into the burning woman's chest, pushing her toward it.

The last of the purple light flickered and died. I saw Lauren, just for one split second, in its wake. Not a transformed monster, not consumed by the Garden's plants, not anything at all. Just a would-be goddess with a shattered throne.

The cracked window gave under the mannequins' weight, and she fell with them, smoldering and broken, thirty-six floors to the concrete below.

I didn't say anything. There wasn't anything to say. We just ran for the fire escape.

We went up, not down, emerging onto the windy rooftop. A cold night breeze whipped through my hair. The helicopter was waiting for us, just as planned, with the twins on pilot duty. I clambered into the back row of seats, and Meadow got in next to me, with Jennifer taking a seat in front. She slammed the door shut behind us.

"Agnelli Airlines, cleared for takeoff!" Juliette chirped as the helicopter lifted from the roof. "Sorry, there will be no movie on this flight."

As we veered away, I looked out to the blazing building below and the swarm of red and blue lights strobing in the distance. It was finally over. Lauren Carmichael was dead.

The helicopter flew into the dark, away from the lights of Vegas. Out into the desert.

"I've been thinking," Meadow said, breaking the silence. "Witness protection is some bullshit. What am I gonna do, become a florist in Albuquerque? And give up all my money? Forget that. I'm going to Costa Rica. You paid me to work for you until Lauren bit the bullet. She's done, so I'm done."

I nodded up at the twins. "Here's good, I think."

"What's good?" Meadow said. Her scar twitched.

I reached under my seat. Under the cushion, my fingers closed on the gun Nicky had planted there for me. I pulled it out and jabbed the barrel into Meadow's ribs.

"She's done," I said. "So you're done."

We landed on a lonely outcropping of rock in the middle of nowhere. I pushed Meadow out of the helicopter. Jennifer got out behind me, reloading her revolver.

"Walk," I said.

We stood in the helicopter's headlights under a canopy of pitiless stars. Meadow took a few halting steps back, looking around as if there was anywhere to run.

"You can't do this," she said. "We had a deal!"

I shook my head.

"Come on, Meadow. We were never going to let you walk away."

"You've got too much of our family's blood on your hands," Jennifer said. "We don't let that go. Ever."

"That was *Lauren*! That—that was all her. *She* gave the orders!"

"And you did the killing," I said.

She waved a hand in front of her face, like she thought it could stop a bullet. "Just—just hold on a second. What about the confession? I disappear, my lawyer sends it straight to the feds! You'll go to prison, Faust!"

"Should have checked into that. Those two murders I confessed to? I *didn't* commit them. In fact, I have rock-solid alibis for both. That confession is worthless. The only thing it'll do is waste Agent Black's precious time."

"I have money, okay? I have a *lot* of money. I skimmed more off Lauren than she ever realized. You can *have* it. Just let me walk away. You'll never see me again, I swear it!"

I looked at Jennifer. She looked at me.

"That last part," I said. "That was true."

When we flew in for the landing, I'd seen lights in the distance. A campfire to cut the cold of the desert night. They must have been hikers, camping far from civilization. I wondered what it sounded like when Jennifer and I raised our guns and emptied them into Meadow Brand's body, sending her staggering back in a stream of billowing bloody gunshots until she crumpled, glassy-eyed and dead, on the sand-swept rock. Did it sound like distant fireworks? I wondered. Or just the finality of a book slamming shut at the end of the final page?

We left her corpse for the coyotes and the vultures. In a week's time, nothing but sun-bleached bones would remain.

45.

I jogged through the glossy halls of the Metropolitan with slot machines jangling at my back. My watch said 11:59 as I swept down an unmarked hallway lined with old vinyl record sleeves, around the corner, and into the little pizza joint that didn't show up on any of the casino's maps. The place smelled like hot pepperoni and warm beer, and the tiny counter was thronged with drunks hungry for a late-night snack.

Caitlin looked up from a high-top table in the corner, and her smile lit up the room. Or maybe it was just me, floating on air all the way into her arms.

"You're right on time," she whispered and kissed me. I could have held that moment forever. Two greasy paper plates sat out, laden with pizza, one for her and one for me. She hadn't doubted me. While I sat down at the table, she took out her phone.

"Cancel Case Exodus," she said crisply. "Repeat, *cancel* it. Order is restored, business as usual. Get back to work."

She hung up and turned her attention toward me.

"Job's done," I said.

"It's funny." She reached out for a glass jar of hot pepper flakes, sprinkling them on her slice of pizza. "All the time I've known you, we've been veering from one crisis to another. We might have to shift gears now."

"We might have more time to spend together," I said, "like a normal couple. We might even need...hobbies."

"Oh, I'm sure we can keep each other busy."

"Agreed." I took a bite of my pizza. The melted cheese singed the roof of my mouth, but the flavor was worth the pain. "And now I can actually look for a new place to live without being shot at."

Caitlin reached out to her paper cup of soda. She didn't drink it. She just played with the straw, restless.

"Daniel."

"Mm-hmm?"

"I've been thinking. I'm...I'm not inviting you to move in with me. It's too soon. There are too many questions, too many things we both have to come to terms with."

"I would never ask—"

"But I think," she said, cutting me off, "given how you do seem to be spending the night a little more often...you should have a drawer."

I blinked. "A drawer?"

"A drawer. You know, for toiletries, and an emergency change of clothes, and that sort of thing. Just to make it easier. Easier for you to stay with me."

I reached across the table and took her hand.

"I'd like that," I said. "I'd like that a lot."

"You'll have to pick out which drawer you want, of course," she said. "Sooner is better."

"How soon?" I said.

"Why don't you come home with me tonight?"

"You," I said, "just want to drive my car again."

She winked.

#

You couldn't turn on a radio or a television the next morning without hearing the news. The cops had staged a daring moonlight raid on the Enclave, the story went, following evidence that Carmichael-Sterling's management was behind the kidnapping ring at the New Life shelter. A hundred drugged and confused homeless people, some from as far away as San Francisco and Tucson, had been freed from captivity without incident.

The talking heads were having a field day, calling it a "real life horror movie" and speculating about how Carmichael-Sterling's wealthy backers were involved in everything from gladiator fights to snuff movies. The headline on one tabloid site screamed "Unanswered Questions in Carmichael Case: Were the Rich Literally Eating the Poor?"

Harmony Black massaged the news, smooth as silk. She gave them sexy questions to speculate on all day long while hiding the real story. There weren't any photographs of what the first responders found up on that penthouse floor, and the news maintained that Lauren Carmichael—along with her entire board of directors and a laundry list of names Meadow's confession implicated—were wanted for questioning. I didn't know if that meant Harmony had covered up Lauren's death, snaking off with the body for her bosses back in Washington, or if there was just so little left

after the fire and the fall that her remains hadn't been iden-
tified yet.

The Xerxes mercs, the ones who couldn't slip the drag-
net, gave up without firing a shot. Angus Caine wasn't one
of them. The feds flashed his mug around too, as one of the
suspects wanted for questioning, and the revelation of a
British private military company working for criminals on
American soil kicked up a little dust storm of its own.

No mention of Nedry and Clark, either captured or
wanted. They'd gotten lost in the wind.

The doors of St. Jude's leaned wide open to let in the
morning sun. I pulled up to the curb and got out, cupping
my hand over my eyes to cut the glare. Pixie spotted me
from across the room as I stepped inside. She didn't quite
make a beeline for me. I saw the drag in her step.

"Hey," I said. "Looks like business is picking up."

She looked over at the crowd of regulars lining up at the
chow tables, and nodded.

"Yeah." She crossed her arms tight over her chest. "A lot
of people came back last night. A whole lot of families are
back together again. They're still in a rough spot,
but...they're together."

"Told you."

She looked at me and nodded. "Yeah. Yeah, you did."

"So," I said. "We cool now?"

"There's stuff—" she started to say. She dropped her
arms to her sides. "There's some stuff I don't want to get
involved in, okay? Stuff I wish I didn't know, but there's no
changing that. But, yeah. We're cool. And if you need me,
for a job or whatever...you can call me."

"Good," I said. I turned and walked away.

"Faust," she said.

I looked back at her.

"You did a really good thing back there," she said. "You helped a lot of people."

I shrugged.

"Maybe you should think about that," Pixie told me. "I mean...you can do anything you want. It's your choice. Maybe you could turn things around. You know...keep helping people. Maybe it'd feel good."

"Yeah, Pix. Sure. Maybe."

I drove to a cafe a few blocks over, bought a cup of coffee and the morning paper, and sat down at a sidewalk table under the shade of a big brown umbrella. I thought about what Pixie had said, long and hard.

Lauren Carmichael, her cult, and her legacy were gone. The ax hanging over my head was gone with it. Sure, I still had to deal with Harmony Black and her legal crusade, but I'd get through that storm when it came. For the first time in a long while I felt myself standing at a crossroads. Wherever I went from here, whatever I did, was totally up to me. What was it Caitlin had said about Emma? "We all have to be true to our nature." That sounded about right to me.

I flipped through the paper to the local events section. A jazz festival was coming to town. A new art gallery was about to open. A traveling museum collection was on display. I read every detail, asking myself questions, brainstorming ideas.

By the time I borrowed a ballpoint pen and started jotting down actual notes, circling one article and scribbling about guards and burglar alarms in the margins, old habits had their claws buried deep into my skin. I knew exactly what I was looking for.

My next big score.

We all have to be true to our nature.

Epilogue

The rusty sedan clattered down the interstate, heading east.

"Such bullshit," Nedry said, slouching in the passenger seat with his arms crossed over his chest. "Such unmitigated and utter *bullshit.*"

"You know it, buddy," Clark said, driving.

"Years of work, down the drain. Our research money? Gone. Grants? Oh-ho-ho, just imagine us trying to get grants now that we've spent years in the shadow economy. Neither one of us has published a research paper in ages! What are we gonna do? Get teaching jobs? High school chemistry? *Community* fucking *college*? Oh Jesus, we're gonna end up teaching community college, aren't we?"

"Hey, buddy," Clark said. "Chillax."

He turned on the radio. A Grateful Dead tune washed in over the cheap speakers.

"Did you just...you did *not* just tell me to 'chillax.' Tell me you didn't just say that."

Clark leaned his head back and smiled serenely. "All I'm saying is, opportunities are everywhere! We've got our partnership, we've got brains, and you know what else we've got?"

Nedry glared at him, sullen. "What?"

"Science."

Nedry stared out the window, his mirrored lenses reflecting the stark desert wastes, and sighed.

"Yeah," he said, "you've got a point. I guess if we stick together, we can figure something out."

"We can, and we will. Trust me."

Clark looked up to the rearview mirror. He smiled at the smoke-faced man sitting in the backseat.

The man raised one bony finger, putting it to the void where his lips would have been if he had a face.

Shh.

"That's right, buddy," Clark said, turning up the radio. "Everything's gonna be just fine."

AFTERWORD

One story ends, and one begins. Daniel Faust will return soon, with new adventures, new challenges, and, as shadows loom over the Vegas skyline, a new enemy unlike anything he's ever faced before. If you want to be the first to know what happens next, head over to craigschaeferbooks.com and hop onto my mailing list for announcements about new releases. You can also catch me on Facebook (at facebook.com/CraigSchaeferBooks), Twitter (at @craig_schaefer), or just drop me an email at craig@craigschaeferbooks.com. I'd love to hear from you.

Grateful thanks to Kira Rubenthaler and James T. Egan at Bookfly Designs, my amazing editor and cover designer. They're an indispensible part of my team.

Names of certain real-life businesses have been changed for legal purposes. The author has also been politely asked to state that "Justine and Juliette aren't just great pilots, they're great at absolutely everything they do. They are smart and wonderful and awesome. Anyone who says otherwise is just jealous and should feel bad about themselves."

The author hopes they will let him out of this basement now.

Made in the USA
Middletown, DE
28 April 2016